# Song

## of

## Songs

# Song of Songs

Melissa Morelli Lacroix

Library and Archives Canada Cataloguing in Publication

CIP data on file with the National Library and Archives

ISBN 978-1-55483-616-1 (trpb)
ISBN 978-1-55483-617-8 (e-book)

Sections of this book appeared as "In the Sleeping Wood." Between the Lines (ISSN: 1929-7645), edited by Dwayne Brenna, Fall 2012.

A brief excerpt from Step Nine of Alcoholics Anonymous is quoted without endorsement. The official wording can be found at www.aa.org/the-twelve-steps.

**Mature Language**

Some vulgar and racist language is used for narrative and historical purposes. No offence is intended. Some explicit sexual content is included. Reader discretion is advised.

To my family who gave me the bones of this story,
especially my mother, who kept encouraging me to cover
them with flesh and skin,
and my children, who grew up with this book
forever in the works.

**Also by Melissa Morelli Lacroix**

**Poetry**
*A Most Beautiful Deception*
A poignant collection that explores love, health, and music.

**Fiction**
*Adventures of Ivan*
A music-inspired novella offering rare insight into the most
golden decade of one's life:
their 90s.

# Table of Contents

# Stéphanie's Family

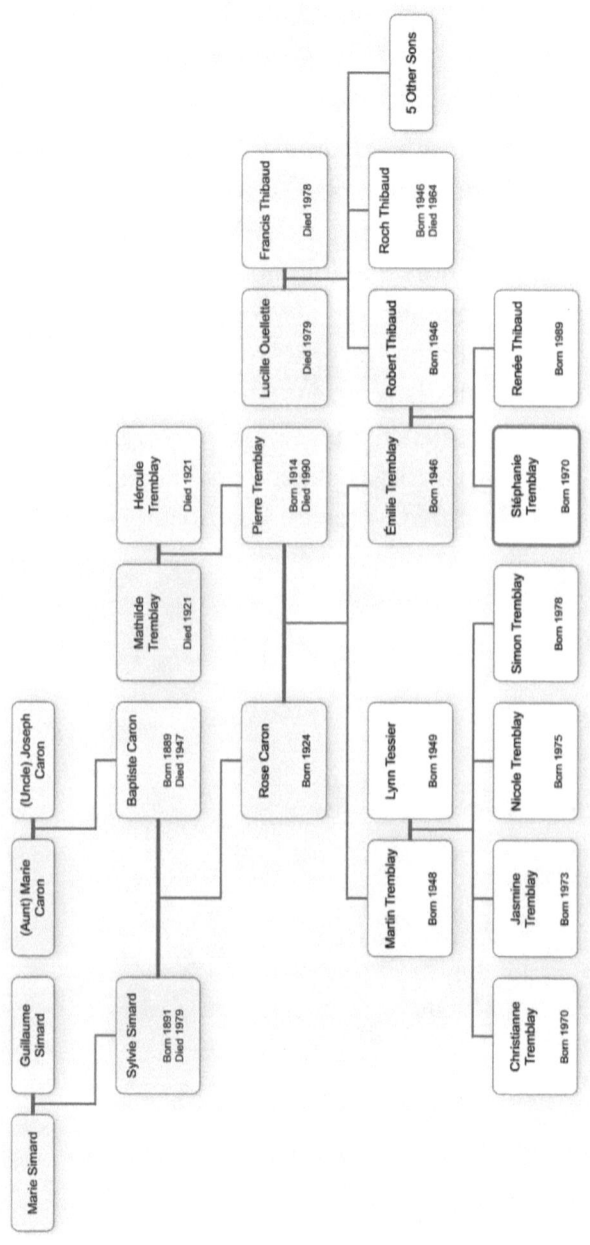

## 1. Prelude
## August 1988

Stéphanie stood under the hot, bright lights at the International Song Festival in Granby, about to begin her three-song set. She was dressed in high-waisted orange pants and a pleated blue designer tee. Her dark mass of curls was piled and loosely clipped up, so it would stay out of her face and off her neck while she performed.

"Voici une vieille chanson," she said into a microphone as she played a slow up-bow on her violin. "Here's an old song that made its way over to what Europeans once called New France. We call it Québec now," she said over her violin and the loud hoots of appreciation from the crowd. A keyboard and guitar joined in as Stéphanie continued, "We call it l'Acadie and le Canada, too. We call it many things. But me, I call it home."

The crowd cheered with agreement; the band swelled behind her. Stéphanie quickened her playing and began to sing an old French song she had always known, "À la claire fontaine, m'en allant promener. J'ai trouvé l'eau si belle que je me suis baignée …"

Across the country in a well-maintained 1920s catalogue house, the eighteen-year-old's family was gathered in the living room. It was warm and cozy and smelled of lemon wood polish. They sat grouped by generation: the eldest in matching stuffed chairs, their two black-haired children on the sofa with their spouses, and Stéphanie's four cousins on the floor. They were cross-legged and arranged by age: eighteen, fifteen, thirteen, and ten. The three teens were girls with long hair, but only the eldest's was the same Tremblay black as Stéphanie's. The other two had wavy, sandy brown hair that flowed about their shoulders. Jasmine's was sprayed into place in front and at the sides, while younger Nicole wore hers in a side ponytail. Freckled Simon had been well-combed earlier in the day, but his after-church shenanigans in the yard had left his mousey brown hair a mess and his trousers dusty and worn at the knee. Each of them stared at their cousin as she made music half a continent away.

"That's my mother's song," their grandmother said. "Isn't it?"

Her daughter, Stéphanie's mother, nodded and smiled. "Oui. If you listen between the notes, that's exactly what it is."

The elder blinked away a prickle of emotion as the warmth of nostalgia spread through her body. "She used to tell that story all the time. Remember?"

"Of course," her quadragenarian children replied in happy remembrance.

Martin took on a high-pitched voice and melodramatic hand gestures in imitation of their late grandmother, "Oh. Mon Baptiste! He never said I love you. Never held my hand nor smiled at me as if I were the only person that mattered to him, but I loved him. Oh! I loved Baptiste Caron before I even knew what that word meant."

Émilie picked up the story, "Oh! And then one day, he was there! Mon Baptiste was there! And he was looking at me!" She placed a hand to her chest and batted her eyes before falling melodramatically into her husband's lap.

He brushed a dark strand of hair off her face. "I always loved that story," he said with sincerity.

"Me, too," she agreed, staring up into his eyes.

"Uh-oh!" Martin laughed. "Look away, kids! Kiss alert! Kiss alert!"

His wife swatted him playfully. "Stop it."

"Why?" He kissed her quickly, then tickled her ribs. She wriggled under his fingers and squealed with laughter.

"Shhh!" their eldest daughter, Christianne, hissed like a pressure cooker as they joked around and jostled about. Six months Stéphanie's junior, and recently graduated from high school, Christianne snapped at her parents, "Honestly! You call yourselves adults! Stéphanie's on national television, and you guys are acting like baboons."

"Ooooo," her younger sisters sounded, both impressed by Christianne's spunk and expectant of their father's reproach, but none came. Instead, he laughed along with the other adults on the couch.

"Shhh!" Christianne hissed again. "She's still on."

On, she was, and so were her violin and bow, as she ripped through a medley of tunes and reels.

"Gawd, this is fast!" Stéphanie's matante exclaimed as she tried to sit-jig to the music Stéphanie played in such a whirl that her fingers blurred as they moved about the fingerboard. "How can she play this!"

"Practice," Christianne and Émilie both replied. Émilie laughed at the unison, but Christianne remained focused on the television. She placed her elbows on her knees and leaned towards the screen. She noticed the sparkle of Stéphanie's sweaty skin, and how it created curlicues of damp black hair about her face. Christianne gaped at the screen as Stéphanie continued to dance her fingers and bow over the strings of her great-grandfather's antique violin.

"I knew she was good," she said, "but seriously Matante, does anyone else play like this?"

"Not many," Stéphanie's mother said with an authority gained from decades of travelling the continents playing classical piano and organ in cathedrals and concert halls.

The family continued to watch in silent awe as Stéphanie played so furiously it seemed she was duelling with the devil. When at last she struck her final bow, the crowd in Granby, and the small one in the country house in southeastern Saskatchewan, went wilder than Stéphanie's violin had been. People screamed and applauded; they stared at one another in disbelief.

Stéphanie had forgotten the crowd was there, and their roar did not bring her back to the stage. She simply launched into another folk song that, with the help of drums and electric guitars, grew into a heavy metal ballad with each new verse.

"Mon petit oiseau a pris sa volée. My bird, she flew, à la volette, she flew away. She flew to an orange tree. She flew, à la volette, to an orange tree. The branch, it was dry, and my bird fell. She did fall, à la volette, she did fall ..."

"Wow," the young Tremblays gasped, wide-eyed and gobsmacked by the transformation of a cheery children's song into something more from a Def Leppard album than one by Sharon, Lois and Bram.

"What was that?" Jasmine, the second eldest asked once it was over, and Stéphanie stood blinking dumbly at the hoots and whistles of the crowd in Québec.

"Your cousin," Christianne grinned. "Isn't she fantastic?"

"Absolutely!" Nicole agreed, utterly amazed by Stéphanie's impassioned performance.

Simon jumped to his feet and began to play the air guitar. Back-combed Jasmine and pony-tailed Nicole joined in the wailing, singing in call and response just as Stéphanie and her backup singers had just done, "Little bird, I want to marry you. Marry you, à la volette, marry you right away!"

They were wild and loud; their mother stood to cut them off before they started head-banging or launched into another verse. "Come on, Bon Jovi," she said with a laugh they didn't notice was forced, "let's go see what Mémère's got in the freezer for coffee time."

Simon dropped his air guitar and sprinted towards the kitchen, calling out for his favourite doughy treat, "Butterrrrr hooorns!"

Jasmine and Nicole followed after him, but Christianne remained in front of the TV even though the program had cut to a commercial. Her mother nudged her.

"You, too," she said.

"What?" Christianne asked with a small start of surprise.

"It's over. Go to the kitchen."

"But there's still the awards," she protested.

Her mother raised her eyebrows rather than her voice. "We'll watch them at home. Go."

Christianne understood the meaning of the look but not the reason for it. She turned towards her father for an explanation, but he was also urging her out of the room with a silent command. She scrunched her face and turned her hands up in question. He gave no further answer but a jerk of his salt-and-pepper head towards the doorway.

Her mother nudged her again. "Now, please."

Christianne obeyed, but she made a quick sweep of the room with her eyes as she walked away. Her matante, Émilie, was paler than usual. Her eyes were hard green gems, and she gripped her once-broken wrist with her left hand the way she used to before she returned to Lasalette and married Robbie.

He, too, had a painful, twisted look on his face that

Christianne hadn't seen since she was a girl, and Robbie spent hours drinking coffee with her father instead of losing himself in the hard stuff she was still too young to buy.

Christianne wondered what had happened to the two of them in the short span of Stéphanie's last song. *Maybe it's a parent thing*, she thought, *like Maman and Papa at my graduation.*

It was a parent thing, but not the way Christianne thought. "That was about us," Robbie said. Émilie pressed her lips together and nodded. "She hates us."

"Non," Pierre, the patriarch of the family, assured. "She just needs time."

Robbie sniffed, but a tear fell from his eye and slid down his face. "How much?"

Pierre shrugged. "I don't know, but she's got her family to help her figure it out."

Two days later, the Tremblay family was assembled at the arrival gate of the Regina International Airport. Jasmine and Nicole held a poster board with the word *Félicitations* written in colourful bubble letters, while their young, freckled brother gripped a helium balloon that read the same thing in English, *Congratulations!* Lynn, their trim, short-haired mother, stood nearby with a *Welcome home!* balloon tied to her wrist.

Robbie held blue and pink hydrangea blooms from his garden in a mason jar of water with his strong, tan hands. Next to him stood Émilie, wreathed in lily of the valley and baby powder amid the airport's strange smell of people, coffee, and jet fuel. She wrung her hands in a mix of apprehension and anticipation for her daughter's return.

Martin laughed at her. "She's only been gone a week."

"I know, but she left so soon after the wedding."

He elbowed her and teased, "Normally it's the couple who goes on the honeymoon."

"Ha, ha," she replied dryly and gave him a playful push, though she remained anxious. "I just want the three of us to be together."

"I know," he said empathetically, then puffed his cheeks and wiggled his eyebrows for no reason but to make her laugh. It worked enough for her to chuckle and shake her head. She pushed him once again.

"You're nuts."

"Walnuts or peanuts?"

"Pfff," scoffed Christianne and rolled her eyes while 10-year-old Simon grinned to hear their dad use the joke he often said himself.

The group of Tremblays twittered and chattered; they shifted weight from foot to foot as they stared at the windowed passageway and arrival gate. "They're starting to come," Robbie said, pointing his chin towards the first trickle of passengers from business class. Martin was often among them, but this day he was on vacation from his SaskTel executive job and among the impatient, casually dressed group waiting for Stéphanie to return from the song festival down east.

Émilie rubbed a blue bead on the rosary bracelet she wore on her long-healed right wrist; she closed her eyes and took a deep breath. Robbie pressed his arm against hers. She nodded at him and his silent support, but she remained in the darkness of her closed lids and focused on the sound and feel of her own breath in the din of the airport. It was a habit, a pre-performance ritual to find herself before stepping in front of an auditorium of strangers. *Or an angry daughter*, she thought.

"There she is!" Christianne cried, pointing to the glass door five metres away. Émilie's eyes burst open like the doors of a cuckoo clock; she felt her heart jump.

"Eeee!" Stéphanie's cousins yelled and surged towards her. Their shoes slapped the cold tiled floor. The five were a coterie of prairie dogs by the time the foursome of parents realized Stéphanie had walked through the door. They hurried over to greet their conquering hero, their grande lauréate of the Granby song festival and of their hearts.

"Ehhhh! Stéph! Bravo! Welcome home!"

Their words were a symphony of excitement and emotion that Stéphanie appreciated somewhere inside herself, but with each successive hug, she became less responsive until she felt like an inanimate teddy bear. "Merci," she said to each congratulations and to every hand of help with her bags. "Where are Mémère and Pépère?" she asked, searching beyond the group around her.

Christianne hooked her arm around Stéphanie's and started to lead her towards the baggage carousel. "Our house. Mémère thought it was too hot for them."

"It is," Jasmine said, following behind the two eighteen-year-olds, near-twins in size but opposites in style—Stéphanie was the girl next door, while Christianne dressed more like Madonna. Jasmine and the younger, pony-tailed Nicole were typical Sears catalogue teens with neon t-shirts and mid-thigh shorts. "It's like thirty-three degrees!" Jasmine complained, fanning herself with the poster board sign.

Christianne swung her head around and snapped, "Were you in this conversation?"

"Chris," Stéphanie reprimanded with a chuckle. She changed her step pattern and turned so she could see the fifteen-year-old and give her her full attention. "Câline. Seriously? Ugh."

"I know, right? Ahh! And it's so humid, too! Look at my

hair!"

Stéphanie smiled at her younger cousin's perception of humidity in arid Saskatchewan and the supposed adverse effect it was having on her shoulder-length, back-combed, and hair sprayed brown hair, "I think it looks great! Did you already get it cut for school?"

"Mémère made pie!" Simon piped up before Jasmine could respond.

"Simon!" she barked. "I was talking."

Stéphanie grinned at the sibling bickering and turned her attention to the youngest. "Mmm! What kind?"

"Guess!"

"She doesn't want to guess," Jasmine said, but Stéphanie was already suggesting the ten-year-old boy's least favourite dessert.

"Pumpkin?"

"Ick!" he cried. "No! Here, I'll give you a hint—it goes with ice cream."

Stéphanie ruffled his shaggy hair, "Everything goes with ice cream, Mon-mon, but is it Rhubarb-saskatoon?"

"Mmm-hmm!"

"Yum! Did you help with the pies, Nic?" Stéphanie asked, turning towards the shyest of the siblings.

"No, I was working on something with Pépère," Nicole responded.

The teens and Simon sounded like chickadees as they continued on towards the carousel and waited for it to start and spit out suitcases. Meanwhile, the parents were quiet rabbits standing on the sidelines. Lynn looked from face to face to face. Martin shrugged and helplessly turned up his hands. She rubbed her lips together as she thought of something to say. "She looks good," she finally offered as a conversation starter.

"Yeah," Émilie agreed, but did not add what was in her head: *Looks can be deceiving.*

After pie and coffee at Martin and Lynn's split-level home in the tree-lined streets of Regina's Whitmore Park, Robbie drove Stéphanie, her grandparents, and her mother home in Émilie's silver Jetta. It was small but had air conditioning, unlike his truck or his in-laws' old Pontiac Chieftain. Still, it felt stifling to Stéphanie.

She sat in the middle of the backseat with her feet on the transmission hump and her hands about her knees. She did not have to hold herself so stiffly, for all three generations of Tremblay women—Stéphanie, Émilie, and Rose—were slender enough not to take up more than their fair share of the seat, but Stéphanie did not want to be beside Émilie, let alone touch her.

*But that's what family does*, Stéphanie reminded herself. *They share cars and give each other rides.* She grimaced at the thought, at the memory of all the rides Robbie had given her over the years, and of all the talks they'd had on the way to and from places. They had shared about their day, about school and music, the land and stars. They had even talked a bit about the past and the future, but Robbie had never told her he was her father, and she had never asked. She clenched her teeth and scowled.

Thinking the teen was uncomfortable, Rose touched her thigh and said, "It's alright, dear. You can put your feet down beside mine."

Stéphanie smiled at her curly, white-haired grandmother. "No, I'm okay. I like it like this."

Rose smiled back and rubbed affection into Stéphanie's leg. "It's so good to have you back. We missed you."

"I missed you, too," Stéphanie replied, touching her head to her grandmother's. Émilie watched them from the corner of her eye; Stéphanie could feel her mother's longing for the same ease of affection but ignored it and said, "I missed my bed, too!"

"You weren't comfortable in Granby?" Rose asked.

"No, I was. But nothing's as good as home." She smiled genuinely at her grandmother, with whom she had lived since the summer before Émilie went to Africa.

Home since late May and recently married, Émilie was settled with Robbie in the Thibauds' home up the road. She said, "We thought you'd stay with us."

*Why would you think that*? Stéphanie thought snidely, but she replied in a polite tone, "I have a room at Mémère and Pépère's."

"Of course you do, dear," Rose said, patting Stéphanie once again. "But you can have two."

"I will," the eighteen-year-old replied, "when I move to Mononcle and Matante's in a few weeks. Besides, you know I don't like my stuff scattered all over the place."

"But, dear—"

Émilie stopped her mother. "No, Maman. It's fine. We're not far," she said with false cheer. "We can see each other every day, and she'll come over. Right, Stéph? Maybe help Robbie with the gardens and check out the piano he bought me as a wedding present?"

Stéphanie forced herself not to laugh at the suggestion or blurt out, "I wouldn't count on it." Instead, she dug into her performer's bag of tricks and pushed out a smile as genuine as her mother's. "Sure!"

She turned and stared out the windshield, at the deep blue sky and the ribbon of grey highway cutting through prairie that had once been home to free-roaming buffalo and the people who followed them. It was parcelled now and worked into a patchwork of pasturelands and ripening crops of wheat and rapeseed, but when Robbie's maternal grandmother had been a girl, her life had been centred on larger, wild bovines than those grazing along the fences. Their hides had provided clothing and shelter, and their bodies meat for sustenance. Their bones had become tools and toys, ornaments and weapons, medicines and broth, and so much more that had been lost to the family.

Robbie had found a small, beaded pouch this kokum of his had made in a box of his mother's things and offered it to Stéphanie just weeks ago for her high school graduation. She had thanked him politely, then tucked it away in her sock drawer for safekeeping, she said, though it was more like safe hiding.

She blinked away the sting of memories and turned her attention to her grandfather sitting in the passenger seat in front of her. She smiled at the back of his grey head and at as much of his profile as she could see. At seventy-four, he was both soft and strong, but he seemed to have shrunk while Stéphanie was gone. *Maybe it's the heat*, she thought, *or all the excitement of the past few months: Mononcle's birthday, my and Chris' graduations, the wedding.* Her mouth soured at the thought of the event just two weeks past, yet she could not stop scenes from the day replaying in her head.

First, it was her mother standing before her in a white eyelet dress with flutter sleeves and daisies from Robbie's garden woven into the crown of braids around her head. She wore but the simplest of make-up, yet she seemed completely made-over—peaceful in a way Stéphanie had never seen without Émilie getting the help of a pill, a drink, or both.

It was as uncharacteristic as Robbie in a suit. He usually wore jeans and a plain cotton t-shirt wherever he went, yet there he was, standing in a charcoal suit at the end of the aisle.

Part of the bridal party, Stéphanie walked towards him. She wore her ruffled lilac grad dress, and her hair was pinned up and sprayed into place with so much hairspray she could still feel the dry, prickly CFC fumes in the back of her throat.

Robbie's face was as radiant as sunshine in the rain. He watched her walk towards the front of the church as if she were a rainbow, but she had felt nothing like a promise from God nor like a noble Noah who had listened to the command to build an ark. Had she received such directions in the dry prairie, she would have built it in the shape of an airplane and flown away.

"But Maman did that," a voice said inside her head, and she kept stepping right foot after left towards the man who had, at long last, claimed his paternity.

When she reached the front of the church, Robbie stepped forward to press his cheek to hers. Surprised, she jerked and stumbled, but he caught her by the elbows, smiled, and said, "It's okay. I've got you."

*I don't want you to have me*, she thought bitterly. Yet his scent—soap and greenhouse plants, warmth and steadiness—wrapped around her, and for a brief, brief moment she softened in the embrace. Then the truth of the past nine years snapped her back: *He knew. He knew he was my father and never said a word.*

Behind Robbie, Martin, her mononcle and the best man, smiled encouragement. The celebrant of the Mass grinned, too, pleased to see her embrace the father she had, just days before, confessed to dishonouring and even hating. "All is right in the house of the Lord," the priest seemed to say.

*But even Jesus was betrayed with a kiss*, Stéphanie thought.

She took her place with the rest of the teen Tremblay

bridesmaids and forced out a smile as if she were on stage. It was the hardest performance of her life, especially when the vows came: I promise to be true to you in good times and in bad, in sickness and in health.

*Pff,* Stéphanie scoffed inside her head. *C'est ben trop tard pour ça. The good and the bad have already passed. And sickness? It never fell on Robbie to take care of Maman when she was sick from pills and wine. That was me! But go ahead—promise all the love in the world you want to one another and just forget about me.*

She was being selfish, she knew, immature and unforgiving, but it hurt to be there. It wrenched and stabbed and burned Stéphanie all at the same time to see them and listen to them.

She focused on the bouquet instead of the bride and groom. It contained cosmos and gardenia, delphinium and tweedia, and smelled sweet, like cotton candy for the olfactory nerves. But she wished there were roses in the bouquet, roses with thorns she could press her thumb against until she bled.

Stéphanie made it through the rest of the service, the receiving line, and photos. She sat through the roast beef supper and the alcohol-free toasts to the bride and groom. But when Robbie led Émilie by the hand to the middle of the room for their first dance and the swooping orchestral opening of *Puppy Love* filled the school gymnasium-turned-reception-hall, Stéphanie grabbed Christianne's arm and said, "Let's get outta here."


Once Robbie had parked the Jetta in front of the Tremblays' two-storey clapboard house and everyone exited, he and Émilie climbed into his blue Ford half-ton and drove away to their home further up the road. By the time the dust had settled in the yard, Rose, Pierre, and Stéphanie were inside the house opening windows, for the air inside was heavy and hot after having been closed all day. It still smelled like home to Stéphanie. She relished the notes of Pine Sol and Pledge, fried onions, and homemade bread as she moved about the house.

"I'll do the upstairs," her grandmother said once they made it to the kitchen. "Then I'm going to wash up and change. Why don't you two catch up? There's iced tea in the fridge, and we have some real lemons you can add if you want."

"That sounds great, Mémère. Thanks!" Stéphanie replied.

Her grandmother's eyes sparkled like dew-covered clover in fresh morning sunlight. She smiled and waved Stéphanie's thanks away as she turned towards the back stairs.

"It's not the powdered stuff," Pierre said as he walked towards the fridge. "Mémère brewed it overnight the way people used to do it."

"Good." She opened a cupboard and removed two glasses. "I like it better that way."

Pierre chuckled. "I know." He set a three-quarter-filled glass pitcher of amber liquid onto the counter, then returned to the fridge for a lemon. Stéphanie filled the glasses with tea. Pierre opened a drawer and took out a serrated steak knife that he used to slice the lemon in half once, then twice. Stéphanie watched him with the adoring eyes of a puppy. He smiled at her attention. "Sit," he said, nodding his head towards the round oak table he had made decades before.

She obeyed, rested her elbows on the table, interlaced her fingers beneath her chin, and watched him squeeze a quarter lemon into one glass and then the other. He wore rubber soled slippers, cotton pants with a belt, and a tucked-in short-sleeved dress shirt with a light blue checkered print. He was tanned from the summer sun and a lifetime of work. He was wrinkled too, and his hair was no longer black. His eyes, however, were still the same deep obsidian orbs that had made Stéphanie fall in love with him the moment they met and, years later, allowed her to absolve him without delay for the role he had played in hiding her father's identity.

Pierre shook the juice from his hands, then licked the tips of his fingers. "Mmmm," he sounded.

Stéphanie laughed lovingly at him and at the pleasure he took in the smallest things, things like lemons and sitting with her at the kitchen table. She liked these things, too, especially the latter—she had traded nine summers on the road and eighteen months in Africa with her mother for it.

Pierre rinsed his hands in the bowl of wash water in the kitchen sink, dried them on the frayed hand towel hanging on the side of the cupboard, then picked up the glasses of iced tea and carried them towards the table. He set one down before Stéphanie and one at the place beside her. He pulled out the chair and sat, smiling at his eldest grandchild with the same awe as if she were a blue jay visiting his feeder. She smiled back, grateful to be home with him once again.

He picked up his glass with his still-strong hand and toasted, "Santé."

"To health," she repeated and clinked her glass to his. They drank. "Mmm. The fresh lemon just makes it so good."

"Mmmhmm," he agreed. They smiled and drank some more, then sat in silence with cold lemon tea and love between them. Finally, Pierre spoke, "You sounded angry when you sang your last song up there in Granby."

She hid her eyes and nodded. "That's because I was," she mumbled.

He placed his strong hand on hers. "I know, and you have every right to be. And you should sing about it, ma fille, but not on stage. It won't do anybody any good up there. Not even you."

She nodded in agreement and closed her eyes against her tears. They still slipped out down her face. Pierre caught them with a thick finger and smoothed her hair as he began to sing a Latin hymn from his childhood, "Stabat mater dolorsa juxta crucem lacrimosa …

*I am seven years old and sit in the corner of a barn near Saint-Patrice, Québec, with my knees drawn up and my arms about them. I sing the songs my mother taught me. It is like the scent of wild roses that have thorns and causes my eyes to well.*

*In the house across the yard, my aunts and uncles are assembled. 'Who are the godparents?' one aunt asks. The faces turn and interrogate one another with glowering eyes.*

*"I'm the boy's," a man finally admits. He runs his tongue over his teeth. 'But I don't want that tuberculosis plague in my house. I have children of my own."*

*"Voyons. We all have children," the others say. "And it's just the parents who have it."*

*"For now," the uncle grumbles.*

*"I'll take the baby," an aunt offers, "but you have to take Pierre."*

*The uncle's eyes turn to black beads. "Tabernak," he swears. "D'accord. But he'll stay in the barn. It's almost summer; he won't be cold."*

*I am cold at night and in the morning, but I warm when I walk past the whitewashed house where my parents lie sick in their bed. I walk towards my home and stare at the curtained window on the second floor. "I love you," I say to the people inside.*

*One day, I go inside. I walk right through the door and up the stairs, then down the hall to Maman and Papa's room. I kneel beside the bed and take my mother's hand. It is cold; her chest is hollow. "Maman," I sob. "Maman. Maman."*

*My father is also in bed. I can hear his heavy, phlegmy breathing. I want to crawl beside Papa, but I am afraid he will wake up and start to cough.*

*I hear the ringing of the church bell off in the distance, and I remember Papa lifting me up to the rope and telling me to hold on as he pulled it. I rode the rope down and up and down. I don't know when this happened, but I remember it, remember the happiness of it, the joy of my father's strength.*

*The door opens below. There are footsteps on the stairs and in the hall. I do not hide. "Mondieu!" a woman shrieks. "Pierre! What are you doing here?" She rushes towards me and pushes me away from the bed. "Don't touch that." She leans over my mother and sighs.*

*I stare at Maman's arm hanging over the side of the bed like a weeping willow. The nurse lifts the limb and folds it across Maman's chest, then makes a cross over her own body with her right hand. "Que Dieu l'accueille." She sighs, then turns to face me. "You cannot stay here." She scoops me up and slings me over her shoulder.*

*"Non!" I cry. "Non!" I pummel her back with my fists, but the nurse is strong, and she carries me out of the bedroom, through the house and out the door. "Non!" I scream. "Je veux rester! Je veux rester!"*

*"You can't stay!" She stalks out of the yard and*

*down the dirt road. The house blurs behind my
tears. I whimper the half mile to my uncle's house. It
is May. The grass is green. The sun is warm. The
nurse sets me down on the top step of the porch.
"Wait here," she orders. "I must speak with your
uncle."*

*I obey. She raps on the door with a solid fist. The
door opens.*

*"What's he doing here?" my uncle demands
without stepping outside.*

*"I found him in his parents' room."*

*"Câlice de merde! Le maudit chien de bâtard de
câline de cri—"*

*"His mother is dead." The man stops cursing and
closes the door in the nurse's face. "Monsieur
Tremblay!" She pounds on the wooden door. "I
have to talk to you!"*

*"Non! Go away!"*

*"Mais, Monsieur, someone has to take care of her
body."*

*"I'll send the undertaker!" He shouts through the
door. "Now take your tuberculosis and get off my
property!"*

*"But what about the boy?"*

*"Take him to his father."*

*"But he's almost dead!"*

*"So? You're a nurse! Tend to him!" He slams the
door.*

*She bangs on it and calls, "Mais Monsieur
Tremblay! Monsieur Tremblay!" He does not
answer. She gives up eventually and leans her head
against the door while she discusses the matter with
herself. At last, she sighs and turns to leave.*

*"Come," she says as she passes me. "I'll take you home."*

*I raise my eyes from my knees and see her hand stretched out to me. I clutch it and follow her lead.*

*We do not speak. Bees buzz in the ditch. Dust rises from our feet. I struggle to keep up. She slows but remains determined. She guides me home, pulls me up the wooden porch and over the threshold, then to the back of the house, where the kitchen is clean and unused. She places me in a chair at the table my father made.*

*"I'll give you a bite, and then I'll go see how things are." We both nod at the unsaid. I run my hand over the surface of the table. I follow the swirls of the wood. My eyes fill. "Why did you come here?" the nurse asks as she opens a cupboard.*

*"I missed them," I say.*

*The nurse blinks away a sting of tears. "I only have bread right now," she says and saws a thick slice, then hunts in the cupboard for something to spread across it. She finds my mother's stash of last year's blueberries made into jam. I had helped pick them. The nurse prepares the bread and sets it before me. "Here. I'll go up." She squeezes my shoulder as she leaves.*

*I remain. I look at the bread and jam. I scan the room that had once been full of happiness: Maman cooking, Papa talking about the deer in a field, my baby sister cooing over peas. My eyes stop on a bunch of dried herbs hanging from a nail. "Smell," Maman had said when she cut them in the fall. "Ahh! It smells like life!"*

*Tears fall onto the bread.*

*There is a knock at the door. I do not move. The nurse's footsteps sound overhead, then on the stairs and towards the door. It opens. She whispers. A man replies. I hear two sets of footsteps climb the stairs and cross to my parents' room, then descend and return to the door. They disappear outside only to return and retrace the same path once again, but much slower.*

*When all the movement is finished, the nurse comes to me. She touches my shoulder again and lowers herself to speak to me, "Your father, he is dead as well." I lower my forehead to the table and cry without making a sound.*

*Later, I find myself curled on the chesterfield under an afghan that smells of Maman. Papa's muskiness lingers in the fabric of the cushions. I close my eyes and drift back to sleep. I dream of my uncle Henri carrying a tan slice of bread covered with molasses on a plate to the barn. He places it on the top of the pen post. "Tiens," he barks, then turns away. When he is gone, I reach for it, then gobble it in an instant. I slip out from my stall, skulk out of the barn, and run up the road. My side aches, but Maman is calling me, so I continue to run and run, but I don't get any closer.*

*"Pierre. Pierre." I jerk awake. "Pierre," the nurse says again. "I made you some porridge."*

*I blink back to reality and nod. I follow her to the kitchen. It does not smell like cinnamon. The brown sugar is not on the table. Nonetheless, I sit and pick up the spoon beside the bowl the nurse has prepared for me. I dig into the thick, gooey mound and raise it to my mouth. It is slimy and without taste. I swallow away the awful mouthful.*

*"I have to take you to your uncle," the nurse says.*

*"Why?"*

*She sighs. "That's just how it is."*

*We walk together down the dirt road to Henri Tremblay's farm. Neither of us notices the bluebells growing along the path nor the robins in the trees. I think of my parents: Maman's cinnamon hair; Papa's square jaw and smiling lips. I try to remember the timbre of their voices, the variations of hazelnut in their eyes.*

*"I can't take him," my uncle says from his porch.*

*"He's your nephew!" the nurse cries.*

*"I don't care. Take him away." My uncle's lips curl, and he flicks his hand. "Take him to the convent."*

*The nurse blinks and gasps but presses on, "Don't you think he should be with his family now that both of his parents are dead?"*

*My uncle's face twitches at the news, but any sentimentality he may have had soon passes. "Fine. Fetch his sister and take her along."*

*"Sale cochon! Do your own dirty work!" The nurse stalks away but stops mid-step when she passes me. She squats down and takes my hands. "I wish I could take you." My eyes ask her why she cannot, but she does not hear them. "Good luck."*

*Soon, my little sister, Émilie, is in my arms. She wants to look over the edge of the wagon and reach her hands out to touch the turning wheel. I tighten my hold on her and sing into her thin dark hair like Maman used to do. Émilie la-las and goo-goos and waves her arms in the air. It has been weeks since we have been together.*

*Our uncle pulls his wagon to a stop in front of a large stone building and jumps down. He storms up the steps and bangs on the door. He bangs and bangs and bangs. After a time, a nun in a white wimple and black flowing robe opens the door.*

*Henri flails and gestures as he speaks. The nun pushes past him and rushes to the wagon. "Mes enfants," she says to me and Émilie. "I am la Soeur Saint-Martin. Come with me." She smiles and holds out her hand. I clutch Émilie to my chest and slide towards the beckoning nun. She takes Émilie, then helps me down. I hide in the folds of her robe as we cross towards the convent orphanage. "You should be ashamed," Soeur Saint-Martin hurls at the man. "Come," she says gently as she leads me past.*

*Henri Tremblay sneers and storms away. I hear the stones crunch under his boots and the sound of the wagon move as the man, my father's brother, climbs in. I hear the horse shift and the crack of the whip, the cry of "Hi-yah," and the reaction of the steed, the rumbling away of the wagon. I do not look up.*

*There are ten steps in front of me and six more inside. I count them to myself as I follow Soeur Saint-Martin into the building. She leads me down hallway after hallway until she finally stops. A door creaks. Soeur Saint-Martin whispers to another nun, then passes Émilie across the doorway. The door begins to close. I lunge forward and reach for Émilie. "Non!" I cry. "Please! Please, don't take my sister!"*

*Soeur Saint-Martin catches me and holds me with her hands. "Ça va aller. You'll see her on Sunday."*

*The door closes. My tears splash onto my dusty shoes."*

Stéphanie and Pierre sat in silence as the last notes of his song died away. Then, he looked at his eldest granddaughter and said, "You should sing that. It'll take away your pain and make you sing like yourself again."

She sniffed and nodded and said, "I'll try."

### Derrière chez nous y un étang

It was the moon, people said, the full moon that caused Lucille Thibaud and Rose Tremblay to go into labour and give birth the same night in November 1946. The twin boys and neighbour girl were wrapped in blue and pink and set into a single bassinet in order of birth: Roch, Émilie, Robert. They were photographed for the parents and the newspaper. The headline read: Les Triplés de Lasalette.

They grew up across the field from one another, five miles from Lasalette, a lively francophone village that boasted a Catholic Church with a Cassavant organ, a school, a skating rink, and a bit more. It was an oasis in the middle of the semi-arid lands of the Palisser Triangle in southeastern Saskatchewan, where the buffalo roamed before they were replaced by French-speaking settlers and the railroad.

The twins were seemingly identical, but baby Émilie knew who was who and always rolled towards Robbie whenever she was placed between them. In time, others came to recognize the boys' differences as well. Roch was the larger of the twins, the mischievous rascal being pulled by the ear or elbowed by his parents during Mass, while Robert was the straight-backed altar server, the thurifer who did not grimace or even flinch when incense smoke billowed up from the loaded censer he carried.

"They're night and day," people said about the boys, but their mother always insisted they were more like dusk and dawn, shades of both and of each other.

Martin wished he were one of them, but he was the fourth born eighteen months later. He was the smallest and the slowest, the last to talk, walk, and run, but he caught up and became part of the group. The four of them trampled through snow and dirt to play tag and hide-n-go-seek, to skate on sloughs and slide down frosted hills. They shared bus seats and mittens, coughs and colds. They annoyed one another, too, and took sides. They often split up two against two: Roch and Martin, Robbie and Émilie. The first two became blood brothers, while the other two thought such a thing was not required, for they were already linked by birth.

It all ended, however, one day when the triplets were twelve and Martin was not yet eleven. The four sat on the carpeted floor of the Thibauds' living room with a game of Monopoly between them and decades of Thibaud family memorabilia about them: framed pictures and family photos, homemade dollies and rag rugs, the television, and a piano on which Lucille Thibaud had taught not only her twins and their five older brothers to play but also Émilie and Martin as well. The four young friends could all play by sight and ear, but only Émilie could memorize a piece by simply looking at the dots and lines of a score and play back a tune she had heard only once.

In the board game, Émilie rolled and passed Go. She landed on Baltimore Avenue, collected two hundred dollars, then paid Robbie two dollars in rent. "Watch my properties for a minute?" she asked him as she stood. "I have to go to the bathroom."

"Okay," he grinned, and she ran off.

The boys each rolled, then Roch called, "Mimi! It's your turn!"

She didn't answer.

"E-em!" Martin sing-sang.

"I'm putting you in jail," Roch yelled.

"You'd better hurry," Martin added, "or you'll never get out."

The two continued to laugh and joke about stealing Émilie's money, moving her shoe piece, and stacking the Community Chest cards.

"I'll go see what's taking her so long," Robbie said, getting up. He crossed through the kitchen to the back of the house and knocked on the bathroom door. "Em? Are you okay?"

"Robbie?" Her voice shook.

He pushed the door open and stuck his head in. "Yeah?"

Émilie was sitting on the toilet. Her face was paler than usual. "I'm bleeding."

"Where?" he asked in a tight, worried voice.

She pointed. "Down there."

"Oh." Robbie stood in silence for a moment, trying to make sense of it.

"Can you get your mom?"

"Mm-hm." He started to back out of the door.

"Robbie?"

He turned back towards her. "Yeah?"

"Don't tell the others, okay? Just tell them I'm sick and go on without me."

Robbie nodded and closed the door. He found his grey-haired mother sewing in the next room. "Maman?" he said.

She looked up from her Singer. "Have you four finished yelling?" she asked, holding pins with her teeth.

"Maman," he repeated. "Émilie's bleeding."

Lucille Thibaud jerked her attention away from her work

and pulled the pins from her mouth. "Quoi? Où? Qu'est-ce qui s'est passé?"

Robbie's words were weak and sticky as he repeated Émilie's words, "Down there."

She touched her chest and raised her eyes to the ceiling. "Seigneur." She sighed and shook her head. "Where is she?"

"In the bathroom. She wants to see you."

"Bien sûr. I'm going right now." She rushed past him.

"Maman?" the boy asked. Lucille stopped and turned back to look at him. "Is she going to be alright?"

The corner of her eyes wrinkled as she smiled. She rubbed his back and kissed his head. "Oh, mon chou. She's fine. She's just becoming a woman." Robbie squinted at her in confusion. She rubbed his back again. "It's what happens to girls. I'll tell you more later, but let me go talk to Émilie first, okay?"

Robbie nodded, although he was still confused. He knew how heifers turned into cows, but he did not think it was the same for girls. *But then why is there blood down there?* he wondered.

He heard his mother knock on the bathroom door and say, "Émilie, chérie, can I come in?" He heard the door open and close, and then he heard Émilie sob. He went to the bathroom door and touched his hand to it.

"You-who!" Roch called from the living room. He and Martin guffawed.

Robbie walked back to them. "Émilie's sick," he said.

"What's wrong?" Martin asked, perking up like a guard dog.

Robbie waved his hands to calm him down, even though he himself felt queasy. "She's with our mom." Martin's forehead scrunched as he considered this. Robbie's heart raced. "She'll be okay," he said without much conviction.

Martin began to stand. "I'd better go see."

"No!" Robbie said too loudly. "It's nothing. She's with our mom. Why don't we go look for Molly's kittens instead?" They did, and Émilie lay in the Thibauds' spare bed until her father came to take her and Martin home.

There was to be no more Monopoly after that, no more skating or sledding, at least not with the boys. Émilie was a woman now, her mother said; she was to stay home and learn how to be one. Rose had Émilie clean more, cook, and bake. She made macaroons and coconut bars to take to school.

"Can't you make nun's farts or cinnamon rolls?" Roch complained when she shared them. "You know I don't like coconut."

She shrugged. "Sorry." She turned to Robbie. "What should I make next? Chocolate peaks? Coconut-cherry squares?"

"Anything," he answered.

"Anything," Roch mocked later at home. "Oh Émilie, I'll eat anything you make."

Robbie's face flushed. Roch scowled and taunted his brother with a crude song and dance, "Coconut. Coconut. 'Tis good for my little nuts." He swung his hips and held his hands to his chest like a Hawaiian bra.

Robbie threw a cushion at him. "Stop it."

Roch caught the cushion and started dancing with it as he continued to sing, "Émilie. Queen of coconut. You drive me oh so nuts." He threw the cushion back at Robbie, jumped onto his brother, and pushed the throw cushion against his face.

"Ow! Stop it!" Robbie struggled to push Roch off.

Roch gave him a final push. "Coconut boy," he growled.

He walloped Robbie with the cushion, then stormed away. Robbie remained alone on the couch, wondering why Roch had gotten so rough.

Despite Rose's insistence that Émilie stay away from the Thibaud boys, she still saw them every day. It was difficult not to since they lived up the road, were on the same school bus, and were in the same class at school. There was the hockey rink, too. Martin always played up a level so he could be with the twins, and since he was an excellent goalie, no one but his mother, who feared bruises and worse from the older and stronger boys' shots, ever complained.

Émilie saw the Thibaud boys at Sunday Mass as well, and sometimes these were followed by dinners at one another's homes. One Sunday in late March, the Tremblays were seated at the Thibauds' table. Lucille had the kitchen window open a crack to cool the house after cooking ham and potatoes, cake, and coffee. The freshness of thawing manure wafted in with the lowing of cows and the meowing of cats. Small waterfalls of melted snow dripped and trickled as they ran off the roof into an overflowing rain barrel. Inside, the kitchen was cozy chaos from the counters to the table. There were dishes, food, and ingredients on every flat surface. Nothing matched except the children and their parents. A stranger would have easily identified the black-haired Pierre as Martin and Émilie's sire, as sure as Roch and Robbie were Lucille's sons.

"Allez," Lucille Thibaud said after a dinner of ham and mashed potatoes, tomato aspic and boiled corn. "Go play outside. Madame and I'll clean up. It's too nice for you to be cooped up inside."

"Woo-hoo!" Roch cheered and pushed himself away from the table.

Martin followed suit. "Merci!"

"Are you sure, Maman?" Robbie asked.

She nodded and smiled. "Yes. Go on."

He smiled back. "Merci."

"Émilie will help clean up," Rose said before Robbie was on his feet.

"Oh, no," Lucille insisted. "No. It's fine. Really. Look at that sunshine. She should go and play, too."

Rose shook her head. "She's too old to play."

Lucille waved the words away. "She's twelve."

Émilie studied the cake crumbs on her plate. Robbie snuck a look at Rose. Her back was straight; her mouth was tight. If ever he had thought Émilie was soft sculpted marble, then surely her mother was a cold, hard slab of rock untouched by an artist's hands.

"Oh, let her play," Francis Thibaud laughed. "She'll have lots of time to do dishes in her lifetime."

Rose made a sound; Pierre touched her knee. She lowered her eyes to look at it. "D'accord," she finally conceded.

Émilie pushed her chair back. "Merci," she said. She rushed to the porch and started to dress to go outside. Robbie waited for her to button her coat and tie her boots. He opened the door and held it for her. "I hate that she does that," Émilie said as they crossed the yard. "She thinks I shouldn't play with you and Roch just because I … you know …" She rolled her eyes to fill in the blanks about her menstruation.

He nodded at her meaning. "Wanna go swing in the barn?"

Émilie's teeth showed as she smiled. "Yeah. Race ya!" She burst into a run and dashed to the sliding door of the wooden barn. "Ha-ha! I win!"

Robbie captured her smile to replay in his mind later on: the soft frame of her blue scarf, the pink of her cheeks, the happiness in her face. He smiled back and pushed on the door to slide it open. She passed through to the dusty shadows.

Roch and Martin, above them, yelped in the hayloft. "I guess they had the same idea," Robbie said.

"Yeah," Émilie said, bending down to pet a thin grey cat weaving between her legs. "Hello there. Who are you?"

Robbie looked over her shoulder. "That's Fanny," he said. "One of Molly's kittens."

"Really? She's so big! What about Nannerl?" she inquired about the cat she had named after Mozart's sister.

"She's big too, but a lot shyer." He tiptoed towards a stack of bales and pursed his lips together as he called the cat with a kissy sound. "Minou. Minou." There was a soft response behind the bales. He squeezed between them and the wall. "Viens, Nanny. Viens voir Émilie." Émilie watched Robbie bend over and scoop up another six-month-old grey barn cat. He held it close to his chest and cupped its head like a protective father. "There, there. It's okay. Émilie's your friend. She named you." The cat dug its claws into his wool jacket as he walked towards Émilie. He turned so she could see the fury being.

"Oh, look at her. She's so scared." Émilie slowly extended her hand towards the cat, but it clawed Robbie and leapt from his arms. She landed on a bale and raced away.

"Ooouf. Sorry."

Émilie shrugged. "It's okay." Fanny wove between her legs again. Émilie's long black braid fell over her shoulder as she leaned to pet the cat named after another composer's sister. "Wanna go upstairs?" Robbie grinned and nodded. Émilie moved to the ladder and climbed. She waited at the top for Robbie.

"You can go first," he said, motioning towards the wall with his chin.

"Thanks." Her entire face smiled. Robbie's did, too.

"Bombs away!" Roch yelled. He gripped the mow rope

with his hands and jumped from his perch on the far wall into the dusty air. "You-who-who-who-whoooo!" he bellowed as he swung across the barn. Émilie cheered and waved her arm over her head. She crossed the hayloft. Roch swung back and forth until his speed slowed, then he dropped to the hay below.

"Wooo!" he yelled, raising his legs and arms into the air.

"My turn," Martin called from his perch on the wall. "Pass it to me."

Roch rolled to his feet and caught the mow rope. He flung it towards Martin. "Okay, Goose! Catch!"

Martin caught it with his arm and wrapped himself about it. He jumped into the expanse of air above the straw. "Ouiiii!" he yelled.

Émilie laughed at him as she scaled the wall. She watched him drop to the hay and jump to his feet with his arms outstretched and straw caught in his hair. "Yeah!" she called.

"Em's turn," Robbie said. Roch scrunched his face and mimicked him. Martin laughed and flung the thick rope across the barn to Émilie. She caught it, gripped it with her hands and one leg, then she jumped from her perch. The rest happened before anyone realized it: she twisted and turned and hit the wall. A gag of pain escaped everyone's mouth. Émilie fell from the air and landed beside the pile of straw.

"Émilie!" The three boys shouted. Robbie shimmied down the wall and ran across the barn. Roch and Martin were already at her side, kneeling and looking at her pale face and mauve eyelids, when he arrived.

Martin touched her arm. "Em? Em?" He looked up at Roch and Robbie. They exchanged wide-eyed stares and swallowed the sickness rising in their guts. Martin turned back to his sister. "Émilie?" She did not move.

Roch shook her. "Mimi! Mimi!"

"Don't," Robbie said, pushing Roch's hand away. "I think she hit her head."

"So? She's okay," Roch shook her again.

"No! Don't! That's not what you're supposed to do. Go get Monsieur Tremblay." Robbie's eyes glared; his face was set.

"She'll be okay," Roch reached around Robbie. "I'll wake her up. She'll be fine."

Robbie grasped Roch's hand and pulled it from Émilie's arm. "No. Go get her dad," he insisted.

"I'll get him," Martin said, pushing himself up from the floor.

"No, Goose," Roch said, "don't."

Martin stopped. "Why not?"

"'Cause she'll be okay."

"No, she won't," Robbie insisted. "She fell hard. She needs Dr. Niells."

"No, she doesn't."

"Yes, she does!" The gold flecks of their eyes glowed yellow in a locked stare. "Go get your dad," Robbie ordered.

"I am!" Martin said as he rushed to the ladder. "Don't move her, okay?" He disappeared down the loft. His running sounded like horse hooves.

Robbie brushed wisps of Émilie's hair off her face. "You'll be alright," he murmured. He held her hand, touched her cheek. The tenderness in his voice riled Roch.

"I'm not taking the blame for this," he said.

Robbie did not lift his eyes from Émilie. "It's okay," he soothed. Roch did not know if he was talking to him or comforting Émilie.

She mumbled and opened her eyes. "Robbie?"

Roch rushed to her side and sandwiched her hand in his. Robbie still held the other. "Shhh," Robbie calmed. "It's okay. You just fell." She held his gaze for a moment before her eyes rolled back, and she lost consciousness again. "Émilie!" Robbie cried.

Roch gulped. "Mimi?" Her hand was heavy in his.

The boys blinked and watched her chest rise and fall. They stared at her pale face and closed eyes. Robbie said, "Monsieur Tremblay'll be here soon. He'll know what to do." His voice was tight and thin; his breath echoed in canon with Roch's in the silence of waiting. Finally, they heard footsteps pounding outside, then rushing down below.

"Émilie!" Pierre called from the ladder. "Émilie!" Robbie shuffled over to make room for him at her side. Pierre surveyed his daughter. His eyes welled as he touched her colourless cheek. "Ma fille ..."

"She hit the wall," Robbie explained, "and then she fell."

Pierre nodded as the information registered. "Okay." He observed Émilie as a patient now, as if he were young and back at a Québec logging camp administering first aid to his epileptic friend, Grenier. "Has she been out the whole time?"

"No. She woke up for a minute. She said my name."

"Good." Pierre leaned in closer to Émilie's face and called her name as if she were a frightened kitten.

Rose's head popped into the hayloft. "How is she?" she demanded as she rushed over. Roch and Robbie scurried away, but they were both seared by her glare. "What did you two do?"

"Nothing," Robbie said. "We were just—"

"You will just leave her alone! And never touch her again!"

"Rose!" Lucille Thibaud gasped. "It's not their fault!"

Roch seemed to slink away, but Robbie was frozen in Rose's stare. Martin draped his arm over his mother. "It was an accident," he soothed. "She fell."

Rose trembled. She turned her eyes towards Pierre and

Émilie. "Is she okay?" she whispered.

"We should take her to Dr. Niells," Pierre answered. He pushed himself back onto his feet and slid his hands under Émilie. He picked her up. Her legs draped over his arm; her head rested against his chest. He motioned to the twins' father with his head. "Francis. Go down first and help me down." Monsieur Thibaud set into motion—he was still strong despite his grey hair and grandfather status.

"You go, too," Lucille told Roch. "Just to make sure."

He went first; Francis followed. They waited, the younger supporting the older, for Pierre and Émilie on the ladder. "Boys," Pierre said. Robbie and Martin rushed to his side. "I can't carry her this way unless you two help. I'll hold her up here, but one of you needs to hold her legs and the other should help support her neck." The boys listened, then manoeuvred and helped carry Émilie down the ladder.

The women watched with big eyes. "Attention. Soyez prudent," they said as if praying in call and response. "Be careful."

At the bottom of the ladder, Pierre paused and readjusted Émilie's body in his arms. Her eyes opened. She looked around at the faces in the grey barn. Her eyes lit on Robbie. "What's going on?"

"You fell. Your dad's taking you to see Dr. Niells."

"Let's go," Rose insisted, touching her hand to Pierre's shoulder. "Martin," she called. "Allons-y."

Francis accompanied the Tremblays to their car. Roch, Robbie, and Lucille watched them from the open barn door. "It was an accident," Robbie mumbled.

"I know," Lucille said. She wrapped her arm about him and followed his gaze across the yard to the Tremblays' Chieftain. Rose sat stiff and straight in the front seat. Lucille clucked, "Cette femme. She had no right to yell at you."

"She's just worried about Émilie," Robbie said.

Lucille shook her silver head. "No. It's more than that." She chewed her lip, but her frustration slipped out, "She always gets her back up about you boys for no reason. I tell you, if her parents hadn't taken in my brother way back when, I'd've told her a thing or two over the years."

"Maman!" Robbie gasped.

Roch chuckled. "I thought Papa was the one with the temper."

She blushed and smiled. "He is." She shook her head at Roch's smirk and gave him a playful swat. "Oh, you. Go finish the dishes. Robbie, come say the rosary with me."

In the car, Rose fumed, "Those boys! She should never have been with those boys!"

It caused Émilie's eyes to run more than the pain, which passed within a few days.

## 2. Chaconne
## April 1990

*H*ome, Stéphanie thought as she stared out the window of her dorm room in Laval. *That's what Maman always called it. 'Let's call home,' she'd say, then we'd count back hours to see what time it was in Lasalette before we called Mémère and Pépère.*

Stéphanie had loved those calls. She'd always hoped it was noon in Saskatchewan and that Mononcle Martin and Matante Lynn were over for dinner with their children. Stéphanie loved to imagine them, her family on the other end, huddled about the phone listening to her sing the German folk songs she had learned at her Swiss school. The way they called "Bravo!" always made her warm inside, and she would sing as long as her mother would let her.

Stéphanie's eyes always blurred when she said goodbye, and the line was cut; the dial tone ground in her ear until Émilie took the receiver from her fingers, placed it on its cradle, and said, "Time for bed."

Stéphanie would nod, walk to the washroom, brush her teeth, look at herself in the mirror and wonder who back home she might resemble. *Who has this square face?* she wondered. *This tan skin? These patchwork eyes?* "Tell me about them," she said when she crawled into bed.

Her mother shrugged and shook her head. "Oh, Coco. I don't know where to start."

Stéphanie touched Émilie's hand. "Sure, you do," she said. "At the beginning. With the blueberries."

Her mother smiled then, and a chuckle rolled from somewhere inside of her that Stéphanie could rarely access. "Saskatoon berries," she corrected.

"I know," Stéphanie grinned. "Tell me."

Émilie nodded in reply and began the story the way her grandmother had years before, "He had never said I love you, had never held her hand, nor smiled at her as if she were the only person in the world that mattered to him, but Sylvie Simard loved Baptiste Caron since before she even knew what that word meant." Stéphanie nestled into the comfort of her mother's side as she went on.

"He had been as present in her life as her brothers—always at the schoolyard or church or even at her home. But it was different with Baptiste. When he walked into the room, Sylvie's ears reddened and her heartbeat quickened. When he spoke, she felt her body tingle and weaken. She thought of him at night, wondered if he got cold sleeping alone. She wondered, too, if he slept on his side facing her house and thought of her, listened to her whisper his name in the darkness of her room across the field.

"And when Sylvie and her younger sister picked blueberries in the bluff along the Simard and Caron property line, she liked to imagine that Baptiste was working close by, and she would make her way to him, wade through the growing wheat and hand him a pitcher of cold water fresh from the well. But he was never there, and she had to carry the heavy pitcher home again.

"Then one day, when she was sixteen, the train whistle

shattered her reverie. 'That must be Baptiste,' her sister Marguerite said.

"Sylvie nodded; she knew it was—their elder brothers had gone to town that morning to bid him farewell. Her heartbeat pounded in her ears. 'Mmm,' was all she could say, and she stood in the sun and listened to the distant whistle. Toooooot. Toooooot.

"Sylvie closed her eyes against the tears welling inside. She imagined the station in town, the heavy smell of the dirty air, the squeal of the locomotive's wheels, the churning of the coupling rods pumping and turning and pushing the train, Baptiste's train, away from the Bas-Saint-Laurent. Away from the blueberries. Away from her.

"She dreamed of him after he was gone, of him stooking hay and sawing wood, of him tapping his foot and playing the fiddle. But more, she dreamed of him dressed in a well-pressed suit, standing tall in a distant prairie church, the sun casting a beam through the wood-paned window as he waited for his bride. He was broad and strong with hair the colour of rich earth and lips like strawberry jam. His reddish-brown eyes were fixed on the bride walking towards him.

"Even as she slept, Sylvie could feel the anticipation, the beating of hearts as the bride walked closer and closer to Baptiste. She arrived at the front of the church, and Baptiste caught her hand in his. Together they turned front and repeated the priest's Latin. 'Volo,' he said.

"'Volo,' she replied.

"Then Baptiste lifted her gossamer veil, and Sylvie would wake with a jerk, with tears and shortness of breath. It was not her beneath that veil. It was never her whom Baptiste kissed, married in that distant prairie church. She rolled and pressed her face into her pillow to stifle her sobs and told herself it was only a dream, a nightmare, that made her cry.

"She had the same dream for months, and then her turn came to take the train west to join her father and the other settlers in this place called Lasalette.

"It took ten days. Hills and trees gave way to rock and lakes, to large, flat expanses of white. She should have been happy, excited at least, but each rock of the train tore at her: what if her dreams were true? What if she found Baptiste married in Lasalette?

"He was waiting for her along with the others in her father's one-room house. The stove was stoked, and the table was covered with meats, pies, and cakes. Prosper Lepine was squeezing out tunes on his accordion, and there was dancing and singing; someone was tapping spoons. It was convivial, a prairie welcome for the Simard women, but Baptiste stood on the fringes of it without his fiddle, sulking at the sight and sounds of another pioneer night for bachelors and married couples.

"Oh, poor Baptiste, there in the corner on the far side of the room, his arms held tight against his sides, his toes scrunched up inside his boots. Despite the stove and the crowd, he was cold; he had been cold since November. He felt it in his back, on the flesh of his nose, at the tips of his feet. He usually took refuge beneath feather quilts and afghans, rolling himself into a ball and lamenting the wind, the darkness, the empty space beside him, and counting days until spring like rosary prayers, but now, one month past the equinox, there was still snow, still cold and emptiness.

"'C'est bien, non?' his friend Théophile asked, putting his arm about his shoulder and handing him a glass of amber liquid.

"'What is?' Baptiste asked, raising the drink to his lips.

"Théophile laughed and elbowed him. 'Ha! The women, of course!'

"Baptiste shrugged. 'I already know them,' he said, 'from back home.'

"Théophile's eyebrows rose with interest, and he pressed Baptiste for details, but he had few to give. He could not recall Sylvie and Marguerite Simard's height, size, or hair colour. 'Ce ne sont que des fillettes,' he said.

"Ah,' Théophile complained, 'girls! Bon Dieu. When will some women come?'

"The door opened then, and a cheer rose up, and Baptiste and Théophile soon saw that Sylvie and Marguerite were not little girls: they had breasts and hips and, Sylvie, well, Baptiste thought she was beautiful with her green eyes and chocolate-coloured hair.

"She did not see him right away, for she was being hugged and kissed by everyone in the room. Then she heard his voice, felt his hands clasp hers, and she was seized, clutched by some internal grip that would either stop her heart from pumping or give it a reason to beat. She looked up to his face, paled from the long winter and shaven for the occasion, and saw that his russet eyes were fixed on her. This, Sylvie knew, was not a dream.

"They did not see each other again for three days: after Mass in the small wooden church made from local aspen and wood carried in by teams of horses. He greeted her with cheek kisses and twinkling eyes. Her mother invited him for lunch and moved her eyes back and forth between him and Sylvie throughout the meal as if she were trying to determine whether the two might fit together like puzzle pieces. It made Sylvie blush and smile.

"In the coming weeks and months, Baptiste was allowed to accompany her to Mass and to soirées in neighbouring homes. He played the fiddle, and she sang along.

"When the snow melted, he picked crocuses for her and

daisies later in the spring. In summer, he showed her the small purple berries that grew in a bluff in his uncle's field. She plucked them from his cupped hand and laughed at the odd prairie blueberries. 'They're not blueberries,' he corrected with a smile. 'They're saskatoons.'

"'Saskatoons,' she repeated, munching the strange word. She pondered for a moment as she chewed the berries, then declared, 'I like them.'

"Baptiste smiled as he watched her lick her lips. 'And me?' he asked.

"The berries were suddenly heavy in Sylvie's stomach, dry in her mouth. 'And you?' she whispered.

"He nodded and took her hand. 'Et oui. Moi. Do you like me?'

"Some berries fell on the ground, but neither noticed nor cared. Sylvie stared at him, stared deep into his shining brown eyes, but she could not speak. Baptiste stared back and said, 'Because me, I love you more than all the berries in the world.'"

Émilie became distant then, sad and preoccupied with something else. "Maman?" Stéphanie asked her once.

Émile tossed her head to clear it of thoughts. "Oui, chérie?"

"Is that story true?"

She brushed a stray wisp of black hair from Stéphanie's forehead. "I don't know, but Grand-mère Sylvie told it to me herself."

"When you were a girl, right?"

"Mmmhmm."

"After a dance? Like in Cinderella?" The girl's voice rose with excitement.

Émilie tapped her nose. "Exactly. Complete with pumpkins and mice."

"Oh, Maman," Stéphanie laughed and swatted the air, "there were not. But was there a prince at least? A Prince Charming?"

Tears came then, but Émile held them back, mustered a response, "Yes."

"Who?"

"Ton père," she whispered.

"My father?" Stéphanie blinked and blinked at that strange pairing of words. "He was your Prince Charming?"

"Yes," Émilie mumbled as she pressed her lips to Stéphanie's dark hair.

"But then he died?" Stéphanie asked.

Her mother pulled away and stood up from the bed. "No. Midnight came. The fairy tale ended."

Stéphanie turned her head to look up at her. She squinted her brown and gold eyes in confusion. "But I thought—"

"It's time for bed," Emile said. She pushed a kiss onto Stéphanie's forehead and rushed away. "Bonne nuit." She switched off the light and left Stéphanie alone in the darkness of her bedroom, then played piano in the other room.

"Hey," Christianne interrupted Stéphanie's reverie. "What are you thinking about over there?"

Stéphanie jerked from her thoughts and blinked to make sense of where she was. Christianne laughed. It helped bring Stéphanie back to the present and to their dorm room, a rectangular box with two twin beds running down the long sides and a large yellow flag transected by a forest green cross and kissed with a red fleur-de-lys on the short side behind the beds. Neither of the young women liked the colour, but the flag was as much a part of their Fransaskoise identity as their accents. In French, they shared the same regional articulations and slanted vowels that caused Quebecers to cock their heads and ask them where they were from. In English, however, Christianne passed as a native speaker except when she was excited, or tired or tipsy. Stéphanie, on the other hand, had a lilting enunciation that betrayed not only her mother tongue but also her early German schooling in Switzerland and a childhood of European travels.

Both young women were five-foot-five and had long, thick hair that flowed down their backs like black oil. They weighed about the same but filled out their shared closet in different ways: Christianne liked short and tight, while Stéphanie preferred simple and chic. Of the two, Christianne was the one people most easily identified as a Tremblay, for in addition to her black hair and ivory skin, her heart-shaped face made her an uncanny replica of her aunt, Émilie, with whom she shared not only a penchant for butting heads with Christianne's father, Martin, but also the green eyes of many female descendants of Sylvie Simard. Stéphanie had the ocular trait as well, but it only showed when she was angry; otherwise, her eyes were a cut-glass pattern of browns and gold just like her father's. Her skin was tawny like his as well, and she furrowed her face like him when she was troubled. She held a guitar like him, too, but she had her mother's small, strong hands, hands that were good for fingering chords on violin strings and playing rapid passages on the piano.

"So?" Christianne asked from her bed.

"So, what?" Stéphanie asked.

"You gonna tell me what you're sighing about over there?"

Stéphanie shook her head and pushed away from her desk by the window. "Just the same old stuff."

"That doesn't mean we can't talk about it," Christianne

said.

Stéphanie walked towards the closet in the corner. "It doesn't mean we have to either. I mean, it's not like it'll change anything."

"It might," Christianne replied as Stéphanie rummaged behind the hanging vines of dresses, skirts, and sweaters.

Stéphanie pulled out a large hard-shelled suitcase. "Why? It hasn't any other time we've talked about it."

Christianne shrugged. "Maybe we just haven't said the right things yet."

Stéphanie scoffed, "Right things? And what would those be? That it's just peachy keen being lied to? That it doesn't hurt that the minute Robbie got a second chance with Maman, he went all in and started a new family, while with me it took him nine years!"

"Stéph," Christianne sounded in sympathy or reason, Stéphanie could not tell.

"I know!" she cried. "It's not about me. But that doesn't mean it hurts any less that all he could give me was lies while Maman and Renée get all of it: a home and family, a frickin' *Little House on the Prairie*, and all I get is some crazy soap opera."

"It's not fair," Christianne said such sincerity that it stopped Stéphanie in her rant. She took a deep breath and tried to gain control of her feelings.

"I told you we shouldn't talk about it," she finally said.

"Maybe," Christianne conceded, then her eyes flickered, and her mouth turned up into a smile. "But you know what we could do?"

"Pack?" Stéphanie suggested, transferring papers and scholastic miscellanea from her desk into her suitcase.

Christianne scowled and batted the suggestion away. "How 'bout we go to Montréal instead? We can see Cats."

"It's still running?"

"Yeah. It's the last week."

"Hmm," Stéphanie sounded with interest as she studied the face of her watch. "But that's like three hours away. We'll never make it."

"No," Christianne agreed, "not tonight but tomorrow. Alex could take us, and we could spend the weekend."

Stéphanie shrugged. "I don't know. I don't want to crash your last weekend together. Besides, we have a lot of packing to do before Tuesday."

Christianne grimaced at the mention of their impending return to Saskatchewan and her separation from her local boyfriend. "Don't worry about Tuesday until Tuesday, okay? Let's go! We can stay with Alex's brother."

Stéphanie stopped packing and gawked at her cousin. "He has a brother?"

"Yes, dodo-head, I told you that."

"You did?"

"Yes. Months ago."

"Really?"

"Yes! Sheesh! Don't you listen when I talk?" Christianne mock complained.

"No," Stéphanie laughed, "not when you talk about Alex and his bone-headed friends."

"Bone-headed!" Christianne gasped with mock horror. "Come on. Be nice."

"That is being nice."

"Ha. Maybe. But listen. His brother? You need to meet him."

"Pfff. Why?" Christianne shrugged in innocence while a grin ran over her face. "No!" Stéphanie insisted. "No! You're not setting me up!"

"Would I do that?" Stéphanie raised her eyebrows;

Christianne laughed, "Okay. I would. But he's nice."

Stéphanie resumed transferring things from her desk drawers. "You say that about all of Alex's friends."

Christianne chuckled. "True. But this is his brother, not his friend."

Stéphanie rolled her eyes. "Ohhh, so much better,"

"He's nice," Christianne insisted. "Really. You should meet him before we go home."

"Why?" Stéphanie demanded again.

Christianne shrugged and raised her eyebrows up and down. "I don't know. Why don't we go to Montréal and find out?"


Stéphanie could list over thirteen reasons why she should not go to Montréal, yet the following evening she was wearing a little black dress and was seated between Christianne and Alex's brother at la Place des Arts. He had straight sandy blond hair and a short goatee the colour of ginger ale. He did not move as he watched the show, but rather he sat as if he were taking notes with his mind or recording melodies and harmonies. Stéphanie did not notice because she, too, was enthralled, gobsmacked by the freedom of the performers, people-cats uninhibited by themselves or conventions. It stung her eyes with longing she had to wipe away while the rest of the theatre applauded at the end of Act One.

Christianne grabbed her hand as soon as the house lights came up. "Let's boot it to the can."

Stéphanie shook her head. "No. I'm good. I just want to sit here and digest it."

"Okay. Suit yourself." Christianne jumped up and wriggled about to adjust her tight, flower-print dress. She touched Alex's arm. "Wanna come with me?"

He flashed a love-sick grin. "Sure." He stood and let her pass, then pressed his hand to her lower back and followed her out of the row.

Stéphanie watched after them: an engineering student, Ken, and a raven-haired Barbie dressed to impress rather than to suit the occasion, as Stéphanie had learned to do from her mother.

Stéphanie's dress was black velvet with crepe straps and a sweetheart neckline outlined with a thin diamante strand, but classic. Her ebony hair was twisted into a side chignon with a fringe of curled tendrils about her head; her make-up was judiciously and skilfully applied with perfectly blended tones and exact lines around her lips and eyes.

"What do you think?" the brother on her left asked.

Stéphanie jerked at the sound and turned towards him. "I'm sorry. What?"

He smiled patiently. "Do you like the show?" She nodded but had no words to explain to a stranger how overwhelmed she was by the freedom of the performers, so she turned towards the stage and stared at the curtain. Her chest ached as she thought of the activity going on behind it: the stage crew rushing about placing props, the performers fanning themselves and drinking water, resting their feet, chatting about how the first act had gone and what they would do after the second one was over. "It's different," Alex's brother said, interrupting Stéphanie's thoughts, "the combination of jazz and standard Broadway fare."

This gave her a wealth of words; she turned to him. "You know music."

He chuckled. "Seriously?"

"Yes. Why?"

"No reason," he said, still laughing. She tilted her head and squinted at him, trying to make sense of his response. He met her stare and said, "You know music, too."

She nodded and shrugged. "I'm in Music Ed."

"And you play a mean fiddle," he added.

She shook her head. "Not that mean."

"Don't be modest. I saw that video of you."

She blinked and shook her head in surprise. "What video?"

"The one of you at the festival in Granby."

Her insides twisted. "There's a video?" she squawked.

He nodded and grinned. "Mmmhmm. And you were good. Very good." She swallowed down the sickness she felt as Michel went on, "Me and the boys, we really liked it."

"Boys?" she managed to ask.

He rolled a laugh and shook his head. "Really? Christianne didn't tell you?"

Her forehead creased. "Tell me what?"

"Who I am?"

"Of course. You're Alex's brother."

"And?" He looked at her, expecting bells of recognition to go off in her head, but she just shrugged. "You really don't know?" he asked.

"No."

"Hmm. So, Clem and Jonny were right—the beard does make me look different."

She blinked at the names. "Wait. Clem and Jonny? As in Clem Clemenceau and Jean-François Boucher?" His eyes sparkled, and he nodded. She gasped to find herself seated next to the lead singer of Plumeau, French-Canada's award-winning folk-rock party band. "Sorry! Chris never said, and yeah, the goatee. Plus Beauchemin ... Alex has a different last name."

He sloughed it off with a laugh, "Yeah. Same mom, different dad." He shifted in his seat and leaned closer to her. "And you? Tremblay, right? Like Christianne?"

"Yeah. We're cousins."

"Nice. Any siblings?"

"Me?" He nodded, and she swallowed down a rise of bile so she could answer. "A sister. Same parents. Different last names." She looked away and brushed non-existent lint from her lap.

Michel kept asking questions, "She's married?"

"No. She's not even two."

"Oh?" One of his eyebrows rose with voice.

She shook away the question. "It's complicated."

He nodded. "Okay."

His quick acceptance loosened her tongue, "They had me. I mean, my mom did. Then later, much later, they got married and had another kid."

His eyes lit with understanding. "Ahh. *À la volette*."

She was pierced by his perception. "What?" she choked.

"*À la volette*. You sang it at Granby. It was about your parents."

"No," she tittered, "no, it was just a song."

"There's no such thing." He put his hand on the back of her seat and leaned towards her. He smelled of bergamot and cardamom. Her heart raced, and her ears turned red. "So, tell me, why'd you pick it?" The question winded her; she bit her lip and turned away. Michel squeezed her hand. "Sorry. Too personal. I didn't mean to pry."

She shook away the swell of emotion and looked at him. "You didn't. It's just I ..." She lost the rest of her words when their eyes met. They stayed locked on each other until Christianne and Alex returned.

"Well, I hope you two had time to chat," Christianne said as she plopped down, "because Alex and I sure didn't. I spent the whole bloody time in the line-up."

"I met a nice blonde while I was waiting for her," Alex

laughed, raising an imaginary beer bottle. "She was a thing of beauty."

"Stella Artois?" Michel asked, cocking his eyebrow. "Really?"

"Yes. Some of us still like to drink, you know?" Alex said. Michel changed the subject even as Alex went on, "A rockstar who doesn't drink …"

"Clem's cooking," Michel said.

"He's home?" Alex asked. "I thought he was with—Oh, câlisse. Not again."

"Yep."

"But everything seemed so good. What happened this time?"

Michel shrugged. "You know."

"Oh, merde."

"I don't," Christianne said. "What?"

"Clem and Alice. They've been off and on since Cégep," Alex explained. "What is this, like the fifth time they've broken up?"

"Fifth!" Christianne exclaimed. "Why do they keep getting back together if they're just gonna break up?"

"Twoo-love," Alex laughed.

Christianne scrunched her face. "Huh?"

"It's complicated," Michel said. He smiled at Stéphanie; she blushed and hid her eyes, unsure whether he was teasing or mocking her for using the descriptor when he asked about her parents—either way, it warmed her.

"So, what's he into this time?" Alex asked, unaware of the exchange between Stéphanie and Michel. Laughter tumbled from him as he thought of Clem's creative ways of trying to get over a breakup with his on-again-off-again girlfriend.

Michel shot Alex a sharp look to silence him, then he turned sweet and explained things to the women, "He cooks when they break up. He cooks a lot." He patted his tight stomach. "It's really good, but we all end up looking like Pavarotti by the time he's over it."

"Ha. Lumberjack Pavarottis," Alex snorted.

"Eh!" Michel protested with a laugh. He pointed towards his turtleneck and sports coat, a change from his Plumeau attire of denim and plaid. "I can get just as fancied up as dear old Luciano."

"Sure. Nice threads there, Armani," Alex joked. "So, what if he's fat anyway? He's still got pipes."

The laughter fell from Michel's face, and he set his eyes on Alex. "You've been listening to opera? Why? Are you having trouble sleeping again?"

Alex wrapped his arm about Christianne. "Nope. I've got a little teddy bear now who helps me out with that." She snuggled into his embrace.

"You sure?" Michel rubbed his lips together as he surveyed his younger brother and his even younger girlfriend.

"Yeah. Don't worry," Alex assured.

Michel scanned them one last time, then turned his attention back to Stéphanie. "Italian opera. It's the only thing that gets him to sleep when he's stressed."

"Not the only thing," Alex said. He pressed his nose into Christianne's ear.

She wriggled and laughed, "Stop that." They kissed and giggled and cooed.

Stéphanie turned away from them. She fiddled with the corners of her program and spoke to cover her discomfort at their public displays of affection and their sexual innuendo, "My mom played Bach when she couldn't sleep. I don't know why. It can be pretty busy."

"What did she play?" Michel asked.

"Usually the preludes and fugues," she said, recalling the

sound of her mother in the other room playing piece after piece of contrapuntal keyboard music rather than sleeping.

"She played them," Christianne burst in. "Literally. She's a concert pianist."

"Was," Stéphanie corrected, her voice rising sharply. "Now she stays home. Takes care of her kid." She bit her lip and looked away, stared at the yellow eyes on the program—the pupils were dancers, she realized.

Michel watched her take a breath and let it out. He covered her hand with his. It made balloons float inside her. She felt him waiting for her to look at him, but she could only do so once the house lights began to dim. She could see the white of his teeth as he smiled. He squeezed her hand, then turned his eyes to the stage. Stéphanie's head spun.

Christianne elbowed her and leaned over to whisper in her ear. "I told you he was great."

Stéphanie turned to answer, but the sound of an oboe rising from the orchestra pit stopped her, and she turned towards the stage instead. She was mesmerized by the people-cats slinking onto the stage through billowing smoke and rising blue lights. A long-haired baritone cat began to sing. The richness of his voice pulled Stéphanie from the auditorium like one of Dickens' Christmas ghosts and transported her through time and space to when she was nine years old and freshly arrived in Lasalette from Switzerland.

The sun had not yet set, but after Grand-mère Sylvie's funeral and visits from more family than Stéphanie ever knew existed, she and her fast-friend and black-haired cousin, Christianne, had been sent to bed in one of the empty bedrooms upstairs in the house their great-grandfather Baptiste had built. The girls were sitting cross-legged on the bed in their cotton pyjamas, playing Connect Four, when a vehicle rumbled into the yard.

"Someone's here!" Christianne cried, bounding off the bed and rushing to the window like an excited house dog.

"Who is it?" Stéphanie asked.

"Oh, just Papa's friend, Robbie," Christianne said, still looking out the window.

"Oh?"

"Yeah. And listen. It sounds like he's yelling your name." Stéphanie made a face of surprise and followed her cousin's beckoning to the window. "Oh, there's Papa," Christianne said. "Wait. What's he doing? Oh, my God! They're fighting!" Stéphanie arrived in time to see the grown men tumble to the ground. She let out a cry. "Don't worry," Christianne said. "It's just like in hockey. They fight, they get back up, and they keep on playing." Stéphanie grimaced at the behaviour. Christianne was too interested in the fight to notice. "Wow! Papa's pretty good. Look!"

Stéphanie's eyes obeyed the command before she could stop herself. Martin held Robbie in a pin on the gravel of the driveway. Her stomach knotted. "Why are they fighting if they're friends?"

"Beats me," Christianne replied. "What's that they're saying? Daughter?"

Stéphanie shrugged. "Maybe."

"Who's that?"

"I don't. I hardly know anyone."

"True. But you know me," Christianne laughed, "so that's good enough."

"Yeah," Stéphanie agreed. "It is. Wanna finish our game?"

"Sure!" Christianne spun on the ball of her foot and charged towards the bed. She jumped up onto it and caused the game to topple over and spill its contents of black and red disks. "Shit. Sorry."

"That's okay," Stéphanie said as she climbed between the

covers of the old bed their great-uncles had once occupied. "We should probably just go to bed anyway."

"Why? It's not even dark yet!"

"I know. But I'm kind of tired. Aren't you?"

"Nope." Christianne scooped up the game and all the pieces and put them into the thin square box where they belonged. "But if you wanna sleep, sleep." She leaned over the edge of the bed and placed the game on the floor, then she reached underneath the bed.

"What are you doing?" Stéphanie asked.

"I've got some comics," Christianne said. "*Archie* and some *Jugheads*." She wormed back into bed and held out a comic to Stéphanie. "Want one?"

"Sure. Thanks." She took the thin review and opened it to explore the colourful world of Riverdale. She squinted at the words and tried to make sense of them, but her English was too limited, so she looked at the pictures and made up her own story about her mononcle Martin and her mom and the people of Lasalette.

In the morning, Martin was gone. "He had to drive a friend to the city," his wife explained as she snuck a look at Émilie. Stéphanie knew from the creases in her mother's face there was something in her matante Lynn's words that Émilie did not want to address. Stéphanie knew, too, from the way her mother hid her eyes and held her coffee cup, that she had broken her promise of no pills in Canada. It stung Stéphanie like a thorn prick and swelled painfully inside of her even with cousins to play with and grandparents to hug.

Clem was in the well-preserved 1970's avocado green kitchen when the cousins and brothers arrived after *Cats*. His face was a Picasso of emotion—a goofy smile with sad, bloodshot eyes. His hair was a beige puffball; he wore a ruffled flower apron over a blue dress shirt and jeans, wool socks, and Birkenstocks. The kitchen was a similar collage— a perfectly set table with linens and silver placed in the middle of the chaos of meal preparation. Onion and garlic turned in the air along with a pungent, skunky odour that reminded Stéphanie of many of her mother's sleepover visitors. Her insides churned, but Clem greeted them with a happiness that displaced her discomfort for a time, "Hey! You're back! How was the show?" He pressed his cheeks one at a time to Christianne's and smacked Alex in the chest. "Salut, toi." Then he scanned Stéphanie from head to toe and grinned. "So, you're the girl from the tape."

"Stéphanie," Michel said.

"Right. Stéphanie. Come in! Come in!" He spread his arm out and waited for her to step forward before he crossed back to the counter to pick up an open bottle of pinot noir next to an almost empty wine glass. "It's not quite ready. Have some wine while you wait."

Alex caught the bottle from his hands. "Sure, if there's any left." He slapped Clem's back and caught his eye. "Sorry about Alice, man."

"No worries." Clem sniffed and blinked away a wave of tears. "It happens. Ha! It happens a lot!" He tried to laugh, but it fell flat. He blew away the attempt and strode to the old avocado green stove. "Look! I made my special sauce." He dipped a wooden spoon into a pot, then held it out to Alex. "Taste."

Alex slurped at the tomato sauce. "Mmm. Good."

"Good? Good?" Clem shoved the spoon in his own mouth and cleaned it. He kissed his fingertips. "Délicieux! Now sit down and try my bruschetta!" He moved to the table and pulled out chairs. "Christianne, here. Tape girl, here. Michel.

Alex. Sit! I'll get more wine!"

"Come on," Christianne urged, pulling Stéphanie's wrist. "I'm famished."

"You'll be even more famished after his special sauce," Alex chuckled as he picked up a slice of bruschetta. Christianne shot him a look of reprimand and jerked her head towards Stéphanie; he shrugged and reached for another appetizer. "Nice oil on here, Clem."

Michel's eyes narrowed at Alex's sampling of Clem's illicit herb-infused food. He turned to appraise Stéphanie. Her jaw was tight, her steps reluctant. "Hey," he said, crossing towards the fridge, "don't we still have that cantaloupe? Prosciutto and melon. That would be nice, wouldn't it?" He looked over his shoulder like an owl as he rummaged for the food. "Something clean and fresh?" He stood in the coolness of the fridge and waited for Stéphanie to respond; she accorded him a nod. He grinned. "This cantaloupe's pretty good for out of season. And the prosciutto—Do you like prosciutto? Christianne doesn't."

"I don't not like it," Christianne said. "I just didn't know what it was when you served it last time."

"Ohhh," Michel teased.

"We just ate plain old ham at our house," Christianne said.

"Us, too," Alex added. "It's just his big shot ways." He reached out and smacked Michel's back. "Right, bro?"

Michel chuckled, "Whatever you say."

"I like it," Stéphanie said.

Michel held her gaze for a moment. He smiled. "Me, too." Stéphanie hid her eyes and tried to hold back the blush spreading over her face. Michel turned to the cantaloupe. Christianne kicked Stéphanie under the table and danced her eyebrows up and down as a comment on Michel's considerate behaviour.

"We have an excellent prosecco to go with that," Clem said, turning towards the fridge.

"Or sparkling water," Michel rushed to add. "It's what I'm having." He looked at Stéphanie as if they were alone. She had trouble finding words under his attention.

Clem grabbed the knife from Michel's hand. "Give me that. I'll get you your melon." He jerked his head towards Stéphanie and batted his eyes like a lovesick Pepé Le Pew. "You get that girl a drink."

Michel moved his jaw as he considered his friend's state and the steel blade in his hand. "Okay," he agreed with a quick nod. He tapped Clem's back. "Thanks." He crossed to the fridge and pulled out a bottle of Perrier. He turned the cap as he walked towards Stéphanie. "Sorry," he said, leaning over her as he filled her glass, "I should've offered you something sooner."

She tried to steady her breath under the heat of his body and the sweet musk of his cologne. "It's okay."

"No, it's not." He filled his own glass and set the bottle down. He sat beside her, raised his glass, and tilted it towards her. "Tchin-tchin."

She picked up her glass and clinked it against his. "Salute." She turned her shy eyes away from his shining orbs as she sipped the fizzy water.

"Do you speak Italian?"

"A little, but mostly just music terms."

"And full operas," Christianne teased with pride. "She lived in Switzerland when she was a kid and went to Italy a lot."

"Yeah?" Michel's head tilted with interest. He looked at Stéphanie as he waited for more, but she held her past to herself. "I came to Montréal when I was five," he offered when she remained silent. "It blew me away. All the people and cars. The tall buildings."

Stéphanie acknowledged his words with a nod, but she was thinking about winding through the Alps with her mother when she was five, of the rocking and bumping of the train and the chain smokers around them. It had made her sick. Émilie had given her ginger ale to quiet her stomach, but Stéphanie spilled it on her dress and on her shoes, so she was wet and nauseous and afraid the mountains would slide down and crush them to death. She burrowed into her mother's side and hid her face in her abdomen. Émilie stroked her hair, kissed her head, sang Joni Mitchell songs sotto voce until Milan appeared.

"What did you think when you first came here?" Michel asked.

Stéphanie blinked away her thoughts. He was leaning towards her, eager for her words. "What? Oh. I was born here actually, but that doesn't really count. The first time after that I only saw the airport." She had no intention of saying more, but Michel's smile caused words to tumble from her like candies from a lonely widow on Halloween, "I was nine. We were coming home. Montréal was just a stop. A long one. Eight hours, I think. I got all excited because there were Smarties in the gift shop. We didn't have them in Basel, but my mémère used to send them to me for my birthday. I asked my mom if I could have some, and the woman behind the counter talked to us in French, a French almost like mine and my mom's. I liked that, but I was surprised by how much English there was, too."

"It's a fucking disease!" Clem barked.

Stéphanie laughed. "That's what my mom said when we moved home. Well, not the eff-ing part, more like, 'Don't worry, English is like a cold; you'll catch it.'

"Ha!" Clem squeezed her shoulder as he set a plate of

cantaloupe and prosciutto on the table. "That's good."

"You didn't speak English?" Michel asked as he served her.

"No, we spoke French at home, and I went to a German school."

"That must've been hard for you when you came to Canada?"

"Not really. I mean, sure, the German wasn't so practical, but I got by with French at school and in Lasalette."

"Out west?" Michel said. "Really?"

"Yes, really," she laughed to temper her frustration that Quebecers knew so little about the French populations around them. "There are pockets of French all over this country, you know?"

"What country are you talking about?" Clem asked, leaning against the Formica counter, folding his arms about his chest.

"Uh-oh," Alex laughed before Stéphanie could answer.

"Uh-huh," Christianne nodded in agreement.

Michel rushed in to change the subject, "Hey, how's your sauce coming along?"

"Simmering," Clem said. "Like the people of Québec."

"Not tonight," Michel warned.

"Why not? We dream at night, man."

"Yeah, but we're awake right now, okay? So how about we eat, hmm?" Clem grumbled and rolled his eyes, but he turned back to the stove. Michel turned to Stéphanie. "Sorry."

Her nose crinkled. "He's a separatist?"

"Nationalist," Clem corrected over his shoulder.

"She doesn't get that," Christianne said.

"I get it, I just don't agree with it any more than I agree with the Meech Lake Accord."

"Uh-oh," Alex laughed again.

Christianne cringed as Stéphanie set off, "I mean, sure, I'll admit that Québec is distinct, but so is Newfoundland and the Yukon and everywhere in between. But if you think it's French that makes Québec so unique, then you're wrong. There's French all across Canada, Clem. From Acadie all the way to the Pacific. And that's more distinct, wouldn't you say, remaining French in a huge sea of English?" Clem began to speak, but Michel glared at him. Stéphanie continued without noticing the exchange, "French-Canadians used to be the largest European population in the west. Now, in Saskatchewan, we're two percent. Two percent! And that's with constitutional rights. And speaking of rights, what about Native Rights? All those Europeans taking their land and resources, and the government trying to squash their language and culture five ways to Sunday."

"Spoken like an Indian," Clem muttered.

"Don't be an ass," Michel said.

"What? She's Indian, isn't she?"

"Native," Michel corrected while his brother offered another word.

"Indigenous."

"Whatever."

"No," said Michel.

"Pfff."

"I'm Métis," Stéphanie said, "on my father's side, but that doesn't have anything to do with it. It has to do with respect for treaties and of people."

Clem opened his mouth to respond, but Alex beat him to it, "You know what I think needs to be respected?"

"Our stomachs?" Michel suggested.

"Yes!" Alex cried. "I'm starving!"

"How can you be starving?" Clem asked. "You ate all the bruschetta!"

"That was just an appetizer. Come on. Is it ready, or what?"

"Yeah, yeah. Keep your gitch on, man."

Stéphanie chuckled at their banter. Christianne leaned towards her and reprimanded her, "Do you really need to talk politics right now?"

"It's not politics," Stéphanie replied. "It's life."

"Ha!" Clem guffawed. He turned and grinned at her. "That's a good one." He clucked to himself and turned back to the stove. He sang Stéphanie's words to a Gilles Vigneault melody, "La politique ce n'est pas la politique, c'est la vie."

The scent of basil and garlic rose into the air as he emptied one of his saucepans into a serving bowl. Stéphanie's face creased as she watched him. "Don't," Christianne warned.

"I'm not." She wondered whether Clem was mocking her or floating along on a wave of private humour like she herself used to do.

Clem continued to sing, "La vie ce n'est pas la vie, c'est la sauce ..."

Michel pulled at Stéphanie's attention, "So, how do you like the cantaloupe?"

She turned back to him. "Sorry. What?"

He smiled at her fluster. "Do you like the cantaloupe?"

She looked at the melon wedge on her plate and felt herself warm with embarrassment once again. "I haven't tried it yet."

He gestured to it with his hand. "Try it now." She obliged and picked up her knife and fork. He watched her with a smile of anticipation. "So?" he asked after she had chewed a few times.

She nodded and swallowed. "It's good."

He grinned in agreement. "I know, eh?"

"That's high praise," Christianne burst in. "She's such a fruit snob."

"I am not. I just know what ripe fruit is."

"Right," Christianne teased. "And what it looks like. And feels like. And smells like."

"It's not snobbish," Michel said, fixing his maple eyes on Stéphanie, "to know what's the best and to want it." Her heart caught. He held her gaze even as she tried to look away to still her pulse.

"Did you say 'best'?" Clem asked, approaching the table with a large bowl of spaghetti. "This is the best!"

"He made it himself," Michel boasted for him. "From scratch. No Catelli for him. No, sir."

"Ach! No way! Now," Clem said as he placed a small bowl of tomato meat sauce in front of Michel, "I have two types. One Milanese for our special guest, and one special Milanese for the rest." He laughed at his wit and placed a larger bowl at the other end of the table where he sat down. "Bon appétit and dig in."

Stéphanie's anxiety returned with a surge as Christianne served herself a spoonful of Clem's special sauce.

"This one's clean," Michel said, trying to pull her attention back to him. She nodded but remained transfixed by the eating at the other end of the table. "Here, let me serve you." He clutched up a tong full of spaghetti and dumped it onto her dinner plate while she watched Christianne turn a forkful of pasta and raise it to her mouth like Stéphanie's mother had raised glasses of wine to wash down her painkillers.

Stéphanie pushed away from the table. "I'm sorry," she said as she stood. "I ... need to freshen up." She rushed from the room.

"Idiot!" Michel barked once she had passed into the hallway. "I asked you not to do that."

"Do what?" Clem sounded with surprised innocence. "I made you some without. Besides, we're not working."

"I am."

"You always are."

"Yeah. And aren't you glad? Or would you rather still be playing every shit hole from here to Gaspé?"

"We all work," Clem responded with the sound of a bruise.

Michel started to respond, but Christianne spoke over him, "Don't worry. She gets like that. It's baggage from her childhood."

"Yeah, take it easy, man," Alex added. "Just because you don't want to get wasted doesn't mean we don't."

"Well, just because you want to, doesn't mean you should, shit head," Michel retorted.

Alex responded with a fraternal insult that Stéphanie did not hear. She found a doorway at the end of the hallway, stepped through, then fumbled on the wall for the light switch. "Oh," she gasped at what was not the bathroom but rather a spacious room filled with musical instruments, a well-worn floral couch, and a Queen Anne coffee table littered with papers, pencils, and several drinking glasses with varying amounts of water in them.

She walked farther into the room, fingered the wood of a guitar, but stopped herself from thrumming the strings. An accordion sat closed on a chair; a violin slept in its case on a dusty Lesage piano in the corner. She took a breath and closed her eyes. She heard echoes of Plumeau's folk-rock mix and smelled a mélange of sweat and cologne.

When she opened her eyes and looked about. Old portraits covered three walls; a print of *The Last Supper* was on the fourth. She stared at it for a long time, first wondering what it was doing in what appeared to be Plumeau's practice space, then remembering seeing it in Milan with the daughter of one of her mother's boyfriends, a cellist, Stéphanie remembered, though she could not remember his name. His daughter was Chiara, however. She was a curly-haired, twenty-something art history student who had spoken as much French as Stéphanie spoke Italian, but they had managed to understand each other and found a way to laugh together at the pigeons on the roof of the Duomo and at each other as they turned in circles on the bull's scrotum in a fancy galleria across the way. They stopped for stand-up espresso and cornetti alla crema at the café Chiara's boyfriend's uncle owned. Then they visited the Castle Sforza and ended their day eating gelato by the fountain out front. As they waited for their parents, Stéphanie wondered what it would be like for all of them to go home together like a family, to have Chiara as a sister instead of having to say goodbye and never seeing her again.

"There you are," Michel said, popping Stéphanie's reverie.

She jumped and turned to face him. "Sorry," she stammered with the guilt of a five-year-old rising to her face. "I was looking for the bathroom."

"Across the hall," he said. He kept his eyes set on her as he walked towards her. "You found my favourite room," Michel smiled like a beam of sunshine. He tugged at her hand and led her to the couch. "It was a dining room before Jonny's grand-maman took us in." He pointed to an oval black and white portrait of a high-collared woman. "That's her. Marie-Geneviève." His eyes lingered on the woman's face before he continued to point out other pictures. "That was her husband, Jean-Louis. Those are the children. The grandchildren are over there. Jean-François' the one with the bowl cut and the missing teeth." Michel's own teeth were straight and white inside his pink lips. "His aunt took the dining suite, but everything else is the same." He chuckled. "Well, maybe not as clean, but the decor at least, except for this couch here that we moved in from the living room."

"So that's why you have that?" she asked, pointing to *The*

*Last Supper.*

He followed her finger. "Yeah. It was Marie-Geneviève's." He considered it for a moment. "We're not real churchy, me and the boys, but we like it. It reminds us of her. And of each other. Of how far we'd go for one another."

"How far would you go?" Stéphanie half sang.

Michel's voice rolled with pleasure, "What's that?"

A tint of pink rose to her face. "Sorry. I do that sometimes."

"What? Burst into song?"

A laugh floated from her. "Yeah."

"Me, too." He chuckled and sang like Pete Seeger, "How can I keep from singing?"

She felt herself quiver and blush. She turned away and stared at the aquiline-nosed men in Da Vinci's painting to steady herself. She tried to recall which one was supposed to be him; she had known once, had liked the idea of inserting oneself into history through art.

Michel leaned towards her. "Was that a real song? What you sang?" She could feel his eyes on her and hear the interest in his voice, but in such close proximity to him, all she could manage was a nod. He hummed the phrase back. "Not bad. What's the rest?"

She shrugged and shook her head. "It's just a folk Mass thing."

"Folk Mass? What's that?"

Stéphanie shrugged as she considered it, then offered an answer, "Kumbaya meets Catholicism, I guess you could say."

"Huh," Michel sounded. "I could maybe get into that." He touched his hand to her knee as he stood up. She looked at it, big and strong, and slipped her fingers over the warm impression it left behind as he strode across the room. He hummed as he picked up his guitar and settled onto a stool.

"Sing the rest."

"No," Stéphanie tittered.

"Yes," he urged, already picking out the melody.

"It's a church song," she reminded him.

He shrugged. "You said it was folk. We dig that here." He set his eyes on her. "Please?"

She shook her head even as the song flowed from her, "In the beginning, there was the Word; a love ever flowing made into man."

"Hmm. I like it. Is there more?" She felt the warmth of his eyes on her and sang the rest of the verse. Michel joined in with an improvised guitar accompaniment and sang along with her on the refrain, nodding at her to repeat it in a loop. She obliged without reserve. Michel played around with his accompaniment, then suddenly stopped the strings of his guitar with his hands. "There's something wrong."

"It needs a descant," she said, "and an ostinato pattern in the bass."

Michel's eyes shone. "Exactly!" He adjusted himself on his stool and began playing again. "Okay. Why don't you sing the refrain and let me see what I can find?" She sang as requested while Michel played with various patterns and added some vocals. When it seemed they had it, he dampened the strings with his hand again. "I like it," he said. "Let's try it tomorrow when Jonny gets back. He's got a good bass."

She nodded, wordless from the music. Their eyes caught, and Stéphanie was aflutter. She wrestled through it and said, "I should go see how Christianne is."

Michel caught her hand as she turned towards the doorway. "No, you shouldn't." His touch enveloped her like the fragrance of a flower. "You should stay and talk with me." He put his guitar aside and led her to the couch. She had no resistance. They sat side by side; their knees touched. She rubbed her lips together and tried to keep her eyes off him so her heart would not race.

"I didn't know they did that," she said, nodding towards the kitchen and Clem's secret sauce. "Did you?"

He brushed a tendril of hair off her cheek with his finger. His touch coursed through her. She took a breath to steady herself. "Know?"

"Yeah."

His eyes flickered as he considered the most appropriate response. "For Alex, yes. For Christianne, no, but I've only met her a few times."

Stéphanie rubbed her lips together as she tried to think when that might have been. "I've been distracted this semester with our pépère being sick and everything. I kind of lost track of her."

He chuckled, "I think Alex's been keeping tabs on her."

A flat laugh rose from her. "Yeah."

Michel squeezed her hand. "And I'm keeping tabs on him." She snorted. "I am," he assured, "but that doesn't mean he always does what I think he should."

Stéphanie bobbed her head in agreement. "Sounds like Christianne. She never does what I think she should."

"Oh? And what's that?" She meant to answer, but he looked into her eyes, and then he leaned towards her and touched his lips to hers and kissed her softly before pulling away and trailing his hand down her arm. "Why don't we go for a walk?" She had no resistance and nodded, followed him to the doorway and into the hall. "We'll go this way," Michel said, steering her away from the kitchen and the sauce.

She stopped and caught his wrist. "Wait."

"What?" His caramel eyes turned her knees weak and caused her to forget her objection. She met his gaze and held it until there was a burst of laughter from the kitchen.

"They'll be fine," he assured before she could voice her worry.

"I know, but do you think we should tell them? I mean, what if they notice? I wouldn't want them to go out looking for us."

"They won't, but sure, I can tell them." His smile filled her with a warmth that lifted her like a hot air balloon. He led her a few steps up the hall and reached inside a doorway. He flicked on the light switch. "Why don't you go in here? Freshen up like you said? Alex left your bag in the corner."

She blushed at his attention and his use of her words from earlier. "Thanks."

"No problem." He flashed a smile and squeezed her hands like a promise. "I'll meet you back here when you're ready."

"Okay." She slipped into the washroom and closed the door. She leaned her forehead against it and let out a breath that came from the tips of her feet. A new wave of air filled her, then emptied and filled again and again like the sea. She wished Christianne were with her so she could ask her what to do to keep from melting every time she looked at Michel. She would also ask her whether she thought Michel really wanted to go for a walk or if that was code for going to the backyard and making out. Her heart flitted at the idea, but she forced it away and decided that either way, she should change out of her sleeveless dress and into something more appropriate for going outside in the dark with a man.

She turned about and did a double-take to find that the room was pink—from tile to toilet, tub to sink—the same pink as the bathroom at her father's house. "My mom liked pink," he had explained to her the first time she had seen it. "The mother of seven boys, Papa thought she deserved a little frill." Stéphanie had decided, then that she liked pink, too, but she had lost such affinity the day she learned that the branches of her family tree had been misplaced. She grimaced at the thought and ground it between her teeth as she stalked towards the duffle bag Alex had left sitting on top of the clothes hamper. She yanked the bag open and rifled through it until she found something casual to wear. She regretted her choice of jeans and a t-shirt as soon as she opened the bathroom door and saw Michel still in a tight turtleneck and sports coat, waiting for her. "Sorry," she stammered as his eyes scanned her, "I changed."

"No problem." He grinned and walked towards her. "I want you to be comfortable." He offered her his hand. "Ready?"

"Yes."


They were only two blocks from the house before Stéphanie said, "I have no idea where we are."

"That's okay," Michel said, "I do." He chuckled and made a joke about his last name, "But then, I am the Beauchemin."

She laughed; he wrapped his arm about her and pulled her into his side. *Mondou*, she thought, *I don't know if this is the right path, but you're certainly good looking.*

"It's pretty dark tonight," he said after a time.

She looked towards the sky. "It must be the new moon." She tittered and warmed with embarrassment when she felt him look at her. "The moon's kind of a thing in my family," she explained.

"Oh?" A smile waxed upon his face.

It caused words to fall from her, "My parents were both born on a full moon. The same full moon, actually."

"That's cool."

She shrugged and nodded at the same time. "It's been kind of a mixed-up thing."

"I gathered." His eyes shone like maple taffy in the yellow refraction of the streetlight and kept Stéphanie talking.

"Everyone says it was destiny. Providence. The way things were supposed to be. But a lot got in the way. Kind of like Draco cutting through the Dippers."

Michel laughed in non-understanding. "What?"

"You know? Like the constellations?" He shook his head, and she said, "It's not important. It's just something Robbie says."

"Robbie?" he asked with interest. "Who's that?"

"My dad," she answered flatly. "He's into that kind of thing."

"What kind of thing?"

"Astronomy. Mythology."

"Oh?" Michel said with surprise. "He's not Catholic?"

"No, he is," Stéphanie replied. "But God created the heavens, right?"

"Umm. Yeah, I guess." He rubbed his lips together as he considered what to say next. Her stomach knotted with worry that she had sounded like a religious fanatic, then she wondered if she was one, if following dictates and praying made her one. "Do you believe in all that?" Michel asked, breaking her thoughts.

"In what?" she choked.

"God. Heaven. That kind of thing."

Seven answers and their potential fall-out with God and Michel turned about her head. She picked the simplest one, "Mostly."

"Me, too." She raised her eyebrows. "What?" He laughed. "You didn't think I did?"

She shrugged and tittered bashfully. "You said you weren't really religious."

He chuckled, "Religious, as in go to church, no, but I

believe in God."

"Oh." She nodded at the concept and offered a smile rather than question his theology.

He smiled back and launched into a story, "A couple of years ago? The boys and I were out on this little island in the Bas-Saint-Laurent doing a show. It was good enough. We played well, and the crowd had a good time, but we got paid in accommodations and beer. Pfff.

"Anyway, I took my payment and wandered around until I ended up at the shore, and I stood there listening to the waves hitting the rocks for a bit, then I sat down and looked out into the darkness, feeling sorry for myself, feeling like I was drifting in circles and getting nowhere real fast. I mean, beer and accommodations? I wanted so much more. I wanted records and tours, and I wanted my music to mean more than just a good time out at the local bar.

"Then, just when I'm really feeling low, like it's all a waste of time and I should just pack up my guitar and call it quits, the sun started to rise, and there was this inky blue in the sky that turned mauve and then pink. Then the whole thing, the sky, the water, everything, it was all these colours I'd never seen before, and it just gripped me, you know? Right down to the core: I could do better. Could *be* better."

Stéphanie's heart pressed against her chest as she floated with Michel on the glory of the experience before he continued, "I hoofed it back to the hotel, and pulled the boys out of bed, laid out this whole plan of what we had to do to get where we wanted to go." He chuckled as he recalled their reaction, "They grunted and had their eyes half closed, but they knew I was right, knew we weren't going anywhere doing what we were doing, so they agreed to get serious, to work towards something instead of just pissing around, hoping success would fall from the sky between parties and gigs." He laughed again. "They'll tell you they only went along with it to get me outta their hair so they could go back to sleep, but I think they felt it, too, felt that we could be more, you know?"

"Yeah." She held his smile until his joy pushed her into a funk. She looked away and clenched her teeth against the doubt and regret churning inside of her. *It's worthy*, she told herself, *teaching music is worthy, even if it's chosen rather than commissioned from above.*

"Hey," Michel said, rubbing her arm.

She pushed away her thoughts. "Sorry. I was just …"

"Thinking?"

"Yeah."

"It's a good thing to do," he teased. "I do it from time to time myself." He bumped her hip and clicked his tongue. "So, what were you thinking about?" She shrugged and held the answer to herself. His eyes danced like bubbling syrup. "Let me see if I can guess. You were thinking about pancakes, right? About how we should stop and get some because you're so hungry you're ready to eat my arm, right?"

"Exactly," she laughed. "How'd you know?" She growled and pretended to bite his bicep. He stepped out of the attack and caught her by the waist. He was warm and smelled of bergamot and cardamom. He looked into her eyes, and her laughter fell like a skin.

"I was thinking the same thing, except that it was more like if we don't eat, I'm gonna have to kiss you." She quivered at his look but did not pull away. They kissed long and deep until Michel slipped out of the embrace and cupped her face. He waited for her to open her eyes before he spoke. "You sang a song at Granby that'd be perfect right now."

Her heart sank to her feet. She slid his hands off her face and stepped back from him. "I don't like to talk about

Granby."

"Why not?" She shook her head and stalked away. He followed her. "Did something happen when you were there?" She pressed her lips together and kept walking. He kept pace and rubbed his finger over the back of her hand. "Did someone hurt you?"

"No." She moved her hand away from his and quickened her step. He followed suit. Their feet struck the pavement at the same time; the rubbing of their jeans filled in the beats like a shaker. Stéphanie's jaw moved as if she were grinding words between her teeth. Michel wondered if they were curses telling him to mind his own damn business, but then he noticed that her hands were beating rhythms on her thighs. *It's rock*, he thought, *she's thinking in rock. Guns N' Roses, maybe, or Bon Jovi.* He was going to ask her when she said, "I shouldn't have sung like that."

"Like what?" Michel asked. "You were amazing! And the way you played? My god! Smoke practically came out of your fiddle!"

She shook her head at the compliments. "No. It was crap that wasn't meant for a toilet let alone a stage!" She started to storm away again, but Michel stopped her.

"Someone said that, right?" She gasped at his insight and trembled, trying to hold back the answer as he continued to pry, "Someone you love?"

She sniffed and nodded. "My pépère," she whispered. "How'd you know?"

"Because it happens a lot. Our families, they see us up there, and they can't believe it. Can't believe that we, their son or daughter or whatever we are to them, that we can do that. Can make those sounds. Can be so free."

"No, my pépère heard me all the time."

"Maybe, but not like how you were that night with *À la*

*volette,* right?"

She pruned with emotion. "No," she admitted.

He smiled in reassurance. "That's because it was one of those once-in-a-lifetime things when all you've gotta do is show up and the music flows right through you."

Stéphanie shook her head and scrunched her eyes. "That wasn't music. It was anger."

"It didn't sound like anger to me," he said. "It sounded like love. Deep, raw, bleeding love."

She considered his assessment. "Maybe, but love's not supposed to be like that. It's supposed to be patient and kind. It's supposed to forget all wrongs."

"Sure, but it can also hurt and bleed." He wiped away one of her tears with the softness of a honeybee looking for nectar. "And it can be a seed that needs the sun in order to bloom as well."

"*The Rose*?"

"Yeah," he tittered. "Is that lame?"

"No." They stared at each other like the moon and its reflection. The streetlights hummed. A breeze rustled through the unfolding buds of a nearby maple tree.

"Do you still want pancakes?" he asked after a time.

She nodded and blinked to free herself from his gaze. "Sure."

"Good, 'cause I know this place just a few blocks from here."

"Great. Lead the way."

He took her hand, and they moved on in contented silence until they came to a corner. Michel turned about, trying to get his bearings. "Oh, shit. Sorry. We went too far." He jerked his head towards a side street a few meters behind them. "We should've turned back there." He squeezed her hand and started to backtrack.

"You got lost?" she laughed. "And here I thought you were the pretty path."

Michel's face beamed. "Oh, I am." He slipped his arm over her shoulder. "I just got distracted, is all. Here," he said, stopping at the second door from the corner. "Chez nous."

He opened the door and ushered her into an urban sugar shack replete with wooden floors and walls, a potbelly stove, and a display of bottled maple syrup glistening in the electric light. It smelled of bacon and coffee and home. He led her to a small booth in the corner.

"Great place," she said, as she looked about and settled in.

"Yeah," he grinned with pride. "And they're open all night instead of all day."

"That's interesting," she replied.

"Well, you catch a certain clientele." She raised her eyebrows, and he explained, "Like students and night shift workers from the hospital getting lunch in the middle of the night or going for dinner in the morning after work. It's better than fast food and kind of nice for us rock-around-the-clock types to have a decent place to get a meal." He pushed his straight hair behind his ear and opened his menu. "So, what'll it be? Meat loaf? Pea soup?" She laughed at his suggestions. "What? They have a very thorough menu."

"I see that, but I thought you said pancakes."

"I did, but that doesn't mean you can't have liver and onions if you want."

Her voice rolled with laughter. "Tempting, but I think I'll stick with pancakes."

"Me, too." He closed his menu and smiled at her. "And coffee?"

"Coffee," she agreed.

Their fingers touched in the middle of the table until a waitress in a long navy skirt and white embroidered cotton blouse came to their booth to take their order. "Macaroni!" she greeted, spreading her arms to give him a hug and to press her cheeks to his. "What're you doing in town?"

He slid into her presence as if it were an old slipper. "Just getting ready to tour."

"Still? How long does it take?" The wrinkles around her eyes spread like chicken feet. "You just gotta get up and go-go." She pulled a pen from her apron and clicked so the ballpoint tip was exposed. "So, what's it today?"

"Two orders of pancakes and a carafe of coffee. That good city roast, you know? And could you make it fresh, please?" he asked with an extra sweet smile.

"Macki." She tsked at the offensive request for fresh coffee. "I'll even bring warm whole milk." She clicked her tongue and turned to Stéphanie. "This one likes what he likes." She danced her eyebrows and patted Michel on the back. "I'll bring that right out."

"Thanks, Lise."

"What was that?" Stéphanie asked. "Macki and Macaroni?"

His face wrinkled with laughter. "She's Jonny's aunt."

"The one with the dining set?"

He smiled, pleased that she remembered something he had said earlier. "No. Another one. He has six on that side."

"Nice. I only have one: Christianne's mom. Do you have any?"

"Aunts?" Michel shrugged. "No. My mom's an only child, and my dad … I don't know. When he split, so did his family." Her heart wrung for him, and she felt compelled to tell him about the years she had lived without her father, but Michel lifted his eyes and smiled before she found the words.

"Alex's dad has a huge family, though, so I can't say I'm wanting in that regard."

"You get along with him then? Your stepdad?"

"Absolutely, but he's not my stepdad. He's, my dad."

She forced a smile, but her heart still burned with the talk of fathers. She stifled it with a question, "How old were you when he came on the scene?"

"Five, and Alex came when I was six." She did the math: he was old, twenty-eight, maybe twenty-nine, depending on when his birthday was. "Man, that kid," Michel went on, "he followed me around from the time he could crawl until the day I left home. It was annoying, but nice at the same time, you know? Kind of like having a puppy, only he didn't chew my shoes." They both chuckled, then fell silent and smiled at each other across the table. Stéphanie's mind raced with all kinds of things to tell him about younger siblings and leaving home, but Lise appeared with coffee and mugs, milk and sugar.

"I don't know if you take it," she said to Stéphanie as she placed the sugar dispenser on the table. "This one's been saying he's sweet enough since he and the boys started coming in here, isn't that right, Macki-doodle?" She pinched his cheek.

He laughed. "Lise, this is Stéphanie."

"Oh, so now you're gonna introduce me?" She chided playfully. "Took you long enough." She held out her hand to Stéphanie. "I'm Lise. Macaroni's favourite aunt."

Stéphanie shook her strong, dishwater-worn hand. "Nice to meet you. Mind if I ask why you call him Macaroni?"

Lise's face brightened. "Not at all!" She wrapped her arm about Michel's shoulder and launched into her answer, "He used to wear this hat with a feather in it back in the day when Plumeau got started. What were you? Sixteen? Seventeen?"

She turned to Michel for an answer, but he held all words behind a grin. "Anyway, we teased him about being Yankee Doodle, you know, like the song?" She hummed a few measures. "Only, none of us knew the words, except that it had something to do with macaroni at the end. By the time all the joking and singing were over, that's what stuck." She squeezed Michel tighter and bopped her hip against him. "Hope you don't mind me telling stories, Macki. Warn me next time. I'll bring pictures!" She gave him a final squeeze and hurried away to tend to a man holding his bill in the air.

Stéphanie chuckled, "You may want to tie her up if Musique Plus ever comes snooping for stories about you guys."

Michel laughed and reached for the carafe. "Coffee?"

"Please. City roast, eh?"

"Yeah. Good character. Not too dark, not too light."

"Exactly. But not many people know about it."

He rolled his eyes at people's ignorance. "I know. They get stuck in a run-of-the-mill medium roast. But you need to be a bit more precise, don't you think? Here, have a taste." He poured her a cup with room left for milk.

Stéphanie studied the amber-brown tones in her mug. She picked it up and breathed in the freshness, then pursed her lips and took a sip. She held the hot liquid in her mouth before swallowing. "Nice," she finally decreed.

"You drink it black?"

She shrugged. "Usually, but it depends."

"On what?"

"The roast. The brew. My mood."

"Ah, so you like what you like, too, eh?" he teased.

She looked away to hide her blush. She rubbed her lips together and cupped her hands around her coffee mug to calm the fluttering in her stomach. He reached across the table and touched her knuckle. Then, slowly, like the sunrise, she raised her eyes to look at him. They smiled at one another until Lise reappeared.

"Here you are, my dears," she announced, presenting plates to them. "Fresh from the griddle." She clicked her tongue at Michel. "Just like you like 'em." She placed the food in front of them.

"Thanks, Lise."

She squeezed his shoulder. "Anytime. Anything else? More coffee? Milk?" She turned to Stéphanie, "There's maple syrup here, but we also have blueberry and strawberry."

"Maple's great. Thanks."

Lise smiled in approval. "'Tis thicker than blood," she quipped.

"What?" Stéphanie laughed.

"It's what my mother used to say: Blood may be thicker than water, but maple syrup is thicker than blood." Michel joined her on the punch line, "So pancakes are more important than family." Stéphanie laughed; Michel glowed with pleasure. Lise wiggled her eyebrows at him and clapped him on the back. "Bon! Je vous laisse. Bon appétit!"

"Merci!" Stéphanie and Michel answered in unison.

"I've never heard that before," Stéphanie said still laughing.

"Marie-Geneviève used to say it. It was completely ironic coming from her, but she said it every time we had pancakes." His face lit at the thought of her. "She took us in like family, even me and Clem, who were just her grandson's bum university drop-out friends playing four-day weekends and trying to do something with ourselves the rest of the week." He poured a flow of amber syrup over his pancakes. "Sometimes she'd come into the music room when I'd be fooling around trying to come up with something. She'd just set a cup of tea down on the table for me and go prop herself up on the couch with another. She'd sit there and listen until I stopped. Then she'd say something like, 'T'es vraiment bon.' The way she said it … bin, it made me feel like she meant more than just my music, you know? That she meant that I, me, Michel Beauchemin, that I was good." He turned to her and set his eyes on hers. "Did you ever have that with someone?"

The question hit her in the gut, and the answer slipped out before she could stop it, "Yeah, with Robbie. Before I knew he was my dad."

"You didn't know?" Michel asked with the same warm softness as the pancakes before them.

"No. He never told me." She grimaced and picked up her cutlery. "We should eat."

Michel's eyebrows rose, but he did not ask any more. Instead, he nodded and said, "Okay." He watched her stab her pancakes with her fork, saw them into strips, and cut them into squares that she moved about her plate, but did not eat, for her stomach was churning and her mind was swirling with memories of all the moments Robbie, or her mother, or any adult member of her family could have told her the truth but didn't. "Are you okay?" Michel asked after a time.

"No," she admitted without looking at him. "Sorry."

"It's okay. Wanna talk about it?"

"No," she said again. "It's long and complicated, and it doesn't matter anyway."

"Are you sure about that? I mean, it seems to bother you."

She tittered and shrugged. "I'll get over it."

"Will you?"

She shrugged again and bit her lip. He reached across the table and touched her hand. She looked at his, so clean and well-maintained, but thick leather on the underside from guitar strings, just like her own. *And Robbie's,* she thought. Her eyes burned. She closed them, and Michel squeezed her hand, causing words to tumble from her, "I was ten. I'd just gotten to Lasalette for the summer and was making the rounds, hugging everyone—Christianne and her family—and then he was there. I mean, he was always there, I just hadn't really noticed because I was so excited to see everyone else. Anyway ... I knew who he was, 'cause I'd seen him the year before, but we'd never met. He was too drunk for that." She stopped for a moment, rubbed her lips together, and then went on, "He was sober that summer, though, and his eyes were all welled up. He kept scrunching up his face, too, so he wouldn't cry. I didn't get it, get why some guy I didn't really know would be there and all emotional like that, but Mononcle Martin took care of it. 'This is Robbie,' he said. 'He lives up the road and is just like family.' Just like," she scoffed. "How 'bout *is*?"

"Your uncle didn't know?"

"No, he knew. They all did. They just didn't tell me."

"Why not?"

"That's a long story," she muttered.

"I've got time," he said with a smile that warmed her, melted the last vestiges of reserve she was trying to cling to.

## Trois beaux canards s'y vont nageant

When the Freshie Dance arrived, Rose agreed that Émilie could go, but only because she and Pierre would be chaperons. Pierre was relegated to door duty, while Rose stood near a wall and surveyed the action on the dance floor, which served most days as the gymnasium at Lasalette High School. It had an interesting architecture that reminded many parents of their old one-room schools, except this one room was a gym that had a stage at the far end and three doors that led to classrooms on both side walls. The doors were closed and locked for the evening; the local students and the odd out-of-town guest were to stay inside the lined wooden floor and dance like mature and respectable young adults in the dimmed room that, between the perfumes, hair products, and stored away gym equipment, smelled of all the departments of an Eaton's store at once. It sounded like one as well to Rose, whose greatest outings were Sunday Mass and Émilie's piano recitals. Oh, she went to the city once every month or two, and attended Martin's sporting events, but this was different. This was a place where the devil could be lurking in every thought, gesture, and word.

Émilie was ten weeks shy of fourteen. She wore a straight skirt and the new sweater set she had gotten for the first day of high school. It was sensible and nothing like the full circle skirts she saw on television, for they required at least twice as much fabric and could twirl so high a girl's panties showed. She did have navy and white saddle shoes, however. Her father cleaned and shined them for her every Saturday so they would look good for Sunday Mass. She wore her black hair long in a soft half pony.

Dressed in a navy dress with three-quarter length sleeves and closed buttons from waist to collar, Rose watched Émilie like a cat surveying a mouse hole. There was a jive with Roch, then a swing and a bop with Robbie. When the record was switched from *Johnny B Good* to *Puppy Love*, Robbie was still holding Émilie's hand; he raised his eyebrows to ask Émilie if she wanted to stay for the dance.

She nodded, and they stepped closer. He placed his hand to her back; she rested her hand on his shoulder. She was about to ask him if he was having fun when his eyes caught hers. Her stomach fluttered. She looked away, but her heart still raced. Her back burned where he held her; her right hand felt fused to his left. She breathed and dared to look at him again; he was staring at her. She turned her eyes away and tried to slow her heartbeat. Over his shoulder, she saw her friends swaying in place with boys in their hold. She saw the chaperones—the Lecomtes, the Tessiers, her mother—surveying from the edge of the room.

Rose's face was taut and white, yet her eyes seemed to glow. Émilie's stomach churned, but Robbie's hold was warm, and everything, save his proximity, ceased to exist. She felt his stare, and she turned back to him. His eyes were golden honey, and she could not stop looking into them. He leaned towards her; she leaned towards him. Their lips touched for a soft, brief moment. She felt peaceful and tethered to him. They swayed until the music faded and was replaced by the Big Bopper's elongated, "Hey-loooo, baaaay-bay!" and the rollicking back-up of the bass and piano. Émilie and Robbie both blinked and stepped out of their hold like everyone else on the dance floor, but they did not swing into motion and start to jive. Instead, they stood for a moment, hand in hand, until Rose snapped Émilie's name and announced, "It's time to go. Go get your coat."

"But Maman …" Émilie raised her hands to indicate that there was a dance taking place around them.

Rose was unchanged. Her eyes were hard. "Now."

Émilie started to leave the dance floor, but she turned back to Robbie to apologize. "Sorry," she mouthed.

He shrugged and nodded, dared, even, to offer a smile. Still, she thought he looked hurt, crushed even. She wanted to run back to him and squeeze his hand, say she was sorry, and kiss him once again, but her mother's heavy palm was on her shoulder.

Émilie's eyes burned as Rose marched her out of the gym. Their footsteps echoed down the hallway to the front door. Her father was waiting for them. He smiled encouragement at Émilie, but his eyes were troubled. He put his hand on Rose's elbow and led her to the car. No one spoke until the car doors were slammed and the motor engaged. "That was absolutely inappropriate!" Rose lambasted.

"We were just dancing," Émilie cried.

"That was not dancing!" Rose cut the air with her hands. "You will never see that boy again!"

"Maman!"

"Rose," Pierre soothed. He reached across the seat and took her hand.

Her face scrunched, and she shook her head before covering her face with her hands. "C'est trop!" she cried. "Trop!"

"Shhh," he consoled. "Shhh."

Émilie watched them. She wanted to ask what was too much for her mother to handle, but she had no hope of an answer. She swallowed her words, slumped in her seat, and watched the flat, dark fields pass by from the backseat window until her father turned down their driveway. He stopped the car in front of the house. They sat for a moment and breathed. Finally, Émilie slid towards the door. "Bonne nuit," she muttered as she pushed it open.

"Bonne nuit," Pierre replied. Her mother sniffed. "We'll talk in the morning," he said.

Émilie nodded. She hurried away, up the back steps and through the screen door, which banged behind her. She winced at the noise, afraid it would wake her grandmother; she was more careful with the door that opened into the kitchen, but her caution was for nothing—Sylvie was seated at the table, grasping a mug between her thin, wrinkled hands. Her grey-white hair flowed in loose waves down her back. She wore a high-collared flannel nightgown.

"Grand-mère?" Émilie said with surprise.

"Back so soon, dear?"

"Mmmhmm. Maman didn't feel well," Émilie replied.

"Oh? Is she alright? Where is she now?" Sylvie pushed her chair away from the table and moved to stand, but Émilie went to her side and touched her shoulder.

"Ça va. She's just getting some air."

Sylvie nodded. "Bon. Air's good. Does wonders. Your grandfather, mon Baptiste, he liked his air, too." Sylvie clutched her mug and smiled. Émilie forced her lips upwards as she sought a way to escape the imminent stroll down her grandmother's memory lane. The stairs were close, but she could not just run away and leave her grandmother there alone so abruptly. She sighed and sat next to the older woman.

"Mon Baptiste, he'd wander the fields for hours. Come back with dirt caked in the corner of his eyes. Then he'd take out his violin and play until his fingers were numb." Sylvie's green eyes glistened over as she stared at a film of memories. "I always loved him, mon Baptiste Caron. But him, bin, he didn't even know I existed. I was just one of the little Simard sisters, but which one? Bah. He didn't know. He had chores and school and girls his own age, but, oh, he could make my heart race and my knees tremble."

Émilie fixed her face into an attentive mask, but she hardly listened as her grandmother repeated her favourite tale. It changed from telling to telling. Sometimes she included the part about once tending to a cut on Baptiste's, how she had shaken at the sight of the bright red blood that had pumped through his very heart. Other times, she told how her brothers and sisters teased her for going dumb whenever Baptiste was at the house. She talked about seeing him at school or church, or at the skating pond as well. There was a variety of details she might include, but Sylvie always included the one about coming west and seeing Baptiste for the first time in months: "And there he was! Mondou! Mon Baptiste, strong and tall and handsome. Oh, how I stared at him! At his eyes and his face, his thick brown hair, his pink-red lips! It was not proper, but I didn't care. He was there! Baptiste Caron was there in front of me, and he was looking at me! Seeing me! Smiling at me! Oh, it was the best day of my life. No! No! It was the first day of my life."

Émilie nodded, truly understanding for the first time in her life, for she had felt the same way dancing with Robbie not even an hour before. "Do you still love him like that even though he's been gone for so long?"

Sylvie smiled as if she were smelling a rich perfume and

touched her hand to her chest. "He's not gone. And of course, I still love him. I was born to love him." The two locked eyes and smiled in a communion of spirits.

The morning after the Freshie Dance, Émilie dressed in home clothes—jeans and a cotton top—and tied her long, black hair into a ponytail. She slipped down the front stairs to limit the chance of seeing her mother. The living room was tidy except for the empty popcorn bowl, and the Marvel comics Martin had left out the night before. *He missed a show*, Émilie thought. She wondered how long it would be before he would seek her out and demand the play-by-play. *Maybe he's already getting it if he's over at the Thibauds'*. It was likely that he was, for Francis liked it when Martin helped with the cows, and he paid him a little something, too. It drove Roch to complain, "He doesn't pay me anything."

"Well, you're his kid," Martin would reply. "My dad doesn't pay me to sweep his shop or carry his pieces either."

"Ah, that's sissy stuff. Farming's hard physical work."

Martin took offence and straightened his five-foot frame as tall as he could to challenge Roch, "Are you callin' my dad a sissy?"

Roch laughed, clapped Martin's shoulder, and smiled. "Nope. I'm calling you one." They jostled and wrestled, but nothing ever came of it; it was just how they were: Roch five inches taller, twenty pounds heavier and eighteen months older, and Martin, the wannabe twin. Émilie and Robbie watched and rolled their eyes at each other over the display.

The thought of Robbie caused tears to spring to her eyes. She had gone over everything from the day they were born until the night before, and she was certain they were meant to be together, but she was also sure there was no way her mother would ever allow her to get within touching distance of him again. It made Émilie angry, made her want to seek out her mother, grab her by the shoulders and yell right into her face, "What's your problem?" Instead, however, she slipped out the front door and crossed the yard to her father's workshop. She could hear neither his saw nor his lathe. She pushed the door open and stuck her head in.

He raised his eyes from the spindle he was sanding and smiled at her. "Bonjour Fille-fille."

She accepted his nickname with a smile and stepped into the shop. "Salut, Papa." Pierre put the spindle down and brushed his hands together to clear away the dust. Émilie plopped down on the stool on the other side of his workbench and traced her finger in the curled wood shavings and dust on the table. She skipped all small talk and cut straight to what she wanted to know, "Why did she act like that?"

His face crinkled with a wince. "She had her reasons."

Émilie sighed at the answer she had heard before. She searched her father's face for more, but it betrayed nothing but patient resolve. "Did she really mean what she said? About me never seeing Robbie again?"

He fingered the spindle and wet his lips with his tongue. "That was a bit much. You can still see him, but you know you can never be alone with him. Nor with Roch."

Her heart was heavy, but she accepted that it was the only concession she would get from her parents. "I know."

He reached over the dusty table and squeezed her hand. "You're a good girl."

"And he's a good boy, Papa. You know that. Just because we danced …"

He raised an eyebrow; Émilie lowered her eyes in guilt. "It was more than dancing. You're too young."

"We're almost fourteen! And we've known each other our

whole lives!"

He patted her hand. "I know, but it's better to wait."

"Why? For how long?"

He answered the second part, "Until you're sixteen."

"Sixteen?!"

Pierre averted his gaze from her round green eyes, for they could weaken him, and he had to stay the course he had set with Rose. "That's not long."

"Not long? Papa! It's more than two years!"

"Everything gets better with time." She wanted to ask him what needed to get better—she and Robbie were already a perfect match—but Pierre squeezed her hand and said, "You go practice now."

She swallowed her words and acquiesced. "D'accord." She slid off her stool and left his workshop. Nannerl and Fanny, the cats Robbie had given her after her accident on the mow rope in the barn, met her at the door. They meowed and circled about her ankles. She squatted and picked up Nannerl and held her to her chest. Tears rose to Émilie's eyes as she rubbed the grey cat behind the ears. "Go practice," she muttered. She sniffed and blinked, but tears still slipped from her eyes. She loosened her hold of Nannerl and let her jump to the ground and run away. She stroked Fanny's short fur, then gently pushed her in the same direction. "Go play."


The following day, Émilie stared at Robbie all through Mass from her spot in the choir loft. She studied how the light caught the bronze highlights in his hair and how the muscles in his neck lengthened when he bent his head in prayer, how his skin was the colour of tea with cream. She had seen these things for years, but they had never made her melt until now. Before, they were just characteristics of someone she saw every day.

*Every day*, she thought. *My god! And now I love him! Of course, I do! I always have! He's so kind and smart and interested in everything I do; I can talk to him about anything, and not just school and the people we know—everything!*

She had told him once that she wanted to walk the paths that Johann Sebastian Bach had taken and play all his preludes and fugues on both a clavichord and a harpsichord. She wanted to wander Paris, too, she had told Robbie and play in the same salons as Chopin and Liszt, and visit Notre-Dame, hear its organ and bells, maybe even play there if she kept up with the organ. "I wanna go there," she had told him. "Wanna sleep and breathe and live in that world of artists and musicians, but I can't really imagine being anywhere but here."

Robbie had nodded in understanding. "Maman says I should go to university. Learn everything I don't know. Maybe we can go together? That way it'd be like never leaving home." They had smiled at one another for as long as Rose had allowed.

A nudge roused her from her thoughts. Émilie turned to her left and stared blankly at her friend Marie. "What's wrong?" Marie asked with a small movement of her head and a lift of her eyebrows. Émilie frowned and shook her head. "Come on," Marie insisted in their silent language of facial expressions. Émilie shrugged and motioned towards the congregation. Marie smiled. She raised and lowered her eyebrows to signal that she had heard about the kiss. Émilie frowned.

"What?" Marie asked in their silent way. "It wasn't good?"

Émilie could not answer. She turned away and watched Robbie again. He stood; he sat; he raised his shoulders as he recited prayers. He looked up towards her when he turned around to shake hands with the people behind him at the sign of peace; he smiled at her when he walked back to his pew after Communion. He lingered there after the closing prayer and the recessional hymn, then moved to the front of the church to light a prayer candle. He peeked up at the choir loft to see if Émilie would be descending soon. He could not tell, but he made his way to the back of the church and pretended to meditate on the seventh station of the cross while he waited for her.

Émilie saw him there. Her heart fluttered, but the wings of such excitement were clipped with each stair she descended. "Wait," her father had said. "You have to wait. Wait. Wait."

Robbie watched her from the corner of his eye—her shined shoes, her shaped calves, the neat hem of her skirt—until he could not contain himself, then he turned completely towards her. She stopped on the second last stair, frozen in his gaze. His face transfigured as he grinned at her. "Hi," he said in a whisper so as not to disturb the grandmothers still kneeling and fingering their rosaries.

She smiled at him and descended the final two stairs. She was opening her mouth to speak when the door burst open, and Martin appeared. "Em," he whispered, walking over, "Maman wants to go." She nodded but did not take her eyes off Robbie. Martin looked back and forth between the two ninth graders with an amused smile, but then he shook it away. "If she sees you two."

"Shhh!" A grandmother hissed.

Émilie and Robbie just smiled and stared at each other. Martin tugged at Émilie's sleeve. "Come on. I'm hungry, and I want more than tears for lunch." Émilie sighed and turned to her brother. "Tell her I'm coming."

"Em."

"Shhh!"

"Please," she whispered.

He rolled his eyes and let out his breath. "Okay." He left the two of them alone at the back of the church.

The sun shone a beam through the window. Jesus carried his cross along the wall. A blue-cloaked Mary stood on a serpent and held her hands out towards them. Grandmothers' voices flowed in incantations of prayers, "Je vous salue Marie, pleine de grâce …"

Tears spilled from Émilie's eyes. Robbie reached for her hand. His touch was a bandage and a burn. "I …" she gasped. "The dance." Robbie smiled and nodded. She hid her eyes from his. "I can't date until we're sixteen," she mumbled.

"Shhh!"

"What?" He mouthed. She tore her hand from his and ran away. "Em."

"Shhh!"


They still saw each other every day, but Émilie kept her distance, and Robbie respected that until the day he came upon her slumped face down on a table in the school library. Her long black hair fell over her face and books like a curtain. Her shoulders shook, and she whimpered. He rushed towards her. "Em?" he asked in a hoarse whisper. He sat in the chair next to her and touched his hand to her back. "What's wrong?"

"I don't get it!" she cried.

"Don't get what?"

"This!" She sat up and motioned towards her papers and books.

"What is it?"

"Geometry!"

"Oh." He looked at the tear-smeared pencil markings in

her notebook.

"I failed our last test!"

"You did?"

She sniffed and nodded. She closed her eyes and wiped away her tears, but more streamed down her face. "I just don't get it! All those letters and shapes and angles! And the way they ask those questions! I mean … ah!"

He squeezed her hand. "I got ninety-six. I can show you."

"You can?"

"Of course." They smiled at each other until the bell rang. "Um," Robbie said as if waking up. "Sorry. I guess we don't have time now. How about after school? I could come over?"

She shook her head. "My mom."

"It's for school," he pointed out. "She can't mind that, can she?"

Émilie shrugged. "You know how she is. It just depends on the weather."

"Well, let's hope it's sunny then," he said with a smile.

Émilie laughed for the first time in weeks.


Rose's chest tightened when she saw the Thibaud boys get off the school bus with Émilie and Martin, but she looked out at the four of them and watched them walk towards the house. Martin's face was animated and bright; he threw back his head in laughter. Émilie smiled too; her black hair bobbed in a ponytail. Their happiness softened Rose, and she almost smiled as she watched Roch walk backwards in front of the other three, gesturing as he talked. Robbie trailed a pace or two behind the others, gripping the strap of his school bag with a tight hand. *He looks so unsure,* Rose thought, *like a boy testing his skates on the fringes of a game of shinny.* It squeezed her heart, but she pushed the tenderness aside. *He is not a boy*, she reminded herself.

She studied the teenage neighbours coming up the way with their bronze-brown hair cut in two different styles and their five-foot-six frames developed in different ways: one lanky, the other thick. "Dusk and dawn," she remembered Lucille Thibaud saying about them, not unlike Lucille and herself: the former was sure-footed and wise, while Rose was treading frantically in the hidden depths below.

The teens laughed again. Rose shook her head and took a loud, deep breath. She nodded to herself in an act of resolve not to drown in her thoughts. She turned from the window and made her way to the back of the house to find food for the extra guests. The group of them burst through the back door with thumps and laughter.

"Salut Maman!"

"Bonjour Madame Tremblay."

"Oh, Roch! Robbie!" Rose greeted with a smile pushed onto her face. "I saw you get off the bus."

"Is that okay?" Robbie asked, stopping at the door like a scared dog.

His timidity squeezed Rose in a band of guilt. She pushed on a bigger smile and continued to tread like a pen swan. "Of course! Sit! Sit! I think we have some macaroons in the freezer. Émilie, go check."

Émilie blinked in surprise at her mother's hospitality. "Ah, okay." She turned back towards the porch where the Tremblays, like many of their neighbours, kept two deep freezers. "Okay!"

"Roch," Rose continued, "don't worry. I have peanut butter cookies for you. And chocolate chip. Émilie, bring the butter horns! Martin, get some glasses." She opened the fridge and reached for the milk. "Now what about fruit? Apples or bananas?"

"Ban-apple," Roch and Robbie answered one over the other.

Rose laughed. "Of course. Still the same: completely different. Isn't that what we used to say?" She bustled about. "Shall I cut your apple, Robbie, and sprinkle it with cinnamon?"

He blinked at the attention not bestowed on him for years. "Uhh. No, that's okay, Madame Tremblay. I don't want to be a bother."

She waved the words away and took up a paring knife. "No bother! Here, Roch, take two. Émilie, put those macaroons on a plate. Is that all that's left? Martin! Have you been snitching?"

Martin grinned bashfully. "Yeah. Sorry," he mumbled through his mouthful of cookies.

In less than ten minutes, the snack plates were crumb-covered, and the drinking glasses were coated with the dredges of milk. "Merci, Maman," Martin said, standing up. "Roch and I are gonna go work on some football passes."

"Alright. And you two?" she asked, facing Émilie and Robbie.

"Homework?" Émilie ventured. "Robbie's gonna help me with geometry."

"Oh, gloire à Dieu! Merci, Robert!"

"It's nothing, Madame. I'm sorry she's been struggling."

"Yes. Me, too." Rose gathered up the dirty glasses from the table. "I tried to help, but, well, I had trouble with it at her age, too." A brief remembrance of sitting in the back row of the schoolhouse through the depression of the 1930s flashed through her mind: looking at geometrical shapes and thinking they looked like pie, or cheese, or roast beef. It had made her stomach growl; the sound had reverberated in the classroom, but no one had laughed, for no one could determine whether the sound came from Rose or from themselves. "It was hard," she said to Robbie of those long-ago school days spent trying to solve for missing cellar provisions rather than missing angles: how would she and her siblings and parents get through winter with only six quarts of canned beans? She turned towards the sink and busied herself with the dishes.

Émilie turned to Robbie and raised her eyebrows. He smiled back, and they pulled out their books from their school bags and set to work. "A polygon is a shape made of straight lines," Robbie said, leaning towards Émilie.

Rose closed her eyes and tried to conjure up a polygon, a square, or a box in which to put her thoughts of the dust storms of her childhood—black blizzards in the heat of summer—and the lack of food, the rationing and reusing of water, her father's wrinkled eyes, the tight lines of her mother's lips, the desolation and the loneliness after her older brothers and sisters, her aunt and grandmother, the Forciers, the Dahlquists, the Painchauds, and the Ouellettes all left in search of rain and the promised land. Her father had always insisted that they had found it there, five miles east of Lasalette, but sometimes it had seemed more like Hell, especially when the devil himself showed up, sly and smooth as gravy, when Rose was about Émilie's age.

She had not recognized the loose and dirty clothes at first, nor the weathered face. He raised his hat as he walked towards her. He had a smile that could melt hard candy. "Mondou, Marie, you haven't changed a bit." The voice was familiar, but the hollow, stubble-covered face was not.

"I'm not Marie. I'm Rose," she said, eyeing the older stranger.

"Rose! By-golly! You're all grown up!" He grabbed her by the arms and kissed her cheeks.

Her heart raced, but she did not know if it was from fear or excitement. "Who are you?"

He chuckled. "A-ho! It's me. Serge. Serge Ouellette. Your brothers' friend. I used to live just over there." He indicated the greyed, wind-blown house across the road. "It was different before." His eyes clouded then, and his jaw tightened. "Is your father here?" he asked after a moment.

"He's in the field. He'll be back for supper."

"Can I wait for him? Maybe get some water? Something to eat?"

Rose shrugged. "I don't know what we have. Come see Maman."

He chatted as he followed her to the two-storey catalogue house her father, Baptiste, had built back when crops grew and the rain came when it should. Serge's talking sounded like a chickadee in winter; it sounded how Rose's older brothers might have sounded were they to come back to the wind-blown farm.

When Sylvie saw the old neighbour boy, she clapped her hands together and shrieked, "Mon Dieu Seigneur! Viens! Viens tant!" She took his coat and hat, gave him two glasses of water and a thick slice of bread. "How are you? Where have you been? Have you seen my Guillaume? How are your parents?"

Rose stood by the wall and listened to his answers: he'd been riding the rails, had gone across Canada twice, but had found little work, little comfort.

"Mon pauvre petit!" Sylvie comforted, patting his strong, dirty hands. "Stay here tonight. We don't have much, but we can share."

"Merci. Merci beaucoup."

She nodded and patted him again.

He stayed for days that turned into weeks, then months.

He helped Baptiste with the fields and the fences. He carried water for Sylvie, played with the younger sons, chatted with Rose and her sister, Louise.

Rose had liked it, liked his presence, his smile, his fingers brushing hers when she passed him the bread at dinner. She had not known it was all an act, all butter and sugar and lies, there in the very kitchen she now used to make meals for her own family, and where her teenage daughter sat with a boy, trusting him as she had trusted Serge.

"Well, that's not so hard," Rose heard Émilie say. "Why don't they just say that in the book?"

"They do," Robbie said, "It's just kind of hard to follow. Kind of like Greek."

They laughed and smiled at each other. Their fingers touched, and Rose barked, "Émilie!"

She looked up. "Oui, Maman?" Robbie cocked his head, too, but Rose's glare made him cower and turn back to his books and pencils.

"Come and cut this," Rose ordered.

Émilie scrunched her nose at the gold-skinned onion her mother held out to her. "Why?"

"Because I said so."

"But I'm studying," Émilie pointed out.

"Not anymore." Rose turned to Robbie. "Émilie needs to help me now; you'll have to go."

"I ... uh ... okay." He stood and collected his text and notebook. "Maybe we can pick it up tomorrow?"

Émilie nodded, but Rose snapped, "No. She needs to practice."

"I can practice after supper," Émilie said.

"Yes, and you can practice before, too." Rose strode to the stove like a führer and picked up the wooden spoon. "And every lunch hour at the church. Soeur Saint-Sacrement wants you to play the organ at Christmas." She lifted the lid off a pot and plunged the spoon into its basin. "You're fine with geometry now. You'd best concentrate on other things." Émilie opened her mouth to protest, but Rose continued with her orders, "Say good-bye to Robbie, and thank you for the help."

Émilie emitted a gasp of disbelief, but obeyed. "Bye. Thanks for your help."

He nodded as he made his way to the door. "Merci, Madame," he said before he left.

Émilie's eyes stung before she even began removing the dry, shrivelled skin from the onion.



"Our hands touched," Pierre said later that night when Rose told him what she had seen between Robbie and Émilie. "Remember? When we were shelling peas."

Rose sniffed and shook her head at the words. "It's not the same."

Pierre covered her hand with his and continued, "Maybe it's like your papa and maman then, eh? They knew each other as children, too."

She pulled her hand away and scowled. "Maybe it's like Serge."

Pierre sucked in his breath as if he had doused a cut in iodine, but he took her hand back. He rubbed it and kissed it. "Please, don't think of that. Think of me instead."

She scrunched her face and tried to oblige, tried to force all thoughts of Serge Ouellette away and replace them with memories of Pierre, kind, gentle Pierre, who had arrived too late to spare her pain, but early enough to assuage it like an angel in disguise. "I'm scared," she whispered. "Not everyone's like you."

Pierre squeezed her hand. "Not everyone's like him."

Rose bobbed her head in quick nods. "But he's his nephew."

"And I'm my uncle's," Pierre replied. "That doesn't mean anything."

"No," she agreed. "But I know things. I can protect Émilie like my parents couldn't protect me."

"Maybe, but it's Robbie. You don't need to protect Émilie from him."

She accepted his assurance; still, it was easier to keep Émilie occupied with music and household chores than it was to trust the boy across the field.


Émilie cooked and cleaned and went to school. She practiced the piano and the organ. She discovered the Romantics and the Impressionists. She liked their stories and their passion: she admired Debussy's spunk, his refusal to follow rules. She wished she could be more like him, wished that she could throw up her hands and cry, "Pleasure is the law!" But she was too compliant for that. So was Robbie. They both kept their distance from one another and prayed for their sixteenth birthday to hurry up and arrive.

When it finally did, the Tremblays went over to the Thibauds' for lunch and cake. Robbie grew flush as the meal progressed. Émilie thought it was the excitement of turning sixteen and finally being allowed to date—whatever that might look like with her mercurial, uptight mother.

Émilie snuck peeks at Robbie and smiled at him throughout the meal. Roch growled and bumped her with his elbow as he forked mashed potatoes into his mouth. She ignored him, continued to ogle Robbie even as Francis Thibaud set into his annual story, "It was the full moon …"

"Oh, not again," Roch groaned, pushing his plate away and crossing his arms across his chest.

"Oui," his father laughed, "encore." Émilie smiled at the good-natured reprimand and the ritual of it all. She grinned at Robbie. He smiled back, but his eyes seemed to be elsewhere. Her heart wrenched, but she kept her eyes on him as Francis Thibaud continued with the story he told every year at their birthday celebration. It changed that year, however, when he got near to the end, "Bon sang!" he cried, as he touched the baby who had grown into Robbie. "You're a bloody furnace!"

Everyone turned towards Robbie. His eyes were glassy, and his face was as white as the wall, but he forced a smile and sloughed it off, "Non, non. It's just warm in here."

"Non." Madame Thibaud rushed to his side. "Non. You don't look well." She touched his forehead and then his cheek. "Mon Dieu! You're burning up! Go up to bed. I'll get you some Aspirin."

He shook his head. "No. It's the story. And I have a present for Émilie." He started to stand, but he stopped suddenly, and his face went blank. He pitched towards the floor.

"Robbie!" Émilie shrieked, jumping to her feet.

Francis caught him mid-fall, then laid him down. Robbie shook and jerked. "Mon Dieu!" his father gasped. "What's happening?"

Pierre rushed towards Robbie and signalled for everyone to make room. "Allez. Get back," he said. "Move that chair." He crouched beside Robbie and touched his hands to his head. "Ça va, Robbie. Come back."

"What's happening?" Émilie cried.

"A seizure," her father replied, calm as ever. "It's okay." He turned back to Robbie and soothed him, "Ça va, mon grand. Viens tant. Come on. Come back."

Madame Thibaud held one hand to her mouth, the other to her chest. Monsieur Thibaud gripped the edge of the table to steady himself. Rose wrapped her arm about Émilie, who turned her face into her mother's shoulder. Roch watched rigidly and wide-eyed.

"Martin, aide-moi," Pierre said. Martin strode across the kitchen and helped him turn Robbie onto his side. "You're okay, Robbie," Pierre said. "We'll get Dr. Neills." He jerked his head as a signal towards Rose; she had already released Émilie and was hustling towards the telephone. He turned back to Robbie, who was still once again. "There. There. Can you say something?" Robbie mumbled but did not stir. "It's okay. Just stay there. Someone, get him a blanket. Rose, call the doctor."

"I am. I am!"

Robbie convulsed again, with everyone's eyes still on him. When it ended, Pierre repeated the command for someone to get a blanket, but they were all still seized themselves, cold and scared. "Émilie!" he ordered. "Get a blanket!"

She snapped out of her trance and hurried to the living room. She returned with an afghan throw she had found on Monsieur Thibaud's TV-watching chair. "Is he gonna be okay?" she asked in a trembling, shallow voice as she handed the blanket to Pierre.

"I hope so," he answered, "but he seems to have a high fever. Lucille, do you have a thermometer?"

"Oui." She scurried off to find it.

Pierre ran his hand over Robbie's face and spoke to comfort the others, "This man at my logging camp had seizures, and he told me what to do. But Robbie, he's not like Grenier. Non. He doesn't have anything wrong with his brain. He's probably just sick. Really sick."

He was sick; he had mumps with encephalitis and was

transported to Regina. Roch and his parents followed in their Fairlane; the Tremblays stayed back, tended to the Thibauds' cattle and waited for news.

Émilie and Martin were put into quarantine. They spent days turning about the house and the yard, waiting for 6 o'clock and the phone call from Monsieur Thibaud.

Rose said, "He's very sick. We should pray for him." So, they did, on their knees with rosaries in their hands and holy candles lit about them. The fact that Robbie could die was only shared after he had made a turn for the living. "Merci Seigneur!" Rose exclaimed, clutching her hands together and raising them to the ceiling. "Thank you for saving our dear Robert from the clutches of death!"

Émilie's eyes rounded and her mouth dropped open. "What did you mean by that? Did Robbie almost die?"

Rose nodded. "Oui. They couldn't get the swelling of his brain down."

Émilie gasped and blinked. "But now they have?"

Rose took her hand. "Oui. Grâce à Dieu! He's going to be alright." Tears streamed down Émilie's face. Rose brushed them away. "Bin voyons. Why are you crying? He's fine. He's going to be alright."

Émilie shook her head and pulled away. "But he might not've been! He might've died! And I might not've ever seen him again!"

Rose hugged her. "Oh, ma fille. It's okay. Everything's alright now."

Émilie pulled away from her mother again. "Non, Maman! Everything's not alright!" She ran from the room.

Rose held her hand to her mouth and stared at the air before her. "Mon Dieu," she whispered to herself. "Mon Dieu, mon Dieu."

Émilie and Martin went to see Robbie the day after he came home. He was propped up on the couch in the living room so he could be close to the bathroom and to his mother who was bustling about the kitchen simmering soup and preparing a meatloaf for supper. She smiled at the two of them when they appeared in her kitchen. She seemed both tired and relieved. She jerked her greying head towards the living room, "Go on in."

"Merci," they responded and traversed the savoury warmth of her kitchen to the living room. The curtains were drawn, and the television was off. Robbie looked smaller to them, for he was sunken into his pillows and covered with feather quilts. "Hey!" he cheered when his friends walked in. "Salut!" He shifted about to free himself from the pillow indentation and sit up.

"Salut," Martin said. "How are you? Are you okay?"

"Yeah." Robbie nodded his assurance.

Émile sat on the edge of the couch and clasped his hand. She surveyed his face and caught his eyes; she held them in hers for long, long seconds.

"I almost died," he said to her, forgetting about Martin. Émilie bit her lip to keep from crying. "I don't remember it, but that's what the doctors said."

She tightened her clutch on his hand. "I know."

He swallowed and looked down at their conjoined hands. His face scrunched with pain as he pulled his hand away. He tucked it to his side and said, "It made me think, you know? About life?"

Émilie nodded; her stomach churned at his nervous yet serious tone. "Uh-huh?"

His forehead furrowed into deep creases. He licked his lips for courage. "Like in Confirmation class? Père Letendre, he talked about why we're here, what we're supposed to do with our lives?"

"Yeah?" she squeaked.

He squeezed his eyes closed as he spoke, "I think maybe I'm supposed to be a priest."

The room fell cold and silent. Émilie stared at him like he had spoken in tongues. "What? No! We're sixteen! We can date!"

He nodded, opened his tear-filled eyes. "I know, but …"

She stared at his long, serious face and water-logged eyes until all the connections in her brain were made. "No!"

He sniffed and nodded, hung his head. She dropped his hand and ran from the room. The front door banged behind her.

"I should go after her," Martin said.

Robbie shook his head. "No. She needs to digest it. I did."

Martin did not know what to say, so he simply looked about the room, cramped and cozy with family photographs, worn furniture, and Madame Thibaud's piano in the corner. She had taught Émilie her first pieces back when she and Martin spent as many hours there as they had at their own house. He studied the crucifix and the image of Our Lady of Lourdes. The words *Je suis l'Immaculée Conception* were written beneath the woman in white and blue. Martin pumped his lips. "So," he finally said, "you want to be a priest?"

"God wants me to," Robbie replied.

## 3. Gigue
## April 1990

"Woah," Michel said, "that's pretty heavy for sixteen." Stéphanie blinked herself back to the conversation, to the coffee and the syrup-logged pancakes before her, and to Michel sitting across from her with his ginger-coloured beard and maple eyes. "Is it?"

"Yeah, I mean, giving up girls? Becoming a priest? Not a lot of guys think of that when they're sixteen."

She shrugged. "I suppose not, but it was how he was raised."

"How's that? School, church, skating rink?" he said with a lightness that made her smile.

She chuckled at the well-known phrase from *The Hockey Sweater*. "Christianne calls it the Fs: faith, family, French."

Michel smiled; his sandy hair fell like a curtain as he tilted his head to look at her. "That sounds like you." Her face pruned, and he rushed to apologize, "Oh, I'm sorry."

"No, it's okay. Christianne says it all the time."

"And I guess it's not a compliment?"

"No." Her brow furrowed as she thought of Christianne and of their differences that night and in general: their clothes, their plans, their opinion of Stéphanie's decision to give up performing and become a music teacher ...

"It was double A-H for me," Michel said to pull her from her thoughts. "All About Hockey."

She was buoyed. "Right. I read about that." She tittered. "Sorry. That was lame."

"No, it wasn't. It was kind of hard to miss the way *Musique Plus* did that whole thing about me and Roch Voisine having played against each other."

"Was it true?"

"Mostly, but there wasn't any big rivalry. And there isn't now either. I mean, really, what do I care if he's on the top of the charts or Plumeau is? As long as good French music's being made and listened to, that's all that matters."

She smiled at him, at his attitude and the joy that shone upon his face. *And that's why I should teach*, she told herself, *to equip the next generation of Fransaskois kids with the necessary tools to express themselves through music.*

"Bull shit," Christianne scoffed inside her head exactly as she had when Stéphanie had proclaimed the statement the year before. "If you really want to help Fransaskois kids, you'd perform. Show them that we can play in the big leagues and that good French music isn't just made out east but here, too." It had bridled Stéphanie then, and it left her wordless once again there with Michel.

He nudged her hand with his fingers. "What about you?" he asked, trying to bring her back.

She blinked and shook her head. "What?"

He smiled like a light at the end of a tunnel. "What were you into when you were sixteen?"

"I don't know," she tittered. "That was a long time ago."

"Not really. Aren't you and Christianne the same age?"

"Yeah, but it seems a long time ago. A lifetime, actually."

"Why?"

She let out a long, heavy sigh before she spoke. "Because a lot's changed ... Sixteen ... That's when I moved to Lasalette."

Michel waited for more, but it did not come, so he asked, "With your mom?"

"No. She had this project in East Africa. She asked me if I wanted to go, but I didn't. Not with her anyway." She scowled at herself and tried to shake down the rest. "Sorry. I didn't mean to sound so bitter."

"There's nothing wrong with bitter. Isn't that why you take your coffee black?"

She chuckled and nodded, but Stéphanie still sank into a funk. "She had these pills," she said like a spirit leaving the dead. "Painkillers because of an accident in high school. But the pain mustn't've ever gone away, because by the time I was in high school, she was downing handfuls at a time and drinking wine like it was water."

"I'm sorry," Michel said.

She shook away his sympathy. "It could've been worse."

"Yeah, and it could've been better, too. How's she now?"

"Now?" Stéphanie snorted. "Now she's fine. Doesn't need pills or wine."

"That's good."

"Yeah. A little late, but good." She tittered and rattled her head; she looked down at her plate, at the syrup-logged remnants of pancakes and the abandoned silverware. "I used to pray for it, pray that she'd be happy and settle down, and we could be a family with a long-term dad and maybe some siblings and a dog. And now I have that, have it with my actual, live father, but it just feels like a joke. A sad, sick joke the devil's playing on me because I prayed for this, but it's not right, you know?"

"Yeah." He reached across the table and set his hand on

hers, then slid his fingers between hers. She looked at the back of his hand, so clean and manicured and strong. "It's like getting a Leafs jersey instead of a Canadiens."

"Exactly," she agreed, still sullen.

He went on, "It's a perfectly good sweater, but it's all itchy and scratchy and blu-uuuue." He sang the last word as two syllables divided into two and six beats each.

The clouds lifted from her face. "Joni Mitchell."

"Yep," he grinned.

"She's from Saskatchewan."

He danced his eyebrows. "I know." They held eyes for a long time until Lise came over and asked them if they wanted more coffee. "I don't think so," Michel said, "unless you do?" he asked Stéphanie.

"No, I'm fine," Stéphanie answered. "We should probably get back anyway. Check on the others."


The sun had already risen when they left Chez Nous. The sky was a thin, pale blue. Birds sang in the trees overhead. A freshness hung in the air despite the cars and activity already on the streets. "I'd like to take you someplace before we go home," Michel said, "but it's totally out of the way. Do you mind?"

She floated on the caramel seas of his eyes. "No. Not at all."

"Are you sure?"

"Yes."

They exchanged smiles and continued walking, savouring the sunshine and the comfort between them. "It's a bit odd, the place I'm taking you."

"Yeah? Where is it?"

He tittered and winced with sheepishness, "The

cemetery?"

"Sounds good," she answered brightly.

"Really? You don't mind?"

"No. I like cemeteries." He raised an eyebrow in surprise, and she added a bit more, "They tell the truth. Especially once you move the tree branches out of the way and rub the dirt off the stone." She grimaced and shook away her extra words.

Michel rubbed her hand. "Sounds like a story there. Maybe even a song?"

She chuckled at his astuteness but shrugged coyly and stayed on topic, "Which cemetery?"

"Notre-Dame-des-Neiges. Do you know where that is?"

"No, but I will once we get there." He chuckled at her logic. "I'm a landmark kind of person," she explained. "Once I've been somewhere, I can usually find my way back, but until then ..."

"You need help finding the Beauchemin?" he teased, slipping his arm through hers.

"Exactly," she chuckled at his joke from hours before and nuzzled into his side. He fit comfortably around her angles and curves and still smelled faintly of bergamot. She closed her eyes and breathed it all in: his smell, his warmth, the sound of their feet moving in cadence with her heartbeat.

He pulled her to a stop at the corner, and she opened her eyes. They exchanged smiles and walked on. Cars passed. Birds flitted from tree to tree. A woman pushed a stroller towards them. The toddler inside let out a wail and writhed in his seat. Stéphanie and Michel both watched the child reach for a stuffed elephant that had fallen on the ground. The woman pushing him, his mother, they both assumed from her lined eyes and impatient curse, stopped and picked up the precious thing. "Tiens," she said as she handed it to the child. His face split into a slobbery grin. He kicked his feet with excitement as he reached for his toy. The woman touched his cheek and patted his head. "Mon petit chou." She returned to her place behind the stroller. Her face was brighter then and held a smile. Michel watched them continue past.

"You like kids," Stéphanie remarked.

He tittered, "Yeah. You?"

She raised a shoulder and said, "I guess," even as her heart swelled with memories of holding her baby sister for the first time—there, at last, was a sibling for her to love. She shook the thought away and breathed in the sunshine and energy of the street. People scissored up and down the sidewalk: professionals with suits and attaché cases, students with backpacks slung on a single shoulder, most with cigarettes, all with coffee cups in their hands. She turned towards Michel to share her observation just as he let out the question he had been chewing on since the stroller had passed, "Do you want kids?"

The overlapping of their words made her laugh. She answered him without much thought, "I suppose. You?"

His face pinched. "I don't think it's in the cards."

"Why? Because of Plumeau?"

His head rattled in surprise. "No. Why would you say that?"

She ground the bitterness from her answer before she spoke. "Because it's not fair when you're a travelling musician."

"Speaking from experience?"

She snorted and changed the subject, "Look at that cyclist! He's already wearing shorts, and it's only April!"

Michel followed her conversational detour but circled back, "It's unseasonably warm. What's not fair about it?" She shook the question away. "Please?" Michel pressed. "I'd like to know."

She sighed like old wood before answering, "The kid either gets trotted around or left behind. Sometimes she gets to choose, but how does she know which one'll be better?"

"Is one?"

She held her lips together as the answer pieced itself together. "It depends," she said at last.

"On?"

"Where you're going and for how long. Who else will be there. That kind of thing." He nodded again; Stéphanie continued talking like butter melting over a hot cob of corn, "It wasn't easy living with her, with the pills and the wine and the parade of men, so travelling could be …"

"Tricky?" he suggested as she shrugged looking for the right adjective.

"Yeah." She accepted the word with a nod, then rubbed her lips together before asking him a question herself, "What about you? How's traveling with Clem?"

"Clem?" He laughed. "Easy. Why?"

She tittered sheepishly, "His sauce?"

"Oh," he shook his head and laughed, "no. He doesn't do that when we're on the road. He doesn't do it at all, really. That's just a break-up thing."

"Really?" she asked almost like a wish.

"Yeah. We have a rule. Have ever since the Bas-Saint-Laurent."

She tilted her head and looked at him with interest. "What is it?"

His eyes glinted with playfulness. "That's a band secret, but let's just say it's something like you can do whatever you want as long as it doesn't hurt the band."

"That's pretty wide-open," she remarked.

"Yep, but it works. We're still together, and we have a gold record."

"But they're your friends," she said. "Don't you care what they do to themselves?"

"Of course. But when we're Plumeau, we're Plumeau. Everything else stays out the door."

"It's that simple?"

"Yep." He squeezed her hand and smiled in reassurance.

She raised an eyebrow in surprise and scepticism. "It never was for my mom."

"Well, it is for us." He stopped walking and looked squarely into her swimming, patchwork eyes. "Music's enough, Stéphanie. It soothes and heals and makes everything alright."

"Not everything," she said.

He ran the back of his fingers down her face. "Maybe that depends on what you sing."

"Or how," she muttered.

He rubbed comfort into her arms. "I don't think there should be any rules for that. I think it should just come out as it comes out." They stared into each others eyes until Stéphanie looked away. Michel took her hand again and said, "Come on. We're almost there." He led her a few more blocks, then through a set of open gates and onward past plots of statues and headstones, crosses and trees. "Here," he said at last.

She read the inscription before them, "Mary Travers, dit La Bolduc. Wow! Vraiment? My grandparents love her!" She turned to him to share her excitement, but her face froze when she saw him raise a harmonica to his lips. "What are you doing?" She pulled on his arm, but he danced his eyebrows and began to play a tune. She looked about the walkway, but no one was rushing towards them to reprimand him or order him to stop. Michel signalled her to sing, and she obliged despite herself, "Monsieur, monsieur, je voudrais danser. Oh, la bastringue, pis la bastringue. Monsieur, monsieur, I'd like to dance the bastringue in your café."

Michel's eyes glinted as he played the interlude. Then he lowered the instrument and sang the response to Stéphanie's verse. She marvelled at his abandon there in a cemetery on a Friday morning and did not notice the people gathering about. She sang the next verse, then tapped a rhythm on her thighs as Michel continued with his response. Then she sang hers, and he sang his, and back and forth until her final verse, "Viens dans mes bras mon cher André. Ah la bastringue, pis la bastringue. Come in my arms, my dear André. Come so I can kiss your lips."

Michel caught her about the waist, and she thought he was going to kiss her; however, he sang the final verse for the handful of mourners who were listening, "Vous allez vous fatiguer. Non, Monsieur, je voudrais danser. La bastringue, la bastringue. No, sir, I want to dance. I'm ready to start la bastringue again."

The small crowd applauded. Stéphanie hid her red face in Michel's chest. "Don't be shy," he said. "It was for La Bolduc." He turned her about to face the others and made her bow. "Merci," he said to them. "Sorry if we disturbed you. We were just paying our respects to la grande dame of folk music." Michel smiled and nodded and led Stéphanie away from the grave.

"Do you always carry a harmonica in your pocket?" she asked with a laugh once they were away from the crowd.

Michel smiled as if he were an eight-year-old who had just popped a wheelie on his bicycle. "Of course. You never know when you might need it." Their hips banged as he pulled her towards him. They laughed like squirrels. "You know what I like about La Bolduc?"

"Her turlu-tu-tus?" Stéphanie teased.

"Of course. And how she made it. You know?" Stéphanie shook her head; he filled her in, "She was like a lot of our grandparents, you know? From a family with too many mouths and nothing but songs to put in them. But our little Mary, she took her father's Irish tunes, and her mother's French ones and fed her kids with them."

"I'm sure it wasn't as easy as that."

"Bin, oui, pis non. It all happened pretty fast. One night she was filling in for someone and the next thing she's selling records faster than hotcakes, and in the middle of The Depression, too.

Stéphanie nodded at the details. "My mémère always said La Bolduc made the Thirties bearable, just like her father whenever he pulled out his fiddle. It drove Mémère's mother to tears, the way he could just play as if everything was right in the world."

"She wasn't a musician," Michel said.

"Why do you say that?"

His eyes crinkled as he smiled. "Because she would've understood that music was the only way for him to make things better."

"Hmm." Her forehead creased and her steps quickened.

Michel kept pace with her. "Are you thinking about Granby or your mom?" he asked.

She clucked at his perception. "Both I guess, but mainly Maman, about how for all her playing, nothing was ever any better."

He squeezed her hand in comfort. "How do you know? I mean, what would it have been like if she hadn't had the piano?"

"I don't know. Worse, probably, judging from Robbie."

"Why? What happened to him?"

"My mom," she snorted, then tried to shake off his interest, but it was sticky and thick and held her like glue. "They were born together—same hospital, same night."

Michel nodded. "It was the full moon. I remember."

"You do?"

"Yeah. You told me on the way to Chez Nous."

"Right." She fumbled under his smile and glistening caramel eyes; she turned away so she wouldn't disappear in them. She took a breath to steady herself and searched for something other than Michel to look at. She tried the grass, the trees, the cauliflower forms floating in the sky.

"So, what happened with your mom and dad. He didn't become a priest, did he? I mean, you're here."

"I am," she agreed flatly. "And no, he didn't."

"Why not?"

Her forehead creased as she shook her head. "That's another long story."

"That's okay. We still have a way to walk, and I'd love to hear it."

She tittered sadly. "Thanks, but I don't love telling it."

"What about singing it?" He suggested. He released her hand and dug into his pocket. "I happen to have a harmonica on hand."

Stéphanie caught his wrist before he could raise it to his lips. "Please don't."

The timber of her voice and the green in her eyes made his acquiesce. He worked the harmonica back into his pocket, then wrapped his arm about Émilie's shoulders. They walked the rest of the way home in silence, but the story ran through Stéphanie's mind.

### Y'en a deux noirs, y'en a un blanc

*A priest!* Émilie ran from the Thibauds' living room as soon as Robbie's announcement reached her brain. She flew through the kitchen and out the door. It banged behind her without her noticing. The air was cold and crisp. It stung her hands and face, but she ran from their home to hers.

"Émilie!" her mother shrieked when she burst through the door. "Mondou! What's the matter?"

"Nothing," she said, as she panted for air.

"It's not nothing. You're freezing, and where's Martin?"

"Still at the Thibauds'."

"Why?"

"He didn't feel like coming home."

"But you did? Why?" she demanded in a high-pitched voice. "Did something happen?"

Émilie snapped, "What could happen? I'm not allowed to do anything!"

Rose gasped at the outburst but maintained her stance, "There are reasons for that."

"Yeah? Well, there are consequences, too! Did you ever think of that?"

"All of the time. That's exactly what I'm trying to protect you from."

"Well, it's too late!"

Rose's eyes bulged. "Why? What happened?" She clutched Émilie's arm. "Did one of those boys hurt you?"

Émilie pulled free from her mother. "No, Maman! It wasn't them! It was you! You made us wait, and now Robbie's gonna be a priest!" She spun away from her mother's shocked face and stormed away before Rose could chastise her rudeness or comfort her or offer any words of contrition.

Émilie plopped down on the piano bench and began to play without even knowing what was in her hands. She dropped her right hand into an octave, then pushed down into another with an added fourth and a running arpeggio in the left. She attacked with her right hand, played chords over arpeggios, explosions of sound shattering and rippling up in one key and descending in another. She raged through the piece marked *allegro non assai, ma molto appassionato*; she paid no heed to the qualifier for speed—not too quick—but went full steam with the indication for passion.

She maintained the intensity for over a minute, pushing out chordal bursts and contrapuntal tension until the fury and the sound died away. It left her wrecked. She hung over the final chord until it had completely dissipated, then, as if in a trance, she extended her arms to the far reaches of the piano, spread her hands, and dropped into a new canvas of tonality.

It sounded like practice to her mother who remained in the kitchen, clutching her chest and raising her eyes to the heavens until she was stilled. Émilie's grandmother, however, stopped her knitting and listened to the sound coming from the living room. She did not know what it was, but it was much too lugubrious for a teenage girl to be playing after seeing her beau.

Sylvie set aside her needles and yarn and followed the sonorous brume to the living room. It grew more tonal as she approached, but a heavy sadness remained. She watched Émilie from the doorway: the girl was rooted on the bench and swayed like a weeping willow; she moved her hands like rustling leaves. Her eyes were closed, but her face ran with tears as she raised a mythical cathedral from the depths of the second-hand Heintzman Pierre had bought for his daughter.

Sylvie watched, enraptured by the sound and the movement. Émilie was unaware. Her hands found the chords they had learned the year before; her body undulated with each harmony. She drooped over the keys as she transferred her feelings into the ivory, wood, and steel. The cathedral returned to the bottom of the sea.

Émilie remained bent like a fruit-laden tree long after the piece was over. "C'était magnifique," Sylvie said, approaching her granddaughter. "What was it?"

Émilie tumbled back into herself. "Huh? Oh, Grand-mère." She sniffed and wiped away her tears. "That was nothing. Just something from last year. I played it at the festival."

"I remember." She sat beside Émilie on the bench. "You won." Émilie nodded with modesty. "But you didn't play it the way you did just now."

"I haven't played it for a while. I'm kind of rusty."

Sylvie touched her hand. "No. It was wonderful. But very dark, like mon Baptiste on his fiddle back in the bad days. But him, he had a lot to cry over—crops and storms and babies—but you? You are young. Why do you play like that?"

Émilie looked at her hands. "I don't know," she mumbled.

Sylvie rubbed her arm. "Oh, I think you do." She waited for Émilie to look at her, but she did not. Sylvie went on, "If I played an instrument at your age, it would have been Baptiste that made me sound like that, mon Baptiste Caron leaving on the train, chugging away to some faraway place while I picked berries for jams and preserves that he would never eat." Émilie nodded at the old story she had heard as often as a perfect cadence. "I'd've played like you, if I knew how, but instead I waited and waited for my papa to send for us, and then we came here, me and my mother and sister. We came to this place for les Canadiens-Français on the prairies, and there he was, mon Baptiste, with his aunt and uncle." Émilie scrunched her eyes to stop her tears. "Oh, chérie," Sylvie said, wrapping her arm about the girl. "Your Baptiste, he's here, too, you know? You just wait and see."

Émilie thought she had waited long enough, and all she could see was that it was not fair.


"Why?" she cried to the ceiling in her bedroom later that night, "Why Robbie? Why not Martin or, if it has to be a Thibaud, why not Jacques, or Mathieu, or Roch?" That idea made Émilie snort: there was no way Roch would make it through the juniorate, let alone the seminary—he had not even lasted a year as an altar server, and he was forever being summoned to the principal's office over some prank or infraction. *No*, Émilie thought, *there's no way he'd ever be called to be a priest. He's too irreverent, too gregarious with his stupid pompadour and leather jacket, his cigarettes rolled up in his sleeve like he's some French-Canadian James Dean.* "Ha!" she barked and tossed over in bed, causing something to fall onto her head. She felt around and found what it was: a stuffed bear Robbie had given her on their tenth birthday. She traced her finger over its marble eyes, green like hers, he had said, and pressed her face into its fur, brown-bronze like Robbie's hair, she had said.

"And mine," Roch had interjected.

"Of course," she had conceded without taking her eyes off

Robbie.

There had been a pink ribbon about the bear's neck; Émilie had untied it and worn it in her hair until it had frayed and unravelled. Robbie had given her another one and then another. "Here," he said, passing them to her over the seat of the bus, "I see you need a new one."

Émilie squeezed her eyes against the memory of his thoughtfulness and sweet gestures of love. Still, she spilled tears onto the teddy bear's plush body until she fell asleep.


Émilie still held the teddy bear when her father knocked on her bedroom door early the next morning. "Eh-oh," he called in a whisper, "Your tea's ready."

She sniffed and rubbed her eyes. "Okay," she answered. "I'm coming." She rushed through her morning routine of washing, changing, and brushing, then joined her father in the kitchen below.

"Are you alright?" he asked when she appeared. She shrugged, but her face rolled, and her eyes welled. He rubbed her back, "Oh, Fille-fille, chérie. I know. It'll take time."

"But I already gave it time! We both did! Like you and Maman said, and now he's gone!"

"He's not gone."

"No, but …"

"There, there," Pierre calmed rubbing her back. "You have your studies and your music. Maybe it's better this way, eh?" She nodded acknowledgment of his words and headed to the other room before her eyes rained again. She made a beeline for the piano and sat on the hard bench, then held her hands on her lap and breathed to find a score inside her head.

She chose a Bach sinfonia that was soft enough for a sleeping house yet still a good balm for her aching teenage heart, but her spirit revolted, and the subject and countersubjects came out as little more than notes. She abandoned the work for something more suitable to her stormy mood: the third movement of Beethoven's Fourteenth Sonata, the Moonlight, so named for the slow, sustained first movement Émilie had poured herself into after the Freshie Dance.

She had gone on to learn the second movement, "A flower between two chasms," her teacher had called it, quoting the flashy nineteenth-century pianist and composer, Franz Liszt. "It's a simple minuet and trio between the oozing passion of the first movement and the raging fire of the third." Émilie liked the middle movement, but she needed more than *allegretto*; she needed the fire of *presto agitato* so she could cry and yell without anyone knowing.

"What the hell was that?" Martin asked later as they waited outside for the school bus.

"What was what?"

"Your morning wake-up. It sounded like a bunch of banging."

"Gee, thanks."

"Oh, it wasn't bad. Just loud. Couldn't you've picked something a little more matinal?"

"Matinal?" she scoffed.

"It's a word."

"So is shut up."

"Actually, that's two," he teased. She sputtered and rolled her eyes at him. "Look, I know you're upset, but don't take it out on old Heintzey. Sheesh; he didn't do anything, and besides, he doesn't really have the guts for it."

"Ha," she sounded, not at all amused by his attempts at

humour nor his pet name for her piano.

Martin elbowed her. "Come on," he prodded. "You know I'm right."

"Sure." She blew out a gush of air. It rose before them in a billow. "Getting cold," she said.

"Yeah. They're forecasting snow for the weekend."

"Great," she groused.

"Yeah, well, it's not like we had any plans anyway, right?"

"Pfff. That's for sure."

"But maybe we could," Martin suggested, brightening with slyness.

Émilie remained sullen and repined, "Yeah? What? Clean out the shed?"

"No, silly. The basement."

"Oh joy."

He elbowed her. "Oh, I'm kidding. Gilles? He's having a party."

"Whoopty-do. What does that have to do with us?"

"Well, maybe we could go?"

"Yeah, sure, and maybe I can become queen."

"You already are." He elbowed her and grinned, "Or at least daddy's little princess."

"Ha-ha."

"Oh, you know you are, and I bet if you asked him, he'd let us go. Especially now that Rob—" She sniffed and scrunched her face. "Sorry."

She wagged her head to keep down her tears. "Do you know if he's going to school today?"

"He's not. He's supposed to stay in bed for another week."

"Oh."

"Yeah. And then he'll probably go to Saint Boniface. His uncle's a priest there."

Émilie blinked at him like a doe in a beam of light. Robbie

was leaving? She knew he would have to, but she had never thought of him leaving Lasalette without her. They had planned on going to university together, then travelling to Europe for Émilie so she could visit the salons and concert halls of the masters, and to Australia for Robbie so he could see the sky upside down. Her eyes stung; her breath rose like a cloud of incense.

"Hell of a thing, eh?" Martin said.

"Yeah," she replied, staring towards the Thibauds' farm. Her heart ached with Robbie's impending departure.

"So, I'll ask Papa."

She sniffed in the crisp air. "About what?"

"Gilles' party." She snorted at the idea; Martin was undeterred, "It'd be easier if you were coming though …" His forehead furrowed with suggestion, and his eyes danced. "You know? A big sister to keep me out of trouble. Papa'd really go for that, and you'd get to go out, too."

"I don't want to go out."

"Why? Do you just stay at home for the rest of your life?"

"No. But ..."

"But what? Câline, Em. Buck up a little. If there's something you want to do, do it."

"That's easy for you to say: you're a boy. They let you do anything. And you do *do* anything." He laughed; she rolled her eyes. "I know all about your little escapades with Roch."

"Yeah, well, Maman and Papa don't, and if you ever want to go out before you die, I suggest you don't tell them."

Émilie sputtered in response, but she knew he was right.

Pierre drove Martin and Émilie to the Tessiers' house on Saturday evening. "I'll come back at ten thirty," he said.

"D'accord," the teens agreed. "Merci."

Once they had made their way inside, Martin went one way, and Émilie went the other. She sat on the edge of the sofa holding a glass of ginger ale she never drank and watched the goings on, which seemed no different to her than the lunchtime goings-on at school except that the Coke was spiked with rye, and Robbie was nowhere to be found. She held her mouth in a line and scowled at Martin's every sip. He shrugged and grinned, turned up his hands in innocence. Roch was not any better, for he was the one who had brought the mickey, procured, Émilie had heard, using fake ID. She pursed her lips and narrowed her eyes at him; he scowled and turned away. She ignored the slight and looked about the room for her girlfriends and found them when Shirley lifted the needle off the record and called out, "Seven Minutes in Heaven!"

Émilie's stomach tightened. She knew about this game; it was one of Roch's favourites, she had heard, and he was good at it, "If you know what I mean," Shirley had told her with dancing eyebrows a few times. Émilie did not know, not really, but she supposed it was what she and Robbie did in her dreams.

"How's this work?" someone asked.

"Marie'll go first and show you," Shirley said.

"Me?" Marie's ponytail hit her cheek as she spun her head to look at Shirley in fake reprimand. "Why me?"

There was hardly a pause before Shirley offered an explanation, "It's alphabetical by last name. André. You go first."

"Well, isn't that nice?" Marie said sarcastically, brushing her hands over her lap. Émilie offered her a sympathetic smile, but Marie raised a shoulder and grinned. Émilie looked away.

She stared at the amber liquid in her glass as she ran

through the last names of the girls present. Bertrand. Chabot. Dupont.

"Go," Shirley ordered.

"Where?" Marie asked.

"The kitchen," Gilles suggested.

"It's not for sandwiches," Shirley laughed.

"Well, I might work up an appetite."

"Yeah, right."

"Good one."

"The bathroom."

"Ooou."

"Gross."

"No."

"Gilles' room?"

"No. It stinks in there," Martin laughed.

"His sisters' then."

"No," Gilles insisted. "Not upstairs."

"Where then?"

"The porch."

"Perfect." Marie smiled and clapped her hands. "We can keep the light off and shut the door." She turned to Shirley and gave her a push. "Get going."

"Okay, okay. Sheesh. Don't be so pushy." She headed towards the kitchen porch. "Send me someone good."

"Oooo," the others taunted. "Someone good."

"That's me," Gilles said, scrambling to his feet.

"Oh, sit down, Major Lewis," Martin laughed, pushing him back down.

"Well, who then? You? Ha!"

"We'll let the cards decide," said Shirley. She rummaged around in her purse.

"You carry a purse?"

"Never mind that. She carries cards in her purse!"

"Shut up. Marie, go." Shirley began to shuffle, raising and lowering cards like an expert dealer. "The cards'll send you a king."

"Or an ass!"

"You say ace, you idiot."

"I know what you say, ass hole."

"That's ace hole. Ha-ha."

"This is lame. Why don't we play strip poker instead?"

"Marie, will you just go?"

"I'm going. I'm going."

"Come on, Marie. I'll hold your hand."

"Aïe! That's not my hand!"

"Just go already! Câline. I'll deal the cards." Shirley slid cards from the deck and snapped them one after the other onto the table.

"Okay. She's in."

Émilie looked at the other girls as Shirley dealt. They had smiles and glistening eyes. She squeezed her glass of ginger ale and continued running through their last names: Frechette, Maynard, Mercier. She hoped Gilles' parents would return before they got to the letter T.

"Do you even know what you're doing?"

"Of course, I do, you ass."

"You mean ace."

"Boo. That's already been said."

"Hurry up, or I'm coming out."

"Oh, keep your panties on!" Shirley called back.

"No! Take 'em off!"

Shirley fanned the remaining cards in her hand and held them out to Gilles. "Pick one."

He grinned and reached for the card in the middle. "Ten of clubs," he said, turning it over.

"What does that mean?"

Shirley raised a shoulder and smiled.

"It means you spend too much time in the clover field," Martin said.

"Sowing my wild oats," Gilles answered over the laughter.

"Whacking your gopher more like."

"Keep it in your pants, boys," Shirley said. She held the cards out to Martin. "Marty, you're next."

He plucked a card from the left-hand side. "Five of hearts. Does that give me five more minutes?"

"It's not kaiser."

"You pick next, Roch."

"Jack of Daniels."

"Spades, Romeo."

"How does this work, Shirl?"

"Just take a card and all will be revealed."

"What will? That you don't know what you're doing?"

"Shirley!" Marie called.

"Hold on!" She yelled back before turning to the group again. "You'll see. Tommy, take a card. Jean. Okay. Everyone ready?"

"Yeah."

"Yep."

"Okay. Watch." She flicked her hair and stepped back to the coffee table. She flipped over the first card. "Queen of diamonds. That's Marie." Whose got a diamond?"

"Me."

"Me, too. But she's my cousin."

"So, why'd you take a card, ace hole?"

"'Cause Shirley told me to."

"You do everything she tells you?"

"Oooo."

"Shut it. Jean, you're Marie's king."

"He's only got a three!"

"It's an eight."

"Whatever."

"Get going, Jean, before Marie faints."

"She'll faint when he gets in there."

"Swoon, buddy. Swoon." The lanky seventeen-year-old extricated himself from the legs and feet of the circle and walked across the room. Émilie fixed a smile on her face, but her stomach churned, and her eyes burned.

Shirley counted down minutes while the rest of the group joked and laughed about what was going on in the porch, until finally, she shouted, "Times up!"

Jean and Marie reappeared. "Ah, there he is, Mr. Seven-minute miracle."

"Hey Marie, what colour's your red face?"

Shirley wagged her finger. "Uh-uh. What goes on in the porch, stays in the porch. Who's next?"

They arrived at T before Gilles' parents returned. "Come on," Shirley said, pulling on Émilie's arm.

"I don't want to."

"You have to."

"Don't be a goodie-goodie," Marie said.

"Em!" The others chanted. "Em! Em!"

"No."

"Don't worry, we'll send you someone good."

"The best are yet to come, baby."

"But I—" She looked about, white, and bug-eyed. She silently begged Martin for help, but he just shrugged and sipped his rye.

"It's okay," Roch said, flipping over cards on the table, "Look, you're a spade, and so am I." He threw his jack on top and took her hand. There was immediate ooing and teasing, but he continued without comment or reddening. She followed his lead like a meek puppy. He closed the porch door behind them and turned towards her. It was dark, and their eye had not yet adjusted to it. He squeezed her hand. "We don't have to do anything," he said.

Her voice quivered and squeaked, "We don't?"

"No."

She heard her heartbeat and felt Roch's breath on her. It was warm and sweet and sour from his drink. Her stockinged feet grew cold on the porch floor. She placed one foot on the other and then reversed. "Do you like these kinds of parties?"

"Yeah."

"Why?"

"They're a good distraction," he said, stepping closer towards her.

"From what?"

"You," he whispered, touching the side of her face.

"Me?"

"Yes, Mimi. You." She quivered at the old pet name he had given her as soon as he could talk. Robbie and Martin had used it as well, but they had moved on to Emmy and then to Em. Roch, however, had persisted with Mimi through the years. He stroked her hair. "We're twins, too, you and me."

"I know," she mumbled.

"Then why don't you ever choose me?"

Her stomach tightened and her head reeled. "What?"

"You never choose me," Roch said, "even when I'm the only one."

"That's not true," she insisted.

"Yeah, Mimi, it is. Blood brothers? Remember?"

Her eyes stung with the memory of the two of them in the saskatoon berry bluff when they were eight years old. Roch had taken her hand in his and pressed the blade of his jackknife to her open palm. She had pulled away and cried, "No! It's not right!"

"Not right!" he had scoffed. "Ha! What's wrong with it?"

She had not known; it had simply felt wrong, like taking a dime from the coffee canister, or smoking a cigarette, or being with him at that very moment.

"Why didn't you do it?" he asked there in the Tessiers' porch.

"I don't know," she mumbled.

He stepped closer. "Well, what if I'd done this?" He pressed his lips to hers, then removed them before she even realized what he was doing. "Would that've been better?" he asked. Her entire body quivered. He traced his finger down her cheek. "It would've been," he said. "Much, much better."

"Roch," she gasped. "I ... I ..." She blinked and stammered at him in the darkness that was soon broken by Shirley.

"Hey, love birds," she called as the door burst open. "Times up."

Émilie blinked in the sudden light. Roch smiled with the glow of Christmas morning. Her chest shook, and her mind swirled. Her fingers felt tangled in his. "I think my dad's here," she announced, pulling away. "Someone tell Martin."

People said things, warbled, and screeched like magpies, but Émilie only heard ringing in her ears as she riffled through the pile of coats lying on the deep freezer in search of her pea jacket. She found it and fumbled with it, flapped it about trying to get her arms in the right holes.

"Hey," Roch said for the crowd, "I'm good with buttons. Let me help." He pressed himself against her and whispered in her ear while the others clucked a what he had said, "It's okay. No one saw anything." He touched his lips to her ear and added, "And so what if they did?"

Her chest was closing in. "I have to go," she said, pulling

away to find her shoes. She pushed into them and rushed out the door.

"Hey, Thibs," Gilles laughed, smacking Roch on the back, "what'd you do to scare her off?"

Roch danced his eyebrows. "No, man. I scared her on."

"Hee-hee. Sure."

Roch tapped Gilles' chest. "Give me a minute, okay?"

"Sure. Gotta cool down, eh? Héhé." He turned back towards the others. "So, is there cake, or what? I'm starving."

"Oh, Gilles," Shirley laughed.

"What? I told you I'd work up an appetite." He moved his hands like lobster claws and reached for her. She shrieked and ran away from him. Roch slipped out the front door as the others headed back into the kitchen. Martin followed Roch. He found him turning about in a small circle; smoke and steam rose from him. The boys' feet crunched on the frozen gravel.

"Hey, Goose," Roch said as if Martin had just happened upon him in the hallway at school.

"Where's Em?"

Roch's face scrunched. "Walking home," he said with the bitterness of vomit. He pulled on his cigarette.

"It's three miles!"

His exhale was the instant flat of a slashed tire, "Yep."

"It's freezing. Why'd you let her go?"

"Let? You ever try stopping her? Here," he passed Martin his cigarette. "It's a long walk."

Martin scoffed, "Gee, thanks." He took a long drag off the cigarette and let it out slowly. "The least you could do is drive her."

Roch sneered, "Yeah, and the least you could do is piss off." He bumped into Martin's shoulder as he stormed away. "Make sure she gets home."

"Of course. That's what brothers are for."

"Brothers," Roch grumbled, "damn pains in the ass."

Martin scowled and took another drag from the cigarette. He examined the remaining length of it and raised a foot, scraped the burning ash on the side of his shoe, and touched the tip to make sure it was out before he slipped the cigarette behind his ear and hoofed it towards his sister.

He caught up to her soon enough, for despite her head start, he was the athlete, not she. "Hey," he said, falling into step with her. "What the hell?" She scissored ahead without looking at him. "Câline," Martin grumbled, but kept pace. He touched her arm to make her stop. "What's wrong?" She chewed her lip and shook her head. "Did he hurt you?"

"No! Gawd! Why does everyone think they'll hurt me?" She jerked back into a quick march. Martin sighed and caught up again.

"I don't."

She exhaled like a dragon and kept on. Martin grumbled but followed her. Their feet chewed up the gravel. Their breath rose in plumes. Émilie let out sighs and gasps as they walked. "He says he likes me," she said at last.

"I know."

She stopped and looked at him in the star-lit darkness. "You do?"

He snorted. "Yeah. I've got eyes."

"What does that mean?"

His throat rumbled with a laugh. "Nothing. Just … You see up there?" He asked, pulling out his snuffed cigarette and placing it between his lips. Émilie scrunched her face with distaste. "Look hard."

"At what?"

"The stars," he said with the cigarette between his lips. He rolled his lighter wheel to produce a flame, then set it to his cigarette and pulled it to life. Émilie waved at the smoke that had not yet floated her way. "Beautiful, eh?" She snorted in reply. "I mean the sky," he said.

"Oh." She turned her eyes back to the globs of glitter in the dark sky. "I thought it was supposed to snow."

"The forecast changed."

"Hmm." They stared in silence at the darkness.

"There're twins up there," he said.

Émilie's eyes burned. "I know," she mumbled. "Robbie showed me."

"Me, too. They're hard to find, but they're there ..." He squinted and turned in a small circle. "See?" he said, pointing almost overhead. "Those two bright ones? They're the heads. Now go down and draw their bodies."

Émilie followed his finger and searched the sky. "Which two?"

"Those two."

She squinted at the far away dots. "I don't see them."

"No," Martin chuckled, "you can never see for looking, can you?"

His laughter weighed her heart like a judgment. She turned towards home. "We should get going."

He shrugged and nodded without concern. "Yeah." They set in motion.

"There're a lot of stars," she said after a few paces.

He chuckled, "Yeah, but only one moon."

Her eyes leaked. "Robbie says that."

"Yep."

"What do you think he means?" Martin snorted at the question. "What?" Émilie asked with genuine innocence.

He sloughed it off, "Nothing. He's just poetic like that. Not like Roch."

"No," she agreed, "not like Roch at all."

## 4. Gavotte
## April 1990

"Here we are," Michel said, turning up a path.

"Where?" Stéphanie asked, looking at the two-storey brick house and overgrown landscaped yard before them.

"Home."

"Really? I don't recognize anything."

"Well, things are different in the daylight. Especially Clem. See?" She followed the direction of his chin-point to the man sitting on the front step with a fresh set of clothes and a mug of coffee between his hands. "All better."

"How can you tell?"

"His shoes. Birkenstocks mean funk; running shoes mean ready to work."

"Huh," she sounded. "Maman never had such a tell, but then, she was always in a funk."

Michel rubbed her hand in sympathy, but Clem called out before he could offer any words, "Hey! There you two are."

Stéphanie reddened with the realization that they had been out all night. Michel, however, chortled and replied, "Yep." Clem's face danced with teasing. Michel ignored him and led Stéphanie towards the front door.

"Coffee's on," Clem said.

"Good. Stéphanie here's a real connoisseur."

"Yeah? Well, grab a cup and let me know what you think."

"Okay. Thanks. I will." She continued towards the door.

Clem caught her hand. "Hey, Video Girl—"

"Stéphanie," Michel corrected.

"Right. Sorry. Stéphanie. Got a sec?"

She shrugged. "Sure."

"Good." He hemmed for a moment and licked his lips. "About last night …"

She shook away his words like she used to shake away her mother's apologies and promises. "Forget it."

"No. I'm sorry. That wasn't a good way to meet you. It's just how I get when I break up with Alice, but it's over now, okay?"

"Okay," she answered without meeting his gaze and expertly changed the subject, "Say? Have you seen Christianne?"

"No, but I think she's upstairs with Alex."

"Okay. Thanks." She started away.

"I wouldn't bother them, though," Clem added.

"Ohhhh," Stéphanie sounded.

Clem laughed. "No, not that. More like the opposite."

Her voice rose with surprise, "Fighting?"

Clem scrunched his face as he considered the question. "Nnnn. It's hard to say. But, no, I think it's more like a discussion. A serious discussion."

"Ah."

"Ah, what?" he asked.

"We're going home on Tuesday."

Clem's face twisted like plastic in fire. "Long distance sucks."

"Did you say there was coffee?" Michel interjected.

Clem shook his head clear. "Uh, yeah. Help yourselves."

"We will." He turned the doorknob.

"Oh," Clem called out yet again, "Jonny's back."

Michel stopped. "Already?"

Clem rolled a laugh. "Yeah. Quiet night, I guess. Plus …" He jerked his head towards Stéphanie and danced his eyebrows. Michel shot him a look of reprimand that made Clem laugh even more. He raised his coffee mug to smother it.

Michel turned back to Stéphanie to divert her attention. "Clemmy gets this breakfast blend from the roaster down the street. It's kind of weak, but he makes it strong." He scoffed at his bumbled speech and tried again, "I mean, it's a mild roast, but he puts two scoops of grounds per cup."

"Gotcha." She shook her head at her own response and rushed to add something more intelligent, "I'll take it black, and go from there."

"Good idea—take it one sip at a time." It made her smile for some reason, which made him smile in return.

The house was dark after the brightness outside, so Stéphanie and Michel stood in the entrance blinking to adjust their eyes before advancing to the kitchen. The air was still heavy and pungent from the night before, but there was music playing in the kitchen, so she set her attention on that instead of the discomfort rising in her belly.

It was a Jean Leloup song, *Printemps été*. "Geezus," Michel muttered as the music video played inside his head: a houseful of people lying about the morning after a party; a couple on a mattress on the floor, their pants discarded beside them; a woman passed out in a bathtub of water; another couple stretched out in post-pleasure slumber; a third awake and looking at each other, revving up for a morning romp.

"It's catchy," Michel said, "but ... meh. It's not really our thing." Stéphanie chuckled in agreement and started to offer her own comments when a series of sexual grunts and groans reached them from upstairs. "Uhhfff," Michel gasped. "Are you kidding?" He grabbed Stéphanie's hand and pulled her up the hall. "Come with me."

"Where?"

"To make our own noise."

Her stomach twisted. "No," she said and tried to dig her feet into the floor. "I don't … I'm not … No …"

He chuckled at her misunderstanding and at her stammering. "Not that," he said with a smile. "You'll see." He tugged her hand again with the patience of a service dog. She followed him towards the back of the house and through the doorway on the right. "Ta-da!" he cried and threw open his arms to indicate the dining-room-turned-music-room they had left hours before. "Take your pick. Anything but Jonny's squeezebox—he doesn't like to share."

She forgot her discomfort and marvelled at the array of instruments. She walked directly towards the open violin case sitting on top of the piano. She reached to pick up the instrument but clasped her hands together in restraint. "Is it Clem's?"

Michel arrived behind her. "Yeah." He pulled the violin from the case and presented it to her like a baby. "A Burgess."

She nodded acknowledgement of the luthier. "Nice."

He moved it closer towards her. "Try it."

She shook her hands in protest. "No. I couldn't."

"Sure, you could." He pressed the instrument on her. "Violin's your favourite, isn't it?"

"Yeah." She traced the curve of the violin with her fingers. "How'd you know?"

He shrugged but smiled at the tidbit he had gleaned. "The way you play."

She looked at him. "And how's that?"

He set his eyes on hers. "Like your heart's on your shoulder."

They were still smiling at one another when Jean-François burst in. "Fuck. Your brother, man. It's not even his house." Stéphanie jumped with surprise; she pushed the violin back towards Michel. He fumbled to maintain a grip on it. Jean-François laughed at their awkward movements. "You must be Stéphanie," he said, walking towards her. He was two inches of hair, two inches of boots, and seventy inches of muscle. Everything, save his skin, teeth, and eyes, was black. He offered her his hand. "I'm Jean-François. Gonna show me what you got?" he asked as she shook his hand.

"No. I was just looking."

"Why look when you can play?" He started towards his accordion. "Do you know *Valse de Valérie*?"

"Yes, but ..."

"But what?" Jean-François picked up his instrument and slipped his arms through the straps as he sat down. He opened the clasps and started to pull the bellows as if they were taffy. He played the first verse, then swivelled to look back at Stéphanie. "What? Don't you like it?"

"I love it," she assured.

Jean-François' face lit with pride, but he remained steadfast, "So what's the problem? Clem's fiddle?"

She laughed at the idea, "It's a Burgess."

"Signature," Michel added. "Hand made by the master himself." Her hands moved towards the instrument as if it were a magnet and she were iron. "Go ahead."

"Yeah, fuck, go ahead," Jean-François grumbled.

Stéphanie ran her hand over the carved maple. "Clem won't mind?"

"Not if you actually play the damn thing," Jean-François

said.

Michel covered Jean-François' gruffness with warm caramel, "No. Go ahead." He presented the violin to her again. It was on her shoulder within a heartbeat. "Here's the bow," Michel said. She pinned the violin in place with her chin and reached for the horsehair stick. She adjusted the tension and set herself into position. She licked her lips and closed her eyes, then took a deep breath, raised her right arm, and bowed the instrument. She fiddled with the tuning pegs and bowed some more. Once the instrument was set, she repeated the waltz Jean-François had played. Michel watched her with the radiance of the man in the moon.

She sang when she arrived at the chorus, "Valérie, Valérie. Veux-tu valser? Valérie, Valérie, ce n'est pas si tard." Jean-François joined in on the second verse. She nodded at his presence and kept on, "Ton père t'attend depuis notre départ. Il peut donc attendre un peu plus pis un peu plus encore ..."

It was not Beaudelaire, but it had gone to number one. Clem wandered in as Stéphanie and Jean-François played. He stood with Michel and assessed the *Teen Angel*-esque ballad with nods and eyebrow raises. "If I'd only listened; if I'd only kept my word; if I'd only stopped my waltzing, you would still be here. Valérie, Valérie ..."

Jean-François stopped at the end of the final chorus, but Stéphanie continued to the solo Clem played in concert and on their album, though it was often cut from the radio. "Geezus," Clem gasped. Stéphanie did not hear him over the music still roaring through her head. She ripped off into a jig that became a five-minute potpourri of folk songs that wowed the others without her even remembering that they were there.

"Holy shit," Jean-François exclaimed after her final stroke of the bow.

"What?" Stéphanie asked, jerking back into herself.

Clem laughed, "I think I'm out of a job."

"No, you're not," Michel said, "but she's good, eh?"

"Fan-fucking-tastic," Jean-François concurred.

Stéphanie shook away the compliments and held up the violin. "It's this. It plays itself."

Clem grinned at the assessment of his hand-crafted instrument but ignored her modesty, "Only in a magician's hands," he said; she turned to hide her blush.

"How are you at the piano?" Jean-François asked as she headed towards the Lesage to return the violin to its case.

"My mom's the pianist, not me."

"But you play, right?" Jean-François asked.

She shrugged. "Yeah."

He pointed his chin at the piano. "Well, go on. You can't be worse than Michel."

She turned towards him. "You play?"

He laughed it off, "It was mandatory."

"For what?"

"Music Education," Clem answered for him.

Her eyebrows rose. "You were in Music Education?"

"Yeah," Michel admitted with a laugh.

"We both were," said Clem. "You know, 'just in case.' That's what people say, right? 'Get a degree; you can always teach if it doesn't work out.' But how the hell can it work out when you're in a classroom ten months of the year?" He turned towards her, expecting nods and shining eyes, but her brow was knit as she considered the future ahead of her. Clem did not understand her reaction, but he went on, "Mitch did better than me. He made it through what? Two years?"

Michel lulled his head and chuckled at the mention of his university career. "Yeah."

"Then he was asked to leave," Jean-François laughed.

"Because he missed all his finals," Clem said. "Not like you, who flunked out."

"I didn't flunk," he replied, "I failed to attend."

"Oh, that's better," Clem teased. He turned towards Stéphanie and explained about Michel, "We had this little tour in the Laurentides ..."

"Lanaudières," Jean-François corrected.

"Whatever."

"They're two different regions, fuck-head."

"Ach. Like dick and balls, man. It all goes together."

"Clem!" Michel cried over Jean-François' laughter.

"What?" Michel tilted his head towards Stéphanie, and Clem grimaced with embarrassment. "Sorry."

"It's okay," Stéphanie said. "It reminds me of high school."

Michel and Jean-François laughed at the comparison; Clem ignored them. "As I was saying, we had a tour, and the cocksucker university wouldn't give Michel any deferrals. It was a total load of horse shit—jocks get them all the time, but a musician asks and no-oooh."

"He's not bitter, eh?" Michel teased.

"Well, it's unfair!"

"He got kicked out after the first semester," Jean-François said.

"No, I chose to leave," said Clem.

"Right. Just like me." The men chuckled and snorted over the past.

Clem waved it away, "Never mind. That's old news. What about you, Stéphanie? Christianne says this year out here is part of an Ed. degree?"

"Yeah," she nodded, "Three years at the U of R and one out here."

"And how'd you make out? You get all your assignments in? All the lesson plans and teaching journals?"

She was not sure if he was teasing, but she answered anyway, "Yep. I even handed in this essay on Soeur Thérèse Potvin."

"Who's that?"

"This nun in Edmonton. She created a bunch of Kodaly-based pedagogical aids we use in French schools."

"Out west?" Clem asked.

She laughed at his surprise. "Yes. I told you last night, we're everywhere, les Canadiens-Français. Plus, there's immers—"

"Oh, fuck, whatever," Jean-François interrupted. "Are we gonna get on with it, or what?"

Stéphanie's face scrunched. "With what?"

"Joni," Michel rushed to answer.

"Huh?"

He pointed at the piano. "Joni Mitchell. I heard you like her." A smile responded for her. He teased her with his eyes and sang the opening of *Blue* to her once again. Stéphanie froze in his attention.

"Geezus," Jean-François muttered as Michel continued to croon.

"Oh, leave him alone," Clem whispered. "He's been waiting a long time for this."

Jean-François grumbled again but let Michel have his moment.

It was like a movie, Stéphanie would tell Christianne later, the way he walked towards her as he sang and got so close that she could feel his breath on her face. He slipped his fingers between hers, then replaced the song with a kiss that lasted until Jean-François tired of waiting and pumped out *Cantina Band* on his accordion. She pulled away and hid behind the curtain of her hair.

"Tabarouette," Michel muttered.

Clem danced about like a vaudevillian and added words to the music, "I say piano. He says sing. They say kissy-kiss-kiss-kiss-kiss." Laughter leaked from all of them. Stéphanie stole a look at Michel. The way he shone made her head spin.

Jean-François emptied the bellows of his accordion. "Alright. Now that we're back on track, how 'bout Stéphanie shows us how she can play?"

She laughed, "You don't stop, do you?"

"Nope." His lips popped with agreement, then set into a smile.

"Fine," she pulled out the piano bench and slipped in. "How's this?" She played the opening of *Jingle Bells*, then set her hands in her lap and turned to face him with playful smugness.

"Ha-ha," he responded. "How 'bout the rest?"

"How 'bout it," she teased. Clem and Michel rumbled approval of her cheekiness. She chuckled, too, then turned back to the piano and turned the tune into Joni Mitchell's *River*.

Stéphanie's playfulness slipped off like a shawl as she shared the melancholic anthem of too many Christmases spent alone with her mother. Tears rose, but she closed her eyes and diverted them to her voice—a full-bodied Shiraz with notes of classical training and eclectic listening habits. Michel and the others were captivated sommeliers swirling and assessing the colours and tones poured out before them. Stéphanie circled back to the opening theme and drifted to a sorrowful close.

"Viarge," Jean-François sighed.

"Indeed," Clem agreed.

Michel smiled. "I told you."

Jean-François nodded. "You sure did."

Stéphanie squirmed under their stares. She was not sure

whether they were hungry wolves or adoring Labradoodles. She looked to Michel for a hint, but he simply stood there grinning and nodding. Her insides flittered; she turned back towards the keyboard to hide her bashfulness. "How 'bout some Piaf?" She played three chords before the men could respond, then sang in the clear whisper of a confidence set to music, "I live on a corner of Montmartre …" She rolled her Rs in satin and poured her voice out like melted chocolate.

"Tabernak," Jean-François breathed when she had finished. "You can fuckin' go all over the place, can't you?"

"Jonny!" Michel barked.

"What? It's a compliment."

"I know but come on. Your language."

"Pfffuck. Whatever," he grumbled, then turned towards Stéphanie and asked, "So how'd you get so versatile?"

She shook her head at his interest and shrugged it off. "I grew up around music."

"Sure, but you obviously had training and what? You do some musical theatre or something?"

"Or something," she smiled; he raised his eyebrows at her coyness, and she gave him a few more details, "Lessons and camps and boredom, really. I was alone a lot growing up, so I had a lot of time on my hands."

Jean-François nodded. "That's important, eh? Time?"

"Yeah. And passion." She scrunched her face at the word and the excitement she was feeling and shook it away. "What about you?" she asked to regain control of herself. "You've got an awesome bass. Did you have lessons?"

"No. That's why I'm such shit for the high notes."

"You're not," she said, "but you don't really need them— Michel and Clem can cover them."

"And you," he said, pointing at her with his chin.

Her voice and her eyebrows rose. "Me?"

"Yeah. You," he said.

"What?" She tittered.

Jean-François grimaced. "Câlisse. I didn't know you were gonna play hard to get."

Michel jumped into the conversation, "She's not. I didn't ask her yet."

Stéphanie looked at him. "Ask me what?"

"You didn't ask?" Jean-François exclaimed. "Weren't you two out all night?"

"Yeah. But we didn't get that far."

"Ohhh," he danced his eyebrows. "Well, how far did you get?"

"Ta gueule," Michel sneered.

"Tabernouche les gars," Clem interjected. "That's how you're gonna ask her?"

"Ask me what?" Stéphanie asked again.

"If you'll join the band," Clem said.

"What?" Stéphanie blinked in bewilderment as Michel cursed at Clem.

"The band," Clem explained. "Plumeau."

"Ca-riste," Jean-François grumbled.

"You want me to join Plumeau?" she said, her voice rising higher than usual.

"Yeah," said Clem. "We've been talking about it ever since Christianne showed us that video."

"Uhhh, that video," she sighed.

"Yeah," Michel said, suddenly at her side. He squeezed her hand and smiled. "That video. I've never seen anything like it. Never seen any*one* like it."

She blinked at him for a moment, then pulled away. "Wait! Was that what this was all about?"

"What?" he asked.

"Last night. The pancakes. Everything! Was that all just to

get me in your band?"

"No! No, that was to get to know you."

"Why?"

"Because I'm amazed by you," he avowed.

"Câlisse," Jean-François mumbled.

Michel went on without notice, "Your talent, your beauty, your ide—"

She raised her hands and backed away. "I need some air."

"We have a backyard," Clem said.

"Tabarnak," Jean-François mumbled.

"What? She's from the prairies. She probably likes that kind of thing."

"Fffu ..."

"I do," she said. "Where is it?"

"Back door. End of the hall."

"Want me to show you?" Michel asked.

"No. I need to be alone." She hurried away.

"Geezus, Mitch," Jean-François barked before she was out of earshot. "You can't go mixing business and pleasure like that."

"I'm not mixing anything. I like her, *and* she's an awesome musician."

"Ffffuck, all the women in the world, and you fall for her?"

"Yep."



Stéphanie's head spun, and her fingers shook. She pushed on the latch of the back door, but it did not open. She tried again, then fiddled with the lock until, at last, the door swung open onto a verdant expanse of uncut grass and unweeded flower beds. She blinked at the colour and the sunlight as she walked into the overgrown Eden of shrubs and trees and perennials. A maple tree spread up and out in the far corner; clematis climbed the garden shed. A row of hydrangea bowed with colourful blooms along the fence. She was drawn towards them like hummingbirds to sugar water. She stood before them, admiring the mauve puzzle balls for minutes, until her heart steadied, and she could truly enjoy the beauty of the blooms.

They were persnickety plants on the open prairie—Stéphanie's grandmother did not even try them, but Robbie had planted three of them on the east side of his house after Stéphanie had told him about the hydrangea her dear landlady, Frau Köhler, had kept in Basel. Stéphanie had not known what they were called at the time, but she had explained them so well that Robbie knew not only which flower she was describing but the variety as well. He had kept his well-watered and showed Stéphanie how to change their colour: add limestone for pink, aluminum sulphate for blue. The white ones would not change colour, he had told her, nor would certain coloured varieties, but the mopheads he had planted would. "It's about the soil," he had said, "but also about the individuality of each plant, how each one absorbs the nutrients around it."

*God*, Stéphanie sighed, *the way he looked at me when he said that—I didn't know if he was talking about himself or me or the plants. Maybe it was all three.*

She sniffed and tried to hold back the memories stinging her eyes, but they came and came like Robbie coming to Sunday dinners at her grandparents' every week. He was quiet and looked at her, held his lips pressed together so words would not accidentally escape them. He visited other days as well: on hot days, he drove her and Christianne to town for ice cream or pop or to the pool in Appleton for a swim. When it rained, he stopped by for games of checkers and crib. The summer she was fourteen, he picked her up at

Red Deer College on the last day of music camp. "Hey!" she had said with happy surprise as they hugged. "What are you doing here?"

"Your matante's father had a stroke, so Martin asked if I'd pick you up."

She nodded at the details and pressed for more, "Is Monsieur Tessier gonna be okay?"

"He'll pull through," Robbie said as he picked up Stéphanie's suitcase and led her towards his truck. She kept her violin and back-pack with her in the cab; Robbie lay the suitcase down in the back, and off they headed towards the southeast. "Do you want the scenic route or the fastest route?" he asked.

She shrugged and smiled. "Doesn't matter to me."

He smiled back. "Let's take the long way then. The scenery's amazing."

It was, for as much of it as she had stayed awake for: the rolling hills and grasslands that gave way to hoodoos and badlands. "It's like Tatooine," she had marvelled as they drove through Dinosaur Provincial Park. Then it was flat for miles and miles. She drifted off to sleep listening to him talk about what you couldn't see from the highway: the Cypress Hills, and the little towns, the creeks and rivers, the history of the people who lived there now and long ago.

"Things get forgotten," he said, "if you don't talk about them." He looked over at his passenger for her thoughts, but she was asleep. He turned his eyes back to the road, then back to Stéphanie. His body shook as words bubbled out of him, "I'm not supposed to tell you unless you ask, but I need to say it—I'm your dad." He drove blind for a mile until the tears cleared from his eyes.

Stéphanie grit her teeth against the unheard words and against the recent memory of Robbie telling her about them.

"That doesn't count as telling me," she had sneered.

"I know," he had murmured back with such guilt and sadness that she had almost forgiven him, but then she remembered her classmates in Basel teasing her for looking so different than her mother.

"Did she steal you from the gypsies?" they asked.

"No, we're Canadian," she protested, yet she asked Émilie about it sometimes before bed. "Why am I so dark and you're so light?"

Her face creased with something Stéphanie called the *no talks*, but Émilie pushed it away with a forced laugh and said, "Cause I spend too much time inside, and you, you get to play outside all the time."

It had seemed logical to Stéphanie when she was seven, but as she grew older and crossed the Atlantic, she needed more ammunition than that. She needed a stock of words like the ones she had for frog and peasouper—French, French-Canadian—to counter squaw and bastard Indian girl. The best she could ever do for that was, "I'm Fransaskoise. My father died before I was born."

It angered her, the racism she had not been equipped to counter correctly, and she blamed her parents for it, even if Robbie had said, "I didn't know much more than you," when she had confronted him about it. He went on, "And I had my mother a lot longer than you had me. She just never talked about it. About her grandmother being Cree, and her mother coming out here with a brood of kids. I do have a picture of her, though. Of my kokum. I found it after Maman died. We look a lot like her, you and I."

Stéphanie growled at the memory and grabbed up clumps of quackgrass in the Montréal garden to calm herself. The tops broke off, but the weeds' roots remained. She would need to paint the stems with herbicide to truly get rid of them, but yanking out the visible weeds was a satisfying solution for the moment. She grabbed another clump and then another until her thoughts were no longer on plants or memories or ludicrous ideas spurted out by Michel and his friends but on the smell of the earth, the mélange of rot and rebirth. It calmed her, caused her to sing without even realizing it.

## Le fils du roi s'en va chassant

The night after Gilles' party, Émilie dreamed of dots and lines, of stars that connected to make twin brothers holding hands. They came to life, released their grip, and marched in opposite directions like sentinels of the sky until they met up again on the other side of the world. Then they turned their backs to one another and doubled back. They met once again and turned, marched and met and turned again, and again, until her brain finally switched tracks and she dreamed of jiving in the school gymnasium. Her skirt flared as her partner spun and twisted her about. She followed along, laughing and smiling with the ease of a doll. Then the song transitioned into a slow, mellow ballad, and she and Robbie, for that's who it was, she saw, moved towards each other like molecules. He caught her about the waist, and she wrapped her arms around his neck. They locked on one another's eyes, then slipped into a kiss that went on and on until Robbie became Roch, and it scalded her throat and caused her to wake with a start. She cried and turned and flipped. She sweated, then shivered, then sweated again. Her throat ached and burned and seemed to close in on itself. She curled into a ball and tried to force the pain away, but it remained. She fell into a feverish sleep only to awaken in the dark with a start.

"Émilie," her father called between taps on the door. "Supper."

"Papa," she croaked in response. Her chest felt pressed between an anvil and a wrecking ball. She tried to take deep breaths to ready herself for getting up, but the air racked her throat. Her eyes burned and ran with tears.

"Émilie?" he asked, opening the door.

"Unnng," she sounded.

He rushed to her side, "Are you alright?" Pierre clicked on the lamp; she groaned in protest.

"Mon Dieu! Émilie!" He touched her cheek, then laid his palm to her forehead. "You're burning up. Let me see." She squeezed her face as she sat up. He touched his hands to her neck and felt for swollen glands. "Open." She obeyed. "Ooou. That's not good. You stay in bed. I'll call the doctor." She shook her head and began to speak, but her words were squashed by the confines of her throat. Pierre squeezed her wrist. "Shhh. Stay put. I'll bring you some tea and honey."

She stayed in bed for weeks. She missed school and Christmas and did not leave the house until New Year's Day once she had finished a third round of antibiotics. "I'm glad you're better," Robbie whispered as everyone around them in the Thibauds' living room sang *Mon Dieu bénissez la nouvelle année* to his mother's accompaniment on the piano.

"Thanks," she choked, weakened more by his presence than by the weeks of illness.

He held out his fist. "I want to give you this." She raised her hand to receive it. He poured in a gold chain with a pendant heart engraved with a scrawl of music.

"I gave you that," she choked.

"I know, but now that I—"

"No." She forced it back into his palm and fled from the

room, crowded with the five eldest Thibaud sons and their wives and children, wishing one another happy new year and toasting with Monsieur Thibaud's lemon gin even though it was not yet noon. She pushed through the kitchen to the west bedroom, where she anticipated flopping face down on the bed and smothering her sobs with a feather pillow; however, she stopped just inside the door when she saw that someone else was already in the room. "Oh," she gasped, "Roch. Hi."

He was seated on the floor, hugging his knees and staring up towards the window. He wiped his eyes and sniffed. "Hi."

"Are you okay?" she asked, crossing towards him.

She sat beside him on the large, braided rug his mother had made and touched his arm with the same concern she had had when they were children and his father had shot his dog, Hugo, after repeated run-ins with porcupines.

"He won't learn," his father had said.

"It's the only way to keep him from hurting himself again."

Presently, Roch clutched her hand but did not turn to look at her. "He's leaving tomorrow," he said.

"Oh." Her hand would have slipped from his arm had Roch not been holding it.

He nodded and rolled a sound in his throat like an old motor. "Yeah." They stared at a stack of clothes piled in the corner: Roch and Robbie's old shirts, ripped and worn and outgrown; their mother would probably make a quilt out of them, spread it over a bed, kneel beside it, and pray for them. "I don't hate him. Everyone thinks I do, but I don't. It's just … I always come up short next to him."

"No, you don't."

He turned to look at her. His face was strained and pale. "Yeah, I do."

She blinked until she found words. "You're just different. Dusk and dawn."

He scoffed, "Yeah. That's what Maman says." He started to stand. "I gotta go. She wants pictures with all us boys."

Émilie caught his hand. "Rocky."

He stopped and looked at her strong, white hand. "You haven't called me that in a long time."

"Really?"

"Yeah. How come?"

She shrugged her shoulders and wagged her head. "I don't know. Maybe the bluff? Blood brothers."

"Oh," he said and sat back down. The memory of the day hung between them: his knife pressed to her palm, her pulling away. "I didn't want to hurt you. I just wanted to be close to you."

"We were already close. We're tripl—"

"Triplets?" She nodded, and he soughed. "I don't want to be triplets." He petted her hair. "Or twins. Or anything like that. I want …" He kissed her; it caught her like a gust of wind. She raised her hands to his shoulders to push him away, but he pressed in against her, and he smelled of cedar and tasted of lemon, and he was there and not going away to the juniorate, and her head spun, and her lips opened, and she kissed him back and back and back until the door popped open and a gaggle of children ran in.

"Mononcle! Mononcle!" They cried and jumped on Roch and pulled at his hands. "There you are! Grand-maman's been looking for you. She wants you for the pictures. Come on! Come on!"

He gave them his attention. "Ha. Ha! There *you* are," he laughed, tickling their ribs. They cried with delight. Roch wrestled and rolled about with them, then chased them out of the room. "Tell Grand-maman I'm coming." Once his nephews and nieces had scuttled away, he turned back to Émilie with a grin. He rubbed his nose against hers. "I have to go, but I'll see ya, okay?"

"Okay," she agreed.

He tickled her chin and kissed her lips. "Good."

## 5. Loure
## April 1990

"What are you doing?" someone laughed.

Stéphanie jerked at the sound. "Huh?" She squinted in the sunlight to see who had spoken. He was nothing but a blur until he walked out of the shadow cast by the brick house. "Oh, Alex. Hi." She wiped a line of sweat from her forehead and left a smear of dirt in its place.

"You look like a singing scarecrow," he teased.

"What? Why?" She tapped her head with her hands and plucked out the hydrangea petals she found there. "Oh," she laughed.

"Here." He stuck his cigarette between his lips and pulled out a few more petals from her hair and brushed her shoulder clean. A plume of du Maurier smoke snaked up Stéphanie's nostril and reminded her for a moment of her uncle, Martin, back when she was a child and he still smoked. "I think they forgot they even had a garden," Alex said. He caught his cigarette with his index and middle fingers as he pulled out a drag, then lowered it from his mouth.

"Me, too." She brushed her hands over her arms, then splayed her dirt-rimmed fingers out in front of herself. "Looks like I've found it, though, somewhere beneath all that quackgrass."

Alex bobbed his head; he let out a gush of smoke. "You and Christianne know about that kind of stuff, eh?"

She fingered her flow of hair for stray hydrangea petals. "Yeah. We worked on Robbie's berry farm a couple of summers, and our mémère has a really big garden."

"Right. But Christianne, she doesn't really like it, does she? Farming and gardening and all that?"

Stéphanie rumbled with a laugh. "No. She likes the produce, not the producing."

Alex nodded at the assessment. Stéphanie noticed his resemblance to Michel: the same ginger ale hair and golden complexion, the same symmetrical nose and slightly rounded chin. Alex's had a small dent; Stéphanie tried to recall if Michel had one on the last Plumeau cover before he grew his goatee. "But she likes it out there, right?" Alex asked.

"Out where? The farm? Yeah, of course, but she's a city girl, needs her pavement and Slurpee runs." She smiled at her cousin's traits.

Alex nodded but did not smile. "Saskatchewan I mean. She likes it there. Wants to go back?"

Stéphanie shrugged and nodded in confirmation. "It's where we're from."

"It's where she's from," he corrected. "You're from Edmonton."

She shook her head at the idea. "I'm not from there; I just lived there. Like I lived in Basel and was born in Montréal. I'm from Lasalette. I'm Fransaskoise."

"Oh, you two," he muttered.

"What? It's who we are."

"Yeah, I know," he sighed and ran his fingers through his shaggy hair. "Tabourette."

"What?"

"She has this whole plan, this dream of helping build a Francophone school system out there and teaching in it her whole career."

"I know. It's about the only thing she and her dad've ever agreed on." She chuckled, but Alex soured and pulled heavily on his cigarette.

"She said, she'd stay. If I wanted her to. She'd stay."

Stéphanie's throat tightened at the thought. "Really?"

"Yeah. But I told her I wanted her to go back, wanted her to become the person she's always dreamed of being."

"Oh, Al," Stéphanie soothed.

"We didn't break up," he threw away his cigarette and ground it out, "but I didn't say I'd transfer to the U of R either."

"Why would you? You only have a semester left."

"I know. But I should've offered or at least given her this." He reached into his front jean pocket and pulled out a gold diamond ring, then held it up towards Stéphanie.

"Oh," she gasped.

Alex shrugged and sniffed. "I couldn't," he said as he tucked the ring back into place. "Not in bed! I mean, she'll have to tell her parents about it, and maybe we'll tell our kids about it someday, and I don't want it to be embarrassing. I want it to be something romantic. Something that'll sweep her off her feet."

"I think she's already swept off her feet."

"Really?"

"Yeah," she laughed.

"So, you think she'll say yes?"

"Yes!"

"Woo-hoo!" He squeezed her up in a hug and swung her around. They laughed and hugged and made joyful sounds.

"So, what's your plan?" she said once he placed her back

on the ground.

"I'm glad you asked that 'cause I need your help."

"Sure! With what?"

"The music."

She chuckled, "Yeah, I guess I can help you with that."

"Great. So, I was thinking tomorrow after supper, you and the boys—"

"Me and the boys?" she choked.

"Yeah," Alex steamed on without noticing the colour drain from her face, "I was thinking I'd get down on one knee, and the four of you could be playing in the background."

She tittered and trembled at the idea of the quartet, "I don't know …"

"No?" he sounded with disappointment. "Not Michael Bolton? Not *How am I Supposed to Live Without You?*"

She shook her head. "No."

"Oh," he sounded with disappointment.

"No, it's a good idea," she assured. "It's just I don't think I should play with them."

He cocked his head and asked, "Why not? I heard you guys earlier. It sounded like you really jibed."

"We did, but …" She trailed off at a loss for words.

Alex offered his, "Jean-François?" She shrugged and shook her head, but he kept on, "He talks like a trucker, but he's a good guy. You just gotta know how to take him."

"It's not that."

"Then it's Clem, right? Because of the sauce?"

"No, but since you brought that u—"

"It's just pot," he interrupted.

"It's illegal is what it is," she said, clinging onto the new subject, "and it could really mess you and Christianne up professionally if you ever got caught with it."

"Yeah."

She raised her eyebrows waiting for more, but when it did not come, she sighed, "Al."

"It's nothing. Just a way to unwind every now and then."

"Well, why don't you try yoga and make it never and again?"

"You sound like Michel," he laughed. "No wonder you two were out so long. Oh, shit! That's it, isn't it? Michel? He's the reason you don't want to sing with them. He said something, right? Came on way too strong?"

Her head and voice shook, "No."

Alex continued to explain, "He does that, you know, puts the buggy way before the horse, but he's usually right about things."

"Not about this," she mumbled.

"About what?"

She inhaled all the air from the yard, then exhaled it all back out before she answered, "Me."

Alex grinned. "You're exactly his type."

"And what's that?"

"Nice, smart, pretty. A girl with a head on her shoulder and a mouth that works."

"Oh, it works alright," she mumbled.

"That's good," Alex assured. "He likes good conversation."

"I'm not talking about conversation."

"No? Then what?" She shook her head for an answer, and his eyes bugged. "Shit! You gave him a blow job?"

"What?" she cried. "No! Why would you think such a thing?"

"Because you got all weird there, talking about your mouth."

She shook her head at him. "I meant singing, you bonehead. Granby."

"Oh. That video? Are you kidding? He loved it! He watched it like twenty times in a row."

"I know, and I wish he hadn't. I wish he'd never seen it at all."

"Why?" Alex asked. He tilted his head and squinted at her with confusion. "You were really good."

She shrugged it off. "No, I wasn't."

His face and eyes turned bright. "Yeah, you were. And that last one? *À la volette*? It—"

"It was crap, okay? And I don't want to talk about it."

He raised his hands in surrender. "Okay. Sheesh. You Tremblays." He elbowed her and teased her with a smile.

"Ha," she replied and made a face at him that made both of them laugh. A series of clicks sounded before either could go on. "What was that?" she asked, turning her head about to locate the sound.

"Squirrels," Alex said, pointing at two bushy-tailed rodents chasing one another along the top of the fence. They jeered and taunted like Chip and Dale as they scurried about the periphery of the yard. One slipped off the cross beam and veered down the side. The other one laughed like a high-pitched machine gun. The fallen squirrel raced up the fence and chased its nasty companion to the neighbour's yard. Alex smiled after them.

Stéphanie said, "Do you know we don't have squirrels in Lasalette?"

"Uhhh. No." He turned up a hand, waiting for more.

She sighed at his confusion and at her own words. "It's just a point of interest."

"Oh-kay."

Stéphanie went on, "We have gophers, though. They're these cute little things that stand at attention in the middle of the prairie only to scurry down their holes at the faintest noise."

Alex's face wrinkled as he tried to understand her. "Are you making an analogy or something?"

"No. I'm trying not to tell you that Michel and the guys asked me to join Plumeau."

Alex's eyes rounded and his mouth dropped open. "Holy shit! No wonder you're like this. Do you want me to get Christianne for you? She'd probably be better to talk to about it than I am."

She spoke with the listlessness of a flag in the heat of summer, "No. I already know what she'll say."

"And what's that?"

Stéphanie snorted and tried to shake off the answer, but it held to her like a tick. "Go for it."

Alex's face spread into a smile. "I'd say that, too."

"So would I, if I didn't know myself."

"What does that mean?"

"That I'm still mad," she replied without looking at him. "And hurt. And that I'd never go home if I joined Plumeau."

"Of course, you would. They take days off."

She blinked back a smart of tears and shook her head. "Yeah, but I don't wanna go home."

"So why are you?" he asked with the gentleness of the air.

"Because I have to. It's the only way I'll ever be able to forge any kind of relationship with my parents and sister."

Alex cocked an eyebrow. "Forge? That sounds kinda brutal: lots of hammering and beating."

"That's exactly how it feels," she said with the heaviness of Hamlet.

"Then maybe it's not right. Maybe instead of forging, you need to let things fall into place like leaves or snowflakes or something."

"That's not how it works."

"Why not?"

She scowled at the question. "It just doesn't."

He raised his hands in surrender. "Okay. Sheesh."

"Sorry," she mumbled.

"No worries," he assured.

They exchanged nods and smiles before Stéphanie went on, "It's how our pépère raised us: family comes first."

"I know, and that's great. Really. It's one of the things I love most about Christianne and you, but how is your misery going to make the rest of your family happy?"

"I won't be miserable," she insisted.

"Maybe, but will you be happy?"

She shrugged and looked away. The leaves of the maple tree danced as the squirrels scurried across its branches. "I'll be with them."

Alex watched the squirrels with her until he found something to say. "When Michel got injured, you know, playing hockey? He came home, and for the first time in my life, he didn't have practice or games or anything to do, so he played with me. Battleship, Lego, whatever I wanted. He played play anything and everything I suggested. Man, I loved it. And he was great! Patient and fun and easy-going, but you know what? He never smiled. Not once. And it wasn't because of the pain. It was because even if he liked being home with me, it didn't fill him up." Stéphanie sniffed and shrugged, willed the words and the tears welling up inside her down. Alex went on, "Then he came to Montréal. Took up with Clem and Jean-François, and suddenly, a Sunday night phone call with him was better than all those hours we'd spent together at home."

Stéphanie was tongue-tied with emotion. She wanted to tell him about her own Sunday phone calls home from across the ocean, how for all the distance they covered, they were not the same as in-person conversations, and she wanted to say that she had not called her mother or father in weeks and that she felt she could go on that way for months and maybe even years. She wanted to tell him, too, that her sister could hardly talk, and while that was fine right now, maybe one day Renée would want a sister just as Stéphanie had once. She sniffed and snickered, "Who's making analogies now?" She swiped at a stray tear and turned to face the hydrangeas blooming larger than melons against the fence.

He chuckled without injury, "Maybe I am, but maybe I'm right?"

"Maybe," she choked, then tossed her head, and wrestled her tears back into place. "Câline. You're gonna fit right in with us Tremblays, you know."

"Good," he grinned and nudged her. "And how 'bout you? You gonna fit in with Plumeau?"

"It's not an exchange program," she replied.

"No, but maybe you could try the Michael Bolton and go from there?" he suggested.

"Maybe," she agreed. "But I need sleep first. Is there some place I can crash?"

"Sure. Come on. I'll take you up to Marie-Geneviève's room."

"Marie-Geneviève's?" she asked as they started towards the house.

"Yeah. It's the only room left. Chris and I took the spare."

"Isn't that gonna be weird for them?"

"What?"

"Someone sleeping in her room."

"Why? She's been dead for years."

"Yeah, but it was hers."

Alex shrugged at the concern. "I don't know. I mean you could ask them if you want, but I really don't think they'd've offered it if any of them had a problem with it."

"Really?"

"Yeah, that's how they are," Alex said, pushing open the door.

"Whoa!" Clem laughed, backing out of the way. "Watch it."

"Oh, shit. Sorry, man. I didn't see you there," Alex chuckled. Stéphanie tried to hide behind his shoulder as he continued to talk, "What are you doing?"

Clem held up a white cotton rag and a bottle of Windex. "Washing windows."

"Sure. Nice cover," Alex teased. "You were spying."

Clem laughed, "No, I was cleaning. But who's they, and what are they like?"

"You guys," Alex said with a laugh, "and you're pains in the ass who make guests smoke outside."

"Take it up with Michel," Clem replied.

"Oh, I will. Say, look who I found in the backyard." He stepped sideways and tried to nudge Stéphanie forward.

"Alex," she hissed even as Clem addressed her.

"How you feelin'?"

"Fine," she answered from behind the dark veil of her hair.

"Actually, she's kinda tired after all her gardening."

"Gardening?" Clem asked with confusion.

"Yeah," Alex laughed, "you know these prairie girls. Hee-hee. Anyway, mind if I show her to her room?"

"No, go ahead. Marie-Geneviève's."

Alex squeezed Stéphanie's hand and moved his eyebrows up and down as if to say, "I told you so." She shook her head at his silent gloating. "Sounds good," he said and led her onward.

A well-worn floral carpet runner ran the length of the hallway, and another mounted the stairs. Beneath was dark wood flooring that matched the panelling on the walls. A crystal chandelier hung in the foyer. It was opulent but dusty and unlit. Some light came into the foyer through the windows around the door and from the kitchen off to the side, where the windows were still wide open, causing the curtains to blow and snap like sheets on a line. Dishes clanked, and the water ran. The scent of fresh coffee wafted in the breeze. Alex turned up the stairs; Stéphanie followed; she ran her hand along the warm, worn banister that generations of Bouchers had held and slid down.

"Well, well, well," Christianne chortled from the large landing at the top of the stairs. "If it isn't my long-lost cousin." She wore a towel on her head and a pink velour bathrobe that Stéphanie had never seen before.

She blushed and mumbled, "Hi, Chris."

"Hi," Christianne sing-sang. "Decided to come in, eh?" Her voice rolled with teasing, and her eyes glistened like polished jade.

"Yeah."

"She wants to take a nap," Alex said, "You know, since she was out all night?" Stéphanie jabbed him, but he still laughed.

Christianne did, too. "Oh, I know."

"We just walked around," Stéphanie said.

"Mmhmm."

"We did. And anyway, we've been home for hours."

Alex and Christianne made teasing sounds like squirrels. "Why don't you take her to her room?" he suggested. "Help her get settled?"

"Sure," Christianne agreed, snatching up her cousin's hand. "My pleasure."

"Great," Alex said. "See ya later, Stéph."

"Yeah. Thanks."

"You bet." He turned his attention to Christianne, her

happy face, her creamy skin exposed by the décolleté of the belted bathrobe. "I'm gonna go help in the kitchen."

"'Kay. I'll be down when I'm dressed."

He traced his finger up and down her breastbone. "See you soon." He kissed her lips, then headed back down the stairs.

Christianne pulled Stéphanie in the opposite direction. "Tell me everything," she said once they had crossed into the room at the top of the stairs and the wooden door had closed behind them.

"What everything?" Stéphanie asked, looking about the carpeted bedroom furnished with a set of walnut dressers, end tables, and an armoire. The scrolled sleigh bed was made up with a ruffled bedspread that matched the drawn pink curtains. "We went for a walk."

"For eight hours?" Christianne's eyebrows angled like acute and grave accents from the tightness of her towel turban and her curiosity.

"Well, we stopped for breakfast," Stéphanie replied, keeping her eyes focused on the shoes she was prying off her feet.

Christianne's voice rose with excitement, "At Lise's?"

"Mmmhmm."

"Eee! That's their place! Alex told me all about it. How was it?"

"Neat," Stéphanie said, entering further into the room, "like a sugar shack in the middle of the city." She turned from Christianne, who was bubbling with excitement, and undid her jeans.

"Cool. And?"

"And the food was good." She shimmied down her jeans and stepped out of them one leg at a time. "The coffee, too. They had a nice city roast."

"What about the company?" Christianne pried, perching

herself on the bed. "How was that?"

Stéphanie blushed. "That was good, too," she admitted as she picked up her pants and placed them on the wing chair in the corner.

"Eee!" Christianne cried once again. "He's wanted to meet you ever since he saw that video!"

"I know."

"You don't sound very happy about that."

Stéphanie snorted and twisted about to undo her bra without taking off her shirt. "Why should I?"

"'Cause he's great! And Alex's brother. And—"

"In a band! Câline, Chris! Is that what this whole thing's about? Trying to convince me to sing?"

"No!"

"Right!" Stéphanie pulled off her undergarment and threw it onto the chair.

"It's true!"

She crossed towards the bed and pulled back the covers. "Whatever. I'm going to bed." She climbed in.

Christianne scrambled out of the way of Stéphanie's legs. "Fine, but come on, tell me what you thought of him!"

Stéphanie sighed with the heaviness of the afflicted. "I thought he was great, okay? A perfect guy who talked and listened and really seemed to care about everything I was saying, but then he brought me home, and ..." She shook her head at the rest and wrestled with the bedding and pillows.

"And what?" Christianne asked gently.

"We played," she mumbled, "he and I, Jean-François, and Clem."

"I know," Christianne said with a grin. "I heard."

"Yeah." Stéphanie was filled with tears thinking about it. "Well, it was good." She shifted about to look at her cousin. "It was really good. I haven't played like that in a long time.

And it was fun joking with them and fooling around, but then they asked me if I wanted to join Plumeau."

Christianne's towel fell off her head, and her hair spilled about her shoulders. "What?" she gasped.

"I know. It's nuts. But that's what they asked. Clem and Michel. Jean-François, he just stood there expecting an answer."

"Did you give him one?"

She laughed at herself, "Yeah. I said I needed some air, and then I went out back and pulled weeds until Alex came out for a smoke."

"Weeds?" Christianne repeated with confusion.

"Yeah. It's overrun back there, and I needed something to do."

"Sure, but gardening? Câline." She shook her at her cousin's coping mechanism but asked with genuine concern, "Did it help at least?"

"Not really, no, but Alex did."

Christianne rolled a sad laugh, "Yeah, he's good like that." She pushed out a smile to stay the tears about their looming separation and turned to scootch off the bed. "I'll let you get some sleep."

"No. Stay."

"Why?" She rolled back to face Stéphanie. "You, okay?"

"Yeah. I just don't wanna be alone."

"Okay." They smiled at one another and settled into the bed like cooked shrimp on rice. The bedding smelled of lavender, and the room was still and dim.

Stéphanie made starts and stops at words until she finally said. "Do you think Michel even likes me?"

Christianne's face turned as bright as a full moon. "Absolutely!"

"Really?" Stéphanie asked, blind to the light in her

cousin's eyes. "You don't think it was just some act to get me to sing with them?"

"No," Christianne assured with the conviction of a god. "He's crazy about you."

"Humph," Stéphanie snorted. "That's what he said, but I think he's just crazy."

"Why? Because he's in love with you?"

Stéphanie bolted upright in a panic. "He's not in love with me! He doesn't even know me!"

"He knows your music," Christianne said, "and everything I've told him about you."

"You told him things about me?" Stéphanie cried.

Christianne chuckled, "Of course. You're my bestest cousin, and besides that, you should've seen him—the way he just stood there with his mouth wide open watching you perform at Granby."

"Granby!" Stéphanie spat. "Why does it always come back to Granby?"

"Because you were good," Christianne said, squeezing her cousin's hand in comfort. "I know, you don't think so, but you were, Stéph."

"Pépère didn't think so," she mumbled.

"Yes, he did!" Christianne said. "Just because he didn't want you to use the stage as a platform for your anger doesn't mean he didn't like it."

"What does it mean then?"

"That he loved you."

"I loved him," Stéphanie choked.

"Me, too," Christianne said. She forced away her grief and tried to look into Stéphanie's eyes. "He'd want you to be happy, you know?"

Stéphanie nodded. "I know, but ..." She shrugged instead of finishing the clause.

Christianne pushed on, "Michel's a great guy, and he's really into you. Alex says he's never seen him like this before."

Stéphanie's mind swirled as much as her heart swelled. "Like what exactly? Because I thought we were on a date, and then suddenly he says he wants me to be in his band. Mondou, Chris! What am I supposed to do with that?"

"I don't know," she admitted, "but there's something you used to do that could help ..."

Stéphanie nodded at the unspoken suggestion that she sing. "I know, but I don't think I can," she said.

"You did last night," Christianne gently reminded her. Stéphanie shivered at the memory of singing with Michel while the others ate pasta in the other room. Christianne squeezed her hand, "Look, I know I'm not a great singer, but how about I start, and when you're ready, you join in?" Stéphanie wagged her head but did not stop Christianne from singing.

### Avec son grand fusil d'argent

Émilie and Roch saw each other every day for the next three months. It was mostly on the bus and at school, but Roch also took the initiative to find better ways to be with her as well. He met Pierre on the steps of Notre-Dame-de-Lasalette Church on Sunday mornings, shook his hand, and said, "Excuse me," and "Please," and "May I," in smooth, polite tones, and he always included Martin in any request to spend time with Émilie: "S'il vous plaît, Monsieur, can Martin and Émilie accompany me to the Appleton theatre next week? May I take them to a little gathering chez Dupont? May we go to the café together?"

Pierre was taken. He touched Roch's shoulder and smiled at the man-boy he had watched mature. "Bien sûr. You three. Oui, oui. Go have fun."

"It's because of Robbie," Martin said one day on the bus, "because he's gone. Papa thinks you must be lonely without him."

"Yeah," Roch sneered, "as lonely as a dog for the fleas he just got rid of." Émilie's eyes stung; she turned away from Roch. "Pfff," he sighed.

She sniffed and turned back to him. "What?"

"You're not over him," he sneered.

"What? No. I … I …"

Roch's eyes were hard amber marbles. "You what?"

She floundered for an answer, "New Year's. You said you di—"

"Never mind what I said." He glared at her with hard, marble eyes. "Do you even like me?"

"Of course! How can you ask that?"

"That's not the question, Mimi. The question is, why do I have to?"

Her stomach turned to cement, but she squeezed his hands in reassurance. "You don't," she said, then kissed his lips for good measure. "You don't. Okay?"

He made a sound of agreement and moved his head forward and back like a gliding rocking chair. "Okay."

She smiled and nodded and snuggled into his side for the rest of the ride to school. It was not comfortable, but it was easier than talking.

Martin saved the conversation, "So what are we doing this weekend? Going to Jean's?"

"Sure," Roch replied.

Martin said something Émilie did not hear over her conscience: *It's wrong* to go *out like that. If Maman and Papa knew what we did* …

What they did was teenage foolery: Roch picked up Émilie and Martin for a party, but only Martin went. Roch and Émilie drove away to find a place to park. It was an abuse of trust, Émilie knew, but she had followed the rules with Robbie and look where that had gotten her. Still, the guilt of it seized her each time she watched Martin jog off to catch up with friends at a party or dance.

"What?" Roch would ask leaning towards her and nestling his chin into her shoulder.

"Nothing. It's just … Maybe we should go in."

"Why?"

"Because my parents think we're with Martin."

"We are," he would chuckle and press closer towards her.

She would hold him off, "We're supposed to look out for each other."

Roch would stroke her hair. "Oh, I'll look out for you, and Goose'll look out for himself. Okay? Now," he would kiss her neck, "let me look."

She would squirm, but their lips would catch, and their tongues would touch, and soon their hands would undo buttons and find skin and even coarse hair. The windows would steam, and she would be on her back, and he would be on top of her, and then she would catch his wrist and say, "We should stop."

He would answer, "No, we shouldn't," and continue kissing her.

She would wiggle and squirm and pull away from him. "Yes, we should."

"Fine," he would sigh and fall back to his side of the car. Until one night as spring drew upon them, Roch did not move away. He hovered over her and asked, "Why?"

"Because!" She cried, trying to squirm out of his embrace. "Because it's a sin."

"No, it's not," he scoffed and tried to kiss her again, but she pushed herself to sitting. "Geez-us, Meem!" He pushed back to his side of the car and gripped the steering wheel.

"I'm sorry," she mumbled.

He glared at the night before them. His jaw moved as he ground his teeth. "Is it because it's me?"

"What?" she gasped.

He turned towards her. "If I were Robbie, would you still make me stop?"

"Roch!"

"What? It's a simple question. Would you make me stop?"

"Of course!" she cried. Her heart raced; and her head shook at the idea.

Roch continued; his eyes were set and almost glowing. "Are you sure?"

"Yes! It's a sin!"

"Ffff! That's the only reason? Because it's a sin?"

Her eyes were round, wet saucers. She felt sick. "Wh— What? No! I'd make him stop because I wouldn't even be with him! I'd be with you."

"Really? If he was here? If he wasn't some priest boy? You'd still be with me?"

"Of course!" Her answer came without hesitation, but she shivered down to her insides as she said, it.

He X-rayed her for a long moment. Her pulse pounded in her temple, and her throat constricted as if she had been caught with her hand in the cookie jar and crumbs on her blouse. He let out a slow deep exhale and turned away. "It's time to get Goose," he said, as he turned the ignition. She concurred with a nod he did not see.

He pulled the knob to turn the headlights on. The tires spit up gravel as he drove off. Sleet tapped against the windshield. They did not speak. They listened to the wind and to one another's breathing. Émilie's eyes leaked. She did not whimper or wipe away the rill, but Roch turned towards her. "Are you crying?"

"No," she lied.

"Yes, you are." He sighed with contrition and joggled her knee with his hand. "Geezus, Meem. I'm sorry."

She nodded rapidly to stay off the conversation and the tears. "I know."

"It's just …" He lost his courage and turned his eyes back to the road. He chewed his lip.

"Just what?" she whispered.

"Nothing." Neither spoke again until Roch parked the car at the assigned meeting spot. Then he said, "He had his chance. Now it's mine."

Émilie did not know what kind of chance Robbie had had with all the rules and restrictions her mother had insisted on, but she nodded agreement like a fishing jig until Martin tapped on the window and saved her from the need to respond.

"You, okay?" Martin asked her later as they walked from Roch's car to the back porch.

"Yeah," she mumbled and quickened her pace.

He kept step with her. "You were both pretty quiet."

She pulled the door open and crossed into the porch. "It's snowing," she said, wiping her feet on the mat. "He had to concentrate on the road." She crossed towards the entrance to the kitchen.

Martin snorted. "Right. Since when?" She shrugged and bent to untie her boots. He sighed at her evasiveness. "Em."

"What?" she snapped.

"Did Roch say anything?"

She pried off her boots with her toes and snapped, "He said a lot of things. We don't just make out, you know?"

"Sure. But did he say anything unusual?"

She shook back a spring of tears and pushed down Roch's outburst and jealous questioning. "Not really. Why? Is there something going on?"

He held his lips together and shrugged. "No."

She wrinkled her face. "You're a terrible liar."

"Maybe," he agreed.

Her stomach knotted. "What's wrong?"

Martin pumped his lips before finally saying, "Robbie."

"What about him?" Her voice rose with worry. "Is he sick

again?"

"No, he's fine, but …"

"But what?" she pressed.

Martin winced and shook away the answer that was not his to give. "Nothing. Just … Are you sure Roch's the right one?"

"The right one?" she parroted. "Gawd! What's with you two tonight?" She strode towards the door.

"Robbie's not a priest yet."

"Shut up!"

"And maybe he never will—"

She slammed the door before he could say anything more.


There was a distance between the Tremblay siblings after that, but a week later they found themselves sitting beside one another in the confines of the backseat of their father's car. Émilie set a fake smile on her lips and let the others do the talking on the drive to Lasalette for Martin's final hockey game of the season. Rose and Pierre laughed in the front seat as Martin gave a running commentary and demonstration of how he would block any shot sent his way. He jerked and jabbed about in the falling darkness and hit Émilie in the arm. "Ow!" she cried, grabbing the throb.

"Martin," Pierre reprimanded with a laugh. "Save it for the game."

"You bet." He turned towards Émilie. "Sorry."

She nodded at the apology and at the sentiment behind it. "You're supposed to stop the puck," she teased, "not me."

He raised an eyebrow that said more than any words. She burned from the sting of it and turned towards the window. Martin left her to her thoughts and picked up his colour commentary of the forthcoming game.

Émilie studied the gradient shades of colour in the sky—a

bleeding of indigo to mauve, to pink, to creamy peach. The sun itself was a golden orange ball setting far beyond the village. Émilie sank into the subtle convergences of colour and light. *Dusk and dawn,* she remembered Lucille Thibaud saying about her twin sons. Émilie considered it and easily summoned up Robbie as a pastel twilightscape of pink and orange.

When she thought of Roch, however, all she could see was an oil canvas of bright oranges and reds that were anything but subdued. She swished her mouth as she considered her assessment of Roch. He was undoubtedly the more extroverted of the brothers, the livelier and more aggressive, and it served him well in social circles and in hockey, but it had been the most beneficial in his pursuit of Émilie—that had required tenacity and hutzpah and planning, planning that had made her head spin and butterflies float inside her stomach.

But Robbie was still the one she thought of when the clouds stretched across the sky like pink cotton candy, and when the snow twinkled in the sun, and when she caught sight of a fox trotting through the field, and when she played *Moonlight Sonata.* Robbie was the one she dreamed of, too, the one she danced with night after night in a dizzying twirl of kisses in the school gymnasium.

How he could still infiltrate her dreams, Émilie did not know, for Roch was the one wrapped about her mind when she went to bed. He was the one who made her swell and ache with such desire that she touched herself until pleasure washed over her. Such gratification was a grave sin, Émilie knew, but she considered it a preventative measure to help her remain strong when Roch asked for more than she could give.

"Eh!" her mother suddenly cried. "Watch out for that

deer!"

"I see him," Pierre answered, slowing as a precaution.

Émilie saw the animal's white behind bound away across the field eastward towards Manitoba, St. Boniface, Robbie. She pressed her forehead to the window and obliterated the view with the steam of her breath on the glass.

Little was accomplished on the ice. Breakaways were stopped, passes intercepted, and shots rebounded off goalie pads. In the last moments of play, the Toussaints and Vikings were still tied at zero. Émilie's voice had grown hoarse from yelling, but she counted down seconds along with her friends and everyone else in the building.

She gave a shout when Martin deflected a Viking shot, and Gilles Tessier scooped up the puck and manoeuvred his way up the ice. He passed to Roch, who caught it on the blade of his stick as he powered forward.

They worked almost as well together as Roch and Robbie had the previous ten years, passing the puck between themselves as if they were friends, confusing the crowd as to who was who. "Roch'n'Robbie!" People had cheered for them. "Roch'n'Robbie!"

In time, it had grown into a call and response that the crowd would sing as the boys skated down the ice. "Rockin' Robin!" a few people would start.

"Tweet! Tweet!" another group would answer.

Émilie had never liked the chant, the way people had made the two brothers interchangeable. She knew they were different, knew who glided and who hunched as he skated, knew who calculated angles and who just intuited passes and shots. She never tweeted or sang with the others, not even once Robbie was gone and the chant just meant, "Go les

Toussaints! Go! Go!"

Roch passed the puck to Gilles. He advanced a few strides and took a shot. He missed. The crowd groaned, but Roch picked up the puck behind the net. Émilie leaned over the boards to watch. She heard the ice crunch as Roch swooped around and flung the puck into the corner of the net. She screamed and jumped at the same time as Roch raised his stick in the air. The Lasalette crowd erupted in cheers and yells and stamped their feet. "Tweet! Tweet!" They called beating on the boards with frozen, mittened hands. Émilie squealed and jumped and hugged her friends.

There were still seven seconds left in the game, but the crowd paid no attention to the referee's whistle and the final face-off. At the buzzer, the crowd hooted and shouted louder than before. People jumped and hugged one another. The Toussaints players leapt about the ice, throwing their sticks and gloves into the air. They calmed down enough to line up and shake hands with the Vikings, receive their trophy, and smile for a photo. The crowd moved inside in search of hot chocolate and hamburgers. Émilie and her friends let the others pass. They waited beside the boards and watched the players pick up their sticks and gloves. Roch grinned at her from across the ice.

"You're so lucky, Em," Shirley sighed.

"Me?" Émilie was surprised that Shirley Dupont, who could go to the café for sodas with whomever asked without permission or a brotherly chaperone would call her lucky. "Why's that?"

Shirley scoffed and jerked her head in Roch's direction. "Only the hottest thing since the invention of fire."

"Indeed," Marie agreed.

"Mmmhmm. But no matter how hot he is, it's freezing out here! My tits are turning into popsicles."

"Shirl!" Marie gasped. "You're so crass,"

"What? They are!" She slipped her arm through Émilie's and started towards the door. "Come on, let's go. I've gotta warm-up, and little Émilie-poo here needs to ask Mommy and Daddy if she can go to the victory party."

"Oh shoot," Marie laughed. "I forgot. I better, too."

They stepped into the conjoined hall. It was loud and hazy with cigarette smoke. Émilie scanned the room to locate her parents. She spotted them across the room near the stairs to the dressing rooms. They seemed happy, convivial even. They held one another by the crook of the arm and smiled and chatted with the people about them. Still, Émilie knew it was best to meet them by herself. "Give me a few minutes," she said with a nod in her parents' direction. "Come back when it looks like they've said yes about the party."

"How'll we know?" Marie asked.

Émilie tilted her head. "You'll know."

Shirley laughed. "No problem," she said. "Come on, Marie. Your parents are just over there."

Émilie watched her friends push their way into the crowd. Then she too moved deeper into the room. She smiled at the people she passed and said hello to them, but she did not linger or chat.

"Eh!" her father called to her as she approached. "Quel soir! Quel jeu!" He picked her up in a big hug. "What a night!"

"Oui," she laughed in agreement.

"Another shutout for our Martin!" Rose clutched her hands with pleasure.

"And your Roch's goal there," Pierre shook his head with joyful wonder, "in the last seconds of the game."

"It was wonderful," Rose agreed.

"Et tiens," Pierre said, pointing towards the players coming up from the change room, "there they are."

They were flushed from the victory and the contents of the silver flasks Coach Hudon pretended not to see. They smelled of Brylcreem and rye, sweat and mint.

"Eh!" Pierre cried, raising his arms to grab his son. "Bravo!"

Martin jumped into his father's hug. "Merci Papa!"

Pierre released his hold and held Martin out at arm's length; he smiled and nodded with pride before relinquishing him to Rose and Émilie. "Bon travail, Roch," he said, offering his hand to Roch and patting him on the back.

"Merci, Monsieur."

"Congratulations," Rose nodded towards him.

"Merci, Madame." They stood smiling at one another until Roch cleared his throat, "Excusez-moi, Monsieur," he said.

Pierre looked at him. "Oui?"

"I was wondering if Émilie and Martin could join me and some of the team for a little party at my house. My parents will be there."

Pierre and Rose exchanged looks in a silent discussion of facial expressions. He touched her arm. "She'll be safe," he seemed to be saying, "Martin and the others will be there." Émilie turned her eyes away from his trust and missed her mother's shrug of agreement and her father's nod. She did hear him speak, however, "D'accord, but have them back by midnight."

"Yes sir. No problem," Roch smiled. "I'll have them back safe and sound." He shook Pierre's hand, and they said good night.

The three teens made their way through the crowded room. Roch and Martin were continually stopped and congratulated with pats and slaps and cheers. Émilie laughed at the smiles shining on both of their faces. She received pats for her proximity to the players, "Your brother there! Ho! A real Glenn Hall! And that Thibaud! Our own Rocket, eh? He even wears number nine!"

Shirley and Marie caught her from behind. "So, they said yes, eh?"

"Mine, too. Think Roch can give us a ride?"

"I don't see why not. If you can get a different ride home."

Marie bumped her hip against Émilie's in jest, "Why? Is he going to be too busy giving you a ride later to give us one back home?"

Émilie blushed down to her stomach but rolled her eyes and made a face at her friend's insinuation. "No. It's just ridiculous to expect him to drive all the way to town to take you home when he's the one having the party."

"I guess."

"How's he going to do that, anyway? Have the party? It's not like Robbie's here to take up the slack."

"Yeah," Marie danced her eyebrows up and down, "I don't imagine Roch'll be around much, eh?" She elbowed Émilie, who was still snagged on Shirley's mention of Robbie and did not respond.

When they finally made it outside, Roch draped his arm about Émilie's shoulder and kissed her head. She smiled at him like she was not still thinking about Robbie's absence. Roch raised his hand in response to calls from friends across the parking lot. He chatted with Martin, Shirley, and Marie, "The folks are taking the equipment home with the truck, so I've got lots of room. Émilie's going to sit up front with me. Goose? Front or back?"

"Back," the girls answered for him.

He tittered and rubbed his neck in embarrassment. "I'd like to girls, but—"

"Yeah, yeah. We know: Lynn." They elbowed each other

and guffawed.

Roch clicked his tongue and smiled. "Gilles said he'd bring her if we won."

"Oooo," the girls teased.

Martin blushed. "Let's just get going. We don't want to miss the party."

Roch jostled him. "You bet, Goose." He opened the driver's side of the car and motioned to the inside. "Mimi." She passed under his arm and into the car. He slid in next to her and squeezed her thigh. He gave her a smile and revved the engine. The others climbed in on the other side, the girls slipping behind the seat to the back and Martin taking his place on the other side of Émilie.

"Hey, check the glove box there, Goose" Roch said once Martin was settled.

He did as told and felt around until his hand came upon a square cylinder. He clutched it. "What have we here?" he laughed, holding it up to the light.

"What?" Shirley asked from the back.

"A little something to get the party started," said Roch.

Émilie looked at him in reprimand, but he smiled and raised his eyebrows in explanation. She shook her head, but Roch's hand soothed her. "Not, too much," she said to Martin.

He took a drink. "Don't worry." He mock-whispered in her ear as he passed the flask to the back, "I'll be good. Will you?"

She wrinkled her brow at him. "Hey," Roch cuffed Martin in the head. "You know the rules. You do your thing. And we'll do ours. No questions asked. No stories told."

"I know," Martin raised his hands in innocence. "I'm just keepin' tabs."

"Yeah? Well, keep 'em to yourself. Lynn might want them

later."

Martin chuckled and reached for the flask. "I hope so."

"Oh, she will," Marie sounded from the back. Martin turned to her for the details, which she and Shirley freely gave. Roch added a few comments, too, but Émilie remained quiet trying to determine when Martin and Lynn Tessier had become an item. *I should know this*, she scolded herself, *should know what Martin's doing when we go out together. We're supposed to be watching out for one another*. Still, when they arrived at the Thibauds' she mutely went along with the routine they had established over the course of the winter.

"See you at eleven-thirty?" Martin asked.

Roch jerked his head in agreement. "You bet. Out front."

"Okay." Martin opened the door and slid out.

"You comin' Em?" Marie asked as she pushed the seat forward.

"Yeah. In a bit."

"Ohh-kay. Don't stay out too lon-ong."

"Have fu-un," Shirley called in the same playful way.

Roch and Émilie watched the others cross the yard. "Don't you think maybe we should go in?" she asked. "It is your house after all."

"Nah. Maman put some food out, and Goose'll take care of things until we get there." He twirled a strand of her hair around his finger and leaned in to kiss her. She pulled away.

"Are you sure? 'Cause we can go in."

Roch set his eyes on hers and smiled. "I'm sure." He swooped in for a kiss, and Émilie relented. After a few moments, he touched her cheek and pulled away, tucked her hair behind her ear. His eyes glinted in the glow of the yard light. "I have a surprise for you."

"You do?"

He nodded and took her hand. "Come with me."

She followed him out the driver's door and into the cold dark. The crunch of their boots on the packed snow echoed in her head like her mother's voice: *No! No! No!* Her intestines twisted into pretzels. Roch kept turning and smiling at her. She kept dodging his eyes but continued to walk with him.

He led her to the barn, pushed the door open and stepped inside to light a kerosene lamp. Then he held out his hand to her; she took it and stepped towards him. He smiled. Their breath rose in the air. He reached behind her and pulled the door closed. His body lingered against hers. Her blood raced through her.

"It's upstairs," he said, pulling her towards the ladder to the hayloft. "You go first," he said at the base. "I'll light the way."

She nodded and climbed up, shivered as she waited for him in the dust and the straw, and the heavy air smelling of cattle and hay and manure. "What's the surprise?" she managed to ask when he poked his head up into the hayloft.

"You'll see," he teased. He climbed the rest of the way up and then illuminated the loft with his lamp. Émilie saw it then: the blankets spread over the bales. She chewed on her top lip. Shivers ran through her. Roch approached her from behind and wrapped his arms about her. He rested his chin on her shoulder and his cheek against hers.

"I got us this," he said, slipping something into her hand.

She went numb as she clasped it and processed the rubbery ring she could feel through the wrapper. Her gut wrenched. Her throat constricted. "Is that a …?"

"Yeah."

"How'd you get it?"

He stepped in front of her and touched a finger to her lips.

"Shhh." She trembled; he rubbed her arms, slid his hands down to hers, and took the condom back. "Let's just see how things go, okay?"

Her head bobbed at the suggestion, but a breath like a drowning woman's gasp escaped her; her eyes watered and blinked. Roch's did, too.

"Please, Mimi. I need you. I need you tonight." Her ears rang, and her chest ached. She wanted to ask him why that night, but he leaned in and kissed her. "Please," he repeated.

His breath made her dizzy. Her head moved. She thought it was from side to side, but he pulled her towards him and pushed his tongue into her mouth, so perhaps she was wrong, perhaps it had been up and down.

Roch moved his hands about her body. He slipped them up beneath her layers of down and wool and cotton. He undid her bra and slid his hands over the freed flesh of her breasts. She moved at his touch, but neither knew whether she was pulling away or arching with pleasure.

"Mmm," he sounded into her mouth. He kissed her neck and traced his tongue along to her ear. "Let's go sit down."

He tugged at her hand and led her towards the blanket-covered bales. She obliged, though her mind raced, and her conscience cried, *No! No! No!*

He sat first and pulled her next to him. He kissed her and led her onto her back. He fumbled with the buttons of her jacket, then the buttons of her sweater. "Gawd, there's a lot."

*God*, she thought, *God. God.* It was not a prayer but a bass continuo over which she said, "You, too."

He pulled back and tore open the snaps of his jacket, then shook it off and pulled his t-shirt over his head. "Not anymore. But you," he said, returning his hands to her cardigan, "you have way too many."

Roch finished with her buttons and pushed the layers of

clothing off her shoulders. She squirmed and twisted below him, pulled her arms out from the sleeves. The air was cold, but his bare chest warmed her. Roch pulled off her bra and threw it aside with the rest of her clothes. He explored her breasts with his hands and his lips.

"Uhh," she gasped, still unsure whether it was from pleasure or protest. Roch's groan, however, was the latter. He tugged at the button and zipper of her jeans and slipped his hand inside her underwear. *Ohgodohgodohgod.*

"Roch," she said.

He kissed her nipple before he answered. "What?" She trembled in response. "Are you cold?"

"Yes."

"Then let's get inside." He pulled at the blanket beneath them and moved this way and that with Émilie as he tried to pull it over them.

"Ow," she protested when her hair got pinned beneath his arm.

"Sorry. Okay. Wait." He untangled himself from her and stood. He yanked the blanket off the bales, then spread it over her. "There." He kissed her lips. "How's that?"

"Good." She shivered.

"Kay. Now hold on." He pried off his shoes, then walked to Émilie's feet and tugged at her boots.

"You don't need these," he said.

She made laughing sounds for him, but she was distracted by the patches of the quilt he had lain over her—plaids and checks and stripes; Roch's old shirts, and Robbie's— his favourite blue and yellow one; he had gotten it at the start of grade nine and had worn it to the Freshie Dance. Her eyes stung and blurred.

"We don't need these either," Roch said as he undid his jeans and peeled them off. His underwear went with them.

His penis pointed out from him like Pinocchio's nose. Émilie blinked at it. Roch smiled like a glutton at the pastry shop. "You like it?" He returned to the bale bed. "Touch it."

He led her hand to his hard organ. It was warm and soft, and she could not swallow or breathe or pull away. Roch grinned and said something she did not hear, then he moved about and undid her pants, pulled them off along with her panties and socks. He discarded them on the floor and stared down at her nakedness. She bit her lip to keep from trembling. Roch rubbed the dark swath of pubic hair he theretofore had only grazed.

She closed her eyes against a rise of tears. The blue and yellow stripes of Robbie's shirt were burned on her eyelids. Roch fingered her labia. The colours in her mind swirled into an image of Robbie. She jerked her eyes open. Roch looked down upon her. "What?"

"Nothing," she gasped.

He smiled at the answer as if it were true and leaned over to kiss her.

"Good. 'Cause I think it's time." A choke escaped her; he did not notice. "Let me get the safe." He leaned over the edge of the bales to search for the condom.

Émilie's heart raced; her head spun. She squeezed her eyes closed again to try to gain control of herself, but Robbie's face burned her eyes once again. *No!* She yelled at herself. *No! It's Roch! I'm with Roch!*

He was upon her before she was ready, and was positioning himself between her legs, saying, "Okay?"

She had no idea if she answered, but he jabbed her with his fleshy probe again and again until he found her opening, then he pushed himself inside of her. It stabbed like a thousand knives.

"Owww!" she cried.

Roch stopped. "What?"

"It hurts," she squeaked.

"It'll get better." Her head nodded; he started to move again, slowly at first, then faster and deeper and harder. "Oh," he gasped. "Ohh. Ohhh."

She scrunched her eyes against the sound and the pain and the act he had wanted for so long. She saw nothing but darkness, though her eyes burned, and tears seeped from them.

Roch grunted and gasped, "Mimi. Mimi," until he arched back and cried, "Ohh. Ohhhh." Then he collapsed upon her and panted into the base of her neck.

She tapped his shoulder. "You're heavy."

"Sorry." He shifted himself off her, and she turned onto her side with her back to him. He rolled into her and spooned her. "Mimi," he whispered. "My Mimi." He snuggled closer into her. The patches of the quilt burned her eyes and caused her to sniff. "Hey."

"Sorry," she gasped and tried to pull away.

He held her tighter. "No. I love you."

"I know." The rest of her response was caught in her head. She remained with him under the blanket until a voice shot out below them.

"Émilie? Are you there?"

They sprang apart. "It's Martin." She grabbed for her clothes.

"Shit." Roch stepped into his underwear. He tossed Émilie her bra and put on his pants.

"Émilie," the voice cracked. "It's late! We gotta go!"

"Oh no." She clasped her bra behind her back.

"Don't worry," Roch pulled his head through his t-shirt, "just tell him you're coming."

"Martin," she called, pushing her legs into her jeans, "I'm

com—"

"Hey! Finally!" Martin's eyes popped with surprise when he saw Émilie dressing. "Em." It was a sound more than a name, a slap. Émilie looked away, busied herself with her blouse. Her hands shook.

"Hey," Roch said as he walked towards Martin, "where you been? It's late. I've gotta get you two home."

Martin's lips opened, then closed. His face furrowed. "I'll wait outside."

Roch turned back to Émilie as Martin backed down the ladder. He touched her shoulder. "It's okay."

She shrugged off his hand. "No, it's not."

He let out a sigh, and they finished getting dressed in silence. She went down the ladder first and did not wait for Roch to follow. He caught up to her at the door and took her hand. "It's okay," he assured again. She pinned her lip between her teeth and nodded in answer. Tears blurred her eyes.

Martin was waiting for them in Francis Thibaud's half-ton. The tip of his cigarette blinked red for all his inhaling. He did not look at either of them when Roch pulled the driver's door open. Émilie scrambled in towards Martin, and Roch slid in behind the wheel. "Why the truck?" Roch asked.

"You know why," Martin growled. "So just drive."

"Geezus." Roch turned the ignition and slammed the door at the same time, then sent snow up into the air as he drove away. "We'll tell them it was my fault," he said.

"Good idea," Martin turned his lips up in disgust, "since it *is* your fault."

Roch continued to brainstorm, "We'll tell them I couldn't leave the others. Or I couldn't find the keys. Or the car wouldn't start. Something like that."

"Or," Martin suggested, "we could tell them the truth."

Émilie and Roch both swung their heads towards him. "Please, Martin!" Émilie cried. "Please don't tell them. Please?"

"Why not?"

She struggled not to cry. "You don't understand."

"Oh, I'm pretty sure I do."

"It's none of your business!" Roch barked.

"Of course, it is. I'm her brother."

"I don't care." Roch pressed harder on the gas. "Damn brothers." The truck shot down the dark country road.

Martin looked at him with scrunched, beady eyes, but he addressed his sister instead. "You sure picked the wrong one, Em. Robbie would've treated you better."

Émilie gasped at his words, while Roch yelled, "Shut the hell up!" and lunged across her to grab Martin by the jacket. He fought back and pushed off Roch's hand. Roch growled and moved to grab Martin once again.

Émilie touched Roch's arm. "Roch. Please."

He stopped and shifted his eyes to Émilie's.

"Hey!" Martin cried. "Watch out!"

Roch turned his eyes back to the road and caught sight of a deer. "Shit!" He jerked the wheel to the right to avoid it. The back of the truck swung the other way. Roch tried to correct his steering, but the speed and the snow and the ice caused the vehicle to swerve and turn and flip.

They banged about the cab and slammed into the dash, and the doors, and each other. There was smashing, shattering, and the crunching of metal. Then there was silence except for the rotation of tires in the air and the crackling of broken glass.

Martin blinked. He lay in the darkness while his mind connected the stop-motion of what had just happened. When it came to him, he jerked and twisted, called for Émilie and

Roch.

He pulled himself out of the cab but saw nothing but darkness and snow in the light created by the moon and the single unbroken headlight.

He turned in circles and called out for his sister and friend again and again. He wiped at the stream of blood flowing down his face, then broadened his orbit of panic and walked around the truck.

That's when he saw Roch discarded in the snow.

"Roch!" he yelled and ran to him, fell to his knees beside him, and shook him. "Roch? Roch?"

There was no sound, no motion, no response.

He would never remember leaving Roch in the snow and forgetting to look more for Émilie. He would only remember running home, banging on the door for some reason rather than going in, and calling, "Papa! Papa!"

His grandmother was first at the door. She was startled and bewildered. She screamed at his bleeding head. Pierre and Rose were soon at her side, tending to Martin's gash and squeezing his arm. "Mon Dieu! What's happened?" Pierre demanded.

"An accident. Roch. A deer."

"And Émilie? Where's Émilie?"

"I don't know! I don't know!"

Pierre steadied him with both of his hands. "Get in the car. Mère Sylvie, call the police. Rose, come. We have to find her."

Émilie saw a beam of light, but it disappeared into darkness again. She heard her name, and she opened her eyes. The snow glistened in the moonlight. She heard feet crunching in the snow and her name being called again and again. Then she saw boots, gloves, her father's face. "Papa?" she mumbled.

"Ma fille. Ma fille." He lifted her out of the truck and cried into her frozen hair.

"What happened?" she asked, muffled against the suede of his coat.

"Émilie?" shrieked her mother. She touched Émilie's face, her arm, her hair. "Oh, Dieu merci!"

Pierre carried her like a sleeping child across the snow. Rose opened the car door, and Pierre set Émilie in the back seat. "There. There." He touched her cheek. "Everything will be okay." He stepped back, and Rose slid in beside Émilie and wrapped her arms about her. Pierre closed the door.

"What's going on?" Émilie asked.

"Shhh," Rose rubbed her arm. "Shhh."

Émilie saw her father through the window. He clutched Martin's shoulder—their heads hung and lulled from side to side. Red and blue light swirled in the darkness and exposed three other figures standing along the road: Francis and Lucille Thibaud, and Robbie.

Émilie jerked from her mother's embrace. "Roch! Maman! Where is he? Where's Roch?"

## 6. Aire
## April 1990

"That's not the end," Stéphanie said without moving her heavy head from the pillow.

"I know," Christianne responded, "but I heard a knock at the door, didn't you?"

"No," Stéphanie replied as her cousin called out.

"Hello?"

An answer came, "Christianne? Is that you?"

"Yes," she called, then turned to Stéphanie and whisper-cried, "It's Michel!"

Stéphanie jerked up to sitting. "Don't let him in! I'm not dressed!"

"You have a shirt and gitch on," Christianne pointed out as she swung her legs over the edge of the bed. "I'm the one falling out of this robe." She tugged at the top flap of the housecoat she was wearing to better cover herself and started towards the door. "Just a minute."

"I have Stéphanie's bag," Michel said from the hallway. "I'll just leave it out here."

Christianne opened the oak door. "No, it's okay," she said, peeking her head around it. "You can bring it in." She opened the door farther and signalled for him to come in, but Michel hesitated like a bashful teenager while Stéphanie hissed at Christianne from the bed. Christianne laughed at them both. "It's okay, just don't mind my robe." She tucked and pulled at the flaps, tightening the belt again.

Michel looked at the pink velour garment and blinked away a sudden rush of tears. "Oh."

"It was in the closet," she explained. "Alex said I could wear it."

"Uh. Yeah. Sure. It's just I haven't seen it for a while."

"Old girlfriend's?" she teased.

He moved his head from side to side and answered in a strained voice, "Marie-Geneviève's."

"Oh," she gasped. "I'm sorry!"

He pushed out a smile, though his face remained clouded. "It's okay. She didn't really wear it much. She said it was too warm."

"It is," Christianne agreed, fanning herself with her hand. "In fact, I'm so warm, I think I'm gonna go change." She slipped past him and pointed to the duffle bag hanging at his side. "Why don't you take that in? Stéphanie'd probably like her things." Michel bit his lip and cocked his eyebrow as he considered. "It's okay," Christianne assured yet again. She grinned and squeezed his arm as she started away.

Inside the room, Stéphanie's heart and mind raced; she did not know whether she should stay seated on the bed or lie down and curl up beneath the covers, hiding, for she looked dressed but felt naked.

"I brought you your bag," Michel announced before she could decide. He kept his eyes down as he crossed into the room and turned his back towards her. "I'll put it in the bathroom."

"Thanks," Stéphanie replied. She, too, had her eyes cast downward. She gathered the frilly bedspread up onto her lap out of nervousness.

Michel opened a door on the far side of the room and disappeared inside. His voice echoed inside the tiled room, "There's everything you need here. Towels, soap, shampoo. The taps are backwards on the sink, though, and the water takes a while to heat up. Especially in the shower. You'd be better off taking a bath. Turn the hot water on and let it run. By the time it's full, the water'll be just right."

"Okay." She peeked up to see if he had come back in, but he had not. "Thanks for the tip."

"Sure. No problem." Stéphanie braced for his return to the room, but he remained in the bathroom and talked from there, "So, did Alex talk to you?"

"About tomorrow night?"

"Yeah."

"Uh-uh."

"And what do you think?"

Her nervousness slipped away as she talked, "I think his choice of music is questionable but that his sentiment is good."

"Me, too," Michel chuckled. "I know he does some stupid things sometimes, but this isn't one of them."

"No," she agreed.

"So, tomorrow? Jonny thought *À la claire fontaine* might be better."

"It would," she agreed.

"Especially your version from Granby?" His voice rose like a testing of the waters; her insides twisted and knotted with emotion as he went on, "You called it a Fransaskois love song, and that's what this is, don't you think?"

She trembled at his memory of her words and at his opinion of Christianne and Alex's relationship. She hemmed for a response, "Umm. Yeah. I guess."

"But you don't want to," Michel said from the bathroom.

"Wants not the question. I just don't know if I can."

"Why?"

"Lots of reasons."

"Me?" he asked. She nodded, but he did not see, for he was still giving her privacy and space. "The band?"

"Both."

"Dammit," he muttered, but the sound reverberated off the bathroom tile, so Stéphanie still heard.

"I can do the Bolton," she said.

He made a sound of pleasant surprise, "You sure?"

"No, but I told Alex I'd try."

"Well, that's something."

"I suppose," she said to the pile of frills on her lap. Her eyes filled, and her insides churned with a thousand emotions she could not identify.

Michel walked towards the doorway and said, "They're two different things: me and the band." She made a sound but did not know what it meant and neither did Michel. He kept talking, "I'm completely taken by you. By your talent and your beauty, your intelligence and passion." Stéphanie trembled like a wet dog; her heart raced, and she could do nothing but shake her head at such flattery. "I'm sorry that's so forward, but I need you to know that last night wasn't a game or a trap or anything. It was a date with the woman I love."

"Love?" she squeaked. She trembled as she went on, "You can't love me. You just met me."

"So?" He smiled and crossed the room towards her. "Sylvie Simard loved Baptiste Caron from the moment she saw him, and she didn't even know what that word meant."

"That's a song," she protested.

"And so's this." He set his eyes on her and sang in a voice

that grew like the rising sun, "In the beginning was darkness, a world formless and without light. So, it was with Michel and the raven on the set. She sang a song that won his heart before they even met."

She turned away and tried to push down the swell of emotion rising inside of her. She took a loud, deep breath and tossed her head to keep it clear. "I'm sorry. I shouldn't've gone out with you last night. I … I can't …" She trailed off, looking for the end of her sentence.

"Can't what?" Michel asked as he sat beside her on the edge of the bed.

She shrugged and clenched her eyes, hung her head to hide behind the curtain of her black hair as she asked herself the same question. Michel moved a tress of her hair and tucked it behind her ear. Stéphanie trembled; Michel touched her chin and gently raised it so she could look at him. She did, slowly, and her heart swelled with feelings for him. Her eyes filled, but she did not pull away. In fact, she leaned closer and closer towards him until she touched her forehead to his.

"I'm scared," she whispered.

"Why?" he asked with such patient tenderness Stéphanie almost replied, *I don't want to be like my mom.* Instead, she remained with her forehead pressed to his until a tap on the open bedroom door interrupted them.

"Sorry," Clem said as they repelled away from each other, "but I made some parmigiana, and we should probably get to it if we're gonna get any work done today."

"Right," Michel said, turning towards him. "Thanks. I'll be down in a minute."

"'Kay. And what about you?" he asked, jerking his chin towards Stéphanie. "Are you up for dinner or would you prefer breakfast? I can make you an omelette."

"Umm. I don't know. What time is it?"

He laughed, "Oh, that doesn't matter. We just go with the flow here: eat when we're hungry, sleep when we're tired, work when there's work to do, and hopefully have some fun along the way."

"That sounds nice," she replied.

"It is." They shared a smile for a moment before he jerked out of it. "Ooops! There's my timer. I gotta go. Come down when you're ready."

"I will, but it might be a bit. Like maybe half an hour?"

"That's okay." He pushed his hands down in a wave-like motion. "Go with the flow."

She chuckled, nodded, and thanked him again. "So that's him sober?" she said once he was gone.

"Yeah. A real little homemaker. It's what made him one of Marie-Geneviève's favourites."

"And let me guess, you were the other, right?" she teased.

"Of course. Although she kind of liked Jean-François, too." They held a smile for a time. "I should probably go," he finally said, then leaned forward to kiss her, but restrained himself and stood instead. "I'll be in the kitchen."

She nodded at him and at his consideration. "See you soon." He nodded back and smiled at her as he backed away from the bed and left the room.

Stéphanie shook away the romantic reverie and clasped her hands together in a knot of prayer that she pressed into her forehead. "Jesus," she sighed. "What am I doing?" She replayed the previous twenty hours in her mind. She smiled at the parts where Michel was sweet and showed his interest in her but winced in shame at the memories of their deep kissing and tight embraces. "Forgive me my impurity," she told her god. "And help me! Mon Dieu, Seigneur! Aide-moi!"

She clutched her hands white and tried to force away her fleshly desires. She recited prayers and pleas until she felt both absolved and strengthened. Then she sat in silence until a song rose inside of her. She balked at the inspiration and tried to shake it away, but it remained with her like a glowing ember that refused to die. "Fine," she conceded with a sigh, then she closed her eyes and sang.

## À la claire fontaine

Sylvie always woke after the hallway lights were turned down and the other residents sounded a symphony of snores. They were not overly loud, but she had hearing that, unlike her eyesight and her breathing, had not diminished in recent years. She lay alone in the darkness, tethered to oxygen and to the memory of the dream she had been having of Baptiste, her Baptiste with the raspberry lips and the shiny maroon eyes. *I love him*, she thought. *I always have.* Then she replayed everything from the time he was a boy in Saint-Bruno learning to fiddle in her family's kitchen to the day he left her and the Lower Saint-Lawrence for a piece of paradise in a place called Saskatchewan.

She replayed the day she found him again, tall and broad and looking straight at her. Their courting had been swift, but the engagement was long, for there was no appropriate place for a newlywed couple to live until an addition could be built onto Marie and Joseph Caron's home. It took months, and had it not been for the work and the eyes of God, and those of Lasalette, Baptiste would have taken Sylvie as husbands are wont, and she would have freely given herself to him.

Their wedding day came at last. It rose cool and fresh after a late autumn frost. The trees and ground were sparkling and white. The sky was blue, and the sunlight was bright.

Baptiste shaved his face and cut his hair; he dressed with care: he wore his pressed Sunday suit, a new cotton shirt and a silk tie. His shoulders were broad in his striped vest and dark single-breasted jacket. His chest was puffed with happiness as he stood at the front of the church. His lips held a modest smile.

Sylvie wore a white blouse that was ruffled and pin-tucked; it had long fitted sleeves and a high hook-and-eye collar. It was just like in the dreams she had had those many months after Baptiste had gone west, except that she did not wake chilled with sweat, for she was there, truly there, as Baptiste's bride.

She trembled at the thought. Her father squeezed her arm to reassure her, but her shiver was not from nervousness but rather from something she did not know how to name: joy or bliss, the fulfilment of one's destiny.

She closed her eyes and breathed in the moment, then lifted her eyelids and met Baptiste's gaze. She walked towards him step after step until she was beside him, and his fingers brushed hers. She listened to the prayers and bible readings, but she could not follow them, for Baptiste was beside her and almost touching her.

Père Marchand motioned for them to stand and answer his questions about their will and their freedom, their intention to love and honour, to accept children from God. "Volo," they said. "I do. I give myself to thee."

They slipped gold bands onto one another's fingers; they smiled and stared at one another as if the priest and the church had disappeared. Then, after more prayers, Catherine Painchaud pulled the stops on the harmonium and pedalled the air into the recessional hymn. Baptiste held his arm out to Sylvie, and she slipped hers around it. He rushed her down the aisle and out of the church, where he pressed his lips to hers before anyone reached them. His hand lingered on her back until the hugs and handshakes from the community made him pull away.

After the congratulations and photographs, Baptiste led Sylvie to his uncle's buggy. He helped her up and slid in beside her. His leg pushed against hers, and her arm pressed against his. They turned to each other as Joseph Caron jiggled the reins to make the horse advance. The couple could not speak. Baptiste felt his heart race and his penis stir. Sylvie blushed and warmed; she shivered with happiness and excitement.

The wheels of the buggy whispered and churned over the hard dirt road. The horse's hooves thumped; his breath chugged out in plumes of vapour as he led them to Sylvie's parents' homestead.

Cold roast meats, ham and tourtière, buns and salads, beans, preserved peas and carrots, puddings and pies and cakes awaited them. Whiskey and dandelion wine were passed around. They ate. They drank. They laughed and twirled and danced to the melodies of Baptiste's fiddle under the hands of Zénon Tessier.

Nighttime fell, and after embracing Sylvie's parents, the newlyweds rode with Baptiste's aunt and uncle to the farm across the way. They covered their legs with an old buffalo skin and leaned into each other—Sylvie's shoulder in his armpit, his arm about her—for warmth and support in the back of the buggy after too much dancing and wine. They clutched hands beneath the fur, stared at the stars twinkling like diamonds they could not afford; they looked for the rabbit in the moon.

When they arrived at the Carons' home, Joseph said, "I'll take care of the horse."

Baptiste jumped down and held his hand out to his aunt, then to his wife. Sylvie moved slowly, nervously—soon Baptiste would lead her to their room and close the door; he would unhook her skirt and blouse and petticoats, untie her corset, and find her naked flesh. She had thought of it for weeks, months, years. Thousands of Hail Marys had been said in reparation for such thoughts.

She clasped Baptiste's hand and descended from the buggy. Her head spun as they walked with his aunt across the frosted ground. Her heart pounded ever louder in her ears.

"I'll get the lamp," Marie Caron said as she pushed through the door. Her shape was black in the darkness of the night.

Sylvie heard her rummage and then the shuffle of a matchbox, the strike of an allumette. She saw a small flame, a glow that grew bigger as Marie Caron approached the lit match to the kerosene wick.

The room filled with light and shadows. The elder woman shook out the match, adjusted the lamp, and replaced the shade. "Would you like some tea?" she asked, already seeming to bustle about the kitchen.

"Non," Baptiste answered. "Ça va. Merci, Tantine. Unless," he turned to his bride, "Sylvie, would you like tea?"

"Non," she said, with her eyes on his. "Non, merci."

"Bon," Marie said. "D'accord." She jumped into the practical details of the night, "I put everything you'll need up in the room," she waved her hand in the general direction of the bedroom the couple would share, then fell silent with embarrassment for the impending intimacy.

"Merci," Baptiste said and stepped towards her, hugged her, and kissed her cheek.

"Oh, bin, c'est normal," she said; she smiled though she brushed away his thanks. "Allez. Bonne nuit." She gave him a slight push and turned to Sylvie. "Bonne nuit, ma chérie."

"Bonne nuit, Madame."

"Tantine," Marie corrected. "We're family now."

"Tantine," Sylvie agreed, then pressed her cheeks to the matron's. "Bonne nuit."

Baptiste took Sylvie's hand. Marie Caron turned as if she had household concerns to tend to. Sylvie's groom led her away.

It became darker as they climbed the stairs, but the moon shone through the window, and Baptiste knew the way. He caught her in his arms at the top of the stairs and kissed her. "Je t'aime," he said.

"I love you, too," she answered and kissed him and unbuttoned him and lay with him all through the night.

In the morning, his face shone like an angel's when he looked upon her. "Good. It wasn't a dream."

She touched the scruffiness of his face and looked into his eyes. "Oui, Baptiste. It's a dream come true."

He wanted her almost every night after that, and she wanted him. He kissed her and touched her in places only a washcloth had ever been. She liked it and felt herself soften and warm under his touch; she floated away into an ecstasy that she had never heard of. She held onto the memory of it as she went through the day. Making the bed, emptying the chamber pot, tidying the bedroom—it all reminded her of him, his lips, his tongue, his member inside of her.

No one asked her about it, not Marie Caron, nor her mother, nor even her sister. Sylvie thought they wanted to, thought she saw them open their mouths to ask if it was alright, if she was alright, but no words ever came. She was content to keep it to herself, but she did wonder how long it would be before a baby took form, and how she would know when it did, but she could not ask that any more than the other women could ask her how she was adapting to the demands of marriage.

Christmas passed, and so did the old year, and then a bloodless period. Sylvie felt pain in her breasts and was cloaked in fatigue. She drank tisanes of red raspberry, dandelion root, and parsley, but nothing changed.

Mardi Gras came. It was Baptiste's last night to have her before the forty days of Lent. He lay beside her, fondled her, roamed his hands over her body. "You're different," he said. She pushed his hand away, pulled her nightgown down and rolled towards the edge of the bed. He followed her and wrapped his arm around her. "Sylvie?"

"I'm pregnant," she whispered, then shook like the earth during the release of seismic energy.

He held her tighter. "Oh, my little blueberry, chérie. Why are you shaking?"

"Because I'm scared," she choked.

"Why?"

"Because so much can happen! I've seen it with cattle and my sisters! And your mother, Baptiste! That's how she died!"

He pulled her ever tighter. "Shhh. Nothing will happen."

"You don't know that."

"I know you are bone of my bone, Sylvie, and flesh of my flesh, so God won't take you from me."

"You don't know that."

"I do, because I won't let Him."

She gasped at the blasphemy. "Don't say such a thing!"

"Why not? It's true." He cupped her face and kissed her lips. "If you die, I die."


She awoke to Baptiste playing *Ave Maria* on the violin he had brought west with him from Québec. It reminded her of the first time she saw him: he was six, and she was four; he was standing in front of her father, armed with a too big violin that, by day's end, he had been able to coax into music. She had known then that she wanted to marry him when she grew up. And now she had, and he was playing a hymn for their unborn child.

Months later, however, the hymn became a lament.

"It's my fault," she cried, but her husband's aunt waved the idea away.

"Non, non, Sylvie. Sometimes God just takes them back." Marie Caron rocked the young woman and cried as she herself had years before. "It was a boy," she told Baptiste as she carried away the bedding.

"Can I see?"

"Non. But you can bury him if you want."

"Where?"

"Somewhere where flowers bloom."

Baptiste nodded for a long time, then he took his wrapped, unborn son away and placed him in a shoe box. He buried him under a lilac bush behind the house. There was dirt under his fingernails and tears in his eyes when he went to Sylvie.

"Can you forgive me?" she cried.

He fell to his knees at her bedside and squeezed her hand. "Oh, ma Sylvie. It's not you I have to forgive."

His eyes never shone the same after that, though in time he did smile again, and he kissed her, and touched her, and made love to her again as well.

A second baby took form one rainy night in July, but she also slipped from Sylvie's body too early to survive. Baptiste buried her next to the son beneath the lilac bush. Then he held his wife and, in time, made love to her again.

Sylvie took to reciting Aves whenever Baptiste was inside of her, then she lay awake until morning, begging the heavens for sterility, but God struck her pregnant once again.

Baptiste tried to smile when she told him, and he tried to play a hymn that did not sound like a requiem as well. Sylvie did not begrudge the lacklustre response, for she had as little hope as he. Still, that night, he pressed in close and touched his hand to her stomach and said, "Je t'aime, mon petit bluet."

They made no preparations and chose no names. Even when Sylvie felt the baby kick and Baptiste saw her stomach roll as the baby moved inside of her, they did not speak of it. Sylvie grew rounder and rounder. The weeks passed. No cramps or fluids carried their baby away.

After nine months, her mother came to stay, and one Friday morning soon after, Sylvie lost her waters while stirring soup. "Oh no!" she cried.

"It's alright," her mother assured, wrapping her arms around her. "Come. Let me get you to a bed." A contraction seized Sylvie before they had even made it across the room.

Baptiste heard her cries from outside. He ran to the house, where he found Sylvie lying on the kitchen floor. "It's coming," his mother-in-law said.

"I'll get the doctor." He turned to leave, but Marie Simard stopped him.

"No. There isn't time. Stay! Help me! Help Sylvie!"

Baptiste followed orders. He slipped in behind Sylvie and held her in his lap. "Chérie," he said. "Mon Bluet. Je t'aime. Je t'aime," he repeated without end as she writhed and cried and screamed.

"You're doing good," her mother said. "I see its head. Its shoulder. Push, Sylvie. Push." She held her hands out to catch the baby slipping through Sylvie's folds. "C'est un garçon," she said. "It's a boy," she repeated as she ran her hands over his body to make him cry.

Sylvie and Baptiste held their breath waiting for his wail. "Il est vivant!" they cried seconds later. "He's alive! He's alive!"

He grew dimpled like his father and green-eyed like Sylvie;
his hair was the colour of fertile soil, and he was baptized
Guillaume Joseph. He received a brother while parliament
discussed conscription for the war in Europe. Then, as a tenth
wedding anniversary present, Sylvie conceived again. There
was peace in the world by then, but flu was spreading wider
than the conflict ever had; it even reached Lasalette.
Baptiste's aunt and uncle had succumbed to it, so Sylvie had
not yet told Baptiste of her fifth pregnancy the morning she
found him in bed unable to move or wake himself for
morning chores.

Sylvie nudged and nagged to no avail. "Franchement," she
complained as she lit the lantern. She shrieked when she saw
the blue tint of his face. "Baptiste! Wake up!" She shook his
shoulders, tapped his cheeks. He grumbled groggily. She
rushed to the washstand for water, soaked a cloth, and
returned to the bed. She rubbed Baptiste's face with the cold
dampness. "Viens, mon amour," she encouraged. "Wake up."
He spoke, but his voice made no words. Sylvie swallowed to
stop the knots of anxiety forming in her stomach. "Shhh.
Don't talk." Her voice seemed too calm for someone so
fretted. "Rest."

He closed his eyes again, and Sylvie slipped out of the
room and rushed to the kitchen. She stoked the fire, set the
kettle to boil while she rummaged for a bottle of the
prohibited whiskey he had cached about the house. "No one's
going to tell me what to do in my own home," he had insisted
when the law had passed. She had tsked but had submitted
to his convictions.

She found a three-quarter-full bottle among the store of

potatoes and made her way back to the kitchen, where she pulled out mustard powder, flour, and oil. She found muslin in the drawer and dropped it in boiling water, then mixed up a paste in a small bowl. Her lips moved as fast as her hands, "Je vous salue Marie pleine de grâce ..."

She carried everything—whiskey, water, mustard, and muslin—up the stairs on a tray. "Mon amour," she said as she tended to Baptiste. "Drink this." She raised his head and tipped a tumbler of watered whiskey between his lips. She kissed his head, lay him back down on his back and opened his pyjamas. "I've made a plaster," she told him, "so be still." She applied oil to his broad, tight chest, then wrung out the hot muslin and spread the mustard paste over it. She applied the prepared cloth, covered it with a towel, and buttoned his pyjamas closed. Then she pulled up the covers and tucked them about him. "I'm going for help," she said. "Don't die." It was both an order and a prayer.

She rushed into the children's room, snatched up the youngest and pulled the older behind her. "We have to go see Mémère," she said. Guillaume mumbled and rubbed his eyes but followed without protest.

Sylvie did not take the time to hitch a buggy for the children nor even to saddle the horse. She wrapped young Antoine about herself as she had seen Cree mothers do and set Guillaume on the horse. Then she jumped on behind him and grabbed up its mane and Guillaume's small hands with her own before kicking the animal into motion. He complied and shot forward as she yelled, "Ya! Ya!"

"Pas si vite, Maman!" Guillaume cried, "Not so fast!" but she raced onward.

"There's no time for slower, mon chou. Hold tight. Say your prayers."

Neither would ever recall more than that, but she arrived

at her parents' home and called for her father as soon as she saw the house. He ran out to the frosted grass. "Mon Dieu! What is it?"

"Baptiste. The doctor. Quick!" She passed Guillaume to him and unbound Antoine from her back. "Quick!"

Baptiste seemed bluer when Sylvie returned, and the plaster had turned cold. She threw it aside and washed away the oil and residue. A cough seized him; she helped him onto his side and held him while he tried to clear his lungs. When at last the fit passed, she laid him down, wiped his brow, and wrapped him up with blankets again. She gave him more whiskey and made another plaster.

She had prayed a year's worth of Aves by the time the doctor arrived. "He's lucky to have you," he said as he examined Baptiste.

"It's not luck," she replied. "It's love. Will he be alright?"

"God willing."

"Oui, but what can I do?"

"Not much. It's the Spanish Flu, like with your in-laws. Best keep the children away again. And you, you should cover your face while you tend to him like you did before. And wash your hands with soap before you do anything else."

"Oui. Oui. But for Baptiste?"

"Open the window. Give him this Aspirin. Make him soup."

It was such simple advice from an educated man, and it had not worked for the aunt and uncle. Sylvie wondered if her poor English had caused her to miss something more medical in the prescription, but when her father came in from tending to the livestock, he assured her that it was the treatment of the masses, so Sylvie nursed Baptiste with soup and Aspirin and air.

She sat beside him through the day and lay beside him through the night. Seven nights in, he hooked his finger about hers as they slept. Five days later, she took on his symptoms, and he did the nursing as best he could. She survived, and so did the hidden baby she had not yet told him about.

It was a girl named Marie. Juliette came the following year, then Rose and Louise each in their own time. By then, Baptiste had replaced the piece-meal house he and his uncle had erected with an Ideal Home chosen from the *T. Eaton Company Plan Book*.

It was a large house with porches in both the front and the back. There was a living room and a parlour, a dining room and a kitchen with a bedroom tucked off to the side, and a pantry for the family's provisions. There was hand-pumped running water, but still no electricity as there was back east. There was enough room for eight children to sleep two-by-two, however, and an attic, and enough land and air and sunshine for Baptiste to call his prairie home Heaven on Earth despite the daily toil of living on the land.

He liked spring best—the promises that pushed through the thawed earth and the bare boughs of trees—but summer was fine, too, with saskatoon berry pie and ice cream made if it happened to hail. "It's from Heaven," he would say of the ice, "even if it's smashed the crops and garden to Hell." The fall was always a race against the sunlight and the weather. It pushed humans and beasts and even machines to the limits of endurance. Then winter came, so long and white. Sylvie liked it best: the snow-covered prairie glistening like a field of diamonds, and Baptiste snuggled close beside her through the cold, long nights.

Whatever the season, the prairie sky was an endless canopy of colour: blue or grey; orange, mauve and pink; black velour bejewelled with stars; radiant streaks of green;

dancing white lights. There were powerful storms, too: blizzards that erased the face of the barn; tornadoes that carried off neighbours' homes or the church steeple; rain and wind that blew the hair off your head, Baptiste liked to say; thunder that cracked and growled and rattled windows and shook the ground; lightening that lit the sky in flashes or in zags and zaps. Baptiste marvelled at the power of it; Sylvie quivered with fear. The storms always passed; the sky always turned blue. Rainbows rose in July, and sun dogs haloed the winter sun with the promise of warmer days.

The children grew and helped in the house and field, in the garden and barn. They had shoes and boots, mittens and scarves, hats and coats, sweaters and socks, night clothes and day clothes, church clothes, school clothes, and home clothes. They ate three meals a day and knew of snacks and treats. Baptiste gave them music; Sylvie regaled them with stories of Ponik the lake monster and of flying canoes, of blueberries that grew in the Canadian west. The children joined in—they took up spoons, jigged, and sang. They were happy, even with teasing and petulance and ill-will that flared from time to time. Baptiste and Sylvie were not immune to such variances, both as parents and as spouses, but like birds, they preened themselves after a storm and cooed and sang once again.

Then came a decade of trial straight from Hell: dust storms, tornadoes, hail, blight, drought, grasshoppers that descended in a humming mass to eat through everything, including the leather tractor seat. The sun burned red like a bloody host because of the dirt suspended in the air. Sylvie pulled the children onto their knees in quaking apocalyptic fear and led them in prayer.

Baptiste wandered his cracked fields and pulled on his chin, ground his teeth, and clenched up his fists until he found the strength to hold on to everything that was blowing away.

Then he returned to the house and pulled out his fiddle and played until his hands no longer felt useless. Sylvie could not endure the sound. She fled from the room, shut herself away in their bedroom and cried. Baptiste joined her when he was ready. He rapped on the door like an apology before he slipped in and sat beside her on their bed. "Mon amour," he whispered, touching her back.

"I can't," she sobbed, "can't feed my children gopher anymore!"

"I know," he mumbled.

"Gopher!" she shrieked.

"It tastes like chicken," he lied with tears that made him look away and press his fingers together and pump them until words came, "I've failed you."

"Non, Baptiste! The land has. And maybe even God. But not you." She wrapped her arms about him and pressed her cheek to his. "Not you." He remained like stone.


"The boys are leaving," Baptiste said one day. "Lapointe'll give 'em both five cents a day to ride west with his cattle. And then they'll stay." His back began to shake as he announced their young adult sons' plans, "Get jobs. Send money home." Sylvie took in the news, sucked it in deep to her bones. "What kind of man am I to need my sons to do such a thing? I'm the one who should leave."

"No! I need you. I need you here with me."

They fell into an embrace of tears and kisses and promises from the days of their youth, promises to love and honour for better and for worse. A baby came of it, though Sylvie, not yet forty, had thought she had become as infertile as the wind-gutted land. She did not hope nor pray that he would live, but neither did she want him to join his siblings in the sky—the two she never knew, and her first-born, too, her sweet Guillaume, who, just months after leaving home, fell from a boxcar while riding the rails looking for a better fortune than what he had found in Kelowna and what he had left in Lasalette.

Sylvie made swaddling from the clothes Guillaume had left behind, and she added his name to the baby's when he was born in the spring. Two years later, she added Antoine's name to another baby, for Antoine was also gone, though he was alive and well, making enough money to send crisp bills home every four to six weeks. Antoine had the good fortune that Guillaume had not: work, love, marriage, and children, as well as the inheritance of a grocery store from his father-in-law. He shared the blessings with his family and sent for his sisters, first Marie, then Juliette, to help his wife with the children she and he made.

Rose and Louise stayed home; they were younger and were needed there. They learned the intricacies of reusing water for washing hands and clothes and dishes, the knack of slicing carrots and potatoes paper-thin so to make one or two tubers feed a table of six. They learned, too, that not all men were like their father or their brother.

Baptiste and Sylvie already knew this, but they did not know such a lesson would ever be learned under their roof, especially not from Serge Ouellette, the young man they took into their home one dusty day—he was a local boy, their children's friend; Baptiste and Sylvie had watched him be baptized and receive all his sacraments. Nonetheless, he was Rose and Louise's depraved instructor.

He left before the girls grew tongues and the parents found out, but not before he had left a child growing inside of Rose. She figured out a solution all on her own, and life tumbled onward like weeds in the wind.

The great trials known as The Dirty Thirties ended around that time, once the rain started to fall at the proper time and the rust fungus and hail stayed away, the grasshoppers, too as if they were unaware that anything had once again grown in that corner of the world. Baptiste and the few remaining men of Lasalette cut their first crops in ten years. Sylvie and the women harvested their gardens. Their daughters helped can, pickle, and preserve; they prepared meals for the men who had not been driven away by the dust.

Sylvie and Baptiste were exhausted from the work but relieved to finally see their land produce enough for themselves and for the market. They fell asleep at night with smiles on their lips and their hands entwined. A train whistle, however, would often wake Sylvie and pull tears from her eyes for her son the steam machine had taken from her. She would roll into Baptiste's side and follow the rise and fall of his chest. He too had left on a train, she remembered, but she had followed and found him in a corner of the prairies that he called The Promised Land. Sylvie no longer believed that it was, but when Baptiste turned towards her in his sleep, she knew it was where she belonged.

The baby boys grew. The girls moved on. A new routine took hold of Baptiste and Sylvie's life, along with wrinkles and silver hair, children-in-law and grandchildren. Sylvie liked it, the comfort and regularity after so many years. There were still challenges, of course, and another World War, but it all seemed less daunting somehow than it had during the decades before. *Maybe,* Sylvie thought, *because there are fewer mouths to feed and no more babies.*

Their youngest children, the boys born in dust and drought, were already in their teens. It seemed it would be them, not the eldest, who would take over the farm, continue to work the land on which she and Baptiste had toiled. It pained her sometimes, like an ache, the way things had turned out: Guillaume buried in a distant grave, Antoine two provinces away. They had been the first to cry and to suck from her breast. They had been the ones Baptiste had said would grow up to be farmers, yet both were gone. Their daughters were gone, too: Marie and Juliette down east to work in factories, Louise to nurse in the city, Rose in her own home married to a black-haired man named Pierre.

Sylvie knew their absence made the house quieter and life simpler; still, she thought of them while she worked in the kitchen, prayed for them as she cooked, cleaned, and sewed. Baptiste was the same, though his prayer was cattle and grain, and fiddle music on rainy afternoons.

Then one Tuesday in April, when everything was as it should be that time of year—the sky the colour of Mary's cloak and tree branches swelling with buds—Baptiste crossed to the house from the barn while Sylvie prepared their lunch. She saw him from the window as she moved about, setting the table and stirring pots. He would be at the door in a moment. She would hear his footsteps on the veranda, then the door would creak as he opened it. He would greet her from the porch as he shuffled off his overalls and kicked off his boots. He would kiss her on his way to the sink, where he would wet and lather his hands with soap. "Mmmm! It smells good in here," he would say. "Let's eat!"

Sylvie sliced the bread, salted the potatoes, and stirred the gravy. She dashed and hurried about, then stopped suddenly as if seized by an invisible vice. She stood frozen for a moment. Her ears rang, and her stomach knotted. There, through the window, stood Baptiste, his face twisted and contorted. Sylvie's legs carried her without command into the yard. She saw him fall, heard him thud against the thawing ground. She ran to him, knelt beside him in the muck, and pulled his head onto her lap. "Baptiste! Baptiste!"

"Berry," he said before he slipped away.


These were the things Sylvie thought of while others slept, sounding out a symphony of snores. When she, too, fell asleep, she saw her Baptiste, young and strong again, stooking hay in the eastern field. He was a man of muscle and earth that made her swoon. He always stopped his work and looked at her, smiled, and waved. She waved back and ran towards him, ran and ran until the lights came on and a new day began. Then she lived and dreamed again and again, until at last, she reached him in that golden field.

## 7. Minuet I
## April 1990

While Stéphanie sang, Christianne finished dressing in the adjacent bedroom. She wore a mid-thigh denim skirt and crimson ruffle crop top and attached a black velour choker at the back of her neck before she set about taming her long permed hair with mousse and hairspray. As she was passing a wand of lip gloss over her lips, Alex tapped on the door and opened it at the same time. "Salut," he said with a joyfulness that washed over him as soon as he saw her.

"Hi," she replied with the same happiness, but it fell away as she strode toward him and saw a tightness in his face that did not match his tone from seconds before. "Are you okay?"

He pushed out a smile and placed his hand on the small of her back. "Yeah. You just caught me for a second."

She wrapped her hands about his neck. "Caught you?" she laughed. "You're the one who walked in on me." He chuckled with her, though his eyes were filled with tears. She cupped her hands to his face. "Hey?"

"Sorry," he said. "I know we agreed to just enjoy the weekend, but, like I said, you caught me."

She rubbed the roughness of his stubbly cheeks. "Don't say you're gonna miss me," she ordered to keep her own emotions at bay.

He swallowed back the lump in his throat. "I won't," he promised.

"Good," she said and tossed her head to clear the tears from her eyes as she stepped out of their embrace. "So, I hear you and Stéph had a little chat?" She said to change the topic.

"Yeah," He tittered and nervously ran his hand over his thigh and the engagement ring in his pocket. "She was singing to the flowers when I went out for a smoke."

Christianne's voice and eyebrows rose with interest. "Singing?" she asked with excitement. "What?"

Alex shrugged. "I don't know. Nothing I recognized."

Christianne pressed on, "Well, was it religious or folk?"

"Folk."

"Hmm." She considered the possible meaning behind Stéphanie's singing before asking for more information, "And she talked to you after that, right? Like, about personal stuff?"

Alex rubbed his thigh again. *Very personal*, he thought with a smile that would have betrayed his covert proposal planning had Christianne not been so intent on talking about her cousin. "What did you talk about?" she asked.

"Wouldn't you like to know?" he teased.

"Ha-ha," she responded as she rolled her eyes and sat down on the bed.

Alex laughed and raised his hands in surrender. "Okay, okay. Do you want the play by play or the Coles notes?"

"Coles," she said as he sat beside her, "but I have the right to ask for clarification and details."

"Fine," he agreed. He put his arm around her and kissed her head before he began. "First it was small talk, then she gave me the third degree."

"About Clem's sauce?" she guessed.

"Yep."

"Figures," she scoffed.

"She's not wrong," Alex said. "It is illegal."

"So is underaged drinking, but that didn't stop Miss Goody-Two-Shoes from getting wasted the night of her parents' wedding."

"Stéphanie?" Alex gasped as Christianne cringed.

"Oops. I wasn't supposed to tell you that."

"Why? What's the big deal?"

"Nothing if it were you or me, but Stéph? She holds herself to this super high standard. Plus, her mom and dad … I told you, right? Matante was hooked on painkillers forever, and Robbie's an alcoholic. Sober now, but you know?"

Alex's head bobbed. "Makes sense, but still …" He turned up his hands. "Once. Is it really that big of a deal?"

"I don't think so, but Stéph was so embarrassed by it that she spent the next day hiding from everyone. Then she was off to Granby, and well, you saw the video."

"What does that have to do with it? Did the wedding turn into a bender, or something?"

"No," Christianne laughed at the idea. "No, that was her on music. You don't know because you've never seen her that way, but before all this stuff with her parents? She could really rip right into it."

"Like in that song on the tape? The one Michel likes? *À la volette*?"

"Yeah. That was the last time she sang like that."

"Why?"

She grimaced and sadly shook her head. "Our pépère." Alex rubbed her knee in sympathy for the still-fresh loss. She placed her hand over Alex's and rubbed it. "He told her it was wrong to sing like that in public."

"Like what? She was good."

"Yeah, she was," Christianne said, "but it was a bit too heavy for him."

"So, I take it he wasn't into AC/DC?" he said, like a buoy for her heart.

She smiled at him. "No, but he liked Stéph's music. He even liked that performance. He just wanted her to deal with her pain in private instead of onstage. And Stéph, well, she didn't know how to do that, so she just stopped singing everything but school stuff. And even then …" She shook her head, looking for words to explain herself. "It's just notes, you know? Not fire like it used to be. Like it was at Granby. That was the biggest fuck you, I've ever heard."

He choked at her use of the expression. "What?"

"You heard me."

"I did, but I've never heard Stéphanie say that, and I sure didn't hear it in that song."

Christianne's chuckled. "That's because you weren't listening between the notes."

He raised an eyebrow. "Huh?"

She nodded at his confusion. "It's hard to explain. I don't really understand it myself, except that when she's in the zone, every note means more than you think."

"Okay, so what's inside *À la volette* that makes you think it's an F-you?"

"It's about her mom and dad, about them finally getting together."

"You've told me about that. It doesn't sound very 'Fuck you' to me."

"It's not, except if you're the kid who lost out on all those years, and there was all this secrecy about who your dad was. Maybe it is then?"

"Hmmm. So, is that why she said she doesn't want to go home?"

Christianne's mouth dropped open, and she stared at him as if he had just confessed that he was an alien. "She said that? Holy shit."

"Why? You don't either."

She turned to face him and touched her hand to his cheek. "That's 'cause I don't want to leave *you*." He placed his hand over hers and moved it towards his lips. He kissed it, and their eyes locked and filled with tears. Christianne squeezed hers shut and fought to hold them back. "Don't say it," she said.

"I won't," he replied.

Neither moved nor spoke for a long sad moment until Christianne pulled away and raised her head like a wolf picking up a scent.

"What's wrong?" Alex asked.

A smile spread over her face. "Nothing. Listen."

He cocked his head. "Stéph?" Christianne nodded; her eyes shone like sun-kissed water. "What's she singing? *À la claire fontaine*?"

"Mmmhmm."

Alex touched her cheek and smiled at her misty eyes. "What's it about? The song between the notes?"

"Our great-grandparents. Sylvie and Baptiste. How they lived happily ever after on a quarter section of land out by Lasalette. But it wasn't as easy as all that. There was a lot of loss and pain that cracked them and tried them, and some would even say killed poor Baptiste there on his farm before he was even sixty. But Grand-mère Sylvie ..." She sniffed and wiped away a tear that had slid from her eye. "Bin, she loved him for the rest of her life."

"I'd like that," Alex said.

"Like what?"

"To live with you through good times and bad." She started to respond, but he slipped from the bed and dropped onto one knee. He pulled out the diamond ring from his pocket before Christianne realized what was happening. He raised the ring like a host and said, "Will you marry me?"

She blinked a Morse code for a moment as it all sunk in. Then she cried, "Yes!" and dropped to the floor and threw her arms about him. "Mon Dieu, Alex! Oui! Oui!" They kissed and hugged and tumbled over as Stéphanie sang on in Marie-Geneviève's pink bedroom. They let out hoots of laughter and whoops of joy that Stéphanie did not hear but drew Jean-François and Michel to the room.

"What the fuck?" Jean-François asked squinting at the toppled, giddy couple.

Michel smacked his chest, "Hey, come on man. Language."

He grimaced. "What? Fuck. Look at them."

Michel turned towards them and fell into their happiness. "What's going on?"

"We just got engaged," Alex said as he set himself upright.

"Really?" Michel exclaimed. He rushed towards them and gave them hugs. "That's fantastic! Congratulations!"

Jean-François raised his eyebrows, "I thought that was for tomorrow."

"It was," Alex laughed, "but …" He raised his hand to indicate Stéphanie's singing. "It was perfect."

"You had something planned?" Christianne asked, turning towards him for the details.

"Yeah. Dinner and flowers and the guys and Stéphanie were gonna sing—"

"Bolton," Jean-François scoffed.

"*How Can I Live Without You?*" Christianne asked Alex.

"Mmhmm." He smiled.

"Like the first time we …?" He nodded; she snuggled into him. "That's sweet."

Jean-François plowed on as if they had not spoken, "I thought of this," he said, pointing to the melody coming from Marie-Geneviève's bedroom. "I guess she agreed, eh Michel?"

He shook his head, and his forehead furrowed. "No. Actually, she said it'd be too hard with everything."

Jean-François made a face of impatience and confusion. "What everything? And why the hell's she singing it then?"

"I don't know," Michel said.

"I do," Christianne offered.

"I like the sound of that," Alex said, nuzzling into her.

"Me, too," she agreed and turned to kiss him.

"Fffuck," Jean-François complained at the distraction from the conversation at hand.

"Lay off," Michel chided. "They just got engaged."

"I don't care."

"Yes, you do. You're just being an ass pretending you don't."

Jean-François snorted but said nothing more until Christianne and Alex stopped kissing. "So?"

"So, what?" she asked.

He heaved a sigh at her lapse of attention. "Why's Stéphanie singing this song if she told Michel she couldn't?"

"Because it's what she does."

He rolled his eyes at the vague answer. "What is?"

Michel answered, "Sing when she's working things out."

Christianne chuckled. "Yeah. How'd you know that?"

He shrugged, but his eyes glistened like syrup being poured over snow to make taffy. "We were out all night."

She nodded at the information for a moment before she asked, "Are you sure about her?"

He looked directly at her and said, "Yes."

She held his gaze and continued like a guardian, "For

yourself *and* Plumeau? Because that's a lot."

"I know," he said. "But I want her in my life, and—"

"In your bed?" Jean-François teased.

Michel tittered and flushed. "Yeah, I want her there, but not in the way you make it sound, you sleazebag."

Jean-François snorted at the insult and turned to Christianne, "Do you think she'll say yes?"

"Yes."

His face lit up. "Really?"

She nodded. "Yeah, but you have to give her time."

"Time? Fffuuck. How much?"

"That depends," she said.

"On what?"

She pointed at the invisible melody turning about them. "That."

"What she sings?" Michel asked; Christianne's eyebrows rose with surprise. He chuckled and explained, "We talked a lot when we were out."

"I see that. Did she tell you about *Stabat mater dolorosa*?"

Michel rubbed his lips together as he thought back through their hours of conversation and song. "No. I don't think so."

"What's that?" Jean-François asked.

"Something our Pépère used to sing," Christianne said. "It's powerful, and if Stéphanie sings it, there's a pretty good chance she'll say yes."

"Great," Jean-François replied. "So, we'll just ask her to sing it."

Christianne shook her head. "Oh, I wouldn't do that."

"No," agreed Michel. "She's gotta get there on her own."

Christianne gasped at his insight. "Wow, you two really did talk." Michel glowed.

Jean-François powered on, "How the hell's she gonna get there?"

"That's a good question," Christianne said. "Everyone in our family's been waiting for it for almost two years." Jean-François grumbled; she pointed at the air again and at the sound of Stéphanie's voice, "But we've been waiting for this, too, and here it is."

"So, it could happen?" he asked with the eagerness of a puppy.

She nodded and shrugged. "Maybe."

"Really? This weekend?"

"Possibly."

"Hmm," Jean-François sounded.

Michel clapped Jean-François' shoulder. "That's the best you're gonna get, buddy."

"Pfffuck." He rolled his eyes and turned his attention towards what he did know. "So," he said to Alex and Christianne with a grin, "you two are engaged, eh?"

Alex grinned back with a smile as large as a looming long weekend. "Yeah."

"Well, congratulations!" Jean-François hugged Alex, then turned to Christianne and caught her by the biceps. "And you, too, little miss." He kissed her cheeks. "Did the numbskull give you a ring?"

"Yes!" She held out her hand like a rake; he took hold of it and lifted it higher to his eyes.

"Beautiful. Good choice, Alley. For the ring and the girl."

"Thanks."

Jean-François clicked his tongue, then dropped his arms about the couple's shoulders. "Let's go celebrate. You two okay with Perrier? We're gonna be working later."

"Sure," Alex replied. "As long as we celebrate!"

Jean-François steered them towards the stairs. "Oh, we will! Come on! Let's go!"

"I'll be down in a minute," Michel said. "I wanna listen to

the end of this."

"It could go on for a while," Christianne warned, "if she gets on a roll."

Michel's face rose into a smile. "Well, let's hope she does."

Alex chuckled and shook his head at him. "Gawd, you've got it bad."

"Yeah, I do," he agreed. "Do you mind?"

"What? That you're infatuated with my fiancée's cousin?"

"Fiancée!" Christianne giggled. "I like that."

"Me, too."

Michel smiled at them. "Yeah, it's got a good ring to it, but I meant if I hang up here for a while?"

"Go ahead," Alex said. "We'll catch up later." He turned away and descended with the others, laughing and talking like parakeets.

## 8. Minuet II
## April 1990

When Stéphanie reached the end of her song, she was thinking about her great-grandparents, Baptiste and Sylvie, and of the day after Sylvie's funeral when she and Christianne stumbled upon a black valise in a closet as they were putting away table linens for their grandmother. "Hey? What's this?" nine-year-old Stéphanie had asked, squatting down to get a better look. "A violin?" Her voice rose with excitement, and she pulled it from its hiding place on the floor beneath the shelves.

"Maybe," Christianne had replied. "Grand-père Baptiste had one."

"Well, I'm pretty sure that's what this is! Can we look at it?"

Christianne shrugged. "I don't see why not."

Stéphanie flicked open the clasp and raised the lid. "Wow," she sounded as she ogled the grain of the wood and the handcrafted edges, "what a beaut."

"Really?"

"Yeah. Look." She clutched up the instrument and showed the cinnamon-coloured wood to the other girl. "See the grain? And these stripe marks?"

"Sure," Christianne said, reaching out to touch the violin. "It kind of looks like a calico cat."

"Huh. You're right. It does."

"I've never seen it before."

Stéphanie tilted her head. "Really? Why not?"

Christianne moved a shoulder. "Probably 'cause no one here knows how to play."

"I do," Stéphanie said.

"Really? Cool. Play something."

Stéphanie shook her head as she passed her thumb across the strings. "No. If these strings've been on here since he died, I don't think it's a good idea. I might wreck something."

Christianne waved away the idea. "So? No one's playing it anyway."

"Hmmm." Stéphanie rubbed her lips together as she wrestled with temptation.

"What? You do play, right?"

"Of course. I've had lessons since I was three."

"Three? What are you? Some kind of Mozart or something?"

Stéphanie flushed. "No. Maman just has a lot of musician friends, so I get all kinds of lessons."

Christianne rolled her eyes. "Ugh! What is it with parents and lessons? Sheesh! Mine make me take piano, and I hate it."

"It's not my favourite either. I like to hold my instruments, but it's the base of everything, so I have to do it. Maman says I can quit once I get my grade eight, though."

"That'll take forever!"

"No, just a year or two. Depends on how hard I work." Christianne's face twisted, and her eyes rounded. "What?" Stéphanie asked.

"You're in grade eight piano?"

"Not quite. But probably by January."

"Câline! I'm still in the ABC books."

"That's okay," Stéphanie assured. "We all start somewhere."

"Yeah, but I've been playing forever!"

Stéphanie's face scrunched as she tried to make sense of the information. "How long's forever?"

"Since grade one."

"Hmm." She winced as she dared to ask, "Do you practice?"

Christianne snorted, "Of course! Every Saturday."

"What about the rest of the week?"

"What about it?"

"Do you practice during it?"

Christianne grimaced. "You sound like my dad!"

"Sorry," Stéphanie mumbled

Christianne gave her a playful shove. "Forget about it. Let's just play. Here," she handed Stéphanie the bow, "you be the symphony; I'll be the audience."

Stéphanie chuckled at the idea, yet she took the bow and turned the end screw. "Okay, but this bow's pretty rough, and I don't see any rosin in the case."

"What's that?"

"This sticky stuff you rub on the bow to make it work better."

"Do you really need it? I mean, it's just a game."

Stéphanie sputtered and blinked at her cousin, so similar in size and shape, but completely different in complexion and personality. "Music's not a game."

Christianne laughed at the seriousness, "Oh-kay."

Stéphanie's face flushed with embarrassment. "I can play without it," she said before Christianne could criticize or tease any further, "but I need to tune it first." She set the sculpted wood to her left shoulder and turned her jaw onto the chin rest. It was a quarter size bigger than she was used to, but still the fit was comfortable. She raised her right arm and approached the bow to the strings. They squeaked and squealed as she played. Stéphanie fiddled with the tuning pegs and bowed the strings over and over until, at last, the instrument was tuned. She reeled off a series of arpeggios.

"Ah, so you can play," Christianne smiled. "I thought maybe you were just a duck."

"Ha-ha. Here's some Mozart for you." She offered a few phrases of the sonata she had been working on before leaving Basel."

"That's really cool. Why'd you stop?"

"I gotta tune it again," she answered as she adjusted the tension of the D string.

"I guess that's one good thing about the piano—you never have to tune it."

"Not never," Stéphanie said even as she worked with the violin. "You should get it done at least once a year."

"Oh? We've never done it."

"Maybe that's why you hate it so much," Stéphanie suggested.

"No. I hate it 'cause it's stupid."

"It's not stupid. It's just ..." She made a face and shrugged. "Not the violin." She reset her great-grandfather's instrument into place and began to play again.

"Hey! That's Star Wars!"

"Yep." Stéphanie grinned and continued with a medley of themes from the soundtrack until their grandfather joined them in the hallway.

"Ah, I see you found something." He smiled so honestly that Stéphanie did not feel a hint of guilt for having taken out the instrument and playing it without permission.

"Was it really Grand-père Baptiste's?" she asked.

"Mmm-hmm. But it can be yours now if you want it."

Her eyes rounded and her mouth formed an O. "Oui, Pépère! Oui!" More than a decade later, she could still feel the warmth of his hug and smell his personal bouquet of sawdust, Zest, and bacon. "S'il te plaît!"

"Alright," he chuckled. "But if you take it, you must play it."

"Oh, I will," she promised with the truest integrity of a child. "Every day!"

She had been true to her word for nine years, then Granby happened, and she had left Baptiste's violin in its case for days and weeks, sometimes even months. Now, when she took it out, she did not play it. Instead, she held it on her knees and stroked the striped wood almost as if it were a piece of Christ's cross. She looked at it and wept, but no song worthy of the instrument ever rose to her heart.

Her eyes filled as she thought about it, there in Marie-Geneviève's old pink bedroom. Her throat grew thick with emotion that she tried to swallow away, but it was as strong as her tears, and she could do nothing but choke and sob, collapse on the floor and beg her grandfather to forgive her. "It's just too hard," she told his spirit, "to play like you want me to."

She felt an answer rise inside of her like a thawing, and she turned it about her head for a long, long time. "I just want you to play," it said. "Sing. Make music."

She trembled at the message, then squeezed down her tears and mopped her face with her hands. "I'll try," she whispered. Then she swallowed and breathed and started to sing once again.

### Vise le noir et tue le blanc

Robbie went to the hospital, but he did not go into Émilie's room. Instead, he watched her from the doorway. Her eyes were closed, and her hair was fanned about her like a lion's mane. There was a red scrape on her cheek and a cast on her right wrist. Her lips were parted, and her chest rose and fell as air passed through her. It made him tremble to see her so broken and pale and alive.

"She'll be okay," Martin said arriving behind him.

"No, she won't."

"Sure. The doctor said."

Robbie shook his head. "That's just her bones."

Martin ignored the comment. "Wanna go in?"

"Yeah, but there's some funeral stuff I have to do." He sniffed and started away before Martin could see his tears.

"You need any help?" Martin called after him.

Robbie stopped and shook his head. "No. But Em does. Stay with her, okay?"

"Okay," Martin said, then went in and stood watch over her from the wall. He, too, was scraped and bruised, but he was sewn up and commissioned to be with his family, which he did with a furrowed brow and a pain-filled scowl.

Pierre was much better at it—he sat next to Émilie's bed,

clutching her unbroken left hand and muttering prayers. It reminded Martin of a painting a teacher had shown in school the previous year. Roch had laughed at her slide show and struck a pose with his finger in the air as he mimicked her, "Edvard Munch. A beautiful convergence of Expressionism and Impressionism. Just look at the thick layers of antipasto."

"Impasto," Robbie corrected.

"What?"

"Impasto. It's thick paint. Pasto. Like paste."

Roch pushed him in the arm. "Shut up, Encyclopedia Man." Robbie gritted his teeth.

"I'm playing in the Impressionist class at the music festival," Émilie said to take the attention off Robbie. "*La cathédrale engloutie*. It's Debussy." Roch winked at her and clicked his tongue. Robbie stared at her with adoration. She smiled at him but then turned shy and tucked her hair behind her ear and fingered her earring.

*Câline*, Martin sighed, *those three*.

Back at the Thibaud house, Jean-Jos, the eldest Thibaud son, said, "Maman would like his brothers to carry him."

Robbie nodded, but his face twisted, and his eyes ran. "I can't," he sobbed.

"You don't have to. Maman just thought …"

"It's probably not easy for him," another brother said, "them being twins and all."

Robbie choked on the word. Jean-Jos squeezed his shoulder. He offered his son, six months Robbie's junior, to take his place, "Mathieu can do it for you."

Robbie shook his head and fought for words. "No. It should be Martin."

"Tremblay?" Robbie's head bounced up and down. "But Mathieu's family," his brother said.

Robbie wiped his face with his hand and found words

inside his sticky mouth. "So's Martin."

Jean-Jos raised his eyebrows but bent to his young brother's request. "Fine. I'll ask him."

Martin was speechless when he was asked a few hours later during a condolence call. It seemed wrong to be asked such a thing: to carry your best friend to his grave when you were only fourteen. "It's too hard for Robbie," Jean-Jos explained, "you know, since they were twins and all."

"They don't like that," Martin blurted.

"Like what?"

"Being called twins."

"Oh?" The Thibaud siblings looked at each other, surprised by such an idea.

"But they are," one said.

"No," Martin said, "they just look like it."

The truth of it hit Robbie like a punch. He stumbled away from the conversation and pushed his way through the house, crowded with relatives and neighbours and friends. He met his eldest sister-in-law as he hurried upstairs. She touched his arm like the practiced mother she was. "How are you doing? Do you want something?"

He shook his head and mumbled, "Just to be alone."

She nodded in understanding. "Go to your room. I'll keep everyone out."

"Thanks," he gasped and stumbled away, but he went to Roch's room instead of his own. It was a shrine not yet entered by anyone but him. He looked about at the tidy room.

*Maman must've passed through*, he thought, *when she was getting ready for me to come home.* His eyes filled at the thought of his return a few days before: the long bus ride from St. Boniface to Stoughton, the strange feeling he had had in his chest, and the uncontrollable shaking. Then there had been the strangeness between him and his parents when they met him—disappointment and relief and worry all wrapped in hugs and false cheer that turned to silence as they drove the rest of the way home.

When he saw the lights up ahead, white and blue and red, a heaviness crushed his stomach; a ringing wailed in his ears. His father slowed to a stop on the side of the road. Then it was all slow-motion as the vehicles and the people and the words started to make sense.

It was strange fortune, people said, that Francis and Lucille Thibaud should arrive upon the scene of their son's death with his twin in tow. It was incomprehensible, Robbie thought, a test or a joke. He was not sure which. He could not, in fact, even believe that it had happened, but his mother's face insisted that it had, and so did the sinking pit inside of him that grew deeper and deeper with each passing hour.

He walked about Roch's room and touched his things: his trophies and collection of hockey pucks, his shoe boxes of old baseball and hockey cards. He fingered the bristles of Roch's brush and the tangles of brown and copper hair there entwined. Then he grasped the handle and ran the brush through his own short hair in a futile attempt to change a brush cut into a pompadour. He scoffed at the result and exchanged the brush for the bottle of aftershave sitting out on the dresser. He opened it and slapped some on. The smack felt good; he did it a few more times.

Then he leaned towards the mirror and squinted to see if he could find Roch inside his reflection. When he could not, he turned away and riffled through Roch's drawers and closet in a mad hunt for something that would bring out the elements they shared.

He found nothing but a flask of something he soon learned was rye whiskey. He shook the flask and guesstimated that it was still about half full. He screwed off the lid and sniffed the contents; he closed his eyes and held the scent of his brother on Saturday nights. Then he raised the flask to his lips and drank it down, the whole four shots in one hot gulp. He coughed and sputtered and threw himself face down onto his dead brother's bed and wailed.

Émilie lay miles away in a hospital bed in town. She dreamed of her last night with Roch: his hands and his lips, his assurance that everything would be okay. She dreamed of the accident as well, of the swerving and the screaming, the rolling and the banging, and the silence, the black silence, that followed it all.

It caused her to cry and moan and wake up with tears on her face and in her hair. She tried to push herself up, to untangle herself from the sheets and the tubes, but she was lead and cotton, drugged and fractured. She fell back against the pillow and sobbed.

Then, once the tears stopped flowing, she opened her eyes and stared about her at the clean white walls and tile floor. *I was born here*, she thought, *somewhere in this ten-room hospital, and so were Roch and Robbie. Oh God! Robbie? Was he there, or did I just imagine that? Is he home? Is he really home? Oh! How will he ever look at me again?*

It required another dose of barbiturates to stop her crying.

Père Letendre went to visit her. He took her confession, cursory as it was: "I have sinned …" choked between sobs. He gave her absolution, blessed her with holy water, and anointed her broken wrist with oil. He gave her Communion and practiced his funeral sermon about eternity as she drifted to sleep.

Her music teacher, Soeur Saint-Sacrament, also visited. She touched Émilie's cast and talked about both the lord who heals and the composers who wrote pieces for the left hand alone. "We'll work on them when you're ready."

Émilie did not think she ever would be ready, but she found her way to the hospital chapel one day, Roch's funeral day she later learned, and played on the small harmonium with her unbroken hand until she was breathless and out of tears.

Two nurses accompanied her back to bed, while across town, Robbie stumbled down the church aisle between an aunt and a sister-in-law. He was not fit to be at a funeral, let alone a Mass, but it was his duty, so he went, with the strength of two mothers and a few shots of gin holding him together.

In the pew, the women held his hands, and he held theirs, squeezed them until pain replaced the grief in their eyes. *I will not cry*, he told himself, *not here, not now*. He clenched his teeth and set his eyes on the crucified Christ hanging behind the altar. He counted the sculpture's ribs and stared at the slash chiselled into his side.

There were incense and organ music and long prayers that would have driven Roch bonkers if he had been there. Robbie choked on the thought of Roch's absence even though he was there, lying before him in a fine polished coffin. *Roch would hate this*, Robbie thought. *He'd be bouncing his knee and looking up at the ceiling as if it offered a way out of here.* Robbie looked up and wondered where the exit was.

Émilie went home in time, but she did not go to school. She stayed home instead and played the music for left hand that Soeur Saint-Sacrament had given her and studied the notes and texts Martin carried home from school; she memorized Latin words and solved algebraic problems in a forced ambidextrous slant.

She went for walks in the melting snow and dark muck, wandered through the fields she had played in with Martin and the Thibauds as a girl. She walked where the geese grazed and stopped at the place where the accident had happened.

She stood there at the road's edge and studied the snow as it melted and receded. She saw the first green sprigs of spring sprout from the frozen land, too, and the thin silver crocuses reaching up towards the sun. She plucked one, touched the soft mauve petals to her cheek and remembered the crocuses in the churchyard after her First Communion—it had not been Roch who had picked them for her. She stood there and cried.

One day, a car approached and came to a stop nearby. Émilie did not hear it, nor did she hear the door open, and the driver get out. He stood a distance off, ankylosed by the sight of her: her skin was rich cream; her long black hair was tied in an iridescent magpie's tail.

He moved towards her without realizing it and said her name. The sound startled her, and she turned towards it. The movement and the sight made her head swim, and blackness overtook her.

"Émilie!" he cried, rushing to catch her before she fell.

She clutched him and waded her way back through the dizziness. "Robbie."

He stroked her black satin hair. "Are you okay?"

She nodded even as she trembled in the warmth of his embrace and the familiar scent of cedar and rye that was not his. "You are home," she whispered.

She felt him nod. "What are you doing out here?"

"I come here sometimes."

"Why?"

She shook her head and shrugged. "I don't know."

They stood together, then in the silence of the April wind. She shivered; he rubbed her warm. "You're freezing. Let me take you home." Émilie nodded at the offer, but she did not start towards the car. Neither did Robbie.

After a time, she stepped away, sniffed, and wiped her free hand over her cheeks. "Sorry."

He smiled and wiped the tears she had missed. "That's okay. Come, I'll drive you home." She took his hand and let him lead her to his father's car. He opened the passenger door and touched her back as she ducked inside. He watched her pull her legs in, then closed the door for her. He walked around the back of the car so he could stop for a moment, rub his hands over his own face and breathe. She did not notice the delay, for she was thinking how the car smelled the same as the last time she had been in it.

Robbie pulled open the driver's door and slid in behind the wheel. He closed the door and turned to face her. His hair had grown, and his eyes had sunk. She noticed a scar on the side of his face and reached out to touch it. "When did you get that?"

He followed her finger to his temple and touched her hand. He closed his eyes and sighed, "New Year's."

She was choked by memories of finding Roch in the sewing room, but she pressed on in her concern for Robbie, "What happened?"

"I got into a fight," he admitted without looking at her.

"With who?" she asked with surprise

He shook his head and ran his tongue over his lips. "Roch," he said, at last.

She slid closer and rubbed Robbie's arm in comfort. "He hit you?"

"Yeah," he soughed. "After I hit him."

"You? Why?"

He started to say, 'Because I saw him kiss you,' but he saw his wrenched heart in her pale strained face and said something less direct instead, "It's just how we were."

She rubbed his arm in comfort. "I'm sorry."

"Me, too." They remained there like that until the sky turned mauve and the sun dropped low in the horizon. "I should take you home."

"Yeah, but not yet."

"It's late."

"I know, but I'm not ready."

"Me neither. But your mom … And mine. I don't want her to worry."

"How is she?"

Robbie tittered and pushed out a brave smile, "It depends on the day." He turned the ignition and started the car.

"Papa says it's the hardest, losing a child."

Robbie nodded as he set the car into motion; he performed a perfect arc to turn the car towards the Tremblays' farm. "I think it's all hard," he said to the setting sun. "Especially when you look like him."

"You don't. Not to me." He tried to smile, but it came out as a snort. His head bobbed; he rubbed his lips together to keep from crying, and so did Émilie.

"Dusk and dawn," he mumbled.

"They're two different things," she said.

His breath caught. They remained silent until Robbie turned into the Tremblays' yard. "I hope you won't be in trouble. Maybe I should come in and explain?"

"No. You should get home."

He nodded at the responsibility. "Yeah. But I need to tell you something first."

"Oh? What?" His eyes shone like gems. He touched a lock of her hair. The porch light flicked off and on in rapid succession before he could speak. "Sorry. That's probably Maman. I'd better go."

"Yeah."

"Can you come back tomorrow?" His face grew a smile. "After lunch, okay? I'm getting my cast off in the morning."

He nodded at the details. "Sure. Around one?" Her head bounced up and down, and she smiled again, and so did he.

"What the hell are you doing?" Martin demanded later as he and Émilie did the supper dishes a while later. His sleeves were rolled passed his elbows, and he had soap suds halfway up his forearms. She held a plate in the crook of her casted arm and passed a towel over the face of it with the opposite hand.

Émilie jerked with surprise to hear his voice directed at her after the many weeks of silence between them. "What do you mean? This is how I've been doing it the last few weeks."

He snarled, "I'm not talking about the dishes. But when are you getting that damn thing off anyway? I hate washing."

"And you're not very good at it either," she teased. "Look at all this water. Are you trying to take a sponge bath or something?"

"Ha," he snorted. "Aren't you just Lucille Ball?"

"Sheesh. Sorry." She reached for another plate. He sloshed water about as he rinsed off a bowl. "We used to joke."

"Yeah, well, there's not much to joke about these days, is there?" Her eyes smarted; Martin clanked the dishes about in the sink. He growled and gritted his teeth until he could no longer hold back his words. "Did he tell you?" he demanded.

"Who?"

"Robbie."

"Tell me what?"

He shook his head and pulled his hands from the dishwater. "Nothing," he said as he flicked the water from his hands. He grabbed the tea towel from her and rubbed his hands dry.

"He'll tell you when he's ready to get you on your back."

"Ahhh!" she gasped.

"What?" Martin raged, "You think he's any different than Roch?" She stared at him with round, dripping eyes. "Don't look at me like that, you slut!"

"Mar-tin!" Their father barked from the doorway. Both teenagers spun their heads towards him. Émilie caught her mouth to stifle her sobs. "That is no way to speak to your sister!"

"You're right," Martin said, "but it's the only way I've got."

"Then go to your room and find a different one, because that's not how we talk to each other in this house."

"Fine."

Pierre sighed as Martin pounded up the stairs, then he turned towards his daughter. "What was all that about?" Émilie quivered under his obsidian stare. He wrapped his arms about her. "Oh, chérie. There, there." She sobbed into his flannel chest. He kissed her head and stroked her hair, rocked, and swayed, and sang to comfort her, "Stabat mater dolorosa …"

"Why do you sing that?" she asked when he had finished.

"Huh?" he sounded as if he were just waking. "Oh. You know, my maman, she sang it, and it helps me to sing it, too."

"Hmmm."

"Like you and the piano, eh?"

She nodded and blinked back a rush of tears. "Yeah."

"Your grandfather Baptiste was like that with his violin, but Grand-mère Sylvie, she prefers to talk. And Martin, well, he's like your mother— steeping or stewing or—"

"Boiling over?"

He chuckled in agreement. "Oui. Sometimes."

"I broke my wrist once, too," Pierre said as he drove Émilie to town the following morning, "and my foot."

"I know," she mumbled, still heavy from last night's medication.

He patted her knee and told her the story anyway, "My foot was first. I was fourteen. Working in a logging camp in the Bas-Saint-Laurent. We were loading a cart, and a log rolled off and crushed it. Aïe! Such pain! But it could've been worse: it could've been both."

He chuckled and smiled at her. "The doctor set me up and put me in bed for a couple of weeks. Then he sent me home, even though I didn't have one.

"Les Soeurs de Jésus took me in, though. They didn't have to since I was no longer a child, but Soeur Saint-Martin was in charge of the infirmary then, and she insisted. Let me stay for two weeks. And such glorious weeks they were!

"My sister, Émilie, you know, like you." He turned to give her a quick, loving smile, even though he was driving. "She tended to me, and, oh, she was so sweet and pretty. She brought me cookies and played checkers with me for hours. She had cinnamon hair like our maman, and she sang like her, too."

He paused and flexed his lips a few times, shook his head and sniffed away a wave of tears. "She died not long after. In a fire. The whole convent went up. Émilie and Soeur Saint-Martin didn't make it out."

Émilie had no words of sympathy even after her own experience of loss, but her eyes filled with tears. She turned them to the window and stared out at the fields they passed. They were black and tilled, but few had been seeded yet. The trees, clumped here and there, were in bud. The ditches were verdant and thick.

Pierre slowed for the stop sign at the intersection known as Quatre-Coins, a silly name, Émilie had always thought, for every intersection had four corners, but that was how the people of Lasalette called that particular junction of gravel roads east of town.

"My wrist was here," her father said looking both ways before proceeding, "in Lasalette. Just a few weeks after I arrived. Your mother had been reading in Baptiste's wingback chair there in the living room and had fallen asleep. I saw that her blanket had fallen to her feet, and I thought she might get cold, so I bent down to retrieve it, but the motion awakened her, and she jumped and cried, and somehow in all the excitement, I fell backwards and banged my wrist hard against the coffee table.

"It's solid maple, you know, so if you fall with enough force, you can really hurt yourself. Which is what I did. "It was a strange and painful fluke, and your mother, oh, she was so upset. My heart hurt more for her than my broken wrist did."

"And that's why she fell in love with you," Émilie summarized in an attempt to end the conversation.

Pierre smiled. "It was not so simple, but yes, she did, in time, and we married and started anew."


Émilie was at the piano when Robbie arrived that afternoon. He knocked on the back door and entered at Rose's beckoning. He greeted her with reserve and respect. She invited him to have a seat at the table with Pierre and Sylvie, then served him cookies and milk. Pierre made small chat, but Robbie's attention kept wandering to the sounds drifting in from the living room. "You should go in," Pierre said. "The doctor said she shouldn't play too long."

Robbie nodded at the invitation and pushed his chair away. "Okay. Thanks. Thank you for the cookies, Madame Tremblay."

She smiled at him with a sincerity he had never seen before. "Anytime, Robbie. Anytime." He hurried away before one of them lost a tear.

Robbie watched from the doorway and marvelled at Émilie as she rumbled through the one-handed concerto Soeur Saint-Sacrement had given her. Ravel had composed it for a former enemy soldier who had lost his right arm in battle. Robbie did not know this, nor did he care right then as he watched Émilie play along with an orchestra inside her head.

She was focused and intense; her body and her mind were all consumed as she painted with sound. Her fingers ran over the old ivory keys like ripples of rain, then transformed into mallets to punctuate the ending with a series of solid chords.

"Wow," Robbie sighed once the vibrations had settled.

Émilie jumped at the sound. She pressed her hand to her chest to stop its racing, then turned to him. "Robbie. Hi."

Their eyes locked. Robbie opened his mouth, then reclosed it, then opened it again. "What was that?" He finally asked, walking towards her.

"A concerto," she answered, turning shy.

"Are you gonna perform it somewhere?"

"No. It was just to keep me busy while I waited for this." She raised her thin, uncasted hand. She tittered at the reminder of the accident.

Robbie focused on the music, "Well, I'd say it did. It was amazing."

She rocked her head with modesty. "It still needs a lot of work."

"Probably not as much as you think."

"No. It's a big piece. It's still a couple of years away from me yet."

"Years? Really? What does Soeur Saint-Sacrement say?"

"Nothing. I haven't had a lesson since the acc—" She turned away, stared at the piano instead of finishing her sentence. "This is Middle C," she remembered Robbie's mother telling her years before, "wherever you go, you just come back here, and you'll always find your way home."

Robbie sat beside her on the bench. He smelled of cedar and rye once again. The misplaced scent made her dizzy. "Remember this?" He asked, plunking out a doo-wop progression in the bass.

She chuckled at the old duet they had played as children. "Yeah."

"Can you do it with your wrist?"

She considered it as he played on. "I think so." She raised her hands and joined in with the melody of *Heart and Soul* at the start of the next phrase.

"That's it," he grinned. They played through to the end like happy children, then complimented one another.

"You were always a good partner," she said.

"You, too," he replied. He looked into her gem green eyes. "You were also so patient and tolerant of my mistakes."

She smiled, remembering the carefree days of childhood music. "You didn't make that many."

He moved a shoulder like a shrug. "Maybe. But when I make them, they're pretty major." The intensity of his stare caused a lump to form in the back of her throat; she found it hard to breathe. She looked away; he took her hand and slid closer. "Em? I was wrong."

"About what?" she choked with a nervousness she did not understand.

"Being a priest," he said.

Émilie felt her heart skip. Her ears buzzed, and her eyes

widened. "What?"

"I was wrong," he said, again. "I was saved so I could be with you."

She shook her head and blinked. "But you went away."

"Yeah," he agreed, "but then I came back."

"Because of Roch," she said.

"No," he corrected, "That was just a coincidence."

She stared at him with wild, drowning eyes. "What do you mean?"

Robbie's forehead wrinkled. "He didn't tell you?" he asked with surprise.

She trembled. "Tell me what?"

"I was on my way home when it happened."

Her head shook like a weathercock in the foremath of a storm. "No!" she cried. "No, you couldn't've been!"

Robbie nodded. "I was, Em. It was planned for over a week."

"A week?" she gasped. "Did Roch know?"

"Of course. It was supposed to be earlier, but there was a blizzard, and the road was closed." Émilie trembled and began to sway. Robbie squeezed her hand and wrapped his arm about her back. "Are you okay?"

She shook her head. "No. No! You couldn't've been coming back!"

He bobbed his head. "I was." She gasped for words; Robbie went on, "I'm glad you and Martin were with him. He loved you guys. More than he ever loved me."

"No," she said, again still stuck on the idea that Robbie had left the juniorate, was coming home, was not going to be priest.

He thought the response was to his last statement and continued to explain, "You know it's true, Em. For all my trying, Roch and I were never much as brothers. Even less as twins. But I felt him, you know? That night? For the first time in our lives. I felt him right here." He pressed the palm of his hand to his chest and clutched his shirt.

"Near Montmartre. I got this pain, and my ears started buzzing, and I felt like when I was sick except that it just stopped suddenly, and then there was this black silence, and I couldn't stop shaking, and then when we came upon the accident? I knew, knew before I even saw him, because I'd felt it. Felt him die!"

Robbie fell against Émilie and sobbed, clinging to her like a shipwrecked sailor hanging onto wood until her father came into the room to check on them.

"Ça va?" Pierre asked.

Robbie pulled away and wiped his face. "Oh, Monsieur. Yes. Sorry!" He stood and started away.

Pierre caught him. "There's no need to apologize, Robbie. Come. I'll get you some water, and maybe a hanky or two, eh?"

Émilie went the other way. She made a beeline for her room and threw herself face down on her bed. *He knew*, she cried to herself. *Roch knew and never said anything! That rat! How could I've been so stupid?*

She remained in bed for the rest of the day, and the day after that, and the one after that. She slept and woke and slept again, but she could not distinguish one from the other— the dreams and memories, the voices downstairs and the ones in her head, the secrets, and the regrets, they all seemed to bounce off the walls and off one another.

One moment she stared at a picture of herself, Roch, and Robbie in a bassinet, the next at the prayer card from Roch's funeral. She imagined it in her head: the full church, the rising incense, the sobs and sniffles, Lucille Thibaud's shaking shoulders, Francis Thibaud's clenched jaw, Robbie's bowed head, heavy and hanging with the weight of grief. She hugged the old stuffed bear Robbie had given her on their tenth birthday and cried about the accident and the grief she had caused.

The memory of her night with Roch flooded over her time and again: the kissing and touching, the lie that her shaking was from the cold when, in fact, it was from the face, Robbie's face, that appeared when she closed her eyes. She had tried to force it away, but it had remained even as Roch penetrated deeper and deeper inside of her.

"I'm sorry," she had cried afterwards.

"No," Roch said refusing the apology, "I love you."

She did not know, neither the night he had said it nor weeks later, if it had been true, but she did know that he had never been the one she loved. It wrung her, and she threw off her covers and rummaged on her nightstand for the amber pill bottle Dr. Niells had given her when he had sent her home. She popped off the lid and shook out a pair of white disks into the palm of her hand. She raised them to her mouth, dropped them in and swallowed them down dry. *I need to get out of here*, she thought as she paced about her room waiting for the relief the pills would give.

She turned ideas over in her mind and settled on hitching a ride to Regina and finding work, room and board. She prepared a small bag with a few changes of clothes and some toiletries, her bank book, and her wallet, then she slid the bag under her bed and waited for the right time to leave.

Days passed. She missed meals, practice, and even Sunday Mass. "Sometimes it's like this," her father said in the hallway. "It takes time."

"But what can we do?" her mother asked.

"Nothing. But come, we have Mass." Émilie pictured them: Pierre pressing out a smile of reassurance as he pressed his hand on his wife's back; Rose taking a deep breath and nodding. Tears slipped down Émilie's cheeks. She wiped them away with her hands. Her parents tapped on the door across the hall. "Martin? Are you ready?" Pierre asked.

"Yeah," the teen grumbled and joined them in the hallway.

Émilie listened to them make their way down the stairs, through the kitchen, and out the door. She heard the thumps of car doors and the rumble of the Chieftain's motor. Gravel crunched as they drove away. Their Collie-cross, Rousseau, yipped and gave chase to the departing car but fell silent once it turned onto the grid road.

*Has he turned back*, Émilie wondered, *or is he sitting out there waiting for them to come home?* She had no idea, but she could not waste time thinking about the dog if she were to seize her opportunity.

She threw off her covers, swung her legs out of bed, and pushed herself up to standing. Her head spun. She took a moment to steady herself, then took a deep breath and crossed the room.

She opened the door and strained for sounds of her grandmother, who was either with the others or asleep, for the only sound Émilie heard was her own breathing. She pressed on and made her way to the bathroom, where she showered until the room was full of steam, then she turned off the hot water and shocked herself with cold water to make sure she was awake and thinking clearly. She was still resolved to leave. She stopped the water and towelled dry.

The hallway smelled of beef and onions roasting on low so as to be ready for her family's return after Mass. Her eyes blurred to think of them coming home and discovering that she had gone. *But I can't stay*, she reminded herself.

She quickened her step and reached her room. She dressed and brushed her hair, then braided it quickly. She made her bed and pulled out her haversack hidden beneath. She stuffed the last of her things inside—toothbrush and hairbrush, the vial of pills on the nightstand. She picked up her bag and crossed the strap over herself so the weight of it was behind her right hip.

Her breath quivered as she took a final look about the room: the floral bedspread and curtains, the hairspray and perfume bottles, the prayer cards and snapshots tucked along the mirror of her dresser. It had been a good place, a comfortable corner of the house to call her own, but there were too many memories floating about there.

She shook away her nostalgia and pressed onward. She kept her eyes forward and made her way downstairs. She grabbed an apple and a banana from the kitchen counter and her jacket from the hook by the door as she passed by. She opened the door and walked into Robbie, who was about to knock.

"Hey," he grinned. "There you are." She gaped and blinked. "I've been coming every day, but you were always in bed." Her eyes welled, and she looked away. She bit her lip and squeezed her eyes; tears still leaked through her eyelids. Robbie cupped her elbows. "What's wrong?"

"I'm leaving," she choked.

"What? Why?"

Her chest quaked. "Because it's too hard."

He blinked a well of tears and sniffed. "What is? Seeing me? Because I look like him?"

"No!" she cried. "Never!"

"Then why are you leaving?"

She turned her eyes away and stared down at the worn wooden planks of the sunporch floor. Her tears splashed onto their feet. "You don't know everything," she whispered.

"I know enough."

"No, you don't."

"Yeah, I do. I left, and Roch—"

"Robbie," she interrupted.

He squeezed her arms and smiled at her. "It's okay."

"No, it's not. I—"

"Dated him," he said for her.

She shook her head at the inadequacy. "Slept with him," she choked.

His hands and face fell like sheet ice. "What?"

"That night."

He blinked at her until he found words, "But I was coming back."

"I didn't know!" She reached towards him, but he stepped away and shook his head at her words and her eyes.

"I gave up God for you. And you? You gave yourself to Roch!"

"It's not like that!" He scoffed and snorted and turned on the ball of his foot. "Robbie!" she called as he stormed away. "Please! Let me explain! Please!"

He carried on, climbed into his father's car, and drove off in a spew of dust and gravel.


Robbie was the one who made it to Regina that day. He went to his eldest brother's house and holed up in his basement for a week. Then the brother, Jean-Jos, old enough to be his father, sent him out with one of his paint crews. It passed Robbie's time and gave him an excuse to drink at the end of the day. *The hard work, the sore muscles,* he rationalized, but it was the heartache he was trying to assuage.

After a few weeks, Jacques, the youngest Thibaud son before the twins had been born, took Robbie along to the Okanagan for a summer of fruit picking: cherries, peaches, plums. Robbie worked so well, he was kept on for fall pruning and winterizing. Then he moved on to ski trail maintenance. He hated the cold but liked the ragtag community of ski bums and chambermaids who did not know that he was all that remained of a set.

Émilie stayed in Lasalette. She muddled through her days with music lessons and daily practice. She did schoolwork and wrote the grade twelve departmental exams even though she was only in grade eleven. She passed well enough, and Soeur Saint-Sacrement suggested she go away to a music school or a university. Émilie accepted the suggestion with a rapid nod and made inquiries down east.

She received interviews and auditions. Her mother and grandmother accompanied her to the far-off city of Montréal, then carried on to the Bas-Saint-Laurent, where Sylvie still had family—siblings, cousins, nephews and nieces she had never met.

Pierre had such relations there as well, but his family was west, he told Émilie, "Here, in Lasalette. So is yours," he whispered as he kissed her goodbye. "Remember that."

"I will," she choked, then turned and climbed aboard the east-bound train.

## 9. Bourée
### April 1990

Stéphanie was trembling when she arrived at the end of the song. She closed her eyes and breathed in the name of her god until her heart rate slowed, and her mind was back in the present.

Once it was, she became aware of a pressing need to pee. She hurried to the en suite bathroom, emptied her bladder, and washed her hands.

She was surprised by the reflection of herself she caught in the mirror: despite her lack of sleep and her ride inside a musical tempest, she did not look a wreck. In fact, a splash of cold water and a quick dusting of face powder left her looking as fit and fair as ever. She moved on to her thick hair, brushed it and plaited it loosely at the back of her head.

As she finished, her stomach growled in sudden ravenous hunger that caused her to finish her washing and dressing in a rush so she could make her way to the kitchen and eat the source of the savoury scent that was wafting into the bedroom from below.

She heard her cousin and the men of the house laughing and talking as soon as she left her room. It and the warm smell of garlic and onion pulled her onward without worry about all that awaited her: Michel and Plumeau and singing with them for Christianne and Alex.

"Salut!" Clem greeted her as soon as she walked into the green kitchen. "Grab a glass! We're celebrating!"

She caught his happiness. "Oh? What?"

"This!" Christianne exclaimed, twittering her left hand in the air.

"Oh, my gawd! You got engaged?"

"Yes!"

"Wow!" The cousins hugged and examined the ring. "When?"

"Just a little while ago. We were coming down for lunch, and you were singing and—"

"It was perfect," Alex picked up, "absolutely perfect for me and my little Fransaskoise." He wrapped his arm about Christianne and kissed her head.

Stéphanie blinked at the information. "I didn't know anyone could hear me."

"Well, we could," Christianne chuckled, "and it was exactly what we needed to hear." She leaned towards Stéphanie and whispered, "Was it what you needed to sing?"

Stéphanie shrugged but nodded at the same time. "Partly," she admitted.

"Good." Christianne squeezed her hand, then reached for a flute of sparkling water. "So here."

"Thanks. And shall I make a toast?" she asked, already raising her glass. "Hourrah to Christianne and Alex!"

"Hourrah!" the others cheered.

Stéphanie went on, "L'chaim! Feliz Navidad!"

"What the fuck?"

"Jean!" Michel cried. "Sorry," he said to the women. Christianne waved it away while Stéphanie got stuck in his caramel eyes.

"It's something my brother says," Christianne explained.

"What the hell for?" Jean-François asked.

"He's twelve and thinks he's funny," said Christianne.

"He sounds like he is," Alex chuckled. "I can't wait to meet him."

Christianne's eyes shone. "I think he'll be pretty stoked to meet you. He's always wanted a brother."

"Me, too," Alex replied.

"You have a brother," she laughed.

"I know," he jerked his chin at Michel and Stéphanie, "but I think he's lost."

"Pffuck, no kidding," Jean-François scoffed though his eyes glimmered, and his lips rose. "So, are we gonna eat or what?"

"Yes!" Clem replied. "Sit! Everyone! Mitch. Stéph."

"Huh?" They both shook free of their eye-lock to the amusement of the others.

"Lunchtime," Alex said.

"Oh," Michel chuckled. "Right. Stéphanie? Why don't you sit here?"

She smiled and moved towards the chair he pulled out. "Thanks." She sat down and got settled at the table, "Mondou, Clem! It smells amazing!"

"Does it?" Clem asked with a grin.

Jean-François smacked him playfully. "You know it does." Clem smiled even wider.

"Absolutely!" Stéphanie insisted. "Is that the parmigiana you were talking about?"

"Yep. It's been cooling for a while, so it should be nice and set. You want some?"

"Please! I'm starving!"

"Great! I've got garlic bread and salad, too."

"And meat?" Jean-François asked as he sat down. "Did

you make something we can actually sink our teeth into?"

"I made meatballs," Clem said, "but it wouldn't hurt you to go meatless once in a while."

"Yes, it would," Jean-François replied.

"I go meatless at least once a week," Stéphanie said, slipping into the men's banter.

"Fridays?" Michel guessed.

She nodded at the old Catholic practice and went on, "Sometimes Tuesdays, as well."

"Why?" Jean-François scoffed.

"Spiritual reasons mostly, but there are some very good health benefits, too."

"Câlisse," he grumbled. "Not another granola head."

She laughed at him while Clem picked up her argument, "And environmental reasons. Did you know that billions of gallons of water could be saved if every North American went vegetarian just once a week?"

"Who cares? Fuck. Let's just eat."

"Oh, we can eat," Clem said, "but we're not done here."

Jean-François turned his eyes to the ceiling. "I know."

"You two sound like an old married couple," Alex laughed.

"Hey!" Christianne protested playfully.

"Yeah, man, be careful what you say there," Jean-François teased. "You'll be a married man soon enough."

Alex pulled Christianne into his side and grinned. "Yeah, I will, but we won't be like that."

"Yes, you will," Clem laughed. "Maybe not about meat, but about something: how to fold laundry or how to make the bed."

"Easy," Alex said. "Just throw the covers on."

"No!" Christianne volleyed. "I've told you: you have to pull the bottom sheet tight and smooth, then pull the flat sheet up and make sure it's tucked in at the bottom. Then you can put on the covers."

"Yeah, yeah. I know." He kissed her head. "I'll just let you make the bed, and I'll make the coffee."

"That's what my parents do," Stéphanie said, then she shook her head at the comment and at the fact that she even knew that detail. She jumped off the thought, "Did you tell your mom and dad yet?"

"No," Christianne said, "I'm waiting for six."

"Why?" Michel asked. "The long-distance fees? 'Cause you don't have to worry about that."

"Yeah," Jean-François added, "consider it our engagement present since you won't be needing the Bolton."

"Oh, right," Stéphanie murmured. She chewed her lip and looked down at her plate as Christianne explained that she was waiting for the clock to reach six back home because both of her parents would be home and available to talk.

Michel touched Stéphanie's hand. "We can still play," he said. "No pressure. Just four people making music. Having fun."

She rubbed her lips together and moved her head as she considered it. The men waited for her to speak. "I'd like that," she said, at last.

Michel's face lit like a hot air balloon at a night glow. "Us, too."

"Yeah," Jean-François agreed.

"Absolutely," Clem said, "but after we eat." He turned towards the counter and picked up a nine-by-thirteen Pyrex pan. "Cause this parmigiana is ready!"

The men told stories about each other while they ate. Jean-François was a child entertainer, they said, ever since he had played a jig with his uncles for his grandparents' wedding anniversary when he was eight years old. After that, the uncles took him to weekend gigs at carnivals and cabanes à sucre. Clem was a child prodigy, too, a classical violinist who went rogue one summer after he heard Jean-François and his uncles play at a street dance. Michel, the men teased, just rolled out of bed one day and decided he wanted to be a rock star.

"Yeah, well, hockey's overrated," he said.

"Not for my dad," Christianne laughed. "Câline, the guy's got carpal tunnel so bad he can hardly move his hands, but give him his skates and his gloves, and suddenly he's Jacques Plante again."

"Oh, he's a goalie," Michel said.

"Yeah. Just rec, but he played at university."

"Nice. Where?"

"U of S. You played, too, right? Junior?"

He blushed. His friends sputtered with laughter. "Yep. 'Til he broke his stick," Clem said.

"It's not funny," Jean-François laughed.

"I know," Clem agreed, still shaking with laughter. He stood up and started gathering up plates. Michel sighed heavily and moved his head from side to side.

Christianne turned to Alex. "What's that about?"

He answered with a chuckle, "He took a puck in a sensitive area." He gestured downward until Christianne caught on.

"Ohhh. So that was his injury? Why he quit?"

Alex nodded. "Yeah. It messed him up pretty bad. He couldn't even walk. They took him to the hospital. He needed surgery on one of his balls."

Michel was as red as the sauce on his plate and too embarrassed to speak. The others were not.

"He could've still played," Clem said.

"Maybe," Alex agreed, "but I think the shot kinda knocked

the fun out of it for him."

"It knocked something outta him," Clem laughed. "Good thing he came with a spare."

"Geezus!" Jean-François barked.

"What?"

"What?" he squawked. "You guys get all over me for the way I talk, but you're goin' on about his balls in front of his …" He raised his eyebrows as he considered what label to use for Stéphanie, but then simply jerked his head towards her and said, "In front of her?"

"Oh," Clem sounded. "Right." He smacked Michel on the shoulder. "Sorry, man."

Michel pinched the flesh between his eyebrows with his thumb and forefinger and shook his head. "Whatever." He ran his tongue up and down the ridge between two of his bottom molars, trying to think of what to say, while Stéphanie wondered if there was a word Jean-François could have used to describe her and whether she wanted there to be one.

The potty-mouthed singer smacked his hands on the table and pushed his chair back before she decided. "Enough of this. Let's get to work."

"We gotta put the food away first," Clem said as he stood as well.

"Oh, we can do that," Christianne said, jumping up and into the conversation. She tapped Alex's shoulder, and he stood as well.

"Yeah, for sure. It's the least we can do."

"Great," Clem grinned. "Thanks."

"No worries," Christianne said as she picked up a plate. "Are you gonna take the lovebirds," she asked with a jerk of her head towards Stéphanie and Michel, who were both still in a lovestruck trance, "or leave 'em here to melt into a puddle?"

Clem laughed. "We better take 'em." He nudged Michel in the shoulder. "Hey. Practice. What about you, Stéphanie? You up for it?"

Her face answered before her mouth. "Yes."

"Well, let's go then," Jean-François groused even though he smiled.

Stéphanie and the men spent the rest of the day and most of the next exploring their common repertoire and sharing their own compositions and covers of classics. Jean-François was a jukebox in the chansonnier tradition, for he seemed to know every French folksong ever sung. Clem alternated between jigs and the classical repertoire he still held in his memory. Michel was not as flashy, but his playing was sound, and his voice was warm and rich.

Stéphanie went all over the place, just as Jean-François had said the day they met. She moved from instrument to instrument as well and offered the men opera and art song, folk music, country, and rock. She sat at the piano and played a blues progression that made Michel smile. "We haven't done this yet," she said, looking straight at him with a warm heart and a smile that showed the white of her teeth like pearls inside the flesh of an oyster.

"No," he agreed with laughter as if it were an inside joke, "but we should."

"What is it?" Clem asked.

"Something from back home," Stéphanie said.

"Well, let's hear it."

She embellished her playing in response, then started to sing, "Would you die for a liar? A robber? A cheat? Would you carry transgressions? Suffer defeat?"

"Oh, how far?" Michel sang.

"How far," she echoed.

"Would you go?"

"How far? How far?"

"Hmm," Jean-François said. "Sounds good, but it needs a bass." He sang out a long low G, "Far."

"That's exactly what we said the other night," Stéphanie laughed.

"Well, fuckin' eh," Jean-François grinned.

She smiled back, but Michel jumped to correct him, "Hey watch the mouth, buddy. It's a church song."

Jean-François scrunched his face, "Câlice," he complained.

"Yep," Stéphanie chirped, "and hôstie, too." Her eyes danced as she played with the religious origin of Québecois swear words, "And all the rest: tabernacle, Holy Virgin, Jesus Christ."

He nodded approval of her playful correction. "Okay. Sorry. Why would we sing a church song?"

"'Cause it has lots of potential." Michel grabbed his guitar and threw the strap over his head. "Listen to this refrain."

Jean-François' face contorted as he assessed the blues-infused gospel song. "Aren't you Catholic?" he asked Stéphanie.

She chuckled at his confusion. "Yeah, but we've come a long way since Vatican II."

"What the fu—"

"I like it," Clem burst in. "It reminds me of Marie-Geneviève's hat."

"Her hat?" Jean-François scoffed.

"Yeah, that flower one she wore on Easter. She always hummed when she wore it."

"Yeah, she did," Jean-François said floating on a drift of nostalgia, "but, fuck, a hat?"

Clem shrugged. "Why not?"

"It reminds me of us," Michel said. He finger-picked the strings of his guitar and sang along, "Would you carry the burden of another soul? Would you stretch out your arms across a wooden pole?"

"Geezus," Jean-François muttered and rolled his eyes.

"Listen," Michel said. He continued to play and started the refrain.

"How far?" Stéphanie echoed once again.

Clem and Jean-François moved their heads about as they assessed the possibilities of the song. Then they offered their own echoes and kept going with an improvised verse.

"I'd give a woman," Clem sang, "her love and her home."

Jean-François added, "I'd give my freedom to reap what we've sown."

"How far?"

"How far."

"Would you go?"

Stéphanie filled the sonorous holes of the trio, then began a counter melody that eventually took over the first hymn.

"What the fuck?" Jean-François groused as she riffed off in Latin.

"Shhh," Michel barked. "I think this it."

"*It* what?" Clem asked.

"Her song. Listen."

"Câ-riste," Jean-François complained after two verses, "How long is it?"

"I don't know," Michel said without taking his eyes off her, "but if you want her, you gotta let her finish."

## Stabat mater dolorosa

The first Saturday in June 1969, the Lasalette High School gymnasium was decorated with crêpe paper streamers and tissue flowers. A cutout poster board of two hearts joined together was rubber-cemented to the wall behind the head banquet table. The names Lynn and Martin were inscribed on the hearts, and the couple sat in front of them all laughter and smiles. The room was loud with talking and eating. The smell of roast beef and gravy swirled about the room with a mélange of perfumes and hairspray, Brylcreem and cologne. A cloud of cigarette smoke already muted out the basketball hoops, scoreboard, and pendants.

Robbie sat at the head table between Martin and Pierre. He could see Émilie seated primly before him at a secondary table with her grandmother and some of Lynn's family. Émilie was more beautiful in person—made-up and dressed in green chiffon—than in his memory, even if she never once looked at him.

She bit her lip between responses to the questions about the past seven years, being fired at her by Lynn's brother, Gilles, and his wife, Émilie's old friend, Shirley.

Robbie noticed the spread of Émilie's nose and the long, tight muscles of her neck as she fought off tears. She rubbed her right wrist with her left hand, he noticed as well. That was something she had started after the accident.

Robbie shook away the sting and poured himself another glass of dandelion wine. Émilie did, too. And then another. It was strong stuff, moonshine masquerading as something more refined; most of the other wedding guests had watered it down or lightened it up with a splash of ginger ale, but not Émilie nor Robbie.

Émilie rose from her table halfway through the wedding banquet and rushed through the gym, weaving through tables and chairs like a bumblebee. Robbie watched after her with the same bewildered lovesickness as the night of their Freshie dance in the same room a decade before.

"Are you alright?" Pierre asked. "You look rather pale."

"Yeah. I think I just need some air." Robbie pushed himself away from the table and stood. His head spun, and he stumbled; he caught the back of Martin's chair. "Yep," he chuckled making light of it. "Definitely need some air."

Martin twisted to look at him. "You, okay?"

"Yeah," he said, again. "I'm just gonna get some air."

"Want me to come with you?"

"No. I'm fine. Look." He let go of the chair and straightened up. "Besides, you've got your little missus to look after." He clicked his tongue and patted Martin's shoulder. "I'll see ya later."

He followed the path Émilie had taken and found himself in the hallway, deserted except for ghosts and memories, and then, Émilie stumbling out of the women's washroom. She stopped with a jerk when she noticed him. They stared at each other. He felt light-headed; he touched a locker to steady himself.

"Hi."

"Hello."

They took turns opening and closing their mouths, thinking words, then swallowing them. She was porcelain and emerald, ebony and rose petals. He was rugged, taller and stronger than the last time they had seen each other.

"I'm gonna get some air," he said, at last.

She held his gaze. "Want some company?"

"If it's you." He held out his hand towards her; she took it.

Their shoes clicked on the tile and echoed in the hallway. Émilie let go of his hand and pressed into his side. He draped his arm about her shoulders; she wrapped her arm about his waist, wider than it had been years before. He ran his fingers over the soft skin of her arm. Their heartbeats quickened; their feet clacked faster and faster towards the door. They caught each other in a kiss as they crossed the threshold. She pressed against him; he pulled her tighter, ran his hands over her back and buttocks.

"Let's ..." she said.

"I have my truck ..."

They made their way across the parking lot in rubato time—rushing, then slowing to embrace, then rushing again to get away from the school and the people inside. He pressed her up against the side of his old F100 and kissed her while opening the passenger side door. They sidled towards the opening still locked on each other's mouths. He lifted her onto the seat. She lay back; he followed on top of her. His tongue went into her mouth; his hand went up the hem of her dress. She caught it. "Not here."

"Where?" he gasped. He was hard and full; his heart raced like a bird's.

"Somewhere," she rubbed his swollen groin to assure him of her intentions, "private."

He rumbled a laugh of excitement as he slid from her and back out of the truck. He hurried to the driver's side and climbed behind the wheel. She greeted him with a genital rub and a full throat kiss.

"Drive fast, okay?" she said.

"Oh, I will," he promised, and he did; he left a trail of dust as long as a comet's tail behind them.

She undid his buttons as he drove: his jacket, his shirt, his pants. His pulse raced, his foot pressed harder on the gas.

He kept his eyes on the road, however, for fear he would forget the wheel and veer them into the ditch.

He stopped, at last, at the edge of his father's east field and moved on top of her as soon as he had stopped the engine. She unzipped his fly, slipped her fingers through the slits of his underwear. They both sighed.

He pushed up her dress and followed the crease of her thigh to the warmth between her legs. There were more sighs as clothes were discarded, and flesh touched flesh.

She gasped when he entered her, then moved with him in synchronized motions. They panted and grunted in counterpoint, bayed in unison as they reached climax.

He collapsed upon her when he was empty, buried his face in the curve of her neck. "Ohhh, Émilie."

She trailed her fingers over his back. "Robbie."

He shifted to look at her; they stared into each other's eyes, then kissed with the softness of dew, caressed each other's bodies with the tenderness they had forgotten moments before. He swelled again in time, and she softened. He slipped into her like a key into a lock. They moved as one, inhaled and exhaled each other's breath, drifted into ecstasy like lilies releasing perfume.

They lay together until full darkness was upon them and the air grew chill. Émilie rubbed his arm. "I'm sorry, but I really need to pee."

"Oh. Yeah. Sure." He disentangled himself from her and

allowed her room to sit up and slide towards the door. Her departure left him cold. He leaned forward to retrieve his clothes from the floor. He gathered up hers as well and dropped them on the seat beside him.

"Do you have any Kleenex?" she asked, peaking her head inside the door.

Robbie stuck his arm into his shirt sleeve. "No, but I have paper towels." He reached behind the seat and extracted a flattened roll. "Here."

"Thanks." She reached for it and backed out of the truck, closed the door and urinated, wiped herself and the traces of Robbie away. She shivered and dropped the dirtied towel onto the ground.

Inside the truck, Robbie's chest was tight, and his head throbbed. He reached behind the seat again and felt about for the Black Velvet he had placed there earlier in the day. His knuckles found it. He followed the contours of the bottle, then clutched it by the neck and pulled it out, bringing it to where he could open it. He raised the bottle to his lips, tilted his head back, and let the whiskey flow into his mouth. He closed his eyes so he could feel the warmth spread through him and his senses return.

When Émilie opened the door, he lowered the bottle but did not look at her. "There's your clothes."

She raised her eyebrows at the curtness. "Ummm. Okay." She studied the angles and shadows of his face in the yellow interior light. His forehead was grooved; his eyes were hooded and dark; his jaw moved as he ground his teeth. "I'll get dressed outside," she said to fill the silence, "I need room for the skirt." She grabbed up her pile of clothing and slammed the door.

He sat in the darkness once again and took another drink, then finished getting dressed himself.

Émilie placed her clothes on the hood and rummaged about in the chiffon to find her undergarments. She could not, so she cast about, looking for the opening of the dress, a long evening gown she had bought for her graduation recital at the Conservatoire de musique de Montréal. She found the bottom of the skirt and pulled the dress over her head. Her bra, pantyhose, and panties fell to her feet as she wriggled into the dress. She bent forward to collect them, then stepped into the panties and swaddled up her breasts with the brassiere. The hosiery she saved to stuff into her purse. She pushed her arms through the broad straps of the bodice and opened the truck door. "Can you zip me?"

"Sure." Robbie shuffled across the seat as she turned her back to him. He fumbled with the thin raindrop slider but succeeded at last. "There." He slid back behind the wheel.

"Thanks." She climbed into the cab and pulled the door behind her.

He started the truck. "I'll take you home."

"There's no rush." He made a sound neither understood— a laugh or a cry or something in between—and pulled out the knob for the headlights. Émilie reached across the seat and touched his hand. "What's wrong?"

His breath trembled as it left him. "We were supposed to be better than this."

"Than what?"

"Drunken sex in an old pick-up."

She rubbed his arm. "I'm not that drunk."

"Humph."

"What?"

"You've changed."

"So have you."

"Yeah. But not enough." He moved his arm despite her touch and pulled the gear shift into drive.

"What do you mean?"

He shook his head at her question and held his words between his thin, tight lips as he pressed on the gas. The headlights cut the darkness. Bugs pinged and splattered against the windshield; gravel crunched and flew beneath the wheels.

Émilie studied Robbie in the dim dashboard light and marvelled at his presence beside her once again. "I've missed you."

A bruised laugh rumbled in his chest. "Me, too."

She smiled at him, but he kept his eyes on the road. She swallowed down a hundred different words and stared out the window at the shadowed landscape she had once known so well: the field with the good toboggan hill, the slough that teemed with tadpoles and frogs the year they were nine, the Thibauds' farm, the spot where Roch hit the deer, rolled the truck, died. Her eyes stung, and she began to tremble.

Robbie drove on without a blink or a breath. He slowed to turn into the Tremblays' yard, then rolled to a stop in front of her parents' well-maintained 1920s catalogue house.

"What was this?" he asked without looking at her.

"You mean tonight?"

"Yeah. Was it anything?"

"Of course!" She slid towards him and touched his arm. "It was how things should've been."

Robbie caught her hand and pushed it away. "When?" His eyes were marbles, hard and round. "When should it have been this way? Before or after you fucked Roch?"

"Uh," she gasped.

He shook away her hurt and barrelled right through, "It's what you did, isn't it?"

She sucked back her tears. "Yeah. It is. We fucked, but you and I, we just made love."

"Sex is sex," he sneered.

"No, it's night and day."

He sputtered at her words, spat in response, "Don't you mean dusk and dawn?"

"No!" she cried, realizing what he meant: the old description his mother always gave when talking about him and Roch. "Oh, gawd, Robbie! No!"

He raised his hand to stop her from touching him. "Just get out."

"Robbie, please. Let me—"

"No!" He swung around and punched the back of the seat. "Get out!"

She choked to see the fire in his eyes and hurried away. He drove off in a spray of gravel. She ran inside and up the stairs. She flopped herself on

to her bed and cried into her old, tear-stained pillow.


Ten years later, Robbie sat in the back corner of Notre-Dame-de-Lasalette Church on a warm May day and watched the procession of priests and altar boys, pallbearers, and a coffin. The Carons, including all of Sylvie's surviving children and many of her grandchildren, followed behind.

Robbie knew some of them from birthdays and holidays past, but they were basically strangers to him now, all except Rose and Pierre, who walked in, arm in arm, clutching and holding and supporting one another. Martin and Lynn followed behind with their three girls about them and a baby boy in Lynn's arms. Émilie was next. She was as pale and red-eyed as the last time he had seen her. There was a girl at her side.

Robbie had heard of her, had thought she was his once, but her birthdate was ten weeks off for that. Still, he studied her as she walked by: tan skin, kaleidoscope eyes. She could be his, he thought; his nieces looked about the same.

*But what do I know? I know them almost as well as this girl of Émilie's.* He blinked and sniffed away the water rising to his eyes as he recalled his mother challenging his absence only weeks before.

"Why do you stay away?" she had asked.

"Because," he had choked. The rest came out in tears that fell upon her once ample chest.

She found the strength to raise her hand and touch his head. "Mon fils," she whispered. They remained such a Pietà until her hand slipped away. Robbie stirred, then and saw that she was gone.

He had been in Lasalette ever since, sleeping on the living room couch in the house in which he had been raised. It was unchanged, save the photos of nephews and nieces he had never met. His brothers and sisters-in-law, their children and grandchildren had all congregated there in the hours and days after Lucille's passing, but now, weeks later, it was just him, the long-lost prodigal son, home after ten years, after nephews and nieces had married and a new generation of Thibauds had been born, home months after his father had been pinned against the barn by a bull and died of a ruptured spleen.

It had taken three weeks for Robbie's brothers to track him down and give him the news, and it was only months later when one of them had phoned again to say that their mother's fatigue and weight loss were due to more than grief and depression. "Liver cancer. The doctor says she's got two weeks to two months to live."

"Tell her I'm coming," Robbie had said, then hung up and stuffed a duffel bag with whatever was underhand and headed north in his live-in girlfriend's Chevette.

It had taken him three days to make it from Loreto to Lasalette. He had not seen a single mile for the memories running through his head like movies: his mother's sewing-pin smile, her hands on his when she showed him how to play the piano, her eyes, soft and grey until Roch died, then they were clouded and did not know whether Robbie was a ghost or a shadow or flesh and blood. They had cleared, in time, and the last time he had seen her before his decade-long absence, she had taken his hand in hers and looked him straight in the eyes.

"You should talk to Émilie," she had said.

"Why?"

She cocked her head and smiled compassionately. Wrinkles grooved her face like river systems. Robbie's heart pushed in his chest as she looked at him with the softness of his childhood. "Oh, Bébert, mon petit chou. We never should've let you go to Saint-Boniface. You were too young to know God's will, too young to try to give up that kind of love for Him."

He fell against her chest and cried, "I didn't."

She stroked his thick hair and kissed his head. "I know. And that's why you never should have left." She rocked him and rubbed circles of comfort on his back. "You three," she finally said, "you were written in the sky like the moon and the stars."

After she kissed him and left him alone to think, Robbie pushed away from the table and stalked to the door, got into his pick-up, and drove to town to visit the L.B.S. before Martin and Lynn's wedding ceremony.

Presently, the shuffle of people brought Robbie back to Sylvie Caron's funeral. He blinked and stood like everyone else in the church around him. He did not know the French prayers the others incanted, and the Latin ones they had replaced were nothing but shards in his heart. He could, however, remember the last time he had said them—Roch's funeral half a lifetime ago. He had thought of Émilie back then, too, and had wished that she were next to him, holding his hand, but she had been in the hospital across town, broken and alone.

He slipped out of his pew and left the church before the final blessing was given. *No one knows I'm here, so no one'll know I've gone.* He shaded his eyes with a pair of dark glasses as he stepped out of the church, but the sun was still bright, and the hearse still glinted in the sunlight. Robbie strode past it, climbed into his truck, and headed to a place across town where the lights were dim, and nothing shone but ice cubes and glass.

Émilie followed the others through the rest of the funeral and to the cemetery for the burial rite, but while the others made their way to the parish hall for triangle sandwiches and date squares, she wandered about the graves. They were mostly laid in ordered rows, but there were occasional tombstones that stood apart from the rest—rounded stones and crosses marking the resting places of people who had been buried before the village had been founded or the cemetery planned.

The grass was mowed; the leaves on the poplars rustled in the wind; the lilacs held tight purple buds not yet ready to open. She walked slowly and read the names she had grown up with—Chabot, Grégoire, Painchaud. She did not see Thibaud: Roch, Lucille, Francis. They were together in the far corner Émilie did not visit, for her eyes leaked and her heart ached just knowing they were there.

She turned around and doubled back up the main path to the entrance gate. It squealed as she pushed it open. The plaintive cry of rusty hinges was a comforting sound. Her grandfather, Baptiste, had helped build the gate, she remembered her grandmother telling her, "Il y a longtemps. Bien longtemps. Long before I ever thought I'd put him there."

*And now she's there, too*, Émilie thought. *Finally reunited with him after all these years.*

"Il était le seul," Émilie remembered Sylvie saying, "the only one I ever loved."

Émilie had found it embarrassing when she was a girl, the way Sylvie would fall into a wistful trance when she spoke of Baptiste, but as an adult, she marvelled at how her grandmother had clung to her love from the time she was a girl in Québec until her death out west decades later.

Sylvie had been only eighteen when she and Baptiste had married, yet she had held fast to him through the losses and joys of life.

*I could've had that,* Émilie thought, but she shook away her regret and focused on the gate instead. *I'll tell Stéphanie about it, about how Baptiste built the gate. She'll like that, like knowing she has such roots here.*

Émilie clasped her left hand about her once-broken wrist and sighed, glad for once that Stéphanie was so intrigued by family and Lasalette, for she would be spending the summer there while Émilie got things settled in Edmonton.

She had never had any intention of returning to Canada let alone to Lasalette, but things had aligned that way: a job offer at Alberta College, Sylvie's decline, Pierre's voice over the phone line, "I know it's hard, but you'll have to face it one day."

*One day*, Émilie had tittered to herself. *Oh Papa, when you see Stéphanie, you'll know I face it every day.*

She walked up the main street that ran from the highway straight through Lasalette. She passed the church and the turn off to the school. The parish hall was on the left behind a row of caragana. The branches brushed against Émilie's arm as she walked by. They felt like a tug to turn up the walk, but she pressed on, eager to find something stronger than orange Tang to drink.

The streets were quiet and seemed the same as the last time she had been there, but they were not. People had gone, stores had closed, the bank had reduced its hours, but flowers still grew in front of the village office, and a Canadian flag still flapped on the pole in front of the post office.

Émilie, too, was both the same and different since her last visit for her brother's wedding. She had taken up a career as a practice pianist for the École supérieur de ballet du Québec the week she returned east, and four weeks after that she learned she was pregnant. She told no one about the latter until Stéphanie had been cut out of her ten weeks before her time. Then Émilie had called home and cried, "Maman! She might die!"

Rose had gone to them, flown for the first time in her life, and found Émilie at St. Mary's Hospital. Rose held Émilie until she was allowed to hold her own daughter. It had changed them, Émilie giving birth to such a small, fragile baby who needed tubes to live, and Rose keeping vigil with Émilie, telling her about motherhood and childhood, about Serge Ouellette and other things that had made them both weep.

Émilie's shoes clapped against the sidewalk. Her wrist ached, and her heart raced. *God, I could use a Darvon.* She ground the idea between her teeth. *No. No pills. I promised Stéphanie no pills in Canada … But I said nothing about vodka.*

She climbed the steps to the Lasalette Hotel and pulled open the door. She had never been there, for she had been too young when she had lived in Lasalette, and there had been enough alcohol at Martin's wedding that she had not needed to visit the bar the last time she had been home.

The hotel door led directly to the bar room, a dim room that smelled of cigarette smoke and spilled beer. It was empty except for tables and chairs, a moustached bartender, and a lone figure sitting hunched over a glass. She paid little attention to either.

"Bin bonjour," the bartender said with a smile of happy recognition.

He did not seem familiar to Émilie, and she did not care to rummage through her memory to uncover his identity. "Bonjour," she answered without the nod or smile that would invite conversation. She sat on the barstool farthest away from the other patron. "Vodka on the rocks, s'il vous plaît."

The bartender raised his eyebrows at her curtness but nodded in understanding of her request for service without words—it was common in his profession. He reached for a tumbler and turned for ice. Émilie watched him, listening to the clink of the ice, the glug-shhh of Smirnoff being poured over the top. The bartender turned back towards her. "Te voilà," he said, placing a drink in front of her.

"Merci."

Her mouth was pursed to ask him to start a tab when the other lone drinker said, "I'll get it, Jean." The sound burned her from the inside out. She turned to look at him.

"Robbie," she gasped.

"Émilie," he said, picking up his rye and ginger and sliding off his stool. He walked towards her and leaned against the stool beside her.

She looked at him, at his defined jaw and the same cut-glass eyes she saw every day in Stéphanie. Her chest ached. She looked away and raised her glass to her lips, took a sip and lowered the glass back onto the bar. She cupped it with her hands and stared at the clear ice cubes as Robbie's eyes scanned her thin body and long black hair. The heat of it made her stomach knot and her eyes well. She raised her drink and finished it. "Another, please."

Robbie downed what remained in his own glass and shifted on the stool. "Me, too."

They waited for their drinks in silence. Émilie studied the grain of the bar as she thought of the tableau she and Robbie made. It was not how anyone would have thought it would be: the two of them drinking at a quarter past one in the afternoon while their illegitimate child ran about somewhere playing tag with her cousins. "Tenez," the bartender said, interrupting her thoughts.

"Merci," she and Robbie both said.

Émilie drank without looking at either man. Robbie, however, watched her chew her lips between sips. "I'm sorry about your grandmother," he finally said.

"Merci." She nodded at his condolences. "I hadn't seen her for a long time," she said, then, after another sip and a deep breath, she turned to look at him and added, "nor you."

Robbie sneered, "Did you miss me?"

She felt her knee bounce and her chest constrict. She answered even though his question had been rhetorical and spiteful. "Yes."

He scoffed and met her look. "Why?"

The hard intensity startled her, causing her to look away and study her hands, which were starting to crack from the dry prairie air. She felt parched, too; she could not swallow or breathe, but she felt the need to speak, "Because the last time ... bin nous avons ... et pis ... I had our daughter ..."

"Our?" Robbie spat. "Christ, Em. I know you've never been any good at math, but I think you can count to nine. And from what Marty tells me, your little chou came way too early to be mine."

Émilie felt hit, but she turned to Robbie and said, "She was premature. She almost died." He blinked at the information, swallowed, and shook his head. Émilie thought she saw the old Robbie peeking out like the sun from behind a cloud, and she asked, "Have you seen her?"

The truth hit him deep inside his gut, but he did not have words or bandwidth to deal with it there in the presence of her eyes. He downed his drink, slammed the glass back down on the bar, and stormed away.

"Robbie," Émilie cried.

He carried on, so did she for almost another decade. Then at Martin's fortieth birthday party, Robbie stood by the chokecherry tree at the end of the Tremblays' yard and shook his head at himself, at the difficulty he was having integrating into the festivities. *It shouldn't be so hard,* he chided himself. But with Émilie there with her black hair and emerald eyes, being there was difficult for him. He took a deep breath and clenched his fists until the flimsy plastic cup he was holding cracked and leaked water over his hand. The wetness roused him as did a chuckle from the shadows.

"Don't like the punch?"

He froze, yet his heart raced as Émilie drew closer. He blinked at her as if she were a hallucination. She was tanned from months in Africa, but she was still porcelain next to the darkness of her hair. "It's just water," he managed to say. "I don't drink anymore."

"I know," she said, holding out a can. "That's why I thought you'd like some ginger ale."

He lifted his eyes and reached for the beverage. "Thanks."

Their fingers touched; their eyes locked for the briefest of moments, then she looked away and talked to her feet. "I don't either."

"Oh?"

Émilie swallowed down her nerves and went on, "Yeah. It's not recommended when you're an addict." She snuck a peek at him, already braced for the same look of surprise Martin had given her earlier that day, but Robbie simply nodded.

"The accident?" he asked.

"Mmmhmm. Pain killers. Sleeping pills."

His head bobbed at the information; he offered his own, "I found this flask in Roch's room. I didn't even know what was in it, but it was his, so I drank it, and it felt good, like I had something of him inside of me, something that maybe he could like."

Her heart ached, and her voice cracked. "He liked you."

Robbie shrugged and shook his head. "I don't know."

"I do," Émilie replied as if they were sixteen again. "He told me. That New Year's before you left. He said he didn't hate you like everybody thought; it was just that he was jealous of you." Her eyes burned with the reality of being over forty and still feeling like a teenager, acting like one when it came to Robbie. She ran her tongue over her lips to make them speak. "That was my fault."

"No, it wasn't," he said with a sincerity Émilie did not accept.

"Yes, it was." She blinked away her tears and pressed on with what she had wanted to say to him for decades, "I'm sorry. I never should've come between you two."

He touched her hair. "Oh, Em, you were born between us."

Their eyes met, held one another like moon and reflection. "I wanted him to be you," she admitted.

"And I wanted to be him, but none of that matters

anymore."

"Then what does?"

"Us."

She stared at him. Time had been kind to him, she thought, with his silver-streaked bronze hair and chiselled face. It had a softness, like that of a statue rubbed in supplication for centuries. She had seen such effects in cathedrals and music halls; she had done the same thing to her wrist. She wore a bracelet there now—a single decade rosary from Bujumbura that she had procured during a visit to Regina Mundi Cathedral. She had liked the blue beads but was not ready to pray with them. Robbie, on the other hand, had turned religious—she had heard—and was into some kind of Catholic born-again stuff their daughter called the Charismatic Renewal. Émile did not know what that was, but Stéphanie seemed to enjoy the prayer groups she and Robbie attended, she certainly seemed all the better for them, so Émilie did not object. Stéphanie made music at these things—guitar and vocals usually, but sometimes rhythm instruments or the piano; it depended on how the spirit moved her, she had said. Émilie had likened it to knowing which stops to use on an organ.

Robbie ran the back of his finger over the contour of her face. "What are you thinking?"

"All kinds of things."

He grinned. "Me, too."

"Yeah? Like what?"

"Like this is how it was supposed to be. And like this is how I'd like it to stay."

"Me, too."


They both thought of it upon waking, side by side and fully

clothed on his couch, how their tears had turned to kisses, and how they had felt young and new to the touching of lips, the passing of breath. They remembered, too, how they had even pulled away at the same time.

"I'm supposed to wait a year," Émilie said, "before I start anything."

Robbie chuckled, "It's not really starting, but I know what you mean. I'm a practicing Catholic again anyway, so ..." He shrugged and turned his hands up as an explanation for stopping.

Émilie nodded at the notion. "I'm not."

"I know."

"I don't know that I ever will be."

Robbie shrugged. "That's not my business."

Émilie raised her eyebrows in confusion. "What?"

He chuckled and kissed her forehead. "Loving you is my business. Everything else is God's."

"Oh," she sighed and trailed her hand over his softened, familiar face. "I don't know about the God stuff, Robbie, but I know that I've always loved you."

"Me, too." They kissed and held one another until Robbie felt the need to speak. "I'm sorry I was so hurtful to you. It was inexcusable, but I hope you—"

She touched her fingers to his lips. "I know. I read your letter. I should've written back, but I needed time."

He nodded in understanding. "Have you had enough?"

Her eyes glistened, and a smile spread across her face. "Yeah," she said with a chuckle. "More than enough."

He touched her cheek and stared into her eyes for a long time. "Can we go find Stéphanie then? Now that we're right, I want her to know who I am." Émilie nodded but closed her eyes against a sting of tears. "What?" he asked. "What's wrong?"

Émilie trembled as she took in a deep, steadying breath. "I appreciate all your consideration, but you could've told her even though I couldn't."

His brow furrowed as he wagged his head. "No, I couldn't have."

"Why not?"

He took a breath as he recalled his long struggle with the answer. "You do the steps?" he asked.

"I'm working on them. Why?"

"Step nine. Made amends."

"Yeah?"

"Well, there's the caveat, right? 'Made direct amends wherever possible, *except* when to do so would injure them or others.'"

Émilie nodded at the words but said, "I don't understand."

"Your dad," Robbie said, "he was afraid that if I told Stéphanie before you were ready for her to know, you might keep her away, never let her come out. And he didn't want to lose her. Didn't want to lose you any more than he already had."

"Oh," she sighed and reached for her once broken wrist and turned about the blue prayer bracelet she now wore there. "Gawd, the list of mistakes just gets longer and longer, doesn't it?"

Robbie laid his hand over hers. "Sometimes," he agreed, "but when we're ready and start making amends, it gets shorter and shorter."

"I don't know how to do that yet, but if being sorry and apologizing is part of it, then, I'm sorry, Robbie, for everything: hurting you, running away, keeping Stéphanie from you. I didn't mean to. I just couldn't …"

"Be here?" he suggested as she searched for words. "See me?" She moved her head in a slow, sad nod. He rubbed her arm in comfort. "I get it. I couldn't stand either of those things either until I saw Stéphanie. Then she was all I wanted."

A smile came over Émilie. "She's great, isn't she?"

"Yeah," Robbie agreed. "Can we go find her? Try to make things right between us and our daughter?"

Émilie warmed at the combination of words that linked her and Robbie to Stéphanie. "I'd like that," she said, and so they stood and headed towards the house down the road.

They walked into the kitchen at the Tremblay farm while Stéphanie and her cousins were making French toast and bacon. "Oh!" Émilie gasped with surprise. "Girls. You're all here."

"Mmmhmm," thirteen-year-old Nicole replied. "We always make Papa breakfast for his birthday."

Christianne laughed. "Yeah, but the way he was putting 'em back last night, maybe we should just give him some Aspirin and a Virgin Mary."

The younger scrunched her face. "He's allowed to have fun on his birthday," she said.

"Pfff," Christianne scoffed. "I'd like to see how good that goes down when I try it next month."

Nicole's mouth opened and her eyes blinked. "You're not old enough to drink," she reminded.

Christianne rolled her eyes. "You're not old enough to be having this conversation."

"I am, too," Nicole replied.

"Oh, shut up," Christianne said.

"Shut up both of you," the middle sister, Jasmine, said, then turned towards Robbie with a hopeful face beneath her back-combed bedhead. "I don't suppose you're here to make chilaquiles, are you?"

"Uhhh," he stammered, surprised by the question and the busyness of the kitchen. "No. Sorry."

"That's okay," she said. "Maybe for supper?"

"Maybe," he agreed. "But not now, okay? Now I need to talk to Stéphanie."

"Okay," she accepted as Stéphanie scoffed.

"No, you don't." She snorted, then ground her teeth and tended to the French toast. "I figured out a long time ago what it means when my mom comes home in the morning with a man."

Nicole and Jasmine raised their eyebrows at her insolence; Christianne clucked to hear her cousin talk back to an adult. Émilie trembled; Robbie squeezed her hand. "Girls," he said to the trio of sisters, "Do you mind giving us a few minutes?"

Eager to increase the chances of getting chilaquiles that night, Jasmine quickly agreed, "Sure. No problem." She pulled Nicole along with her and headed towards the living room. "We'll check on Simon."

Christianne was not as compliant; she turned towards Stéphanie for a cue, but her cousin was already ripping into Robbie, "I thought you were better than that! Thought you were a Christian!"

"I am," Robbie replied. "I mean, I try to be."

"Sure." She flipped a piece of French toast with the force of a slam dunk. "How hard did you try last night?"

"Very," he said, stepping towards her. "Look, it's not what you think."

She backed away. "I don't need to think anything! I saw the two of you making out by the chokecherries! Then where'd you go? Huh? I don't think it was church." She pressed her spatula into Christianne's hand. "Here. Take over. I'm going for a run."

"Umm, okay," her cousin replied with confusion.

Stéphanie rushed towards the door, but Robbie caught her hand. "Please. Just give me a minute."

She heard her mother choke on a sob, and her own eyes stung with tears. She pulled her hand free, "Fine!" she barked. "One minute."

Robbie nodded at the condition and tittered at all the words he had to say. "We only talked last night."

"Pff."

"It's true." She scowled, so he added, "And we kissed. A lot. But we didn't sleep together. Not last night. But we did once, eighteen, almost nineteen years ago."

She grimaced at the information and raised her hands as a shield. "I don't need to know this."

He set his kaleidoscope eyes on hers. "Yes, you do, because that was the night we made you."

A siren wailed in her ears, and her head spun. "What?"

Robbie pressed on, "I'm your father."

"No, you're not," she responded as defiantly as if he had claimed to be a horse. "My father's dead." His eyes smarted, and his words got stuck in his throat. All he could do was shake his head. Stéphanie scowled at the motion and ordered, "Tell him, Maman. He died in a car accident when you broke your wrist."

"Coco," Émilie choked.

Stéphanie's face transformed through emotions like patterns in a kaleidoscope. "But you said!"

"No," Émilie responded. "I said I lost your father. It's two different things."

Stéphanie's lungs puffed and contracted like bellows, but she could not breath. "I saw his grave."

Émilie shook her head and looked Stéphanie square in the face. "You couldn't't've. He's right here."

"No! I saw it! Chris showed me."

"I did?" she asked from her post near the stove.

"Yeah. When we were nine. Remember?"

"No. Where?"

"In the cemetery! That grave in the corner. Remember? Your dad's friend? The one who died when Maman broke her wrist!"

"Mondieu," Émilie gasped; she stumbled to find support against the cupboard.

Robbie lost his breath like a punctured tire. "Roch."

"Yeah," Stéphanie said without notice of her parents' pallor and sighs. "He had the same birthday as Maman."

Robbie sucked in a breath and dragged his hand over his face. "Yeah. And as me. We were twins."

"Twins?" she mewled.

"Yeah." She blinked at him like an alarm clock after a power outage. "We were all born together: your mom, Roch and me."

"You never said that."

"No," he agreed. "It was hard to talk about. But didn't you see that he died way too soon to be your father?"

Her face scrunched as she thought back to the grave site Christianne had shown her summers before. "There's Papa's friend," she had said, pointing towards a granite headstone next to a flowering bush. "You remember that guy from the other night? Robbie? Well, this is his brother."

"What happened to him?"

"A car accident. 'Pa was with him. So was your mom, wasn't she?" She turned to Stéphanie for an answer but jumped to see her wide-eyed and pale. "Are you okay?" she asked.

"He has the same birthday as my mom," Stéphanie whispered.

"Wow. Weird."

Stéphanie had choked on the facts as she tried to say more, but Christianne pulled her onward.

"All I saw was the birthdate," she said to Robbie. "There's a bush there."

"Potentilla," Robbie concurred. "Our mother's favourite." He reached for Stéphanie, but she pulled away. He looked crumpled and wounded, and she was glad.

"Did you know this whole time?" she cried.

"Not the whole time," he said, "but for a long time. Since your first summer here."

"That was nine years ago!" she shouted.

His nodded at the truth and swallowed his shame. "I know. I'm sorry."

"Sorry?" she screeched. "Sorry is for spilling coffee on my hand or scratching the car! It's not for this!"

"I know, but there isn't any other word. No word at all that can change it or make it better. But I am sorry, Stéphanie, utterly and completely sorry, and I offer you the rest of my life in reparation."

Her breathing came in pants and gasps. "I don't want the rest of your life. I want mine back! I want it with the truth!"

"Stéphanie," her mother said, touching her arm.

"Don't!" she barked, pulling away. Émilie retreated, pressed her hand to her mouth to stifle a cry. "I hate you! I hate you both!" She ran from the room. Christianne moved to follow her, but Robbie raised his hand.

"I think she needs to be alone for a while."


Stéphanie folded herself into the silver Jetta she had used while her mother was overseas and jabbed the key into the ignition. She turned the motor, then ripped out of the yard with a spray of gravel and a cloud of dust. She did not know where she was going, but she turned left at the end of the yard.

She saw nothing but the grey of the road and the passing blotches of green: ditches and fields and caragana. Dupont Pond was nothing but an annoying shimmer in her eyes, and the red triangle yield sign at Quatre Coins did not even register in her mind. She drove on full throttle until the turn-off to the cemetery made her slow down. She braked and shifted, took the turn, and brought the car to a stop in front of the iron gate.

Cimetière-Notre-Dame-De-Lasalette was wrought in metal in the arch between two fieldstone pillars that her great-grandfather, Baptiste, had masoned in his early years in Lasalette—after his marriage but before his first children were born alive; the others, unborn and unbaptized, were inhumed in a plot beneath the lilac tree behind the house Stéphanie had just left. Baptiste, however, was there before her with his Sylvie—Together, Stéphanie knew the headstone said, for eternity.

The car door cawed for oil as she opened it. She pulled herself from behind the wheel and slammed the door, then stalked towards the gate, decorative more than functional, and entered the parcel of prairie reserved for the village dead. Dupont, Duceppe, Tessier, Simard. She passed them all until she found what she was looking for: Thibaud. Francis, Lucille, Roch.

She knew only the smallest bits about them: they were Robbie's family, his parents and brother, twin, apparently. *Jesus*, Stéphanie thought, *why didn't anyone ever tell me? Why didn't I ask? I certainly could've. Mononcle, or Pépère, or mauzus! I could've asked Robbie himself! I've certainly seen him often enough—prayer group and Mass, and all those lunches and suppers at Mémère and Pépère's. And those summers I worked for him! The rides he gave me! I thought it was because he was my uncle, not my dad! Câline! Why didn't I ask? Why didn't I care?*

She sniffed and wiped away her tears, then crouched before the weathered stone and pushed away the shrubby potentilla branches that hid the date she had never seen: Mar 22, 1964. *Six years. Simple math,* she chided herself, *even for a kid.*

She squeezed her eyes against the barrage of tears, yet they streamed down her face and splashed onto the granite ledger until a voice came to her with the softness of a breeze. "Coucou."

She turned towards the sound. "Pépère," she cried, then scrambled to her feet and threw herself into his arms.

"Tiens," he comforted as she choked and gasped and wailed into his chest. "Tiens. Tiens." He petted her hair and kissed her head. "Oh, ma fille, ma petite-fille. Je t'aime."

"I love you, too," she said into his tear-soaked shirt.

He sucked in her words for strength. "We should have told you."

"We?" She lost her breath. "You knew?"

His head moved like a ripple through a wheat field. His eyes filled with tears. "Yes. Your papa—"

"Don't call him that," she said.

Pierre passed his tongue over his lips and nodded at the request. "Alright," he agreed. "Robbie. He wanted to tell you, but your maman, she was still so broken. I was afraid she would take you away. Never let you visit again."

"Pépère," she whimpered like a kitten, unsure whether she was angry at him or empathizing with his fear of losing more family.

"We'd already lost nine years," he said. "That's longer than I even knew my parents. And Robbie, he wanted to know you, said it was more important for him to have a relationship with you than for you to know that he was your father. He said he'd wait to tell you until you asked to know."

"I thought I already knew." She pointed at the decades-old gravestone.

"Ah, but that's not enough, chérie. Knowing a name on a piece of granite. You need more than that to know who your family is. You need their stories."

Her head bobbed as she tried to make sense of it all. "Robbie could've been a stone for all I know about him. I didn't even know he was a twin!"

"No, but you know other things, like how he scrunches his face when he's full of emotion, and how he closes his eyes when he sings at church. You know, too, that he gave up being your father so he could be with you. Know you."

"I don't know that," she said.

Pierre hugged her into his side. "No, I suppose you don't, but when you're ready, you will. Just don't wait too long, eh? Don't waste a lifetime drowning in the pain."

## 10. Courante
### April 1990

"Holy shit," Jean-François gasped once the final syllable of Stéphanie's song died away.

"Amazing," Clem breathed.

"Indeed," Michel agreed as he crossed the room towards her and touched her arm, "but are you okay?"

She opened her eyes and turned to him. "Yeah. Great. Why?"

"You're crying."

"I am?" She touched her hands to her cheeks and found them wet. "Oh. I guess I am." She chuckled and brushed away the tears.

"Was that your pépère's song?"

She smiled at him. "Mmmhmm. And it worked." His face lit; their eyes locked in happiness. "It worked," she repeated.

"What did?" Clem asked.

"Fuck, no kidding," Jean-François grumbled.

Stéphanie was still set on Michel. "Can I use your phone?"

He blinked at the question and tossed his head in surprise. "Uhhh. Sure."

"The phone?" Jean-François scoffed. "What the hell you gonna do? Order pizza or something? Fffuck."

"Phone home, actually," she said as she turned towards the compact, muscular accordion player. "Is that okay?" She asked in all sincerity.

Jean-François scrunched his face in disgust. "Go ahead. Fuck. It's not like we've been waiting all weekend for you to make up your damn mind or anything. But sure, if you need to phone your mommy, go ahead."

"Jean!" Michel barked in protest at his bandmate's rudeness.

Stéphanie did not notice the reprimand nor even Jean-François' sarcasm and impatience. She said, "Thanks," and walked into the hallway as the men continued bickering.

She headed towards the kitchen with the impulse of a spawning salmon to reach home and was nose blind to the simmering curry in the kitchen; she did not even think of what she would say on the phone—all she knew was she had to talk to her parents. She picked up the receiver of the old rotary wall phone with a stretched-out cord and inserted her pointer finger into the first hole of the dial wheel and then into another and another.

Her heart raced in anticipation; butterflies fluttered in her chest with every sound the dial made. Once the ten digits of her parents' phone number were finally inputted, she waited for the ringing to begin. It came once, twice, ten times without response. Stéphanie sighed and hung up the receiver. She looked about for a clock and found the hour on the microwave: 2:43, which meant 1:43 in Lasalette. Her parents would be at her grandmother's for Sunday dinner.

Stéphanie imagined the scene at the dining table: her parents and Christianne's, her cousins—all teenagers now, even Simon, the youngest and only boy of the family—and her toddler sister, Renée, closed behind the table of a highchair while Rose carried in roast beef and gravy, carrots, and mashed potatoes.

There would be pitchers of Tang and water on the table, and homemade buns, Co-op butter, and the salt and pepper shakers in the shape of a portly old couple—one with a bib-apron that declared *I'm Salt,* the other with a hat that read, *I'm Pep.*

Everyone would be talking and laughing, Stéphanie thought, although Jasmine might be sulking if she had missed a good party the night before or had had to get up too early after an even better one. Émilie would ask her and Jasmine about school, and dance, and volleyball. They would babble back with all the news. Robbie would shower attention on Simon: ask him if he had made any progress in Super Mario Brothers or on learning the song he had shown him on the guitar the Sunday before. Martin and Lynn would talk with Rose and fuss over Renée. They would resemble one of those television families that Stéphanie had always envied: the Keatons, the Seavers, the Huxtables.

Her eyes usually stung at such reflections, but at that moment, there was a blaze of warmth radiating in her chest, and her finger was rolling through the numbers she had memorized as a girl in Switzerland.

"Âllo?" Robbie said after two rings. The sudden sound caught Stéphanie by surprise and left her mute. "Âllo?" he said, again.

"Âllo," she gasped, then added a word she had never addressed to anyone before, "Papa."

He took it in stride, "Oh, Chris! Hi! It's not your dad. It's Robbie."

"It's not Chris," she said with a quiver. "It's Stéphanie."

"Oh." Their breathing echoed in each other's ears. "You said, 'Papa.'"

"Yeah, I did."

The line crackled with his swelling emotions and hers as well. "You've never called me that before."

"No." She squeezed the phone chord in her free hand as she went on, "but I wanted to. Did you know that? Know that I wished you were my dad since I was twelve years old?"

"You did?" he gasped. "Why?"

She smiled, remembering their time together. "Because you were nice and always around and you cared about me. Me, not Maman or music or anything else. Just me."

"I did," he agreed. "And I still do, Stéphanie. I'll always care about you. Always love you."

"I know," she choked. "And I get it, now. The choices. Doing the wrong thing for the right reason. And I forgive you. I hope you'll forgive me, too."

"For what?"

"Being mad," she mumbled. "Saying I hated you."

"That's okay," he replied.

"No, it's not."

"Sure, it is," he insisted. Stéphanie could see his smile in her mind, could hear it on the other end of the line. "If you love me."

"I do!" she said and nodded for good measure.

"Then it's all good," he assured.

"Good." They smiled at each other and breathed in each other's ears. "Hey, Papa?" she asked after a time. "Is Maman there?"

"Yeah, do you want to talk to her?"

"Please."

"Okay. Just a minute." The phone clunked as he set it on the counter. She heard the rustling of his footsteps, the swinging of the dining room door, and the rise and fall of voices in the other room as the door swung in and out. She heard voices down the hall in Montréal, too—Michel, Clem, and Jean-François:

"Be patient."

"Fuck that; it's fuckin' Sunday."

"We need to know, Mitch."

"I know."

Stéphanie bent her ear so far towards their conversation that she jumped when her mother came on the line and called her by her pet name, "Coco? Are you alright?"

"What? Oh! Maman! Hi! Yeah, I'm great! How are you?"

Émilie missed the question. "Oh, thank God! When Robbie said you were on the phone, I got so worried."

Stéphanie chuckled. "Why? 'Cause I don't usually call?"

"No," Émilie insisted, though it sounded like a lie, "that's not what I was going to say."

Stéphanie stared at the orange and brown flowers papered on the wall to avoid the sudden sting of tears. "Maybe. But it's true."

"You have your reasons," her mother said.

"I did," she agreed, "but I don't anymore."

Émilie's voice rose happily, "Really? Oh, honey, I'm so glad to hear that!"

"Yeah! Me too. I'm just sorry it took me so long and that I hurt you and Papa so much along the way."

"Papa?" Émilie repeated.

Stéphanie laughed, thinking of her mother's mouth hanging open in surprise. "Yeah," she said. "I call him that now 'cause that's who he is."

"Yes, he is," said Émilie, smiling at her daughter as if she were standing in front of her in Lasalette.

Stéphanie felt as if she were and spoke that way as well, "Maman?"

"Oui?"

"What would you say if I didn't come home on Tuesday?"

Stéphanie heard her mother inhale sharply and imagined she was fingering the blue beaded bracelet on her once-broken wrist in search of an answer, but one came without delay, "Well, if I knew *before* I made a special trip to the airport, I'd be okay with it."

"Really?" Stéphanie tittered with surprise.

"Really," her mother assured. "Is that the plan?"

"I don't know." Stéphanie was the one who left silence on the line until she found words. "I've met these guys. Friends of Alex, you know, Chris' boyfriend?"

"Fiancé you mean," Émilie corrected with a laugh.

"Oh, so, she told Mononcle? How'd he take it?"

"Well, you know your mononcle," Émilie said, "overprotective and overbearing, but he's happy she's happy. He even talked to Alex for a while, asked him questions and welcomed him to the family. Invited him out. That kind of thing."

"Wow," Stéphanie remarked.

"Yeah, well, it's easier over the phone sometimes, you know?" Émilie said. "At least, it always was for me,"

Stéphanie nodded with understanding. "I loved calling home, but being home is better."

"That's true," her mother replied, "but home can be inside you, too, you know?"

Stéphanie continued to nod. She closed her eyes and inhaled. "I didn't," she said, "but I think maybe I'm learning that."

They lingered in the thought for a moment before Émilie broke the reverie and returned to Stéphanie's plans, "So, what's this about Chris's fiancé's friends?"

"Alex's," she clarified. "And it's his brother, actually, Alex's brother and two friends. They have a band. And they want me to join."

"That's great! And you said yes?" Émilie asked, thinking it was rhetorical, but Stéphanie twirled her pointer finger around the coils of the telephone cord and sighed.

"Not yet."

"Why not?" her mother asked gently.

Stéphanie's nose prickled as tears began to fill her eyes. "What about Renée? She's so young. And Mémère? I should be with them."

"You can be with them without living with them, you know?"

"I know," Stéphanie mumbled. She sniffed and wiped away the tears that were leaking from her eyes.

Émilie waited for her daughter to say more before gently prodding her, "Is there something else?" Stéphanie nodded across the line and made a sound Émilie understood. She chuckled. "You like one of them, don't you?"

"Yeah," Stéphanie admitted with a titter. "And he likes me. But is that a good idea? Mixing music and feelings like that?"

"It can be," Émilie replied. "But you need rules and boundaries and really good communication." Stéphanie's head moved in agreement as her mother went on, "I know I wasn't a very good example, but I do know about this stuff, about music and musicians ..." she trailed off with an embarrassed snicker.

"You know about love, too," Stéphanie reminded her.

"Yeah," Émilie agreed with a contentment that was new to Stéphanie's ears, "I do." The two women smiled at each other across the line once again and listened to each other breathe until a knock startled Stéphanie and caused her to let out a small cry. "What's wrong?" her mother asked.

"Nothing," Stéphanie replied as she turned to find Michel, Jean-François, and Clem standing in the doorway like a strange trio of wisemen in t-shirts and jeans.

"Are you okay?" Michel whispered.

She nodded and grinned, looked into his warm maple eyes as she spoke into the phone, "I need to go, Maman. The guys are waiting. But I'll call soon, okay? I promise."

"Does that mean you're staying?" Clem asked with the excitement of a schoolboy before Stéphanie had even hung up the receiver.

"Yes," she answered with a happy laugh.

"Wooo-hoo!" He exclaimed and lifted her off her feet. He twirled her about as she continued to answer.

"If you still want me."

"We do!" He put her down and turned to the other two. "Don't we, guys?"

Jean-François moved a shoulder and pushed out his lips as if he didn't care, but a smile overtook his face as he said, "I guess." He and Stéphanie chuckled and smiled at one another before she turned towards Michel.

"What about you?" she asked. "Do you still want me?"

He looked into her eyes as he replied, "Yes."

"Good," she said, and moved towards him, wrapped her arms about his neck and kissed him.

He kissed her back until Jean-François grumbled, "Okay, enough of that. We've got a shit load of work to do."

"That we do," Stéphanie agreed with the widest grin of the group. She caught Michel by the hand and pulled him towards the doorway. "Come on! Let's go."

The End

## Tremblay Family Vocabulary

It is common for the Fransaskois (French-Canadians from Saskatchewan) to call the siblings of their parents "matante" and "mononcle" (literally "my aunt" and "my uncle"). This compound word can lead to a seemingly double possessive (i.e., "My matante has black hair") and contradictory possessive articles (i.e. Her mononcle plays hockey), but it is how some of us talk.

Further confusion can arise when reading, for a capitalized relational noun indicates a name (i.e. Matante Lynn held a balloon), while lower relational nouns are simply that—an indication of a relationship (i.e. her matante, Lynn, held a balloon). The same practice is used for talking about parents and grandparents (i.e. my maman, her pépère) and for addressing them or using the relational noun as their name, (i.e. Émilie and Mémère are in the other room; Hi, Papa.)

Note, Pierre intentionally avoids these practices when speaking of his childhood family.

**Terms**

**Grand-mère:** Grandmother; often indicates Grand-mère Sylvie

**Mémère:** Grandma; usually means Rose

**Matante:** Aunt, Aunty

**Mononcle:** Uncle

**Pépère:** Grandpa; usually means Pierre

**Petite-fille:** Granddaughter

**Tantine:** Aunty; Used by Baptiste when addressing his aunt.

## More about Language in this Book

### Capitalization

Just as familial nouns can be common or proper depending on context, religious nouns and interjections can be written in different ways and cases to indicate different enunciations, i.e.

> Mon Dieu: A personal address to or call upon "My God."
> Mondieu: A response or interjection outside of prayer.
> Mondou: A variant of the above to avoid cursing; similar to "My gosh."

Similarly, the city of Saskatoon is capitalized, while the small fruit, the saskatoon berry, is not.

### Spelling

"Jesus" generally indicates a prayer or respectful tone, while "Geezus" is used as a curse. The same goes for "God" and "Gawd."

# French Notes

**A**

**Aide-moi:** Help me.

**Allez:** Go.

**Allons-y:** Let's go.

**Ave:** First word of the Latin version of the Hail Mary prayer; often used as the name of the prayer.

**B**

**Bas-Saint-Laurent:** The Lower Saint-Lawrence region of Quebec.

**Beauchemin:** A last name that means "nice path"; sounds similar to "bon chemin," which means "the right/good path."

**Bien sûr:** Of course.

**Bin:** A Canadian pronunciation of "bien", which means "well or very," depending on the context. It is a nasal sound and pronounced bẽ. Think of the French word for end ("fin") and change the "f" to a "b". Or, if you know the word for bathroom ("salle de bain"), you can pronounce this word.

**Bin voyons:** Come on now.

**Bin, oui, pis non:** Well, yes and no.

**Bin nous avons... et pis... :** Well, we... and then...

**Bluet, mon bluet:** French-Canadian word for blueberry; my blueberry.

**Bon:** Good.

**Bon Dieu!:** Good God!

**Bon sang!:** Literally "good blood;" generally translated as "good grief" or "for goodness' sake."

**Bon travail:** Good job.

**Bonne nuit:** Good night.

# C

**Cabanes à sucre:** Sugar shack.

**Ça doit être Baptiste:** That must be Baptiste.

**Ça va?/ Ça va./ Ça va aller.:** How are things? How's it going? / Things are fine. / Everything will be alright.

**Câlice, Câlisse:** Chalice; French-Canadian swear word.

**Câlice de merde! Le maudit chien de bâtard de câline de cri – :** A string of swears.

**Câline:** French-Canadian expression that can mean "wow" or "darn," depending on the context. It comes from the more explicit word "câlice," which means "chalice" and is used as a swear word.

**Carisse; Câriste:** Variant of Christ; used as a swear.

**Ce ne sont que des fillettes:** They're just little girls.

**Ce n'est pas si tard. Ton père t'attend depuis notre départ. Il peut donc attendre un peu plus pis un peu plus encore:** It's not so late. Your father's been waiting since we left, so he can keep waiting a little bit more.

**Cette femme:** That woman!

**C'est bien, non?:** It's great, isn't it?

**C'est trop!:** It's too much!

**C'est un garçon:** It's a boy.

**C'était magnifique:** It was great, magnificent.

**Chansonnier:** Singer/songwriter.

**Chez Dupont; Chez Nous:** At the Dupont home/house; at our house. The latter is the name of the restaurant Michel and Stéphanie visit.

**Chérie:** Dear, honey, sweety (feminine form).

**Chou:** Cabbage; Term of endearment, especially for children.

# D

**Délicieux!:** Delicious!

**D'accord:** Alright, fine, okay.

**E**

**Encore:** Again; still.

**Es-tu là:** Are you there?

**Et, oui, moi:** And, yes, me.

**Et tiens:** And look.

**Excusez-moi:** Excuse me.

**École:** School

**Église:** Church


**F**

**Félicitations!** Congratulations!

**Fille; Fille-fille; ma fille:** Girl/daughter; Girlie; my girl/daughter.

**Fils, mon fils:** Son; my son.

**Franchement:** Frankly; honestly.


**G**

**Gloire à Dieu:** Glory to God.

**grande lauréate:** Grand winner.

**Grâce à Dieu!:** Thanks to God! Thanks be to God.


**H**

**Hôstie:** Host, communion wafer; often used as a swear word.


**I**

**Il est mort, lui aussi:** He is dead as well.

**Il est vivant!:** He is alive!

**Il était le seul:** He was the only one.

**Il y a longtemps. Bien longtemps.:** A long time ago. A very long time ago.

**J**

**Je suis l'Immaculée Conception:** I am the Immaculate Conception.

**Je t'aime:** I love you (to one person).

**Je t'aime, mon petit bluet:** I love you, my little blueberry.

**Je veux rester!:** I want to stay!

**Je vous aime:** I love you (to more than one person).

**Je vous laisse :** I'll leave you alone.

**Je vous salue Marie, pleine de grâce:** Hail Mary, full of grace.


**L**

**La cathédrale engloutie:** The Sunken Cathedral (see Music Notes).

**La grande dame:** The great dame.

**La politique ce n'est pas la politique, c'est la vie/ c'est la sauce:** Politics is not politics, it's life/it's sauce. See Gilles Vigneault in Music Notes.

**Les Triplés de Lasalette:** The Lasalette Triplets.

**Lui aussi:** He as well; him, too.


**M**

**Ma chère:** My dear (to a female).

**Ma fille:** My daughter, my girl.

**Ma petite-fille:** My granddaughter.

**Mauzus:** Moses; an expression of frustration.

**Merci; merci beaucoup:** Thank you; thank you very much.

**Merde:** Shit.

**Mes enfants:** My children.

**Minou:** Kitty.

**Moi:** Me.

**Mon:** My.

**Mon amour:** My love.

**Mon Baptiste:** My Baptiste.

**Mon Bluet:** My Blueberry.

**Mon chou; Mon petit chou:** Literally my (little) cabbage; my dear

**Mon Dieu:** My God.

**Mon Dieu bénissez la nouvelle année:** a song; the title means "My God, bless the new year."

**Mon Dieu Seigneur!:** My Lord God!

**Mon fils:** My son.

**Mon grand:** My big boy.

**Mon pauvre petit:** My poor little one.

**Mon petit bluet:** My little blueberry.

**Mon Père/ Le Père:** My father/the father; used to address a priest.

**Mondou, Marie, t'as pas changé pan toute.:** Wow, Marie, you haven't changed at all!


**N**

**Ne**: Part of the negative construction "ne…pas." The "pas" is often removed when speaking.


**O**

**Oh, bin, c'est normal:** Oh, well, that's normal.

**Oh, la bastringue, pis la bastringue:** A song; see Music Notes.


**P**

**Pas si vite, Maman:** Not so fast, Mom.

**Pis:** A common pronunciation of "puis" (then); it is pronounced "pee" but has nothing to do with urination.


**Q**

**Quatre-Coins:** Four Corners.

**Que Dieu l'accueille:** May God welcome her (into his kingdom).

**Quel soir! Quel jeu!:** What an evening! What a game!

**Qu'est-ce que tu fais ici?:** What are you doing here?

**Qu'est-ce qui s'est passé?:** What happened?


## S

**Sale cochon:** Dirty pig.

**Salut:** Hi; the t is silent.

**Salut toi:** Hi, you.

**Santé:** To health; equivalent of "Cheers".

**Seigneur:** Lord.

**Seigneur! Aide-moi!:** Lord! Help me!

**Soeur/ La Soeur:** Sister, the sister; used to address a nun.

**Soyez prudent:** Be careful.

**S'il vous plaît!:** Please!


## T

**Ta gueule:** Literally means "your mouth;" equivalent of "shut up".

**Tabernak:** Strong swear word; literally means "Tabernacle." Softer variants include "tabarouette" and "tabernouche".

**Tchin-tchin:** Onomatopoeic expression that mimics the clinking of glasses; similar to the Italians use of "Cin cin," which is why Stéphanie responds in Italian.

**Te voilà:** There you are; it's you.

**Tenez/ Tiens:** Here you go.

**Tiens:** There, there.

**Toussaints:** The All Saints.

**T'es vraiment bon:** You're really good.


## V

**Valse de Valérie:** Valerie's Waltz (Plumeau song title)

**Viarge:** Regional pronunciation of "vierge" (virgin); a soft Québecois swear.

**Viens, viens voir:** Come, come see.

**Viens! Viens tant!:** Come back!

**Voici une vieille chanson:** Here's an old song.

**Voyons:** See now; look.

**Vraiment:** Really.

# Latin

**Ave:** First word in the Hail Mary prayer; often used as the name of the prayer.

**Volo:** I do.

**Stabat mater dolorsa / juxta crucem lacrimosa/ dum pendebat Filius:** A hymn about Mary's grief and suffering as she watched her son, Jesus, be crucified. The title translates as "The Sorrowful Mother Was Standing." A common singable translation of the first verse is "At the cross her station keeping, stood the mournful mother weeping, close to Jesus to the last."

**O quam tristis et afflícta:** Oh, how sad and stricken; a line from "Stabat mater."

# Italian

**Cornetti alla crema:** Cream puffs
**Salute:** Cheers, to your health; similar to "Santé."

## Musical Terms
**Allegretto:** Moderately fast
**Allegro non assai, ma molto appassionato:** Not overly lively but with passion; the performance marking for Johannes Brahms' Intermezzo in A minor, Opus 118, No. 1.
**Ostinato:** A short musical pattern (often rhythmic) that is continuously repeated throughout a piece of music.
**Presto agitato:** Fast and agitated
**Sotto voce:** In a quiet voice or under the breath

# Music Notes

**À la claire fontaine:** A traditional French song that may date back to the 15th or 16th century. It is a sorrowful song about enduring love. The title is translated as, "By the clear fountain." The refrain is, "I have loved you for a long time; I will never forget you."

**À la volette:** A folksong that dates back to the 18th century or earlier. It is about a bird who flies away, then lands on the branch of an orange tree that breaks. The bird's injuries are mentioned, as are her desire to be cared for and to marry.

**Bach, Johann Sebastian** (1685-1750): A German composer who wrote extensively for the keyboard as well as sacred music. His two volumes of preludes and fugues (known as the *Well-Tempered Clavier*) are considered the foundation of western keyboard music and the basis of counterpoint and harmony. The *Sinfonias*, also known as Three-Part Inventions, are short keyboard works that are generally studied before the *Preludes and Fugues*. They were written to help keyboard students clearly voice three lines of music while playing in a clear, singing style.

**Counterpoint:** The combination of two or more voices or melodic lines simultaneously, thereby creating harmonic and rhythmic interplay.

**Chaconne, Gigue, Gavotte, Loure, Aire, Minuet, Bourée and Courante:** Some of the dances/pieces that comprise a musical suite (a group of pieces performed as a single work).

**Descant:** An added melody that is higher than the main melody and often creates a harmony.

**Derrière chez nous y a un étang:** The opening line to *V'là bon vent,* a French-Canadian folk song that is over 300 years old. The song tells the story of three ducks and a king's son who kills the white duck (innocence) with a silver gun. Other lines from this song serve as the headings of many parts of Émilie and Robbie's story.

**Fanny Mendelssohn** (1805-1847) was one of the composer Felix Mendelssohn's sisters.

**Gilles Vigneault** (b. 1928): A Québecois singer-songwriter. Clem refers to his song, *Mon pays,* whose best-known lyric is "Mon pays ce n'est pas un pays, c'est l'hiver." ("My country is not a country, it is winter.")

**Kinderszenen:** Scenes from Childhood Op.15; a set of 13 piano pieces by Robert Schumann (1810-1856).

**La cathédrale englouti:** The Sunken Cathedral; a piano piece by Claude Debussy (1862-1918) that was written in 1909 and published in his collection *Préludes, Book 1* in 1910.

**Mary Travers, dit La Bolduc** (1894-1941): Mary Travers, known as La Bolduc, was a popular French-Canadian folksinger during the 1930s. She sang traditional and original songs in a lively, narrative style. She was well-known for her turlutte, which is a form of vocalizing using nonsensical syllables to imitate musical instruments. **La bastringue** was one of La Bolduc's hits. It is a call-and-response folksong.

**Moonlight Sonata:** Ludvig van Beethoven's piano sonata No.14, Op. 27, no.2; written in 1801.

**Nannerl and Fanny:** Nannerl was the family nickname for Wolfgang Amadeus Mozart's sister, Maria Anna Mozart (1751-1829). Fanny Mendelssohn (1805-1847) was one of the composer Felix Mendelssohn's sisters. Some of her compositions were published under his name.

**Stabat mater dolorsa:** See Latin notes.

## History & Geography Notes

**Bas-Saint-Laurent:** The Lower Saint-Lawerence; a region in eastern Québec along the lower St. Lawrence River.

**Catalogue Houses:** In the early 20th-century, prairie settlers could order ready-to-build homes via mail-order catalogues such as the T. Eaton Company Plan Book. Purchasers received plans and all the necessary materials via rail delivery.

**Fransaskois:** French Canadians in Saskatchewan.
Before the mid-20th century, *Canadien-Français* was the general term for French-speaking Canadians across the country. During the rise of Quebec nationalism, *Québécois* became the preferred identifier within Quebec. In response, Francophone communities in other provinces and territories adopted distinct names, like *Fransaskois*, as well. The first official use of the term was in 1977.

A yellow flag with a red fleur-de-lis and green cross was officially adopted by the Fransaskois community in 1979. This flag hangs in Stéphanie and Christianne's dorm room.

**Francophone Schools:** Different from French Immersion schools, Francophone schools offer full instruction in French as a first language. They are publicly funded and a constitutional right under Section 23 of the Canadian Charter of Rights and Freedoms. They did not exist in Saskatchewan until 1995, but Fransaskois parents and students were already working towards and preparing for a Fransaskois school board when Stéphanie and Christianne were at university.

**Laurentides & Lanaudière:** Two distinct administrative regions north of Montréal, Québec.

## Love Notes

Thank you to:

Mike O'Connor at Ardith Publishing for his guidance, support, and expertise.

The tutors at the University of Lancaster DLMA program, especially Michelene Wandor, who encouraged me to explore French Canadian language and culture in an English program at a British university, and my classmates who joined me in Lake Country and online back near the turn of the century.

Margaret MacPherson for encouragement and feedback on a very early draft.

The Writers' Guild of Alberta Mentorship Program, especially my mentor Jacqui Dumas.

MWG Ink group for years of support and feedback: Amanda Lim, Brett Sheehan, Gregg Koop, Laura Barakeris, Mike Sheehan, and Nikki Stalker.

The many friends, colleagues, and readers who provided feedback over the years. I dare not name anyone for fear of forgetting someone and regretting the blank for all eternity. My heart knows who you are and thanks you all.

Et merci à mon bibliothécaire préféré, Denis Lacroix, pour son écoute et son aide. Merci à nos enfants, pour leur patience et leur présence auprès de ce livre depuis toujours.

S.D.G.

## About the Author

Melissa Morelli Lacroix was born in Saskatoon, Saskatchewan, Canada, and raised between grain fields and potash mines in nearby Viscount, where, as in Lasalette, the school, church, and skating rink were fundamental elements of the community.

Though she was raised in English, Melissa was always encouraged by her father to practice her French whenever she visited her Fransaskois grandparents. Similarly, her mother proudly reminded Melissa that they were French-Canadian, even if they never made tourtière or ate pea soup and only spoke a bit of French.

From these beginnings, Melissa went on to become a Registered Music Teacher and has taught piano for over 30 years. She also earned an honours degree in Creative Writing and French from the University of Alberta and a Master of Arts in Creative Writing from Lancaster University.

Melissa's writing has been performed on Edmonton stages, read on CBC radio, set to music, and published in Canadian, American, and British publications. Her books include the 2014 music-inspired poetry collection *A Most Beautiful Deception* and the 2025 bestselling novella, *Adventures of Ivan*. To find out more about Melissa and her work, please visit her website www.melissamorellilacroix.com

Want More Lasalette?

Visit Melissa's webpage for details about more books about the settlers of Lasalette.
www.melissamorellilacroix.com